Reading the
Sweet Oak

Center Point
Large Print

**This Large Print Book carries the
Seal of Approval of N.A.V.H.**

Reading
the
Sweet Oak

JAN STITES

CENTER POINT LARGE PRINT
THORNDIKE, MAINE

This Center Point Large Print edition
is published in the year 2017 by arrangement with
Amazon Publishing, www.apub.com.

Originally published in the United States
by Amazon Publishing, 2015.

This is a work of fiction.
Names, characters, organizations, places,
events, and incidents are either products of the
author's imagination or are used fictitiously.

The text of this Large Print edition is unabridged.
In other aspects, this book may vary
from the original edition.
Printed in the United States of America
on permanent paper.
Set in 16-point Times New Roman type.

ISBN: 978-1-68324-246-8

Library of Congress Cataloging-in-Publication Data

Names: Stites, Jan, author.
Title: Reading the sweet oak / Jan Stites.
Description: Center Point Large Print edition. | Thorndike, Maine :
Center Point Large Print, 2017.
Identifiers: LCCN 2016044601 | ISBN 9781683242468
    (hardcover : alk. paper)
Subjects: LCSH: Book clubs (Discussion groups)—Fiction. | Female
friendship—Fiction. | Large type books.
Classification: LCC PS3619.T5777 R43 2017 | DDC 813/.6—dc23
LC record available at https://lccn.loc.gov/2016044601

To my brothers,
Ronald James Stites and Steven William Stites,
through whose veins Ozark rivers also flow,
and especially to my husband, Bert Felton,
who is my river, in all seasons

PART ONE

MAY

CHAPTER ONE
Tulsa

Tulsa slipped her canoe paddle into the Sweet Oak, a lazy song of a river that threaded the Ozark hills for miles. She knew every bend, every grove of sycamores, and every boulder and fallen tree that could spill unwary paddlers. From behind her came the deep-throated *wahwk* of a great blue heron. The bird glided into view, tipped its massive wings, and landed on a gravel bar with perfect grace. Herons were her totem bird. Perhaps the heron's arrival meant that this was the day to make that call to Ed. If she did, however, life as she knew it could end.

Tulsa thrust her paddle into the water and cut back hard in a J stroke that propelled her canoe straight for home. Beaching the boat, she thought about all she needed to do to prepare for the upcoming Memorial Day weekend: mow the campground, load thirty canoes the high school seniors were renting to float the river Friday, and stock the cabins.

She sprang up the rock steps that led from the river and jogged toward the white clapboard farmhouse she and her grandmother, Ruby, had shared for the last seventeen of Tulsa's twenty-eight years. Perhaps it would be better if Ruby made that call to their neighbor Ed Logan since the two of them went back decades, to the days of moonshine and one-room schools.

Tulsa reached the door of the two-story house, which sat on the bank overlooking the river and was surrounded by purple lilacs and yellow forsythias, just as she heard the rumble of a large engine coming down the hill. She turned from the door, hoping for a customer. A dust cloud hovered like smoke, marking the trail of the approaching vehicle: a long-bed Chevy pickup that stopped just inches from her. Its driver wasn't a customer. It was Rupert Clancy, a man with the moral scruples of a crawdad.

One of Clancy's two dogs, bulky animals with gleaming teeth, stood vigilant on the backseat, its muzzle poking through the partially lowered window. The other climbed into Clancy's lap. Clancy, who owned the land downriver on the other side of Ed Logan, playfully shook the dog's muzzle before pushing him into the passenger seat.

Tulsa's grandmother emerged from the house to stand beside Tulsa, arms crossed, her wrinkled face furrowed by a scowl that would give fright to saner men. Given their history with Clancy, it was amazing Ruby hadn't grabbed her shotgun.

Clancy leaned out the driver's window and blew a large pink gum bubble. His skin was tanned, his long graying hair pulled back into a ponytail, his eyes the pale green of an old dollar bill. It still stunned Tulsa to think this man had almost become her stepfather.

"What do you want?" Tulsa said.

Clancy popped the bubble. "I guess you heard Ed's selling his place," he said.

Tulsa clenched her teeth to keep from gasping. So the rumor was true.

They'd leased Ed's cabins and campground every summer for as long as she could remember. The people who rented their canoes could float the river and have somewhere to stay. Without Ed's facilities, the Sweet Oak River Oasis canoe rental business could not survive.

"I'm buying it," Clancy said, giving them a triumphant look. "I know you'll want it, but you won't be able to afford it with riverfront land going for twenty thousand an acre. Since I'm in a good mood, I'm offering a consolation prize. Today only. I'm giving you three thousand dollars just for good-will if you don't bother Ed." He held out a check.

"You know damned well that Ed will sell to me," Ruby said. "That's why you're trying to buy us off."

"Everybody knows Ed's in love with you, Ruby, but I offered him seven hundred thousand. Cash. What can you afford? Five hundred thousand? Six? No man's going to let love interfere with that much profit."

Tulsa swallowed hard. Ruby looked aghast.

"So take my three thousand and be grateful." Clancy adjusted his side mirror.

"You're wrong, Rupert," Ruby said. "As usual. Ed *will* sell to us."

"Oh? You have seven hundred thousand cash, do you?"

"Maybe not," Ruby said. "But we have a bank."

"To get a loan to buy Ed's place, I imagine you'd have to put your own up as collateral." Clancy held out the check. "Take it. You'll save yourselves a world of trouble."

Tulsa bristled. "What kind of trouble?"

"Oh, you know. This and that."

Tulsa stepped closer. The dogs snarled. "Are you threatening us?" she said.

"I'm just saying things happen." Clancy snapped his fingers; the dogs fell silent.

Tulsa snatched the check from Clancy's hand and ripped it in two.

"Just so you know," Tulsa said, stance wide, "if you do anything to mess with us, I guarantee you'll regret it." She wadded the ripped check into a ball and tossed it into the cab.

Clancy blew another bubble, then popped it. He held up the balled check and looked bemused. "You should both be downright grateful for my generosity, but if you don't want a free three thousand dollars, I'll just head on over to my bank and have them prepare the check for Ed. Good day, ladies."

Clancy drove slowly up the hill, gravel popping under the tires of his pickup. Tulsa's arms hung limp at her sides.

Ruby appeared lost in thought, but after a few moments, she whirled to face the house. "I'll call Ed," she said. "Give me some privacy."

Tulsa hadn't seen Ruby move that fast in a while. She took long, hurried strides of her own down to the water's edge.

Spring-fed, cool, and clear, the Sweet Oak seemed to absorb all the greens of the trees that lined its banks. After Tulsa's mother died, the river had been her lifeline, and this house the only real home she'd ever known. The closest town of Fiddle, population three thousand, had few people, fewer jobs. If they had to close their canoe business, she would have to move away to find work. Tears stung her eyes. She slipped off her shoes, left on her jeans and T-shirt, waded into the water, and sat. The rocks beneath her bottom had long ago been smoothed by the river's flow. Tulsa let herself feel the steady strength of the current hugging her.

She and Ruby didn't make a lot of money, especially since Ed closed off the cabins and campground during hunting season in fall and winter for his large family's use. Fortunately their own house and land were paid off, and they made enough from the summer months' canoe business to cover their bills and save some for emergencies.

Fortunately, too, both she and Ruby were content with simple living. Life at the river brimmed with the riches that mattered to them both: herons, bullfrogs, trees, flowers, whip-poor-wills, fireflies, and so much more.

A twig struck the surface, swirling the reflections of sycamore, maple, and birch. Leaning back, Tulsa immersed her head and counted slowly to sixty, then sat up. Cold water slid down her face and neck. She hugged her knees, shivering.

If she did have to move away, what would she do? She'd dropped out of college after one semester to help Ruby run the canoe business, having learned she would much rather read a river—looking for the ripples that signaled a hidden rock, a potential hazard for paddlers and bonanza for fishermen—than a book. Maybe Guy would have some ideas.

It seemed like both five seconds and five hours later when she heard someone coming down the rock steps. She stood.

Ruby looked somber. "Ed was going to come by this afternoon to talk to us. He and Clare are moving to St. Louis to be closer to their grand-kids. Ed doesn't want to sell to Clancy, but these days Ozark land isn't worth much more than two hoots and a holler. 'Course, Ed's got the cabins and that riverfront property, and he wants to sell fast. It's Clancy or us. He'll let us have it for six seventy."

"Six hundred seventy thousand dollars?"

"Yes."

Tulsa whistled. That was a lot of money. "Can we afford that?"

"I called George Calhoun over at the bank. I'm meeting him in an hour. We'll have to secure the loan with our place plus most of our savings, but he thinks we can swing it."

Tulsa's throat felt like she'd swallowed sand. "You mean if we didn't bring in enough, we'd lose not just the canoe business, but our land and the house?"

"Well, yes."

Ruby's white hair was thinning, her pale-pink scalp visible in places. She was less than two years from eighty. Tulsa called her grandmother by her given name because even as a child she'd loved the sound of the word *Ruby,* a name that seemed soft and welcoming, unlike the unmelodious *Gran,* which sounded harsh, like *slap* or *trap.* When Tulsa got older, she kept calling her Ruby because her grandmother had always seemed a jewel in Tulsa's life.

If it were just herself, Tulsa thought, she would take the gamble, but if something went wrong, Ruby could end up in some tiny apartment in town or, worse, a nursing home. It was even possible that losing her home at her age could kill her. There was no way Tulsa would let Ruby risk so much.

"We'll just have to close the business," Tulsa said. "You'd still have the land and house." And more. Clifford, Ruby's late husband, and Tulsa's mother, Faith, were buried in the front yard overlooking the river. Ruby had lost them both years before. It could destroy her to lose them all over again.

"And what would you do, Tulsa? Flip burgers? Honey, I love you, but your hamburgers taste like roadkill, and there isn't much else to do in Fiddle."

"This isn't up for discussion, Ruby. You are not going to risk everything. Besides, I can find work in Springfield." Tulsa strove for a nonchalance she didn't feel. Springfield was a city nearly two hours away, too far to commute. She shrugged like it didn't matter, though it did. It really did. "I could still come back for weekends."

Ruby crossed her arms. "Rupert Clancy will not get his claws on Ed's."

"It's too risky."

Ruby's angry face seemed to soften. "You love it here."

"That's beside the point."

"Your happiness *is* the point," Ruby said. "I *will* get that loan, and we'll keep the business open year-round. That should bring in enough. This will be my gift to you, honey. And while I'm at it, I'm going to transfer ownership of everything, Ed's and ours, to you."

"What? Why?"

"I'm almost eighty. I'm not going to live forever. That way, when I die, you can avoid probate."

Tulsa winced. "Don't talk like that."

Ruby just shrugged. Tulsa's mouth opened and closed. Twice. She reminded herself of a fish out of water, trying to gulp air. Though part of Tulsa wanted to hogtie her grandmother until she could talk some sense into her, another part wanted to celebrate Ruby's determination to keep the canoe business afloat. Finally she nodded her head. "I'll come with you to the bank." If the bank's terms were too preposterous, she would have a chance to make Ruby reconsider taking out that loan.

"I'm a big girl, and you've got to be here for customers. We sure can't afford to lose any business now." Ruby started walking up the steps.

Her grandmother seemed a little wobbly. Tulsa jumped up beside her and linked her arm through Ruby's to steady her. "Are you okay?" Tulsa asked.

"I'm fine."

Ruby's face seemed so thin these days. "Maybe you should take a nap first."

"Later." They topped the stairs.

Tulsa stopped, putting a hand on each of Ruby's shoulders to hold her in place. "Ruby, are you sure about this?"

"Life is about taking chances," Ruby said.

"Chances on the weather. On other people. On yourself. On romance and love."

"Love? What's that got to do with anything?"

"Oh, Tulsa." Ruby looked almost tearful. "Love has everything to do with everything."

Tulsa looked away.

Ruby put her arm through Tulsa's. "Come to the house with me before I go. I got you something."

Ruby's pace was much slower than before. They entered the house through the office, which faced the yard. The antler rack on the wall above Ruby's head made it look as if her grandmother had sprouted horns.

Ruby handed Tulsa a paperback novel, *Sunny Chandler's Return* by Sandra Brown. On the cover a pretty woman gazed adoringly at the man in whose arms she was dancing.

Tulsa groaned.

"You'll like it," Ruby said.

"A romance novel?"

"It's about a woman trying to start her own business. You should relate to that."

"Let me guess. She falls in love with Mr. Perfect."

"No one's perfect, honey, even in romance novels."

"I bet it's got a happy ending," Tulsa said.

"Romances do."

Tulsa tossed the book on the desk. "That's not romance, Ruby. That's fantasy."

"True love isn't a fantasy."

All those times when her mom had sat on Tulsa's bed, face flushed, eyes wide, words tumbling out of her about her latest Mr. Right. How many different men had they moved in with? Five? Six? Her mother had loved so fast. Been so sure.

Been so wrong.

"Mom always had a romance novel in her hand. Was that what made her think that every man she met was her Prince Charming?"

"Just because your mom made some bad choices doesn't mean you will."

Tulsa thought of Charles. And Donny. And Warren. "I sure have so far."

Ruby looked near tears. "You can't give up on love, Tulsa. You just can't."

Tulsa sighed. Ruby was risking everything for her. The least she could do was do something to please Ruby. She lifted the book from the desk. "Fine. I'll read it."

Ruby's eyes lit up. "Good." She raised her hand in the air as if swearing an oath. "Promise me you'll keep an open mind."

"It's open."

"Honey, if you've got an open mind, then I'm a rainbow trout."

"I'll try. I promise."

"Good," Ruby said. "Oh, and one more thing. You need to read it by tomorrow night."

That made no sense. "Why?"

"You'll see."

Ruby's smile was maddening. Good thing it was a short book. "Tomorrow, fine." Damn. She didn't have time to waste on some silly book. She would just skim the thing.

"I've got to use the bathroom and put on some lipstick before I go to the bank," Ruby said. She kissed Tulsa's cheek.

Tulsa went back outside and inhaled the late-May morning air, so fragrant with honeysuckle and clover, bees were probably getting drunk. The seventy canoes she'd stacked leaned against one another, their aluminum sides glistening in the sunlight like beached whales. Lose this place? She walked down to the river, where customers had left three boats earlier. She grabbed the gunnels of one, swung it overhead, and carried it up the stairs. Her strong arms made her feel oak hard and deep-rooted.

She glanced at her watch. Guy should be back soon. If the bank did give Ruby a loan to buy Ed's, they would need to come up with ways to increase their business. She would not let Ruby lose her home. She would not.

CHAPTER TWO
Ruby

Ruby stood in their office, car keys in hand, trying to settle her nerves, wondering if she really wanted to risk losing the home that had been her family's through four generations. Her precious, precious home.

She sank into the desk chair and looked around the office at all the familiar, loved things. The ten-point antler rack she'd found years ago when she and her best friend, Pearl, were hiking through woods shushed by snow. The pipe her beloved husband had used, filling the house with the sweet fragrance of cherry tobacco. The cabinets her mother had built from old barn wood, then decorated with elaborate designs of green stems and pink roses. Ruby had recently repainted the cabinets, taking care to bring back the vibrant colors of her mother's handiwork. Despite having no schooling, Ruby's mom was one of the smartest women Ruby had ever known. She'd even taken the seats out of an old junked Ford Model T and fashioned them into the most comfortable porch swing in the hollow.

Ruby picked up the photograph of her daughter Faith, Tulsa's mom, with that thick, curly hair and carefree grin that had made her a heartbreaker even as a toddler. Faith had loved the Sweet Oak almost as much as Tulsa did, spending every spare hour she could in the river. The photo was taken when Faith was eighteen, pregnant with Tulsa, and engaged to Buddy, Tulsa's dad. Faith and Buddy were going to marry as soon as he came home on leave from the army. Faith looked so happy in the picture, her dancing eyes two-stepping through life.

Then Buddy was killed in a helicopter crash. A year later Faith and Tulsa moved in with Rupert Clancy, who was ten years older than Faith and promised to care for them both. As if. Living with Clancy had faded Faith's eyes from bright to pale blue, like a blouse that had been washed too often.

When Faith had had enough of Clancy, she took Tulsa and fled to Kansas City, moving hours away from the river. From Ruby. Faith died a few years later, barely twenty-eight. Ruby's heart still ached with missing her daughter. The only way Ruby would let Clancy get his claws on Ed's place was over her own dead body.

Besides, while she most certainly did not want to risk losing her home, it would be equally painful to close the canoe business, which would force Tulsa to move away just as surely as Clancy's jealousy had forced Faith to leave. She set the photo down gently on the desk, snatched up her car keys, and rose.

The phone's ring startled her. "Sweet Oak River Oasis," she said.

"Ruby, Dr. Morgan here."

She dropped her keys. She'd gone in to see him two days before because of nausea and fatigue. "Yes?" She sank into the desk chair, her body rigid.

"Your blood work and EKG look good," he said. "I think the nausea's from heartburn, which probably means you aren't sleeping well. You need to avoid rich, fried, and spicy foods."

Her shoulders relaxed. "So this is a clean bill of health?"

"Not entirely, no. Your blood pressure is much too high. Given your family history of heart problems, you need to be on medication."

Ruby pictured the small cemetery outside Fiddle where willow trees draped the graves of those she loved whose hearts had given out, including both her parents. "How much will that cost?"

"I'm not sure. You have prescription drug coverage, right?"

"No." She'd never needed pills.

Dr. Morgan clicked his tongue. "Well, we'll start with a generic. It shouldn't run you much."

"Good."

"Come back and see me in six weeks so we can be sure it's working. And, Ruby, you need to avoid stress. It's hard on the heart, and you're not getting any younger."

It didn't take a medical degree to know that. When they hung up, Ruby leaned back in her chair and glanced out the window. A scattering of white and pink dogwood blossoms dotted the woods bordering their house. It seemed that spring had lasted only a minute. She remembered as a child thinking that the school year would never end. Now it felt like Memorial Day followed right after Christmas.

She picked up the copy of *Sunny Chandler's Return* that she'd bought for Tulsa. If Tulsa had been surprised by the request that she read a romance novel in one day, wait until their friends showed up tomorrow evening having also read *Sunny Chandler's Return*. Ruby was certain that the other three—Pearl, Jen, and BJ—would love the book, which she'd given them a few days before. Tulsa . . . maybe not.

Her granddaughter was a striking woman— long, thick hair the color of a brand new copper-bottomed pan, and a figure both slender and curvy—but she didn't give a fig about her looks. Maybe romance novels, with their tales of true love, hot sex, and hopeful endings, would inspire Tulsa. Surely Tulsa could identify with Sunny Chandler. Like Tulsa, Sunny was striving to run a small business. Also like Tulsa, Sunny was doubtful about men and marriage. Hopefully, like Sunny, Tulsa would change and find true love.

Of course there were lots of newer romance

novels, but it was cheaper to read older ones. She could almost always find multiple used copies of older romances at local book exchanges like the shelves at the Fiddle post office and the library's Bring a Book, Take a Book collection. Then, too, she much preferred the older books to newer ones about love affairs with vampires, demons, and ghosts.

Quit stalling, Ruby told herself. *If you're going to the bank, then go.* She grabbed her car keys and shoved open the screen door. She had to see Tulsa settled down before she died, and she might not have all that long to make it happen.

CHAPTER THREE
Tulsa

Tulsa practically leapt off the riding mower to greet Guy when he drove up to the campground in the old yellow bus they used to shuttle canoeists. It seemed like she'd called him days ago to fill him in, but it had been only a couple of hours. Ruby was probably nearly finished at the bank by now.

Guy swung open the bus door. Elvis, his blind, spotted dog, bounded down the bus steps. "Big day," said Guy, Tulsa's half brother on her father's side, sauntering over to her.

"Yeah. Bus running okay?" she asked.

"Yep. Belts held. I filled her up. We're good to go."

"Great, because we can't afford problems. We've got to increase business fast if Ruby gets that loan. I was thinking we could send out flyers to fly shops, bait shops, and sporting goods stores around the state." She was talking so fast the words practically tangled in her mouth, but she couldn't seem to slow down. "I'll work on the flyers tonight. Tomorrow we'll post them in every store and church in Fiddle and West Plains."

Guy put his hands up and took a step back. "Whoa. Did you drink a whole pot of your own coffee? That stuff could fuel fighter planes."

"I couldn't bear it if we failed."

"That won't happen," he said, petting Elvis.

"How do you know?"

"Because we won't let it."

She envied his certainty and looked into his soft brown eyes. Odd to think neither she nor Ruby had even known Guy existed until a year ago. Now he seemed almost as much a part of her life as the river. They paid him a third of their net earnings every summer. In winter Guy did odd jobs for others: repairing vehicles, fixing leaking roofs, building retaining walls and decks, and whatever else needed doing.

"How about we use that energy of yours to finish getting the campground ready for this weekend while we wait for Ruby," Guy said. "We can talk while we work."

"Good idea."

They got a scythe and weed spray from the carport that served as a garage. Guy swung the scythe easily, rhythmically, like it was part of himself, trimming the weeds that bordered the campground while Tulsa sprayed the intermingled patches of poison ivy. The spray's astringent smell stung her nose.

"We might want to offer store owners a one-time thirty-percent discount off midweek prices if they post the flyers all summer," he said.

"I like that," she said. "And I'll put together a list of phone numbers of places like schools, churches, and scout troops. Then when any of us has a couple of minutes, we could make phone calls and maybe offer a ten-percent discount for groups of, say, fifteen or more."

"Good. I'm working on Rich's truck this afternoon."

"Really? We've got so much to do."

"I know. But he's going to pay me by building us a website, which we should have done a while ago."

"There's a lot we should have done a while ago. If only we'd known about Ed's."

"Relax." He put his hand on her shoulder. "You and Ruby won't lose this place." His certainty, his steady gaze, and his hand on her shoulder made her take what seemed like her first real breath since that morning.

"If we do get the loan and the business we need," she said, "you won't have as much time to spend with Wanda."

Guy rested the scythe on his shoulder. "Oh, I'll make time for Wanda. That woman moves her body in ways that are a wonder to behold."

He grinned. Born within five weeks of each other, Tulsa and Guy shared lanky builds and light-brown hair with a reddish tint. While her eyes were green, Guy's were a warm brown that fell on you soft as a cat's breath. No wonder he could bed most any woman he wanted. It wasn't that he was classically handsome. His nose was crooked, his hair beginning to thin a bit. But those eyes made it seem like they weren't interested in anything except the person they looked at.

"I'd advise you to make some time, too," he said.

"Make time for Wanda?"

"Make time for *somebody*."

"You sound like Ruby. She practically begged me to read a romance novel."

"Good. It's been months since you broke up with Warren."

"I didn't. *He* broke up with *me*."

"Which just proves he's an idiot. But there are a lot of men who aren't. And life's a whole lot more fun when you're in a relationship."

"Says the man who wouldn't know a real relationship if it bit your lure and swallowed your cork."

"Says the woman who won't even cast out her line." He started swinging the scythe again. "Besides, I've been going out with Wanda for four months now."

"Is that a record?"

"Could be. Seriously, have some great sex. That will get your mind off Warren."

"It's not on Warren. And lay off. I hear enough about it from Ruby."

They worked side by side in silence for a while, making their way around the eight-acre campground, trimming and spraying and sprucing it up for the crowds they hoped to welcome this Memorial Day weekend.

Elvis rose from lying in the sun near them and howled—a long, mournful sound that seemed to seep inside Tulsa and make her shiver.

Guy scratched behind the dog's ear. "I swear, Elvis, you are one big hound dog, howling all the time. Even if you are a girl." Elvis's tail thumped the ground.

That's when Tulsa heard the rumble of an engine coming down the hill. It had to be Ruby. Tulsa tightened her grip on the rake in her hand. She reminded herself to breathe.

Ruby parked by the house. Tulsa dropped the rake and sprinted toward the truck. She yanked open the driver's door. "Well?" she said.

Ruby grinned. "It's ours."

Tulsa shouted, "Yes!" and thrust her fist into the air.

"Congratulations," Guy said, shaking Ruby's hand. He put his arm around Tulsa's shoulders and squeezed. "What terms did you get?"

"Ten percent down. Thirty-year mortgage. No falling behind on payments."

"And our place?" Tulsa said, sobering.

"It's collateral," Ruby said. "We better make this work."

Tulsa took Ruby's hand. "We will."

"I transferred ownership of everything to you, like I said I would. You call the shots now."

Tulsa shook her head. "No way. I don't care what's on a piece of paper. This is *our* place, Ruby, not mine. We call the shots together. As always."

"Well, we'll see. I'm tuckered out. Think I'll take a little nap."

"Take a long nap if you need it," Tulsa said. "It's been an exciting day."

Ruby nodded her agreement. "I'll say."

Tulsa helped Ruby down from the truck, then opened the screen door for her. As Ruby started inside, Tulsa put her hand on her grandmother's shoulder. "Thank you," she said.

Ruby just smiled and went on inside.

Elvis barked. Tulsa ruffled the dog's ears, wanting to bark along with her. "Give a shout if anybody comes," she told Guy. She stripped off her jeans and T-shirt. In underwear and bra, she plunged into the river, kicking and stroking as hard as she could, battling the current. She wasn't sure if she was propelled more by exuberance or fear, but she found herself able to conquer the current and make her way upstream.

Life took so much away, but then, once in a while, it surprised you by slipping in something sweet. She had lost her mom at ten, but she'd gained Ruby and the river. And then, at twenty-seven, she'd found Guy, a half brother she really liked. She counted herself lucky. And luckier still now that Ed's was theirs. *Sweet river,* she thought. *Sweet Ruby. Sweet Guy. And sweet, sweet life.*

CHAPTER FOUR

Tulsa

Late the next day Tulsa parked the bus near the house. An expensive gray Range Rover was parked by the river. Someone had money. With any luck, he or she would spend a bundle of it here. Tulsa got off the bus, wiping the sweat from her face with the back of her hand. She'd probably streaked her face with the grime she'd gotten when she put the high school seniors' canoes in the river.

A man stood on the bank overlooking the water, his back to her. He wore dark pants and a white shirt with the sleeves rolled up. He turned from the river and started toward her. A large brace covered his left knee. Even with a limp, he seemed to stride rather than just walk, his fluidity that of a man whose life was greased by money and power. Funny how inseparable those two things were.

As he neared, Tulsa judged him to be close to her own age. She took in dark, bushy eyebrows above eyes that were the shimmering blue of a jay's feathers. The stubble that shadowed his cheeks and chin appeared carefully cultivated. He probably shaved only every two or three days. His white linen shirt looked immaculate if out of place. Overall, the man's appearance was one of contradiction—shadow and shimmer, precision and indifference.

When he reached her, he held out his hand. "Morning," he said. "I'm Slade Morrison."

She wiped her hand off on her pants before shaking his. "Tulsa Riley."

"You run the Oasis?" he asked.

"With my grandmother and brother, yes."

"I rented Hideaway cabin for the weekend," Slade said. "I understand it's only one room. I'd prefer something bigger."

"Memorial Day weekend's been booked for a month," she said. "You're lucky we had a cancellation. Hideaway's a large room, and it's got a deck overlooking the river. You can put some gear out there."

"It's safe?"

"Except for the raccoons. They won't steal much."

He nodded like he was taking that in, then said, "I'd be happy to pay extra to upgrade to a bigger cabin."

"Sorry. But you're welcome to reserve the bigger cabin for later in the summer."

He smiled. A dimpled smile, naturally.

Ruby's sedan churned gravel as she came down the hill and parked by the house. She had gone to Fiddle and West Plains to post Tulsa's flyers. Ruby got out of the car. Tulsa walked over to her, followed by Slade. When Ruby's eyes fell on him, they seemed to brighten. "I'm Ruby Riley," she said.

"Slade Morrison."

"I see you've met my granddaughter."

"I certainly have."

"Tulsa, honey, why don't you go wash off some of that dirt," Ruby suggested.

"Dirt is just Ozarks rouge," Tulsa replied.

Ruby looked like she wanted to protest, but she didn't. "Slade, you booked Guy to guide tomorrow, right?"

"Right," Slade said. "Folks at the Perfect Drift Fly Shop recommended him."

"He can't," Tulsa said. "He promised to take

a look at Linda Tucker's roof. It's leaking."

"Great!" Ruby rubbed her hands together like she'd just served them strawberry rhubarb cobbler. "Then you can guide Slade."

"Sure," she said.

"Really?" Slade looked skeptical. "I mean, not many women fly-fish. You know how?"

"It's easy," Tulsa said. "You throw your line up in the air and try to snag some flies."

Ruby chuckled. "Tulsa could cast her line between a mosquito's wings."

"Really?" Slade said.

"Only the bigger ones," Tulsa said.

Slade arched his eyebrows. "They grow that big around here, do they? Should I buy some mosquito netting?"

"Nah. We've got an extra volleyball net. It'll stop the big ones."

"Tulsa," Ruby said, "you're crazy."

Slade flashed a disarming smile; the lines around his shimmery eyes turned up like they were smiling, too. "I'd be grateful if you'd guide me," he said. "I may make an ass of myself at times, but I'm quick to make amends."

Tulsa couldn't really blame him for doubting her. He was right that not many women fly-fished. She'd been lucky to learn from an expert, the man who'd helped out with the canoe business before Guy came. "Ruby says I make an ass of myself with some regularity," she said.

"Two asses. One canoe. Perfect. What time should I be here? Six?"

"Make it nine."

Slade seemed to wince. "That's too late to get started."

"This time of year, trout don't start biting till midmorning. They're waiting for the insect feeds."

"I'm eager to get out on the water. I'll be here at eight."

"It's your money."

"Great," Slade said. "See you tomorrow." He nodded to Tulsa and Ruby. "Enjoy your evening."

He limped to his vehicle. Whatever injury he had didn't seem to slow him down much. Lucky for him the brace covered only his knee. A full leg brace would be harder to manage.

As they walked toward the house, Ruby spoke. "That is one good-looking man, is he not?"

"If you like tall, dark, and handsome. Not my type."

Ruby sighed. "I don't know why I bother."

Tulsa squeezed Ruby's shoulders. "Because you love me," she said.

"That I do," Ruby said, her hazel eyes so full of love they seemed almost blurry. The women stepped into the office. "You go on and shower now, Tulsa. We got company coming later, and you're smelly."

"It's Ozarks perfume. Goes with my Ozarks makeup."

"If you want to eat my Ozarks potato salad and Ozarks hamburgers, you'll shower."

"Throw in some fresh peaches and I'll even use deodorant." Tulsa paused. "Tell me again why Jen, Pearl, and BJ all decided to come by tonight."

Ruby's smile would look perfectly sincere to most people, but Tulsa read in it an ulterior motive so loud it was practically a roar.

"Oh, they just wanted to come by to gab a bit and enjoy some dessert," Ruby said.

"Uh-huh."

"Don't be so suspicious," Ruby said. "Go on and shower."

It was futile to try to pry answers from her grandmother when she didn't care to give them. Tulsa took the stairs two at a time. The white oak outside her bedroom window shaded the room without making it gloomy. She loved the sage-green walls, the white trim, the treasures scattered around: an orange flicker feather, a crimson cardinal feather, dried asters and goldenrod, a river rock with spiral fossil.

She stripped out of her clothes and stepped into the shower. The hot water struck her shoulders, loosening them. She scrubbed her body, beginning with her hair. A good-looking man in her shower could be fun, and Slade was definitely good-looking, but love died, one way or another. It certainly had with Warren, not to mention the many men her mom had loved, Clancy included.

Tulsa was only three when her mom left Clancy, and she didn't remember much about living with him except a vague recollection of how often her mother had cried. Her own choices in men hadn't worked out either. Tulsa flinched at the memory of the Tuesday Warren had come to see her, a night they rarely got together. She'd been excited, looking forward to seeing him, thinking it a sign of how much he cared for her. Instead he'd told Tulsa that he'd reconnected with his former high school sweetheart at their class reunion and realized he'd never stopped loving the sweetheart despite her short-lived marriage to another man. Suppressing tears, Tulsa had literally pushed Warren out the door midapology.

Looking back, his dumping her hadn't been all that surprising. Like mother like daughter. Her mom might have left Clancy, but most of the men she'd loved had dumped her. Tulsa rinsed the shampoo from her hair and watched it disappear down the drain.

CHAPTER FIVE
BJ

In an office in Fiddle's town square, BJ Smith studied her doctor's thin Ichabod Crane face— drawn now, and solemn—and knew what he would say before he could say it. The CT scan had proved her right. The awful pain in her back meant bone cancer. At just forty-six, she was too young to be so sick. Poor Guy. Her son would be devastated, but at least he had Tulsa and Ruby. He wouldn't be totally alone in the world. Besides, she would fight just like Angela Levy, bless her soul, who had been given six months but lived six years until she slipped on her granddaughter's plastic mermaid and cracked her skull on the toilet bowl.

Seated behind his large mahogany desk, Dr. Newton frowned, his furry eyebrows like caterpillars stretching. She was oddly calm to be able to think of caterpillars, but she'd known all along what he would say.

"BJ—" he began.

"I know. Cancer."

"No."

She didn't move, afraid to jinx herself. "Are you sure?"

He nodded then, gently, it seemed to her. "I am."

Thank you, Jesus! she thought.

"You've got ELS, BJ."

She didn't know what ELS was, but his unsmiling face made her heart plummet. "Is that serious?"

"Potentially. Though it's curable."

Her heart settled back in her chest. "What is ELS?"

"Empty Life Syndrome."

Her head began to throb. "What?"

Dr. Newton folded his hands on his desk. Was he praying? "Brenda June," he said, "you've been coming to me with fatal illnesses you don't have for years, both before you moved away and ever since you've been back."

"Just because you can't find what causes my pain doesn't mean it isn't real."

"I realize it feels real."

"For your information, my life is not empty. I've got my son and my job and I've got Jesus. I'm blessed."

"You shouldn't build your life around Guy."

He had no idea how fulfilling it was to nurture a baby inside you, then guide your child through life's many valleys. "You've obviously never been a mother."

"And you've never been a son."

"What are you saying?"

He leaned his forehead against his hands and

peered out like he was begging for strength. "You've got church. Hobbies. A part-time job. Friends. The only thing I can think of that you don't have is a man's love."

She touched her hand to her heart. "Jesus loves me."

"Jesus loves everybody," he said. "You need someone less promiscuous."

BJ stood. She would not listen to this. "You aren't giving me a prescription for my back pain?"

Dr. Newton scribbled something on his prescription pad, ripped the page off, and handed it to her.

Rx: Find a man.
Refills: Unlimited.

BJ stomped toward the door.

"You should also lose thirty or forty pounds," he called after her.

She squared her shoulders and walked away from the room with as much dignity as she could muster. She didn't let herself slump until she got in her car. She sat against the hot vinyl seat back, clenching Dr. Newton's prescription. How dare he suggest she didn't know how to mother her son, that her life was empty! What did he know? She had Guy, church, her visits to shut-ins, the model churches she created. And, yes, she had Jesus.

And how dare he write that prescription! She was no feminist, but she'd bet he wouldn't write a prescription for a man that said *Find a woman.*

She also had back pain, no matter what he thought. Right now. She rummaged through her tote bag until she found the aspirin bottle, then took two and choked them down with saliva. They scratched her throat. Closing her eyes, she leaned back in the seat, letting the minutes pass, waiting for the aspirin to work. Though she would give anything to stop the pain, she knew she deserved it. After what she'd done, it was a wonder God didn't punish her even more.

Was there any chance Dr. Newton was right, that her physical pain stemmed from the emotional agony of loneliness? Lord knew, those nights when she couldn't sleep, she sometimes thought of Buddy and dreamed they were both young, that he held her sweetly. Of course, they'd had only the one night, and he'd been dead for nearly thirty years. Wasn't it a bit pathetic that she was nearly fifty, yet Buddy was still the man of her dreams?

If by some chance there was a tiny element of truth to what Dr. Newton had said—and she wasn't ready to say there was, but if there was— what was she supposed to do about it?

BJ unwrapped a piece of butterscotch candy. The wrapper crackled. She placed the candy in her mouth and sucked hard, wanting its sweet, buttery flavor to explode. Ahh. Next to Guy and Jesus, butterscotch was perhaps her biggest source of comfort.

She reached in her tote bag for Kleenex and felt the book she'd just read. *Sunny Chandler's Return*. Ruby had asked her to read it. Normally BJ had no time for fiction. She'd read the book because of all Ruby had done for her. Actually, she hadn't read the book so much as devoured it. The idea of having a man like the hero, Ty Beaumont, in her life made her yearn for love in a way she hadn't in years.

If Buddy had lived, she'd bet he'd have been a lot like Ty Beaumont. Buddy, with his long-lashed, smoldering eyes, the wounded look that at seventeen had made her want to hold him so much even though he was the beau of her best friend, Faith.

Why was it so easy for some people to find true love and so hard for others? Like herself. And her son, Guy, who had no trouble dating but had never dated anyone he wanted to marry. If only Guy had fallen for Tulsa's friend Jen, who was sweet and loving and would make a perfect daughter-in-law.

BJ wished she understood more about finding love. She had hoped that her job working three days a week at the West Plains hardware store might do the trick. After all, she'd grown up helping out at her dad's store, which she'd inherited and sold. It was why she could afford to work part-time. None of the male customers who had complimented her on her knowledge at the West Plains store, however, had bothered to ask her how she knew so much, let alone whether she wanted to go out.

Well, maybe reading romance novels would help. Not that *Sunny Chandler* had. Sunny didn't go out and find love so much as had it forced down her throat by Ty. Well, no man was likely to want to force love down BJ's throat. She wasn't gorgeous like Sunny. Heck, she wasn't even pretty.

BJ set *Sunny Chandler's Return* back in her purse. She should be happy—no, joyful—that she didn't have cancer, and she was. She really was.

She groaned as she picked the prescription off the floor, where it had fallen by the brake pedal. *Find a man.*

Weren't prescriptions supposed to include directions?

CHAPTER SIX

Jen

In the salon on the main street of Fiddle, Jen Haskell pressed her fingers into the arch of the elderly Delilah Foster's foot and daydreamed that the hero of *Sunny Chandler's Return*, the book Ruby had given her to read, would walk into the salon, whisk Jen up in his arms, and tell her a version of what he told Sunny: that he'd loved her instantly, that he would marry her, take care of her, and let everyone know she was his.

"That feels so good, Jen," Mrs. Foster said.

"I'm glad." Jen's was the only touch Mrs. Foster, widowed two years, knew from week to week, so Jen lingered on the massage part of the pedicure, letting Mrs. Foster know someone saw her. Someone cared.

"I'm ready for you, Delilah," said Marianne Turner, salon owner and chief hairstylist. Marianne's last customer had just left.

Much as Jen disliked her boss's focus on the bottom line, she had to give the woman credit for fashion sense. Marianne wore her thick hair in long, choppy waves, and her pink blouse and white slacks flattered her Barbie doll figure. Jen dressed in vivid rainbow colors, like the tulip-red blouse she was wearing beneath her turquoise smock. Her friend Tulsa claimed Jen dressed like a Christmas tree ornament. Jen took that as a compliment. She liked to think she shimmered.

While Marianne cut the thin, elderly Mrs. Foster's hair, Jen would paint her toenails the same dark red she'd worn for all ten years Jen had been doing them. Jen gently dried Mrs. Foster's feet, then helped her into Marianne's chair. "There you go."

"How about a little different cut for once?"

Marianne said to Mrs. Foster, who wore her hair short and turned under, styled in a fashion as prim as the blouses she kept fully buttoned even when the temperature soared. "Something a little more modern."

"No, thanks. Just the usual."

"I swear, Delilah," Marianne said, "you've been wearing your hair the same way since the Confederates fired on Fort Sumter."

Mrs. Foster looked down at her hands. Jen covered her mouth to keep from blurting out to her boss that she needed to be more sensitive.

Hair Today, Fiddle's only salon, stank of the ammonia-based products they used for permanents. The paint was drab, the magazines old. If the salon were Jen's, it would smell of perfumed oils and offer current fashion magazines and steamy novels, fresh flowers and bright colors, coffee and sweets. It would be a place that invited women to indulge and dream. And it would be a place where a woman could change hairstyles every single time or never. No one would mock her choices.

The phone blared. Jen rose to answer it. "Hair Today. May I help you?"

"Is this you, Jen?"

The rasp of the voice told her who the caller was. "Mom?"

"I'm in the hospital," her mother said.

"What! Are you okay?"

"I'm in the hospital, what do you think?"

Heart attack? Stroke? Diabetic reaction? Cirrhosis? Jen held her breath as she asked, "What's wrong?"

"I broke my leg."

"Oh no," Jen said, her mind spinning. As if her mother hadn't dealt with enough in her life. "How?"

"I fell."

Jen pictured her mother drunk and tripping on the broken pavement outside her trailer. "Did you break it bad?"

"I sure didn't break it good."

Jen winced. "I'm sorry, Mom. Do you need me to get anything for you?"

"No. I need to stay with you and your boyfriend when they release me."

"What?" Jen clenched the phone.

"I don't have anywhere else to go. Tell him."

"I'll come by the hospital at lunch so we can talk," Jen said.

"What for? Just tell your lover boy I need to stay for a few weeks." Jen's mother hung up.

Jen stood staring at the receiver in her hand. If only she could push a rewind button and start over. Or better yet, just erase the whole conversation.

"Is your mother okay?"

Mrs. Foster asked the question with such caring, Jen had to turn away. She brushed her hand across her eyes. "Not really," she said, turning back. "She broke her leg."

"Tough luck," Marianne said. "I've never broken anything. Except a few hearts." She blasted a laugh.

Jen grabbed a bottle of nail polish and pulled her stool up to do Mrs. Foster's nails. She would go by the hospital at lunch and see what shape her mother was in. If she really needed help, what choice did Jen have but to ask Jack?

Maybe this was a blessing in disguise. Maybe it would give her the chance to connect with her mother—really connect. They might talk about their lives, their hopes, their dreams, their disappointments. Maybe they would even laugh together over something one of them said.

"Stop!"

Marianne's command brought Jen out of her reverie. She glanced down. She'd just painted the toenails of the widow's left foot a perky green.

Jen paced the kitchen she'd painted a few weeks ago, transforming walls the color of split-pea soup into candy-apple red. Though Jack had said the brightness practically blinded him, he'd accepted the change.

Jack was the best thing that had happened in her life. He wasn't classically handsome. His ears seemed large, his chin sloping, but she loved his blond hair—natural, unlike her own—and she loved the way his sport shirts fit him perfectly, as if he were a carefully displayed mannequin. Plus, he was stable. Responsible. Reliable. He ran his own insurance company, rarely drank, and treated her pretty damned well. Did she really want to risk all that?

The garage door rumbled open. Jen tried to swallow a thin strand of saliva, but she had to choke it down.

Jack strode in and tossed his briefcase on the kitchen counter. He sniffed the air. "Tuna fish casserole?" he said, his face light, eager.

God, she was lucky! "Made special for you," she said. The aroma of tuna fish was tantalizing.

Jack hugged her, then stepped back. "Hey, cutie," he said.

Jen's smile stretched her lips. She'd long ago become artful at makeup, nails, and accessories. She wore her short blonde hair carefully mussed. Only a little over five feet, she was often called "cute" or "perky." She would far rather be tall, with coltish legs, and move all smooth and confident like a dancer. She didn't remember how tall Sunny Chandler was, but she bet most romance heroines were tall and regal. Jen straightened. "Sit down and I'll serve you."

"Sounds good." He took his seat at the square kitchen table they used for meals when it was just the two of them.

"How was your day?" Jen picked up the

casserole dish to serve him, hoping he didn't notice the slight tremble of her hands.

"Great. I convinced Martha Burris she needed a much better homeowner's policy."

"She does?"

"She did."

"That's wonderful, sweetie. Congratulations. You're so good at what you do."

Jack raised his shoulders as if to show his indifference to praise, but his smile suggested otherwise.

"Was Martha appreciative?" she asked.

"She was a little concerned she was spending too much, but I think she appreciated the security the policy provides."

How was she ever going to persuade Jack to let her mom stay with them? "Not everyone can afford insurance," she ventured after a moment.

"Sure they can. It's just a matter of priorities. So many people are so damned shortsighted." He jabbed the air with his fork. "Insurance should be top, right up there with food and shelter. Without insurance, you could lose both. I tell people they shouldn't start a family until they can provide the basic necessities. Insurance is one of those."

He made it sound so simple, but for so many people it wasn't simple at all. Of course, if her mother had insurance, she could go to rehab. If only. "You're right," she said. "But . . ."

He looked up. "But what?"

"It's my mom."

"What about her?"

"She's in the hospital with a broken leg. They had to pin it. And they're keeping her to get her diabetes under control."

"That's too bad."

The words gushed out of her before she could filter them. "She needs a place to stay. She doesn't have insurance. Could she stay with us just for a couple of months until she can get around on her own? I know it's a lot to ask, but she needs my help and she doesn't have any savings. I realize she's made a mess of her life, but I'm her only child and I don't know what else to do."

Jack chewed a bite of tuna slowly, staring at his plate, apparently lost in thought. Jen didn't even attempt to eat.

"I thought you didn't much like your mom," he said finally.

"Well, I like her. I mean, she's my mother. Or maybe I don't like her all that much, but I love her."

Jack stirred his food on his plate. "If she stays here, she'll make you miserable."

"I don't know what else to do. She has nowhere to go. I can't let her be homeless or starve to death because she can't get around. Please, Jack. Just till she can take care of herself."

"What about your job? Are you going to be nursing her all day?"

"No, I'll fix her food and put it in the

refrigerator, and I'll come home at lunch to check on her. She can call me at work if she needs something."

"She'll understand that this is my house, right?"

His words stabbed her. He still thought of it as *his* house? Not theirs? Of course, it was technically his, but they'd lived together for two years. Her eyes misted over. More than once Tulsa had questioned Jack's ability to commit. *Would* he ever agree to marriage and family?

"What?" he said.

"Nothing." She brushed her hand across her eyes and made herself smile.

"What I say goes," Jack says. "What we watch on TV isn't her decision. She respects our home. And no booze. If she agrees to follow the rules, we can try it, though from what you've told me about her, I just hope you're not miserable for the next two months."

"Thank you!" Jen said, though she shared Jack's concern. "Maybe she'll change."

"People don't change, Jen."

"A little, they do. Sometimes. And if she does, when we have kids, she could babysit."

"Kids? I just acquired a mother."

Why on earth had she brought kids up now, and why couldn't she stop? "*Do* you want children, Jack? Really?"

"Sure," he said, "but I've got to build the agency up first."

As much as Jen enjoyed doing people's nails, it wasn't how she wanted to be spending her days, not at this stage of her life. "How long will that take? I'm turning twenty-nine soon." She squeezed his hand to show she didn't mean to be confrontational.

"A couple of years or so."

Two years sounded like *two decades*. Maybe in two years he would want two more. Then again, what were her options? She wasn't likely to meet a man who offered her all Jack did—the stability, the home. Besides, she loved him.

"I want to raise my kids right," he said. "Give them things you and I didn't have."

Like her, Jack had grown up in a trailer court. Jen would be glad to give their children a comfortable home, but what really mattered was parents who would love them. Unlike her own mother, Jen would shower her children with love.

Her mother had refused to meet Jack. She'd never had that much interest in Jen's life. Jen's stomach felt tight. The casserole on her plate looked about as appetizing as dog food. Her mother was like a tornado that sucked Jen up, spun her around, and spat her out. Jack was his own force of nature, a man accustomed to control. He would no more let a tornado obliterate his house than destroy it himself. Jen wasn't sure if two tornadoes had ever collided, but she had the awful feeling they were about to.

CHAPTER SEVEN
Tulsa

Lowell White, the man at the office door with a squirming toddler in his arms and a slightly older one clinging to his leg, asked Tulsa a question that didn't make sense.

"Have you got some air mattresses we could borrow for bedding?" he said.

Lowell and his family were staying at Treetop, their largest cabin. It had a queen bed and two bunks, plenty for two adults and four kids.

That was when Tulsa registered that Lowell's wife and two more kids were sitting in a packed Suburban, which was even more puzzling given that they'd arrived only the day before and had booked Treetop two months previously for an entire week. "Something wrong with the beds?" she asked. She smiled at the boy trying to hide behind Lowell's thin leg. The boy ducked back farther but gave her a shy smile.

"No, we're swapping cabins." Lowell rubbed his fingers together in the symbol for money. "I was admiring some guy's car, and he offered me a thousand plus the rental price of the cabin to swap. We need to borrow bedding, if you've got any."

Damn Slade. "You don't have to do that, Lowell."

"Are you kidding? That's the easiest money I ever made."

Given Lowell's enthusiasm, there wasn't any point in protesting the cabin swap, though Slade's throwing money around rankled her. "I've got some air mattresses we used to rent for floating. They're in the carport. I'll get them." Tulsa closed the door behind her and walked toward the covered carport that served as storage space.

She yanked the box she thought held the air mattresses off a shelf. People with a lot of money seemed to operate on a whole other level. The last man Tulsa's mother loved had a lot of money. He spent it lavishly, buying Tulsa a shiny red bike and her mother a brand-new Buick Skylark that he presented covered with red bows. But he wasn't lavish with his love. The few times Tulsa had been to his mansion, he'd kept issuing orders: don't sit on anything white, don't wear shoes or sing indoors, don't touch the roses in the garden.

That last day, he came to the tiny cottage Tulsa and her mom were renting and told Faith that he'd fallen in love with his personal masseuse. Tulsa's mom sobbed, clinging to him, begging him not to leave her. He just walked away with a jaunty step down a sidewalk lined with the marigolds Faith had planted to celebrate their promised marriage.

Faith's last lover drove off in the Buick Skylark, never once looking back.

Tulsa could still see her mom sinking to her knees. Sobbing hysterically, she began ripping up the marigolds, smearing her hands with dirt and flecks of orange petals. Tulsa tried to calm her mother by putting her arms around her, but Faith just pushed her away, sobbing even louder. Not knowing what else to do, Tulsa began helping tear up the flowers. "It's okay, Mom," she'd repeated, over and over. "It's okay."

Suddenly silent, her mother keeled over. Tulsa tried to rouse her, then ran inside and called 911.

Faith never woke up. The doctor said she'd suffered a massive heart attack, but Tulsa knew better. Her mother had strangled to death on her tears.

Ruby sped to Kansas City and took Tulsa home to the river. The Sweet Oak had saved her.

Tulsa rummaged through the box. No air mattresses. She set it back on the shelf and pulled down another. The only customers she hated dealing with were drunken louts and people who liked to throw their money around. Unlike her mother, Tulsa would never let herself be bossed around by rich people or lovers. She would rather take orders from a potted plant.

There they were, the air mattresses, folded in a box in the corner. They smelled musty. She carried them out to a grateful Lowell, got him four sleeping bags forgotten by various campers over the years, and headed back to the house. There was so much she needed to do.

CHAPTER EIGHT
Pearl

In the family room of Fiddle's Holy Bible Church, Pearl Jacobs licked salt from the pretzel she was holding while she read about kisses, erotic zones, and fertile bellies. She glanced up from *Sunny Chandler's Return*, the book Ruby had given her. Pearl's eyes fell on the wooden cross hanging on the front wall. Would God mind that she was reading about sex in His church? Hopefully not. She was in the family room, after all, not the sanctuary, and it was a Thursday, not a Sunday.

Sunny Chandler's Return was a whole lot more fun to read than her last book, which was the biography of William Howard Taft.

Pearl again licked the pretzel. Her buddy Ruby joked that when Pearl died, she wouldn't have to be embalmed because she was already brined. Well, she'd made it almost to eighty. If the salt took a few months off her life, so be it.

Muffled voices. Pearl stashed *Sunny Chandler* in her purse and turned up her hearing aid. The other women were arriving, no doubt with their usual contributions to the Thursday potluck lunch: deviled eggs, Jell-O salad, fried chicken, baked beans flavored with molasses.

Pearl never prepared food for the luncheons. She had once calculated that in her fifty-eight years running Sherman's Café with her husband, Sherman, she'd rolled out over three hundred thousand pies and served over a million hamburgers. Her legs and feet ached from all those years Sherman had made her wait tables, wash dishes, mop floors. God help her, there were times when she was glad her husband had passed.

Good thing her grandson didn't mind bringing something for her contribution to the church luncheon from the Wagon Wheel restaurant, where he worked. Last week he'd dropped off potato salad. This week he'd said he'd bring coleslaw.

More women entered the family room, chatting up a storm. There would be a dozen or so of them plus their minister, who tended to ramble. Pearl was more pious than a lot of folks, but she didn't think you needed to pray so long the lettuce wilted.

A couple of the women looked toward the door and grimaced. She followed their stares. Her twenty-five-year-old grandson was entering the room, covered bowl in hand. He greeted the women, who leaned back like he was a leper.

Pearl had a pretty good idea why Minnie Plunkett looked so angry. Daniel had broken up with Minnie's daughter, Bonnie, a good six months ago, but Minnie apparently still held it against him. It was a shame because Bonnie had seemed such a sweet girl. Which just went to show that apples *can* fall far from the tree.

Pearl rose and kissed her grandson on the cheek. Minnie harrumphed so loud, Pearl's hearing aid crackled. She whirled toward Minnie. "Minnie Plunkett, you got a bug up your butt?"

Minnie clapped her hand to her chest like she was trying to push her insides back in. "Sinners don't belong in God's house," Minnie said.

"Then why are *you* here?"

Minnie's nostrils flared so wide, they could suck in a low-flying bird. "I've repented of *my* sins." She glowered at Daniel. "When the rapture comes with the new millennium this January, *I* will be called up."

"Then I hope I'm not," Pearl said.

"Gran?"

Pearl turned back to Daniel. His curly red hair and the freckles spattered across his face made him look young and innocent, like the puppet on that old TV show *Howdy Doody*. "Yes?" she said.

"I need to get back to work."

Daniel looked like he was ill at ease. What with Minnie's scowls, Pearl didn't blame him. She took the bowl of coleslaw and set it on the food table. "Sure thing, Danny. I'll walk you out." She turned her back on Minnie and walked beside Daniel into a day that was warm without being hot. Bluebells lined the church sidewalk, giving off a slightly sweet scent.

"You might want to warn people about the coleslaw," Daniel said. "I put in some Ozark Hillbilly Hot Sauce to make it interesting."

"Good idea." Daniel was certainly a talented enough cook to realize his dream of someday moving from Fiddle to become head chef at one of Springfield's better restaurants. He'd loved cooking since he was old enough to wield a rolling pin and help roll out piecrusts, biscuits, and cinnamon rolls at the café. "I guess Minnie still hasn't forgiven you for breaking up with Bonnie."

Danny looked away.

"Is something wrong? Why *did* you break up with Bonnie? If you told me, I've forgotten."

"She's just . . . not my type."

"What is your type, Danny? If I knew, maybe I could help you find the right girl."

Daniel gave a furtive smile.

"What?" she said. "Did you already find someone else?"

"I did," he said.

"You certainly move fast, young man. Just be careful you don't do anything reckless like I did.

You get to know a person real well before you marry her. Who is she?"

"Nobody you know."

She didn't think there was a girl Danny's age in town whom she hadn't met through her church or her work.

"Did I tell you I moved?" he said.

"I thought you liked your place."

"I did, but the landlord wanted it for his son. I moved in with a friend across town."

"A friend? You're not living in sin with some girl, are you?" she asked.

"No."

There was that funny smile again. "What?"

He glanced at his feet. If she didn't know any better, she'd think he was hiding something, but Daniel had always been one to show his feelings. His smiles were pure sunshine, while his sad expressions just about broke her heart.

"I'd better get going," he said. "I'll come by and trim your bushes this week."

"Great. Thanks. Are you sure you're okay? You're acting as odd as Minnie. When I go back in there, I'm going to give that woman a piece of my mind."

Daniel winced. He opened his mouth to say something, then closed it, then opened it again just as a car turned the corner and came toward them, steel guitars and drums vibrating the air. The clamor singed Pearl's ears. She flipped off her

60

hearing aid. The only word she heard Daniel say was *gay*. She glared at the booming car. When she turned back to Daniel, he was watching her like he was waiting for something. "I'm glad you're happy, dear."

He just shook his head. "I don't *feel* gay, Gran. I *am* gay."

"What?"

Daniel stood straighter, like he was trying to look all of six feet tall, when in reality he couldn't be a centimeter over five foot eight. "I'm gay, Gran. Homosexual."

Pearl was sure her heart had stopped. "You can't be!"

"I've been wanting to tell you, but it never seemed like the right time. A couple of nights ago Minnie saw me kiss a man at a theater in West Plains."

Pearl covered her ears with her hands. "No," she moaned, closing her eyes.

"I wanted you to hear it from me, not her."

It was a minute before Pearl could look back at him. She made her voice sound severe. "You can't be that way. It's a sin. You'll just have to make better choices."

Daniel scowled. "You sound like Dad. You think I'd *choose* to be gay? In the *Ozarks?*"

That was the last thing Pearl wanted, to sound like Daniel's blowhard of a father. She shuddered. Why hadn't Danny's mother, Pearl's own daughter, told her about Danny? Maybe it was shame that kept her daughter silent. Or maybe her daughter's jerk of a husband had ordered her to keep her mouth shut.

Pearl felt so dizzy all of a sudden, she sank onto a bench in front of the church. How could her grandson, her beloved only grandchild, be gay? Of course, he'd always been tenderhearted. Even as a little boy Daniel used to catch spiders in the house and release them outside.

"I've got to get back to work," Daniel said. "Do you still want me to trim your bushes, or would you rather have straight hands touch your roses?"

"Oh, Danny."

"You don't hate me?"

"Of course not. The Bible says to hate the sin but love the sinner. Of course I want you to come over. Alone."

Daniel gave a wistful smile and headed down the sidewalk, back to work.

Pearl remained on the bench in front of the church, too stunned to move, to think.

From the church behind her the choir began rehearsing "Holy, Holy, Holy," one of her favorite hymns. She closed her eyes and let herself float, her body gently swaying, mouthing the words, savoring the melody as well as the message of God's love and perfection. On the last verse the sopranos' voices rose like a descant sung by angels. Eyes still closed, Pearl trembled with the music—the lovely, sacred music, the part of church that had always soothed her most, a balm to her troubled soul.

CHAPTER NINE

Ruby

Ruby didn't think Tulsa had looked so astonished since the time the canoe she was paddling split open and sank.

"Seriously?" Tulsa glanced around their living room. "*Everyone* read *Sunny Chandler's Return*?"

Seated beside Tulsa on the sofa, which was covered with Ruby's multicolored friendship quilt, Jen nodded. So did BJ and Pearl, who sat in the green easy chairs.

The lingering light set aglow the tiny daisies detailed in the wallpaper. Ruby almost always smiled when she walked into this large, airy room, with its warm walls, comfortable furniture, and a wheat-colored rug she'd searched nine garage sales to find. The room was made even more welcoming by the aroma of the still-warm cinnamon apple cake she'd just served.

Jen picked the paperback up from her lap. "This was a *great* book," she said.

"You're kidding," Tulsa said.

Maybe if Tulsa dressed more like Jen, she'd be more receptive to love. Jen's makeup made her eyes seem bigger, her cheeks rosier, her lips fuller. With her short skirts and feminine blouses, her styled hair and painted nails, Jen looked like— well, like a girl. Tulsa, on the other hand, wore T-shirts and jeans. Not exactly clothes to inspire feminine thoughts. Of course, it had taken Jen some years of dating mostly losers before she'd settled in with Jack. Hopefully he would marry her soon. The fact that he was willing to live together for two years without making a commitment was troubling. Clifford would never have kept Ruby dangling.

Pearl, in her usual outfit of long-sleeved blouse with rhinestone snaps and blue knit slacks, turned to Tulsa. "You didn't like the book?" she asked, fiddling with her hearing aid.

"No," Tulsa said. "Sunny's a wimp."

"That's not true," Jen practically sputtered. "She's trying to run a business, just like you do with Ruby and Guy."

Tulsa made a brushing motion with her hand, as if to wave aside Jen's protest. "Somebody tries to break into her house, and she just stands there all helpless? She should have picked up a knife."

"That's what I'd have done." Pearl sipped coffee. "A meat cleaver."

"I'd call nine-one-one," BJ said.

Ruby had hoped Tulsa could relate to Sunny's

struggle to start her own business making Mardi Gras costumes. She'd also hoped that the hot sex might make Tulsa yearn for romance. To Ruby, the book was charming. She should have realized, however, that Tulsa would find Sunny's occasional helplessness downright pathetic. Tulsa was anything but helpless.

"This cake is heavenly." BJ took her last bite of cake and closed her eyes.

BJ worshiped food with the reverence some people saved for God, a fact that meant she amply filled her size 16 white pants and green tunic. Ruby thought the cake too sweet. It practically gummed up her mouth. She should have used green apples.

"A man like Ty could make life a whole lot more interesting," Pearl said.

"You want some man's 'swollen manhood,' as the author puts it, to explore 'the cradle of your femininity'?" Tulsa said.

"A womb *is* a kind of a cradle, honey," Ruby said.

"Oh lord."

"I wish somebody would have explored *my* cradle," Pearl said. "If you'd asked Sherman what foreplay was, he'd have said it was a town in Kansas."

Pearl's once-black hair had turned a lovely shade of silver, Ruby thought. Not white. Silver, intermixed with still-black strands.

"Sunny was lucky to have a man like Ty make love to her," BJ said.

Pearl, Jen, and Ruby nodded agreement.

BJ rubbed her lower back. "And I bet if Sunny's back hurt, Ty would give her a massage."

Ruby knew better than to ask BJ about her back. Sympathy made BJ's symptoms worse and her explanations longer. Of course, when BJ was young, about the only time her mom paid her any attention was when BJ got sick. It was no wonder she kept up the sick act for sympathy.

"I can believe that Ty bets his friend he can seduce Sunny," Tulsa said. "But to think that he and Sunny would fall in love for keeps? Does anyone?"

"Clifford was a lot like Ty," Ruby said, "though not that good-looking. We fell in love for keeps."

Tulsa's expression softened. "I know, Ruby. I'm sure Clifford was a wonderful man. I wish I could have known him. But you're the exception. A whole lot of women would be better off single."

"That's just nonsense," Ruby said.

"No, it's not," Pearl said. "Love between Sherman and me lasted about a minute. The rest was more like indentured servitude. I calculated I walked over twenty thousand miles at that café."

"Now, Pearl," Ruby said, "I know Sherman wasn't perfect. But without him you wouldn't have your daughter or Daniel."

Pearl flinched.

"What?" Ruby said.

Pearl rubbed her left foot, which so often plagued her. "Nothing. Just don't assume that everybody's marriage ends up like yours and Clifford's. Not by a long shot."

Tulsa looked downright pleased. "Exactly."

Ruby glared at Pearl.

Pearl clearly understood her. "What, you want me to lie?"

"*I* don't want to be single," Jen said. "It's just lonely."

"Well, that's right," Ruby said. "I'm glad someone has some sense."

Tulsa turned to Jen. "So you're going to live happily ever after with Jack?"

Jen twisted the napkin in her lap. "I sure hope so."

"I hope so, too," Tulsa said. "But he still hasn't asked you to marry him."

"Give Jack credit, Tulsa," Ruby said. "If allowing your more-or-less mother-in-law to stay with you doesn't qualify as true love, what does?"

"Especially *my* mother," Jen said.

"That practically makes Jack a saint, all right," Tulsa agreed. "But it doesn't necessarily make him a great husband. He doesn't do half as much for you as you do for him, Jen."

Jen looked crestfallen.

Ruby jutted her finger at Tulsa. "Just stop."

"I would have been happier with . . . somebody," BJ said, her voice so tiny everyone had to lean forward to hear her.

What BJ doubtless meant was that she would have been happier with Buddy. The news that Buddy had gotten both Ruby's daughter, Faith, and BJ pregnant had shocked Ruby. She never doubted, however, that it was Faith, Tulsa's mom, whom Buddy truly loved. "If Buddy hadn't been killed in that helicopter crash," Ruby said to Tulsa, "he'd have married your mom. They'd have been as happy as Clifford and me. Besides, Buddy gave us you and gave BJ, Guy. A double blessing."

BJ blushed and looked down at the empty fork in her hand. "Ruby's right," she said. "I'm lucky to have Guy. And the whole thing was my fault. I'm so sorry. I knew Buddy loved your mom."

Tulsa waved away BJ's apology. "You didn't point a gun at Buddy's head and force him to cheat."

Ruby could see the pain that still haunted Tulsa from all those years of her mom's love affairs, all those moves from one man's place to another's, in desperate search of love that would last. Tulsa wasn't Faith. Unlike her mom, Tulsa didn't fall for *every* man; she hardly fell for any.

Of course, Tulsa had seemed to really like Warren, their local conservation agent. Indeed, Ruby had thought perhaps Tulsa was falling in love with him. Ruby had cheered on their relationship. If only Warren hadn't gone to his class reunion and reconnected with his former sweetheart, maybe he and Tulsa would have married. Certainly their breakup had only made Tulsa more skittish about men.

"You've just got to be careful to get the right man," Ruby told Tulsa. "And maybe have a little luck on your side."

The phone's ring made Tulsa bolt up. "I'll get it. Maybe it's my Mr. Right."

Tulsa grinned, but sadness made Ruby sag. It seemed that Tulsa, who was so strong physically, who could handle canoes and guns and fly rods and most anything else, would forever be that lost little girl.

CHAPTER TEN
Tulsa

The caller had seen one of their flyers at Springfield's fly shop and wanted to book six canoes plus two cabins for the third week of June. What a great way to start the official summer!

"Welcome back," Ruby said when Tulsa returned to the living room. "We decided to keep getting together for discussion and dessert."

Tulsa froze. "I thought this was a onetime deal."

"No."

"But I've got so much to do."

"You don't have time for our friends?" Ruby looked at Tulsa as if daring her to say she didn't.

Jen frowned. "It's fun to get together and talk," she said. "Right?" She looked at Tulsa, then at the others.

"Sure is," Pearl said.

"I'm glad you included me," BJ said. "And, Ruby, your desserts are so tasty, I'd read anything. Even the obituaries."

Ruby handed Tulsa a purple paperback. "Here's the selection for our next get-together on June eleventh. That's in three weeks. It's a Wednesday. Be sure to put it on your calendar."

On the cover of the book was a half-dressed woman clasping the leather vest of an otherwise bare-chested, muscled man. "Great," Tulsa mumbled.

"Ruby promised to fix her peach cobbler," BJ said.

"You'll like this book a lot better," Ruby assured Tulsa.

Jen's face was alight. She smelled like roses, her usual fragrance. *Naturally, she would like romance novels,* Tulsa thought. She and Jen had been close when they were younger, both enjoying swimming, canoeing, and hiking. Once Jen started finding boys more interesting than the river, they'd drifted apart some, though until Jen moved in with Jack, they would still float together at least once a month. No longer. Jack wanted Jen to spend her free time with him. Ruby would probably say that was natural. Tulsa didn't think there was anything natural about it.

"Too bad we didn't get to read books like this in high school," Jen said.

"Yeah," Pearl said. "I imagine a romance novelist's version of *Moby-Dick* might be real interesting."

Jen grinned. "I bet class discussions would have been lively."

Tulsa's mind reeled. How was she going to find time to read? And if she was going to have to read, how could she persuade them to at least read something worthwhile? "Fine," she said, "but let's take turns suggesting books."

Ruby's eyes met hers. Tulsa thought Ruby had always had an uncanny ability to read her mind.

"Do you know any romance novels, dear?" Ruby said.

"We could read different types of books."

"With so many problems in real life," Ruby said, "I like to read books I know have happy endings."

"Fairy tales, you mean?" Ruby's eyes clouded. "I'm just kidding," Tulsa said, though she wasn't.

"I may be old and my 'womanhood' withered," Pearl said, "but reading and dreaming about hot sex and true love sure perks up my day. I'm with Ruby."

"Me, too," BJ said.

"And me," Jen agreed.

Maybe it wouldn't be so bad, Tulsa thought. She could just keep skimming the books. It wasn't like they required concentration. She looked back at the new book's cover. *Savage Thunder*. It took every ounce of self-control she had not to groan.

CHAPTER ELEVEN
BJ

The cedar cabin her son, Guy, had built nestled amid sycamore, hickory, oak, and maple should be a perfect love nest, BJ thought as she climbed its stairs beneath a pale crescent moon. With two skylights and floor-to-ceiling windows, Guy's place was like a tree house. Just stepping into the cabin would spark most women's nesting instincts, which was probably why Guy said he didn't bring women there.

If Guy noticed her holding her aching back when he answered her knock, he didn't say anything. He just stood aside and stirred a cup of instant coffee. Blues music played from the stereo, the woeful tune sung by a woeful voice that matched her mood.

"Aren't you going to ask me what's wrong?" she said. "Why I'm here?"

"Nope. You want some coffee?"

"No. Remember Barbara Franklin?"

"Mm."

He was being noncommittal, as always. That was the trouble with his generation. They were unable to commit to anything, even a simple yes or no. "She was the one who drove her car into the mailbox the year we had three feet of snow on Christmas Eve."

"Uh-huh." Guy looked at his watch, which made her check hers. A little after nine thirty. The meeting at Ruby's had ended earlier than she'd expected, so she'd thought she would try to console herself by dropping in on her son.

"Barbara's leg ached, but her husband and doctor and children all ignored her," she said. "Turned out she had bone cancer."

Guy watched her with brown eyes almost as dark as his coffee and exhaled a soft "Oh boy."

"By the time they found her cancer, it had just riddled her whole body, poor soul. She died a month later. Come to think of it, she was forty-six, the same age I am now."

Guy downed the last of his coffee and wiped his lips with the back of his hand. "Mom, you don't have cancer."

"I might."

"Or tuberculosis, meningitis, polio, MS, or

rabies. Or any of the other diseases you've been sure you had. If you want to talk health problems, look at Jackson. He never complains."

Her gaze followed Guy's to the small three-legged turtle pulling itself toward the lettuce Guy had left on a paper towel on the floor. Guy had found the turtle on the road, one leg crushed, nearly twenty years ago.

Her son had always been a sucker for wounded animals. It started with the broken-winged duck he brought home from his one and only hunting trip with BJ's father. They weren't sure whose shot had injured the bird, but Guy begged until BJ reluctantly agreed to let him nurse the duck—which Guy named Lefty—back to health. Even now the local veterinarians knew whom to call when someone brought in an animal they didn't want. Over the years Guy had tended all kinds of critters, including an epileptic dog, a deaf cat, an arthritic horse, and a beaver that had a puzzling aversion to water.

"I've got to go." Guy switched off the stereo.

BJ rinsed his cup. "I'm looking for a design I drew for an old Scottish stone church. I'm pretty sure it's in one of the boxes in my garage. With my back, I don't dare try to get them down. Could you come over and take the boxes down for me? They have some of your old school stuff and family letters. Plus some magazines I keep meaning to read."

"Yeah. I'm out of here. Wanda's waiting."

"Wanda Jennings?" she said. She tried to sound nonjudgmental. Guy had a smile so sweet that when he turned it on a woman, it was like he was giving her a valentine. He needed to be more careful who he gave that valentine to.

"Yes, Wanda Jennings."

"Be careful, honey; her sister got pregnant at fifteen. So did her mother. And even though I really want grandkids, I'm not sure Wanda's mother material. She's a little, well, crass."

"Wanda's twenty-eight, just like me. We're not having kids. And I'm not exactly father material."

"Of course you are. You'd be a great dad. And I'd be a terrific grandmother. You just need to date the right woman. Ask Jen out. She's a sweetheart."

"Yes, and she *has* a sweetheart."

"You should have asked her out long ago." BJ picked up a sponge to wash the few dishes in his sink.

He took the sponge from her and tossed it back in the sink. "Stop trying to run my life. You've been doing that since I popped out of the womb."

"Twenty-one hours of labor is not *popping* out. I thought they were going to have to tie a rope around you and drag you out."

"Maybe I knew you'd drive me crazy."

That stung. "I drive you crazy?"

"Mom, you put a capital *S* in front of the word *mothering*."

She clapped her hand to her suddenly heavy heart. "Are you saying I smother you?"

"It isn't a news flash. I've told you all this before. Remember when I had my hernia operation?"

"Of course. I got to take care of my baby."

"I wasn't a baby. I was twenty-one. You even stood outside the door every time I went to the bathroom asking if I was okay."

"I was worried about you."

"That's the point! Worry about yourself instead. You need to get a life, Mom. Your *own* life."

Had he been talking to Dr. Newton? Those were almost the same words her doctor used when he diagnosed her with "ELS." Well. She was only acting like any loving mother would. If Guy didn't want her love, fine. "If that's how you feel, I just won't bother you." She stomped toward the door, but the closer she got to it, the slower she walked. How was she supposed to find her own life? She'd always been her parents' daughter, her son's mother. Oh, sure, she lived alone now, but that was exactly the problem. She lived alone.

Guy clearly didn't understand. He'd taken off the day he graduated from high school and spent seven years working his way around the West, doing odd jobs, floating rivers, climbing mountains. He came home for an occasional visit and the hernia surgery, but he'd never seemed lonely a day in his life. Nor had he ever lacked for females—girls in high school and women after.

She summoned the courage to face him again. "How?"

"How what?"

"How do I find my own life?"

"I don't know. Look for it. Date somebody."

"Men don't want me. Most of the dates I've been on, the guy was drunk."

Guy took a Sweet Oak River Oasis cap from the counter and pulled the brim over his eyes. "Don't you know any single men?"

She mentally scanned the pews at her church and the shops around town, but what she saw were married women with husbands and kids, and widowed women with kids and grandkids. The only single man she could think of ran the Conoco station. "Jerry Carver." She pictured the hair he gelled to his skull in a vain attempt to cover the bald spots.

"Forget him. All he'd want is sex."

BJ put up her hand to stop him. Sex was not a topic she wanted to discuss with her son.

"I know!" Guy's voice sounded inspired. "Matthew Bonner."

She'd forgotten Matthew. "But he was just widowed."

"No," Guy said. "It was last June. He came to spread his wife's ashes in the river."

A year ago? She felt dizzy and put her hand to her forehead. Though she was only forty-six, the way her life was speeding by, she'd be fifty in what would seem like a month and eighty a few days later. Eighty! Did she really want to be eighty and have loved so briefly?

"Invite Bonner to dinner." Guy put his arm around her, gave a quick squeeze, and opened the door. They stepped into the night. "He'll probably jump at the chance for a home-cooked meal."

"Do you think so?"

"Sure."

They were at her Chevy Blazer now. Guy held the door for her. BJ clambered into her seat.

"And, Mom, when he comes, don't attach yourself to him like a suction cup. That's not a turn-on. And don't tell him about all your ailments." He closed her door.

BJ remembered that her back hurt.

Guy whistled. Elvis bounded from the woods, seemed to hear Guy pat the passenger seat of his pickup, and jumped in.

Guy ruffled Elvis's ears. "See you, Mom." He got in his truck and sped off.

BJ pictured Matthew Bonner, who owned the shoe store in Fiddle. His hair was thinning, his middle thickening. She wanted a man who, like Ty Beaumont in *Sunny Chandler's Return*, knew how to please a woman, both emotionally and sexually. Could Matthew be that man? She hoped he was a kind man, hoped he hadn't started courting another woman. And as she bowed her head to pray, she hoped that Jesus wouldn't mind if she asked for a little help in curing her ELS.

When BJ returned, she was greeted by her latest model church. Each church BJ had designed and built over the past few years was a stab at penitence for her sins. Her great, grievous sins. Whether she was fashioning tiny roof tiles from plaster, routing wood to construct a bell tower, cutting out colored cellophane for stained glass windows, or building an elegant spire with a crowning cross, BJ felt good. Cleansed. Not that building model churches totally made up for what she'd done. She doubted anything ever would. But at least it was one way she could prove that she'd repented.

BJ's back ached from leaning over the table painting the tiny roof tiles of the model Westminster church. She'd come back from Guy's too wired to sleep.

Hungry, she stood, stretched, and went to the kitchen, where she scooped herself out a bowl of vanilla ice cream. She poured butterscotch syrup over it. The first bite of the sweet, buttery syrup tasted so good, she practically shivered. Thank God for butterscotch! She carried the ice cream back to the living room, where eight of the nine model churches were displayed on TV trays.

If only she'd remembered all those years ago what it was to be a true friend, her life might be different now. Seventeen, she'd been, and never been kissed or asked out. Her school announced a Sadie Hawkins dance, where girls invited boys. She waited until a few days before the dance so she could see which boys might be desperate enough to accept her invitation. Two turned her down. Billy Packard, with crooked teeth but lovely golden-blond hair, accepted, although he colored a thousand shades of red.

At the school gym that night, he immediately ditched her. When she tracked him down, he was surrounded by other boys. She summoned the courage to suggest they dance. She and Faith had practiced in Faith's room, and she could dance as well as any girl there. "I don't dance with cows," Billy said. As she slouched away, someone mooed.

Faith insisted her boyfriend, Buddy, drive BJ home. They dropped Faith off first to meet her curfew. BJ had always envied Faith her good looks, her slender figure, and her mom, Ruby. Watching Faith disappear inside her house that night, BJ had felt alone and ugly. She burst into tears. Her crying must have discomforted Buddy, who drove her to an overlook and told her not to cry, that she had just as much sparkle as the stars. She cried harder. "No, I don't," she sobbed. "I'm a cow. No boy will ever want to kiss me."

"Sure they will," Buddy said.

She ached to believe him. Her tears eased but didn't stop.

"You have a pretty face," he said.

She'd never thought of any part of her as pretty. "Really?"

"Yeah." He opened a flask he took from under his seat, unscrewed the top, and handed it to her. She sipped whiskey so bitter she choked. He put the flask to his own lips and gulped, then gulped some more. "Billy Packard's an idiot," Buddy said, his speech slightly slurred.

BJ looked into his lovely, smoldering eyes. She'd always dreamed that someday Buddy and Faith would break up, and that Buddy would ask her out. She closed her eyes and leaned back in the seat, imagining Buddy pressing his lips—his full, moist lips—to hers.

And then he did.

Her eyes flew open. Buddy's eyes were closed while he kissed her. Her! BJ closed her own eyes. What would one little kiss hurt?

Only it wasn't a little kiss. It went on and on, and she felt parts of her body awaken for the first time in her life. She wanted a second kiss. And a third. No! It was wrong. She pushed against his chest. He pulled back. "We shouldn't," she said.

"I know."

BJ held her breath to slow her racing heart. It didn't work. Buddy shook his head as if to clear it. Then he kissed her again. And again. And again.

The night was so cold, and he was so warm. "Hold me," she said, because no one ever had.

Abruptly he got out of the car. She was sure he was doing it to stop himself. And her. Instead he took a blanket from the trunk, spread it out on the ground, then opened her door and held out his hand. He swayed a little, and she knew that he'd had too much to drink. Knew, too, that if she took his hand, neither of them would stop, but BJ had never wanted anyone or anything as much as she wanted Buddy at that moment. She yielded.

He helped her from the car, folded his suit jacket under her head for a pillow, and covered her body with his own, kissing her.

"Oh" slipped from her. And then, "Don't stop."

He didn't.

Buddy climaxed. Not only did she not come close, but the lovemaking scorched her insides. A virgin's pain. A betrayer's pain. What they'd done was wrong.

Very, very wrong.

Before he joined the army three months later, Buddy asked Faith to marry him. Faith was pregnant with Tulsa, BJ with Guy. After Faith said yes, Buddy confessed what he and BJ had done that night. Faith invited BJ over, not revealing that she knew. BJ arrived at Ruby's to see Faith hurling all of the clothes BJ kept at her house for their frequent sleepovers into the river. She watched her favorite pajamas, ivory with tiny yellow flowers, float a little ways, then sink. "I never want to see you again," Faith shouted.

True to her word, Faith returned BJ's tear-smeared letters of apology unopened. BJ lost more than her virginity the night she betrayed Faith: she lost her only real friend.

BJ's parents moved with her and her infant son to a small Illinois town outside Chicago to flee BJ's shame. A year ago Guy visited Fiddle and the river because he wanted to see the area BJ raved about so much. Guy met Ruby and Tulsa and fell in love with the river. When he told her he was fixing up a cabin he'd bought in the woods and that Ruby held no grudges, BJ wondered why she'd never thought of going back. She packed her things and returned home.

It was hard, even now, to believe she'd cheated on her best friend. And that wasn't her only sin.

She'd told so many lies. To her parents, about why she came home late that night. To her favorite teacher, swearing that her weight gain was the result of too many Hostess cupcakes. She'd even shoplifted a maternity dress to hide her condition.

After Buddy, BJ had had a few other pathetic one-night stands that proved almost as painful as her first. She lost all interest in romance. It was only now since she'd read *Sunny Chandler's Return* (twice) that she'd let herself feel her long-buried desire for love. She picked up the new book, *Savage Thunder*. It sure had a suggestive cover.

Did she really have to spend the rest of her life

paying the price for her sins of almost thirty years ago? She licked the last of the golden butterscotch syrup from her spoon and set her bowl on the table beside the partially finished Westminster Abbey. She certainly wasn't going to be able to cure ELS sitting in her own home, churches or no churches.

In a couple of weeks, once she finished constructing this church and had built up enough courage, maybe she would see if Matthew Bonner wanted to come to dinner. In all likelihood he'd turn her down, but at least he wouldn't moo.

CHAPTER TWELVE
Tulsa

Tulsa stared dumbfounded at the amount of fishing gear in the back of Slade's Range Rover. He had every contraption ever invented for fly-fishing and then some. Simms Gore-Tex waders that on an Ozarks summer day were about as useful as snow skis. A gold-threaded bamboo fly rod. A machine-personalized Abel fly reel with several spare spools. Six Richard Wheatley of England fly boxes. An assortment of other rods, two tackle boxes, and three nets for different-size fish, which struck her as incredibly optimistic.

Or arrogant. In her experience, people with the most gear made the worst fishermen. She'd be willing to bet that Slade would hook more trees than fish. But even if he proved to be inept as well as obnoxious, this was a chance for her to float the river. What job could possibly pay more?

"Well," she said, helping him transfer the gear to the pickup she'd loaded earlier with a canoe on a small trailer, "if you decide you don't like fishing, you can always open your own fly shop."

Slade pulled his Aussie hat down till it nearly kissed his eyes. "Keep your options open," he said. "That's my motto." He rubbed his hands together. "Let's go get some fish. I want to eat trout tonight."

As the canoe glided forward, a great blue heron rose into flight from a gravel bar ahead of them and winged its way past light-dappled trees that bordered the rippling water.

"It's a pretty river," Slade said from his seat in the bow of the canoe.

" 'Pretty' doesn't begin to cover it."

"I've seen some spectacular rivers," he said. "The Tambopata in Peru's got white water that will get your pulse up. You ever rafted white water?"

"Yep."

He turned toward her. "Where?"

"Montana. Wyoming." She'd driven there when she turned eighteen.

"Like it?"

"Sure. But I prefer a river that whispers over one that shouts."

Slade faced forward again and dangled his fingers in the water. "I'd rather get my adrenaline going. Extreme skiing. Skydiving. When you jump out of a plane, you feel alive."

"Unless your chute doesn't open."

"But when it does, you know you beat death."

"Nobody really beats death," she said.

Tulsa kept paddling, reading the water for signs of an insect feed that would attract trout. "Is that how you hurt your knee? Jumping?"

"Yeah. Chute opened late. Tore my ACL."

"You going to jump again?"

"Sure. You should try it."

"I'll put it on my list of to-dos," she said. "I guess *your* list includes bribing people into swapping cabins." It slipped out before she could censor herself.

"All I did was make a legitimate offer. Lowell was delighted. Teachers don't make much money, you know."

"So it was a charitable contribution?"

He faced her again, pushing his hat back as if to see her better. "You have a problem with me?"

She dug her paddle deep and pulled hard in an effort to control her temper. "I have a problem with people who throw money around to get what they want."

"If it doesn't hurt anybody, if it actually helps

somebody out, like the Whites, what's wrong with offering?"

He was right about the fact that Lowell White had seemed pleased. Delighted, even. "I don't know. It just pisses me off that some people have so much they can do practically anything, while others don't even have a home. Or food. Or medical care."

"It is unfair," he said. "You're right. And if I could make things equal for everyone, I'd give up my money like that." He snapped his tan fingers. "I can't. And I shouldn't have to feel guilty about not being poverty-stricken. Should I?"

Tulsa stared at the water, at the fractured reflections of trees and clouds. "No," she said, looking back into eyes made even bluer by the sky, "I guess not."

He held her gaze a moment longer, then faced forward. They floated in silence broken only by the trilling of a cardinal from the woods. After a while, he spoke again. "So besides guilt-tripping rich people, what do you do for fun?"

She almost smiled. "Float the river. Swim. Hike. Stare at stars. Pretty tame by your standards." Brush along the left bank made a perfect refuge for smallmouth. If he were lure-fishing for bass, it would be their first stop. "Fishing's pretty tame stuff, too, compared to jumping out of airplanes." She paddled them farther downriver.

"Got to do something while my knee heals."

"So this is your first time fly-fishing?"

"I took a casting class at the fly shop, but yes."

Her eyes surveyed the mountain of gear she'd secured in the middle of the canoe, thankful for shot cords. "You bought all this gear without knowing if you'd like it?"

"Boy toys."

They passed below the heron rookery. The birds had built some sixty nests in that grove of sycamores. She and Warren had liked to stop here to watch the herons coming and going, their hoarse *whawk*ing calls, the flapping of their huge wings that sounded like rumbles of thunder. For a while after Warren ended their relationship, she felt sad every time she passed the rookery. Thank God she was over him. Besides, Guy also shared her love for the rookery. She didn't need Warren to be happy.

They rounded the bend into the first set of rapids, only Class II white water, but overturning a canoe with a hobbled man and expensive gear would be ill advised in any situation. A strong current pushed the canoe toward a fallen tree; Tulsa kept the boat aligned with the deepest part of the fast water. She maneuvered around a rock and by the tree. As they passed through the wildest stretch, she backwatered to swing the canoe around, paddled hard upriver, and stepped out, holding the boat facing into the rapids.

"You can fish from the canoe," she said. "I'll keep us here."

"I prefer the shore."

"The rocks are slippery. This is a lot safer."

"Plenty of time to be safe when you're dead."

"Suit yourself." She pulled the boat up toward the gravel bar at the foot of the rapids, then offered her arm to steady him.

"Thanks," he said. He put most of his weight on his good leg as he rose. She helped him out of the canoe. He let go of her then, his braced knee seeming to hold him steady enough on the gravel. Tulsa studied the river while he prepared his line. Insects darted about the water, stoneflies and caddis flies particularly. A fish surfaced in the shallows to snatch one.

"What fly do you recommend?" he asked. He'd opened all six fly boxes.

She reached into her vest pocket and took out the small, cracked, plastic box in which she kept the dozen flies she knew could attract fish in May on the Sweet Oak. She handed him a fuzzy brown one that looked like a caddis fly. "Try a prince nymph."

"Really? I mean . . ." He looked back at his expensive collection.

"You want to baptize flies or catch fish?"

"You're the guide." He took the nymph and hooked it to the leader more quickly than she would have expected.

She stepped a little to his left and put on

wraparound sunglasses to protect her eyes in case his cast went wild. Slade pulled down his Aussie hat brim, spread his long legs a little apart, whipped his line, and sent it whistling out across the river. The smoothness of his cast surprised her. "Not bad," she said. "You want some pointers?"

"Sure." He reeled in his line.

"You're holding the rod too tight. Hold it lightly, like it's a hummingbird you don't want to hurt. And most of the action should come from your forearm, not your wrist. You want your movements to be small. Less is more."

He tried again, and though he moved too much of his arm, it was a good cast for a beginner. "Better. Still more with your forearm."

He held the rod out to her. "Show me."

The solid-gold thread wrapped around the guides that held the line in place glinted in the sunlight. The rod was elegant and sleek.

"Please," he said. "I'm a visual learner."

The rod felt good in her hands. If she'd been alone she might have run her fingers over its shaft. She moved the rod between the ten-o'clock position and the two-o'clock, ten and two, then flicked her forearm and released the line at twelve. The line rose in a perfect arc. She flicked her forearm again and the fly floated down to rest atop the water.

"Beautiful," Slade said.

Surprised by the passion in his voice, she looked

up. He was staring. Not at the rod or the river. At her. She handed him the rod. "It's all in the forearm."

He still looked at her, eyebrows up, voice down, in a way that seemed intended to be flirtatious. "You've got a real way with a line."

His fingers were long, she realized, a plus for maneuvering flies and rods. And women, no doubt. "Focus," she said.

He looked at her a moment longer, then grasped the rod differently than he had before. Reverently. He spread his legs more and brought the rod back, letting his forearm control it, casting the line out smoothly, bringing the fly down to just kiss the water.

"Much improved," she said. "You're holding the rod perfectly."

"Thanks."

He was eyeing her again. "If you don't keep your eyes on the water," she said, "you'll be lucky to catch anything. Even a cold."

He grinned at her and tipped his hat. "Yes, ma'am."

He might not be inept or totally obnoxious like she'd thought, but she was sure Slade had a stringer full of women, most of whom had no doubt swallowed his bait.

It wasn't surprising that in the first two hours Slade had only a handful of strikes. Trout really didn't bite before midmorning. Fortunately, in the past half hour he'd had several good strikes, though he hadn't managed to land a fish. Hooking them was the easy part, and he was just a beginner. Still, she wanted him to land at least one. Tulsa wiped her hand across her sweaty forehead. The temperature hovered around ninety, unusual for May.

Slade finished changing to the fly she'd suggested, then waded into the river, his stance fairly steady. His wavy black hair curled under his Aussie hat. "Careful," she said. "Current's running fast through here."

"Not to worry."

He gave her his broad smile and cast again. The fly struck the water. A fish struck the fly. The way it tugged the line, Tulsa was sure it was a big one. "Set the hook," she said.

He followed her suggestions precisely: walk with the fish, tighten the line, let a little out, keep the rod tip up. He edged deeper into the water. The fish neared the surface, a large rainbow trout. "Let him do the work," she cautioned. "Be careful. It's deeper here."

The trout fought to run downriver. Slade walked along with him. The fish leapt. Slade slipped, hitting the water every bit as hard as the fish, wincing as he struck something under the water's surface. Tulsa lunged for his arm.

"The fish!" he yelled and thrust the rod at her.

Pain creased his face. She again reached for his arm.

"No! Please!"

If he'd said anything else, she would have ignored him, but the intensity of his plea made her take the rod instead of him. He'd said he wanted to taste his own trout. She fought the fish. Slade pulled himself to shore. He struggled to stand, his weight clearly on his good leg. Tulsa backed up, keeping the fish hooked. When Slade regained his footing, she handed him the rod.

Alert again, he battled the fish until it was exhausted, reeled it in, and held it up, the expression on his face somewhere between delight and pain, but his eyes alight.

Tulsa whistled. "That's one beautiful fish." She hoped Slade hadn't done himself any real damage.

He stared at the fish, which flopped in his hand.

"Got to be eighteen inches," she said. "You don't see many rainbows that size."

Slade cupped the fish. Its mouth gasped open and closed, open and closed. Its green body, speckled pink, glistened in the sunlight. The fish flicked its tail, still trying to free itself but losing strength.

To Tulsa's surprise, Slade unhooked the trout and set it back in the river. At first the fish was still. When it moved its tail, Slade let go. The fish darted for the depths. Slade sank onto the bow of the beached canoe.

She hadn't expected that. "Why'd you release it?"

"Because it fought so hard to live." He wasn't smiling.

"You okay?" she said.

"Fine."

"You sure?"

"Yeah."

She picked up her paddle. "When you're up to it, we need to get going."

"What's the rush?"

"We're only halfway," she said. "A half day's just four hours."

He stood. "I'll pay you double for another hour."

"You can have another hour at the same rate."

Slade waved her response aside. "Contrary to what you might think, I don't take advantage of people I hire," he said. "Double or nothing."

"Fine. But we still need to move. We splashed around so long, no self-respecting fish is going to bite anything."

"You're the boss."

She liked that about him. He was bankrolling the day, and he seemed to be a man used to power, but he didn't try to take charge. He set his rod in the canoe and smiled at her. She couldn't help it. She smiled back.

CHAPTER THIRTEEN
Ruby

The four canoes the Petersons had just requested for the following weekend brought that weekend's total to fifty-one, which was not enough. Not nearly enough. "Got it." Ruby scribbled the Peterson reservation on the booking calendar. "Thanks for calling, Andy. See you next Saturday." She hung up. If they were just leasing Ed's land, fifty-one canoes would be plenty for the first of June. To keep up with their loan payments, however, they needed to rent out sixty-five or seventy canoes every weekend, plus thirty or more on midweek days. Fortunately they weren't that long a drive for vacationers from Springfield and Kansas City, who made up much of their business.

Ruby opened the tin of cherry pipe tobacco that she kept on the office desk of their house and replaced every few months to remind her of her beloved Clifford. Each time she unscrewed the lid, it was like he came briefly back to life. Today she saw his lopsided grin and his unruly hair, which had seemed to have more sprouts than an alfalfa patch. If only he were here now, to put his arms around her and reassure her with the steadiness that so marked him. "We won't lose our home, Starlight," he would say, using his pet name for her. "Trust me."

Clifford's family had moved to the hollow when he was thirteen, a year older than she was. He walked into their one-room school two years into the Second World War and announced that he would escort her home. One of the few kids with shoes, he'd stuffed his socks into the toes and insisted Ruby wear them. In exchange he wrapped the potato sack rags that functioned as her shoes around his own feet.

They set out through the woods. Unaccustomed to walking on rocks and twigs, Clifford tried not to wince, but he was clearly hurting. Ruby made him take his shoes back. He was reluctant but grateful. He kissed her cheek. She teased him for his tender feet and kissed him back for his tender heart. Within a few months, Clifford's feet toughened. His heart never did.

She was just fourteen when he proposed. Her daddy said, "Hell, no." Her mama whispered, "Maybe." Ruby never questioned her own desires. All she wanted was to be Clifford's wife and as good a mother to their children as her own mama had been to her.

They married the day she turned fifteen. Her one big regret in life was that it took her so long to conceive. It certainly wasn't for lack of trying. The doctors were mystified. Then, at age thirty-three, Ruby gave birth to Faith. She and Clifford were deliriously happy. He was as attentive a father as he was a husband. But Clifford had a heart attack at forty-six. Faith was twelve when he died, only two years older than Tulsa was when Faith died.

The phone's ring startled her. "Sweet Oak River Oasis," she said, hoping the caller was a new customer.

"Guess who's joining me for dinner."

There was no mistaking Clancy's raspy voice. "I don't care," she said.

"You should. It's George Calhoun. From the bank. *Your* bank. I'm going to make him my new best friend."

"Lucky George."

"You sure you don't want to reconsider selling to me? Heck, I'd pay you close to nine hundred thousand for your place and Ed's combined."

"You know, Rupert, every time you open your mouth, I like you even less."

"I'm used to getting my way," he said, his voice hard.

"You wanted Faith to stay. How did that work out?"

Clancy chuckled, but he didn't sound amused. "Don't say you weren't warned."

The line went dead. Ruby stared at the receiver in her hand before hanging up. If Clancy did become buddies with their banker, he might find a way to make their lives difficult. And if she told

Tulsa what Clancy had said, Tulsa might retaliate by doing something stupid. Maybe that was the whole point of Clancy's call: to provoke a response that would land Tulsa or Guy or both in jail, costing them dearly in more ways than one. Ruby would keep this conversation to herself.

Someone dragged a canoe up on the gravel below the cabin. Ruby looked up from the cap she was knitting for a charity. It was two o'clock. The half day with Slade should have ended at noon. Maybe Tulsa had given him more time because she liked him. Wouldn't that be lovely.

Ruby pushed herself out of the chair. Lord a'mighty, she was getting achy. Too bad she couldn't just squirt some oil on her joints. Well, there wasn't any doubt about it. Aging sure took the stuffing out of you.

"How was it?" she asked as she walked down to where Tulsa and Slade were gathering his gear.

"Great," Slade said. "I learned a lot. I bet tomorrow we'll reel them in."

Tulsa looked up. "Tomorrow?"

"Sure. I'm thinking a full day."

"Guy's a better guide."

"My money's on you." Slade slung his waders over his shoulder. "What time?"

"I'll have to check the schedule."

Ruby kept the schedule. "You're free after ten."

"Great," Slade said. "Ten?"

"Sure, if you want," Tulsa said.

The phone clamored. Ruby had turned up the volume so they'd hear it outside. Tulsa sprinted to answer it.

"She's a great guide, don't you think?" Ruby asked. She thought she'd managed to not sound like she had an ulterior motive.

Slade picked up his rod. "I do. She's a wonder with both a canoe and a fly rod."

"You should see her off the water," Ruby said. Drat. Why did she go and say that? It didn't sound like what she meant. Or rather, it sounded *exactly* like what she meant.

Slade looked like he was giving it some thought. "I imagine that would be quite interesting."

Ruby's heart skipped a beat. She grabbed up the nets. "You single, Slade?"

"I am."

"What business are you in?" she asked him as they walked up the hill together.

"Commercial real estate."

"You enjoy it?"

"It pays the bills and lets me do things I enjoy more."

He seemed like a decent fellow. If only he would stay around long enough to get past her granddaughter's defenses.

Tulsa joined them at the Range Rover tailgate.

When Slade unlocked the car, Tulsa fumbled his gear, dropping one fly box. All three of them bent over to retrieve it, their faces so close Ruby could feel their breath on her cheeks.

"Thanks for a great float," Slade said as he climbed up behind the wheel of his car. "Where do I go to get cell phone coverage?"

"You have to go to Fiddle," Ruby said. "It's about five miles. But you're welcome to use our landline."

"Thanks, but I've got to make several calls. See you in the morning. And, Tulsa, thank you again."

Tulsa nodded. Slade took off his hat. His black hair was somewhat flattened but still beautifully wavy. He drove the Range Rover up the hill.

Ruby would swear there was a sparkle in Tulsa's eyes. "How was it?" she asked.

"The river was gorgeous."

"That's not what I meant, and you know it."

"*Please* don't play matchmaker."

"Please answer my question."

"No." Tulsa held up her palms up as if to stop Ruby from coming closer. "You push me at every two-legged male you see. Heck, if a dog walked by on its hind legs, you'd want me to marry it."

"I just want you to be happy."

"I *am* happy. I like my life just fine except for you hounding me. Right now it's hot and I'm thirsty and I'm going in."

Tulsa opened the door for her. The cool air sucked Ruby inside.

Tulsa filled two glasses with ice, then poured lemonade for them both. "Any cancellations come in?" she asked.

"Not one."

"Good." Tulsa finished off her drink without clinking glasses. "I've got to clean the cabins. You look tired. You should take a nap."

Ruby did feel tired. She clung to the rail to haul herself up the stairs. Why was she so droopy? She hadn't worked that hard today. She stretched out on her bed.

Slade seemed kind and confident. Honest, too. Tulsa valued honesty almost as highly as she valued the river. It was silly to think this way about someone Ruby barely knew, but she didn't have forever. She crossed her fingers. Of course, she knew that crossing fingers didn't really help, but she wouldn't not cross them when she had high hopes, any more than she would not make a wish when she blew out the candles on a birthday cake or saw her first evening star. Fingers crossed, she made her silent wish: *Please if you may, please if you might, let Slade be Tulsa's own Mr. Right.*

CHAPTER FOURTEEN
Tulsa

Perched on a rock on the rise above the water the next morning, Tulsa sipped bitter coffee and watched a great blue heron stalk fish. The heron moved almost in slow motion along the bank, eyes on the water. Its head snapped forward. Its beak seized a fish that flopped wildly, striving to slip from the heron's grasp, but the bird raised its head and swallowed. The fish squirmed all the way down the heron's thin throat. After a moment the heron flapped its massive wings to pull itself aloft and glided around the bend.

The river's flow through this stretch was like a humming. Tulsa breathed deep.

The ping of gravel against metal made her look up. Guy parked his pickup at the river's edge and soon plopped down on the rock beside her. He drank iced tea from his usual twenty-four-ounce glass. He brewed his tea even stronger than she made her coffee. While her coffee might pickle your taste buds, his tea could corrode them. How he could consume that much caffeine all day and still sleep, she didn't know, though when she looked at him, she wondered how much sleep he'd been getting. Dark bags underscored his eyes.

"You look like hell," she said.

He started to shake his head but stopped as if movement caused pain. "Wanda."

"Did you bring her to the *pinnacle of passion?*"

"Did you have a sunstroke?"

"Romance novels" was all she said. "Pinnacle of passion" was Sandra Brown's term in *Sunny Chandler's Return*. Supposedly the hero brought Sunny to that zenith. Many times. Lord knew what the author of the new book would call it. Tulsa didn't intend to read it until she had to.

Guy's arm brushed hers. She felt a feathery shiver. It was damp this morning but not really cold. Still, she wrapped her arms around herself and looked out at the water. Sunlight made the river gleam.

"How'd the float trip go yesterday?" he asked.

She tried to keep her face impassive. "Okay," she said.

"You've got kind of a funny expression."

She stood. "Your imagination. We need to leave to pick up the Scouts." The troop had put in at the Oasis the day before, planning to spend the night camping on a gravel bar, then float on down to the Possum Springs take-out. "They're due in at Possum Springs in half an hour." She'd attached the canoe trailer to the bus earlier. She paused at the sound of a vehicle coming down the hill. Much as she would welcome more customers on this Memorial Day weekend, they had no space in the cabins and only a couple campsites. Maybe they'd just be people wanting to float the river.

It was a Range Rover.

"Morning," Slade said as he got out of his car to stand before her, clad in designer jeans and a rose-colored shirt, his sunglasses off, his eyes so steady on her that Tulsa felt like the fish flopping in the heron's beak.

He was too early for their float. "What can I do for you?" she asked.

"I can think of several possibilities," Slade said. "Dinner. Dancing."

Guy came to stand beside her. He didn't say a word, but his presence steadied her. She put her hands in her back pockets. Slade held out a hand to Guy.

"Slade Morrison."

Guy shook his hand. "Guy."

"You are . . . ?" Slade asked.

"Tulsa's half brother."

Either Slade's smile widened, or she was imagining it.

"I'm afraid I have to cancel today," Slade said to her. "Business. I need to get back to Kansas City."

She shrugged her shoulders to get rid of a surprising sense of disappointment. "Bye," she said, and started toward the bus.

Slade blocked her. "I'll be back in a couple of weeks," he said, so close she could smell the peppermint on his breath. "Will you guide me again?"

Her pulse seemed to spurt. "Sure, if you want."

"I do. And I meant what I said about dinner and dancing." His eyes lingered on her a bit, then he got into his Range Rover and started up the hill.

"If I didn't know better," Guy said, "I'd think you were smitten."

"The day I fall for slick, you just take me out behind the barn and shoot me."

"Uh-huh."

Tulsa leapt up the bus stairs, took a seat behind the wheel, and turned the key in the ignition. Guy was on the first step when the engine started. Sputtered. Died. She tried again. Again it sputtered.

And died.

Guy jumped down the stairs and flung open the hood. "Try again!"

She did. Same result. She got out and stood beside Guy. "Starter?" she said.

"My guess is water in the tank."

"Can you fix it?"

"Hopefully, if that's what it is, but it'll take a couple of hours. I don't understand. I filled the bus two days ago. Didn't give me any problems before."

She looked at her watch. The Scouts were due in to the take-out point in less than twenty minutes. The kids and their chaperones, at least some of them fried and frayed, would not be pleased to have to wait over two hours to be picked up. It was bad for the group and bad for business.

"I'll call Floyd." She raced to the house hoping that Floyd, who ran the closest canoe outfit, fifteen miles away, could spare a bus to get the kids. They'd have to split the take, but it was better than making the kids wait.

"Can't," was all Floyd said before hanging up.

That was weird. Floyd had never been short with her before. She hurried back to the bus, where Guy verified that he'd found water in the gas tank.

"You think the station's tank was contaminated?" she said.

"Or someone poured water in ours."

Tulsa frowned. "We both know who that someone would be," she said. "Is there any way to tell whether it was sabotage?"

"We can ask around, see if anybody else who got gas at the Conoco had problems."

The gas dripped slowly into a five-gallon jug Guy had taken off the bus. "Can't we do this any faster?" she said.

"I wish."

"Damn. They're a new troop for us. We're going to need to give them a partial refund."

"Let's see how long they end up waiting. Maybe they'll be late to the take-out."

"There are fifty-one people and twenty-five

canoes. If they aren't late, real late, this will cost us several hundred dollars." They had only $15,000 in reserve for emergencies, and they'd need most of that to get them through the sparse months between mid-September and May.

They were in the middle of draining the gas into jugs, buckets, and a huge rubber trash barrel when Rupert Clancy drove up in his pickup.

"Too bad about your bus," he said.

"How'd you hear?" Tulsa said.

"Floyd called. Said you were experiencing some transportation difficulties."

A new bus would run them sixty thousand. Tulsa gripped his driver's-side window. "Did you put water in our tank?"

"Nope." Clancy used a bandana to wipe her fingerprints off his window. "I was busy talking to George Calhoun at the bank. We're buddies now."

Guy moved beside her.

"I don't give a damn who your buddies are," Tulsa said.

"You might if you miss a payment or two."

Guy slapped a wrench against his palm. "Is that a threat, Rupert?" he asked.

Guy's eyes narrowed. If Clancy was smart, Tulsa thought, he'd back off.

"Nope," Clancy said. "I'm just offering to take Ed's place off your hands and give you something to boot. Say, six thousand? Tulsa turned me down before. You might want to reconsider."

"Why are you so eager to get Ed's that you'd pay us extra?" Tulsa said.

Clancy adjusted his rearview mirror. "I hate the whole canoe business. Renting to people who holler and yell all the way down the river. Every time they float by my place, it spoils my peace of mind."

"So you want the river to be for your own pleasure," Tulsa said.

"You can put that however you want. But I'd sure hate to see you and Ruby lose your home if you default on those loan payments."

Tulsa scowled. "The day we let you have any of our land—and it is ours now—will be the day the Sweet Oak runs dry."

"Speaking of dry, have you seen the forecast? They're talking about a real rainy June. Not good for business. 'Course, neither is keeping customers waiting. Good luck." Clancy gunned his engine, spun gravel, and sped up the hill.

A dust cloud marked the trail of his pickup.

"The man's a snake," Guy said, fingers smeared with gasoline and grease. "I just haven't decided if he's poisonous."

Tulsa spat on the gravel. "Clancy's so full of venom, it's a wonder he doesn't poison himself. You think he was telling the truth about the forecast? A rainy summer would sink us."

"He's probably lying. And I've got your back."

She had no doubt he did.

It was a year ago on a day much like this one—

a beautiful late-May morning—that she'd learned she had a brother.

Guy had come to see the area where his mother and her family were from. When he walked into the office to arrange a float, Tulsa had liked his slender build, his easy amble, his warm brown eyes. Over the next few days she floated with him several times. He was the only man she knew who revered the river like she did, like it was alive, like it was a lover, his face lighting up every time he stepped into the water.

When the man who'd been helping run the canoe business moved to Little Rock, Guy took his place. Guy accomplished more most days than his predecessor did in weeks.

And then it all changed. She and Guy had been going over the books in the office. He was sitting atop the desk chewing Juicy Fruit gum. She was in the chair sipping near-perfect coffee: thick and bitter.

Ruby walked in.

Guy noticed one of the photographs under the glass topping the desk. It was a picture of Tulsa's mom as a teenager, arm linked through another girl's. "That looks a lot like my mom," he said. "Who is it?"

Ruby replied, "The one on the left is my daughter, Faith: Tulsa's mom. The girl with her was her best friend, Brenda June. But we called her BJ."

Guy looked astonished. "BJ Smith?" he said.

"That's right."

"That's my mom."

Ruby's jaw didn't just drop. It positively plunged. "BJ Smith is your mother?"

"Yeah."

"Good Lord. That means the two of you"— Ruby pointed to Guy, then Tulsa—"are siblings."

"What?!" Tulsa and Guy chorused.

"Half siblings." Ruby closed her eyes, rubbed her temples, then explained how it was that they had come to share the same father, Buddy.

"I don't understand," Tulsa said when Ruby had finished. "Why didn't you tell me I had a brother?"

"Your mom never forgave BJ. She made me promise I wouldn't tell, and since I had no idea where BJ and her baby had gone, there didn't seem to be any point. Until now."

Tulsa looked at Guy, her half brother.

He pivoted toward the door.

"Where are you going?" Tulsa asked, her voice shaky.

"To call my mother."

Tulsa lifted the phone receiver, which he waved away. "What I have to say, I plan to say loud."

"Guy, tell your mom she's welcome to visit," Ruby said. "I'd love to see her again."

"That makes one of us," he said, then left.

When he walked out, Tulsa stood trying to take

in that she wasn't an only child, that she had a brother. And that brother was Guy. Although it had taken some weeks to fully sink in, she and Guy had gradually relaxed into the comfortable routine and banter of adult siblings.

Guy apparently conveyed Ruby's invitation, because BJ came to visit a month later. Though Guy avoided her at first, BJ felt so much at home that she soon moved to Fiddle, renting a two-bedroom apartment a block away from the home she'd grown up in.

"I think that does it," Guy said now, patting the yellow bus. "Hopefully there wasn't enough water to wreck the engine."

Tulsa froze. "Wreck the engine?"

"It can happen. You don't always know right away. I'll fill it from our reserves and with a little luck, we can pick up the Scouts."

Guy fueled the tank. Tulsa slid into the driver's seat and turned the ignition. The engine sputtered, then caught. Tulsa gave a silent thanks to the universe.

"You'd better start parking the bus by the house," Guy said. "And keep your eyes open."

"I'm not afraid of Rupert Clancy." Tulsa swung the bus door closed.

"You're not afraid of anything," Guy said. "That's what worries me."

PART TWO

JUNE

CHAPTER FIFTEEN
Jen

Her mother sat in a wheelchair, her broken leg in its cast propped up, her T-shirt's logo proclaiming, *Think I'm sarcastic? Watch me pretend to care.* She looked around the kitchen in silence. Though Jen had invited her over for dinner several times, she'd never come, had never even cared to meet Jack.

Jen pushed her through the candy-apple kitchen to the peach dining room, the dark living room, the master bedroom, Jack's study, the pink bathroom, the turquoise master bath, and the yellow-walled room Jen hoped to make into a nursery. "This is yours," Jen said. It had been Jen's sewing room. Now it held a twin bed, dresser, nightstand, and daffodils. A bowl on the nightstand contained a potpourri of dried petals that filled the room with the fragrance of roses. "Do you like it?"

Her mother grunted.

What have I done? Jen thought. Her mother had been in the hospital for nearly three weeks due to diabetes issues and an infection. If only Jen could have left her there. Were Jack and she going to have to live with grunts for the next two or three months? She wheeled her mother back to the kitchen. "Are you hungry?"

Her mother shook her head.

"Let me get us some Coke." Jen busied herself pouring two glasses with soda and ice. "What do you think of the house?"

Her mother didn't respond right away, just clicked her tongue. "I think you scored big-time, Jen," she said. "This is a nice place. Or it was."

Jen heard the sarcasm. Her spirits plummeted. "Was?"

"Till you painted most of the rooms the colors of jawbreakers."

Jen told herself to ignore the sting. Jocelyn in the newest romance, *Savage Thunder*, would no doubt say that Jen's mother was mean. Jocelyn was a lot stronger character than Sunny Chandler, though, of course, Jocelyn, a British duchess who came to America fleeing a killer, had money to help strengthen her. She wasn't dependent on anyone for anything. Except Colt Thunder. She needed him for love. For happiness. But not for self-confidence, let alone backbone. Well, Jocelyn was absolutely right. Jen's mother had a mean streak.

Her mother sipped the Coke. She wore her lacquered hair so short it was almost prickly. "Not bad. All it needs is a shot of whiskey to make it go down smooth." She held out her glass.

Jen sat back, her body rigid. She'd known this

was coming. She just hadn't expected it so soon. "We don't have any," she said.

"Rum, then. I'm not particular."

Jen shook her head. She gestured to a vase full of white calla lilies. "How do you like the flowers? Ruby gave them to me as a welcoming gift for you."

"You gave me daffodils. Ruby gave me lilies. What I really want is booze."

It took Jen a good minute to respond. "There's no liquor in the house."

"You mom-proofed it, did you?"

Jen's throat constricted. This was a mistake. A huge mistake. "Jack said you were welcome if you didn't drink or try to boss him.

Her mother gripped Jen's wrist. "You expect me to live here for two or three months without a drop of anything?"

Jen pulled her arm away, stood, and stepped back. Her mother wheeled herself so that the chair's bulk and her extended leg blocked Jen in a corner. "Go to the store," her mother ordered. "Now."

"Please, Mom." Jen hated the pleading in her own voice. "Your doctor said that with your diabetes, drinking could kill you."

"So you gave me *Coke?*"

"Diet Coke."

Her mother nodded, more to herself it seemed than to Jen. "So it's Jack who calls the shots around here."

"No, not exactly."

"You had to beg his permission to let me stay, did you?"

"It's not like that," Jen said.

"Uh-huh."

The garage door ratcheted open. Jen looked up, hoping for rescue, fearing a fight. If her mother turned on Jack, Jen could lose everything.

Her mother wheeled her chair back to the table and picked up the glass of Coke, which she gulped down. "Delicious," she said, sarcasm again evident.

Jack entered the room. He looked so good in his vibrant green button-down shirt. He'd worn muted colors before Jen convinced him that his blond hair and skin tone went better with jewel shades. He appeared to her at that moment like her own Colt Thunder, riding to her rescue.

Jack set his briefcase on the floor and went right to Jen's mother. "Welcome, Elizabeth," he said, holding out his hand.

Her mother shook hands. Jen prayed that she wasn't squeezing too hard.

"Thank you for having me, Jack."

Jen had to clamp her teeth together to keep her jaw from dropping open. She'd never heard her mother sound so . . . so appreciative.

"You're welcome." Jack nodded to her leg. "I was sorry to hear about your accident."

"Thanks. The sunset was so pretty, I didn't even see that ditch."

Jen's mother smiled a smile that would put a prom queen to shame. It was a lie, of course, what she'd said about the sunset. According to the doctor, her mother had stumbled drunkenly out of a neighbor's trailer and tripped over a dog. Jen hadn't told Jack.

"Did Jen show you the house?"

"She did. It's great. You must work hard. And be pretty sharp."

Jack looked genuinely flattered. "I like to think so."

"I'm sure you are."

Jen just stood there looking between them, wondering if she was delirious. Was this pleasantry really happening?

"The walls are pretty bright, huh?" Jack said.

"Pretty bright, yes. Do you like it that way?"

"Sometimes I feel like putting on sunglasses." He grinned at Jen's mom and winked at Jen.

"I know what you mean," her mom said.

"But Jen's training me. It's cheerful."

Her mother smiled. "That's Jen, for sure. Cheerful to a T. Though I guess that's an odd saying. There's no *T* in cheerful."

"True." Jack looked at Jen. "What's for dinner?"

"I picked up some steaks. How about steak and mashed potatoes?"

"Great." He turned to Jen's mom. "Sound good to you?"

"Sure does," she said. "I'd offer to help, but I'm a little handicapped at the moment."

"No need. Jen's got it under control. Right, Jen?"

Jen could barely suppress her astonishment. Her mother, whose tongue could chill butter, was actually acting pleasant. Jen's pulse quickened. Maybe Jack would be a good influence. Maybe her mother would come to appreciate not just the house and Jack but her own daughter. Jen beamed her brightest smile at both of them. "Absolutely," she said.

CHAPTER SIXTEEN
BJ

If she had any sense, BJ thought, watching the rain spatter her windshield, she would start the car and flee before she totally humiliated herself. The Fiddle town square, where she was parked, was a grouping of a few squat, two-story brick buildings, some red, some brown, some tan. Built in the 1800s, the buildings seemed like fortresses, erected to withstand attack. Not like the flimsy things going up today, which you could practically huff, puff, and blow down. Huff & Puff. What a great name for a children's store.

Quit stalling, BJ, she scolded herself. *Decide.*

If only Guy had never suggested this. It had taken her almost three weeks to psych herself up for it. She picked up her copy of *Savage Thunder*. Bonner's Shoes was on the ground floor of the dark red building across from her car. Matthew Bonner would probably think she was crazy. Dinner? They knew each other by name, yes, but if they'd ever exchanged more than weather remarks, she couldn't recall it. She bought her shoes at the discount Shoe Emporium in West Plains.

Clutching *Savage Thunder* to her heart, BJ closed her eyes and prayed: *Dear Jesus, help. Please. Amen.* When she opened her eyes, she decided she would at least enter the store and check things out. Good thing she'd chosen a Tuesday. There should be fewer customers. Besides, she didn't have to actually buy anything, let alone issue an invitation. Maybe she'd even get lucky. Maybe *he* would ask *her* out.

She set *Savage Thunder* on the seat beside her and picked up her red umbrella. This had been such a rainy June, and it was only the tenth. Was the whole month going to be like this? As she got out of her Ford Escort, umbrella opened, she was glad she'd had Jen give her a pedicure, since she was proud of her narrow feet with their shapely toes. It made her feel a little less ugly. She smoothed her skirt and blouse and started toward Bonner's Shoes, repeating two words over and over in her mind: *Savage Thunder*.

The pungent smell of new leather assailed her as

she stepped into the store and stuck her umbrella in an umbrella stand. Shoes of all colors, shapes, designs, and materials were displayed on shelves and circular tables. Mirrored walls reflected shoes throughout the store, making it seem like there were enough to shoe an entire regiment.

And there, smiling at her amid his wares, was Matthew Bonner. Dressed in dark slacks, powder-blue sport shirt, red-and-blue striped tie, and polished brown wing tips, he looked every inch a shoe salesman. She would bet not a single romance novel featured a shoe salesman as hero. Not that Matthew Bonner was bad looking. It was just that he seemed, well, ordinary. Tame. An average man with thinning brown hair, a slight roll at the middle, though much less than her own, and unremarkable features.

He was certainly no Colt Thunder. But then she was no romance heroine, women who no doubt had thin figures and beautiful, thick hair. Her own body shape resembled an Idaho potato, while the hair she'd dyed to cover the gray had turned out not the expected auburn but more the color of mud.

"Good morning, BJ," Matthew said. "What can I help you with?"

She couldn't just say "dinner." She hadn't really thought this through. "Uh, shoes."

"We have quite a few of those." His gesture took in the store.

He motioned her to a display of canvas sandals, perhaps because it was summer, but it wasn't how she was feeling, not after reading *Savage Thunder*. "I want leather. Deep brown."

"Excellent. Would you prefer heels or flats?"

Heels were sexier, but she'd always been clumsy in them. The last thing she needed was to totter. "Flats, please."

"We just got in some new ones. Over here."

She liked the way he moved, his gestures graceful. Her eyes surveyed the display table. There were at least a dozen styles. "What do you recommend?"

"These are a particularly good bargain." He handed her a pair of brown, strappy shoes. "Very comfortable yet inexpensive."

The leather felt lovely, so soft she wanted to fondle it. It smelled good, too. "Could I try a pair?"

"Of course." He glanced at her feet. "Size seven triple-A?"

His expertise pleased her. "Yes." He was nothing like the young girls at the Shoe Emporium, who never could get her size right. There was something attractive about a man who knew his business.

She liked his unhurried but purposeful stride as he walked to the storeroom, his straight back, the way his bottom filled but didn't balloon his pants. And when he returned, three boxes of shoes in hand, she liked the warmth in his eyes.

"Think it'll clear up soon?" he said.

"I sure hope so." She was ready for sunshine outdoors and in her life.

He knelt before her just like she used to dream Buddy would.

"Let me take those off," he said, slipping her shoes off her feet. "Hmm."

She sat straighter. She didn't like the sound of his *hmm*, like a doctor pondering a strange shadow on an X-ray.

He frowned. "You have a remarkably high arch."

"Is that bad?"

"Not at all. But your shoes need to give you the right support. Let me get you a pair that I think would be a better fit."

BJ ran her hand over her foot, but her arch didn't feel high or low or anything, really. What did she know about feet?

Matthew knelt before her again and guided her feet into a pair of elegant brown slip-ons. "These are a little expensive," he said, "because they have leather straps and sides as well as rubber soles, a padded foot bed, and excellent arch support."

The shoes made her feet look classy.

"Why don't you stand to see how they feel," he suggested.

BJ stood. Straight. She stood straight for what seemed like the first time in years, her feet supported in a way they never had been. And her back seemed to unkink. "Wow," she said, "they even fit my back." *Well, that didn't make sense.*

"You might have gotten backaches from the lack of support in your shoes," he said.

Could it be that simple?

"Let me tighten your left shoe."

His fingers touched her skin. "Would you like to see my pork chops?" she blurted.

Puzzlement wrinkled his forehead. "Pardon?"

"I mean, would you like to *try* my pork chops?"

He busied himself putting away the pair of shoes he'd first taken out. Said nothing. She sank back down.

"Are you inviting me to dinner?" he asked at last.

"Yes." When was the last time she'd given anyone a one-word answer?

"Catherine used to make pork chops every Sunday."

His eyes had a dreamy look. Of course he hadn't gotten over his wife. What was she thinking? She grabbed her purse.

"Yes," he said.

"Yes?"

"I love pork chops, but they don't offer them in TV dinners. I'd love to come. When?"

"How about Thursday?" Two days would give her time to plan their meal and shop.

"Excellent. I'll look forward to it." He slipped the shoes off her feet. "Let me box these up."

"No need. I'll wear them."

"In the rain?"

She'd forgotten. "No, of course not."

He put a can of Scotchgard in the box. "On me," he said. "Treat your shoes with it before you get them wet."

He'd said they were expensive, though she hadn't asked how much. But then it didn't really matter. This was one pair of shoes she'd take at any price.

BJ pressed her garage-door opener. The first thing she realized as the door went up was that Guy was there in her garage, and he'd taken down the boxes she'd asked him to.

Her second realization was that Guy was standing with legs spread wide apart and glaring at her.

Her third was that he was holding a piece of paper, though what it was she couldn't tell for sure. She had the sinking feeling, however, that she knew. It had never occurred to her that his birth certificate would be with his school papers.

Guy remained where he was. She turned off her car, tried to steady herself with two deep breaths, then got out.

"*Travis* is my father?"

BJ winced. Guy was practically shouting.

"You've lied to me my whole life?"

"I'm sorry," she said.

"You're *sorry?* My father is your own cousin's husband. A skirt-chasing, booze-guzzling son of a bitch."

He had his birth certificate; she could see that now. It was all she could do to say a soft "Yes."

"How could you do that to Marjorie?" Guy asked.

Her stomach twisted. "It's a long story," she said.

He sat on one of the boxes. "I have all day."

BJ stared at her feet while she explained that after she slept with Buddy, she'd gotten her period. Then Travis got her drunk and seduced her. She let him because she was so fat nobody wanted to date her, let alone kiss her. "I was just so lonely." She heard the pleading in her own voice. Her story had so much drama. It felt like something from one of the romance novels they were reading, only this was real. Painfully real. Nothing she could do or say would diminish her guilt.

"So you betrayed Marjorie, and then you lied to me for twenty-eight years about my father."

Guy's voice sounded hard. He was right to be angry. "I'm sorry," she said. "I was going to tell you when you turned twenty-one. I went to Marjorie's to confess first, but she was recovering from her surgery, and Travis was so good to her. He was doing all the cooking and cleaning and shopping and was just so sweet. Her eyes seemed

127

to glisten every time she looked at him. I couldn't bring myself to tell her." If only she could hide from her own shame. "I'm really, really sorry."

"Is that what you're going to tell Marjorie? That you're *sorry?*"

"I wasn't going to tell her anything."

"You were just going to keep on lying."

"I didn't think it was hurting anybody. Buddy was a wonderful man. He would have made a great father. I wanted you to have a dad you could be proud of."

Guy glowered at her. "What you wanted," he said, "was not to have to tell Marjorie that you screwed her husband."

"That, too."

"What other lies have you told me?"

"None. You have to believe me."

"Why should I?"

She understood his anger, but she hadn't lied to him about anything else that mattered. "Are you going to tell Marjorie?" she said.

"I don't know! I should. Just so she would know the truth about Travis. And about you. That her own cousin slept with her husband. Damn, Mom, how could you?"

She could offer no good reason. "I was young and stupid and lonely and selfish and drunk." Two nights of booze and betrayal. She hadn't had a drink since. "What else can I say?"

He stood, crumpled the birth certificate, and

threw it against a box. Silent, he stared at the floor a long time. She said nothing, waiting for him to decide whether he would tell, every part of her seeming to knot. Her throat felt so tight, she half thought she would need a tracheotomy just to breathe.

"If I told," he said, "it would hurt Marjorie a lot. I can't stand to cause her that kind of pain."

"And our friends?"

"Is Tulsa's dad really Buddy?"

"Yes."

"So we aren't related."

"No."

Guy didn't answer immediately. "There's no reason to tell that I can see," he said after a moment. "If you did, it might get back to Marjorie. Do you think she knows that Travis fools around?"

"I doubt it," BJ said. "She's always telling me how much she loves him."

"I'm surprised you put down the truth on the birth certificate."

"We were living in Chicago then. And Dad insisted."

Guy picked up the birth certificate. He unwadded it, then waved the wrinkled paper at her. "Understand this: if I ever find out you've lied to me again, you won't have a son."

BJ paled. Her eyes fell on some of the other things Guy had taken out of the box: school projects he'd done as long ago as kindergarten.

She looked back at him. "I won't lie again," she promised.

Guy dropped the birth certificate back in the box. "I'm going home," he said. "You can sort through these boxes yourself."

"Thank you for taking them down."

He shook his head in obvious disgust, walked out of the garage, and whistled. Elvis appeared from around the side of the house. The two of them got in the truck. Guy drove off. BJ just stood in the garage, dazed. Though she felt the familiar shame and regret, she also experienced something she wouldn't have expected: relief that Guy at long last knew the truth.

CHAPTER SEVENTEEN
Pearl

Daniel beamed so bright when Pearl handed him the cast-iron skillet from her kitchen pantry, she'd have thought she was giving him the keys to the kingdom.

He ran his hand over the skillet's trademark: a cross inside a circle, the word *Erie* stamped beneath it. "A Griswold," he said, so reverently he practically whispered. No doubt about it: her grandson was smitten with all things culinary, especially antiques.

Unlike her. What pleased her wasn't cooking or antique skillets. What pleased her, apart from Daniel and her daughter, was music, like the Patsy Cline album playing on her stereo, and putting her feet up on the lounge chair in her backyard to watch the birds that flocked to her six feeders. The curtains over her kitchen window featured white lace with tiny red cardinals embroidered on them. The border across her wallpaper was of songbirds. Even her canisters echoed the theme: brown cylinders that looked like logs, their lids topped by colorful ceramic birds.

"When was the last time you used this skillet, Gran?"

"The Sunday before your grandfather died." Sherman used to say that stepping into their kitchen made him want to go quail hunting. Not that he ever did. He was so obsessed with the café he'd inherited, he rarely left it even to sleep; he kept a cot in the back office.

"Are you sure you want to give it away?" Daniel asked.

His lips were such a deep red, they looked like they'd been colored with a crayon. Many women spent a lot of money trying to acquire lips like Daniel's. "Honey, if I ever say I'm planning to cook another meal, lock me up in a loony bin, 'cause you'll know I have lost my mind." The only foods she kept in stock were ones that required no preparation: cereal, instant oatmeal, canned soup, peanut butter. The kitchen smelled of the bay leaves she scattered around to keep away moths.

"I'll use this a lot," Daniel said. "Thanks."

Was it the freckles, the big smile, or the cheeks that looked clean-shaven even when they weren't that made him seem so young?

The phone rang. Pearl answered it.

"Hi, Mom, it's Lillian."

"How are you, Lil?" That wasn't what she wanted to say. She wanted to ask if her daughter had left her domineering husband, who was practically a clone of Sherman, only worse. At least Sherman hadn't quoted Scripture when he'd insisted Pearl leave her sickbed to work, labor for fourteen-hour days, or refuse her aunt's invitation to go with her to Florida. Pearl had so longed to see the ocean.

In high school, Lillian had been popular, a pretty girl with cheerleader perkiness. Pearl tried to get her daughter to dream big—become an airline stewardess, a cruise ship entertainer, a travel agent. At nineteen, however, Lillian married a man about as loving as a cactus. Though Pearl encouraged her daughter to stand up for herself, Lillian retreated behind silence, even wearing her hair in a bun because that's what her husband wanted. A bun. In this day and age? Perhaps Pearl should buy Lillian a copy of *Savage Thunder*. From what Pearl had read so far, the heroine of that book didn't take guff from anyone.

"Danny's here," Pearl said.

"Oh." Silence. A sob.

That confirmed her suspicions. "So you know?" Pearl said.

Daniel looked down at the skillet in his hands. "Jennifer Landis called. She heard it from Minnie."

Jennifer had been Lillian's best friend before Lillian moved to Omaha when she married. Too bad Jennifer hadn't kept her mouth shut. "Don't you want to talk to him?" Daniel was watching her now.

"I do, but Conrad ordered me not to."

"*Ordered* you?"

"Just till Danny's normal again. But please, Mom, please tell him how much I love him."

"But—" Pearl began.

Lillian hung up. Daniel looked so crestfallen, Pearl's heart ached. "Your mom said to tell you she really loves you."

Tears welled in Daniel's eyes.

Pearl wanted to slap her son-in-law silly for not talking to Daniel and for forbidding Lillian from doing so, but that would require her to see the man, something she would rather not do. Still, he was right about homosexuality. Pearl spoke as casually as she could. "You know, Danny, the book of Leviticus in the Bible says, 'If a man also lie with mankind, as he lieth with a woman, both of them have committed an abomination: they shall surely be put to death.' "

Daniel's expression was somewhere between incredulous and wounded. "You think I should be put to death?"

"Of course not."

He studied her with thickly lashed hazel eyes that made her feel loved. He had so much love to give. If only he wouldn't throw it away.

"Gran, the Bible was written by men. Homophobic men who lived two thousand years ago. Things have changed."

"The Bible is the word of God. That doesn't change."

"But how we interpret it does. Doesn't the Bible say to stone adulterers, kill disobedient children, and cut off the hands of thieves?"

"We changed the punishment, honey, not the crime. Homosexuality is still a sin."

Her doorbell chimed. She needed to beat Daniel to the door. "I'll get it," she said, starting forward.

But he was already through the kitchen doorway. "I got it, Gran."

She moaned. This was not going to go well.

When Daniel reentered the kitchen, leading Cindy Shafer, his scowl could freeze boiling water.

Pearl tried to assume a breezy tone, like this wasn't part of her plot to lure him back to normalcy. "Honey, this is Cindy from church." Cindy's thick blonde hair, pretty face, and short skirt would make many young men whistle.

"Tell me you did not invite Cindy here to meet me," Daniel said.

Wide-eyed, Cindy looked from Pearl to Daniel and back.

Her only choice was to brazen this out. "You don't have anything against female friends, do you?"

"Girl friends, no. Girlfriends, yes. You know that. And that's exactly why you invited Cindy here, isn't it? You hoped I'd fall for her."

"If you just took some time to get to know Cindy, maybe you'd change your mind."

"I'm sorry," Daniel told Cindy. "This has nothing to do with you." When he turned back to Pearl, his scowl dissolved into tears. He left the skillet on the counter, turned, and rushed out of the house. The front door slammed.

"Can I get you something, Mrs. Jacobs?" Cindy asked in a pillow-soft voice.

"No, thank you," Pearl said. She couldn't bring herself to meet the girl's eyes. "I'm so sorry, Cindy."

"I think I understand. I'll see you at church Sunday."

"Thank you for coming."

After Cindy left, Pearl went outside and sat on the lounge chair for a long while, her gaze unfocused, her mind torn between sorrow and despair. She hadn't wanted to hurt Daniel or make Cindy feel bad. She should never have invited the girl over. She tried to think of another strategy, concentrating for what seemed like hours. Nothing. If she thought about it much more, her skull would crack.

A cardinal sang from the maple near the back bird feeder. A blue jay dipped itself in the bird-bath. A robin hunted worms on her lawn. She picked up the book she'd been reading when Daniel came. It was a good book, but it wasn't *the* Good Book.

Was there any chance the Bible wasn't inspired by God, that it was just a work of fiction like the book in her hands? She traced the print on the cover of *Savage Thunder*.

What was she thinking? To equate Johanna Lindsey with Matthew, Mark, Luke, and John? She must be losing her mind.

CHAPTER EIGHTEEN
Tulsa

Rain clattered on the tin roof of the shower house the next morning, creating a racket that was worsening the headache Tulsa had developed from two mostly rainy weeks. Cancellations had cut $9,000 from their normal intake for the first eleven days of June.

And now the damned women's shower-house

tap was leaking. Water seeped up around the base of the shower and dripped onto the floor, where it had pooled, drowning one moth, two beetles, and a spider that looked to be the size of a small jellyfish. The mess had caused two campers to demand a partial refund, which Tulsa had reluctantly given. She couldn't afford to keep doing that.

People had gotten too soft. She enjoyed floating in warm rain when she wasn't worried about going broke. Raindrops dimpled the water, dappled leaves, and turned air sensuous with the fragrance of wet woods. She didn't get why other people didn't enjoy it, nor why locals were canceling at a higher rate than out-of-towners. She would have expected locals to be hardier than city folk.

Tulsa scoured the three shower-house toilets with Ajax and a stiff-bristled brush. Cleaning toilets wasn't her favorite task, but it needed doing. She didn't want Ruby to get stuck with it.

A car was coming down the hill. Tulsa put the toilet brush back in its holder, washed her hands, and went to the doorway. Thankfully it was Jen, bringing the washers. She was opening a bright polka-dotted umbrella as she got out of her car. Jen was dressed in white capris and a tight orange knit shirt. Her gold hoop earrings spangled. Her mussed hair looked casual, but she'd probably spent a good half hour with blow-dryer and round brush to achieve that effect.

"Hey," Tulsa said as Jen hurried to her.

"Hi." Inside the shower house, Jen shook rain from her umbrella. "Get it fixed?"

"Not yet." Tulsa took the hardware store bag from Jen. "Thanks. How much do I owe you?"

"My treat."

"Thanks again. How's your mother?"

"Oh, fine."

"Really?"

"Well, you know."

She did. In the few times she'd met Jen's mother over the years, Tulsa hadn't seen a single act of love or kindness toward Jen. It was one of the reasons that Tulsa had invited Jen for sleepovers growing up. That and the fact that she'd enjoyed Jen's company. It was fun to explore the river together. Before Guy came, Jen was the closest thing she had to a sibling. Tulsa missed her.

"How are your mom and Jack getting along?"

"Surprisingly well. Better than she and I do."

"That's not your fault, Jen."

Jen shrugged and looked around the shower house. "You should fix this place up."

Tulsa took in the gray concrete floor, gray concrete walls, green plastic roof, moths trapped in spiderwebs, and a couple of beetles trundling across the dirt-streaked floor. Nothing awful. She unscrewed the faucet handle. "The toilets flush; the hot water works. It's a shower house. In a campground. People don't expect luxury." She used her adjustable crescent wrench to loosen the nut holding the valve stem.

"Do they expect spiders, bugs, and toilet tissue you could use for sandpaper?"

Tulsa paused from her work. "You think people would stay elsewhere just because we don't supply soft toilet paper?"

"It's not even two-ply. And yes, I do think there are people who care about that."

"Well, I'll think about it. We can't afford anything expensive." She lifted off the valve stem, undid the screw that held in the washer, took out the old washer, and held it up to the light. Torn. No wonder the faucet leaked. She ripped open the packaging on one of the new washers and replaced the damaged one. "I wish we could take a float."

"Me, too. Between Mom, Jack, and work, I'm lucky to find time to breathe. But at least work gets me out of the house and away from Mom. Plus I can save money for buying a crib."

Tulsa whirled toward her. "A crib? You're pregnant?"

Jen slumped against the shower stall. "No," she said.

"Then why save for a crib?"

"I'm saving for when I do get pregnant."

Jen was wearing her usual rose-scented perfume. Tulsa focused on tightening the nut on the valve stem and keeping her cynicism to herself.

"Sometimes," Jen said, "I worry about having kids. What if I turn out like my mom?"

Tulsa put her hand on Jen's shoulder. "There's not a mean bone in your body."

"I can be pretty vicious with spiders."

"Gandhi was probably vicious with spiders. I don't know why so many people hate them." Tulsa turned and gave the valve a final wrench. Given how things were going, she half feared the valve was going to burst. She turned the faucet slowly. Water flowed. She shut it off. No leak. If only she could shut off the rain.

"You read the book for tonight?" Jen asked.

"Yeah."

"It's good, right?"

Tulsa tossed her wrench back in her toolbox. "Jocelyn's a lot stronger than Sunny was. I liked that."

"I liked Colt." Jen started to open her umbrella. "By the way, I was doing a customer's nails, and she said something about your bus not running right. Is that true?"

"No. We got some water in the tank a couple of weeks back, but Guy fixed it. It's running fine now. When was this?"

"A few days ago."

"That's odd," Tulsa said.

Jen opened her umbrella. "I'd better get going. I need to start a pot roast for dinner."

"Thanks again for bringing the washers. And

let me know if you hear any more rumors about the bus."

"Will do. See you."

Jen stepped outside, put out her hand, then collapsed the umbrella as she turned back to Tulsa. "Rain's stopped."

"Really?" Tulsa joined Jen. A patch of blue sky was the first she'd seen in days. "If you brought the sun, we might have to tie you up and keep you here."

"Sounds kinky," Jen said.

"Just desperate."

"Business will pick up."

"I sure hope so." Tulsa closed Jen's car door. "Take care of yourself."

"You, too."

Tulsa watched Jen drive up the hill. If the rumor that their bus was unreliable was spreading around town, it would explain why locals were canceling at a higher rate than out-of-towners. One of the Scouts or Scout leaders must have said something. She would put together some new flyers to post in local shops, maybe feature a photo of the bus. Ruby could call shopkeepers to let folks in town know that the bus was running fine. Tulsa closed her toolbox and headed to the house.

That afternoon, listening to a radio weatherman predict yet another storm for the following day, Tulsa felt like wasps were crawling up her arms.

She'd been so hopeful that June was finally acting like summer. The storm they'd forecast for tomorrow night would bring rain *and* drop the temperature into the fifties.

She slipped on the soft flannel shirt that was hanging from a prong of the antler rack. It couldn't keep raining! If it were dry and chilly, folks would still stay in the campground. They'd roast marshmallows over bonfires and maybe ask Guy to play his guitar and sing for them. If it was wet, though, nobody but die-hard fishermen would come.

A knock at the door startled her. Slade. "Hi," he said, entering. His wide smile revealed teeth so white, they could signal passing planes.

"Afternoon," she said. "Welcome back." She'd wondered if the weather would prompt him to cancel. His brace was gone. "How's the knee?"

"Better. How are you?"

"Soggy."

"Rain must be bad for business."

"Yep."

"You're still guiding me tomorrow?"

She tilted the chair back. "Like I told you, Guy's a better fishing guide."

"I'm not fishing. I caught my fish last time. Thanks to you."

"You bought all that gear for just one fish?"

"I'm fickle."

"I'll say." Tulsa rose and took the key to Treetop

from the antler rack. "So if you're not planning to fish, why are you here?"

"To shoot."

"It's not hunting season."

"I'll show you. Come with me."

He led the way to his Range Rover and grabbed something from the passenger seat. It was a fancy-looking black camera with a singularly long lens. "It's the newest digital," he said. His face lit up like someone had flipped a switch. "Twenty-point-one megapixels. I'm entering a photography contest. Take me out tomorrow, and we'll see what we can find."

"Okay, but I'm tied up hauling folks in the morning. And it'll be cool tomorrow."

"I prefer late-afternoon light," he said. "And cold weather's great for hugging."

"Hugging?"

"Kissing, if you prefer."

She had to admit that his twenty-megapixel smile made both propositions halfway appealing. Not that she cared to confess that. "Let's say four tomorrow."

"That's interesting."

"What is?"

"You didn't say no to hugging and kissing. So why not join me for dinner tonight?"

The damned wasps were back. "Can't."

"Why not?"

"Got company coming." She didn't bother to

explain the discussion of *Savage Thunder*. Shouts rose from the river; canoes scraped gravel as they were pulled up on the bank. It must be the Sanchez family. She'd put them in upriver this morning, only a six-mile float. Apparently they'd stopped a lot.

He pointed the camera at her. Though tempted to turn away, she just kept her eyes on him, as blank-faced as she could make herself.

"Nice," he said. "No wonder they say the Ozarks are scenic."

"Are you always this annoying?"

"Most women find me charming."

"I'm not most women."

"I know. I like that."

Eight-year-old Bobby Sanchez practically flew up the stairs and scampered over to her. Hair shorn in a crew cut, clad only in a pair of cutoffs, Bobby bounced up and down like he was wearing springs on his feet. "Look, Tulsa." He held up a stringer full of good-size smallmouth bass. "Look at all the fish we caught!"

"Wow," she said.

"That's quite a haul," Slade said.

"Did *you* catch some of them?" Tulsa asked Bobby.

"Yeah! The biggest. Only I didn't land him."

"That still counts. I bet you'll grow up to be just as good a fisherman as your dad."

"Better!" Bobby galloped back to the river.

"That kid's going to be a mover and shaker," Slade said.

"He already moves and shakes. I don't know how his dad manages to settle him down enough to keep from capsizing, let alone catch fish. They've never overturned, even once. If I believed in miracles, that would be one."

Slade moved to within an inch of her. "So what do you believe in, Tulsa?"

She drew her lean body up to its full five feet, seven inches. She did not back up. "The river. Sunshine. My family. My friends. And myself."

"That's a good list, but I hope there's room for it to expand."

She didn't know whether there was or not.

"I'm staying through the weekend, so block out as much time as you can," he said. "I want to win that photography contest. See you tomorrow." He reached out to shake.

Tulsa clasped his hand. It was warm and smooth. She could almost feel that hand caressing her breasts. She dropped it, turned away from him, and headed toward the river. "I've got work to do," she said.

"You sure about dinner?" Slade called.

She waved without turning around.

Though she had nothing immediate that she had to do, she felt an overwhelming urge to wade into the water.

CHAPTER NINETEEN
Pearl

Jen's face flamed almost as bright as the fire in Ruby's wood-burning stove, Pearl thought, turning up her hearing aid. She didn't want to miss what Jen had to say.

"That scene where Jocelyn and Colt make love on horseback?" Jen tugged a strand of her short blonde hair. "It made me want to run out and buy a horse."

BJ snickered. Tulsa rolled her eyes. Only Ruby gave an understanding nod, though Pearl was willing to bet that Ruby knew as well as she did how unlikely the horseback scene in *Savage Thunder* was.

"I used to ride a horse over to Ruby's for school," Pearl said. "*Whiskey,* we called him, because he'd been born with one front leg shorter, making him walk like he was drunk." A pinto pony, black and white. Pretty thing. Too bad he hadn't had a smoother gait, because it was a good twenty-minute ride to Ruby's, where they'd pasture Whiskey, then walk together the two miles to their one-room school. "Let me tell you, the way we bounced around on that horse, if people tried to fool around on horseback, a man would be lucky his vitals didn't snap off."

"Really?" Jen said. "It seemed so . . . real."

Pearl buttoned the top two buttons of her sweater. The cold front had started settling in around dinner. It seemed strange to be lighting a fire in June, but the temperature had dropped to the fifties. The cold made her joints ache something fierce. Of course, worrying about Daniel probably worsened the hurt. She still hadn't come up with a way to save him, but she wouldn't think about that now.

"I really loved this book," Jen said. "Colt and Jocelyn make a great couple."

"I liked it, too," BJ said.

Pearl agreed. "Kept me interested." She glanced at Tulsa, who half shrugged and half nodded.

"What did everyone think of Colt?" Ruby asked.

"Dreamy," Jen said.

"I liked him," BJ said, "but he was a little bit rough."

"I wouldn't want to be kissed so hard my lips bruised," Pearl said, "though I'd rather have a bucking bronco than a lame horse."

Ruby turned to Tulsa.

"He's okay, I guess," Tulsa said. "The way he lives in the woods and doesn't care about money, he reminded me of Guy."

Pearl didn't think BJ's smile could spread any farther.

"Thank you," BJ said.

There was something different about BJ. It wasn't just that her toes were painted for the first time Pearl could remember. It was that her eyes were bright. What had BJ so excited?

"One thing I disagreed with," Jen said, "is when Jocelyn's friend says a woman can experience the pleasures of sex with any man. I don't think that's true."

"I don't either," Ruby said.

"Sure you can," Tulsa said. "All guys have the same parts."

"All cars have the same parts, too," Pearl said, "but they sure don't drive the same."

"We're talking about men. Not cars."

"Guess you haven't noticed that some go a lot faster than others," Pearl said. "And a used model doesn't drive like a brand-new one. Just how many 'cars' have you tried out, Tulsa?"

"Enough to know where the throttle is."

"I wish every car drove as well as Colt Thunder," BJ said, then looked confused, like she'd forgotten just exactly what she meant.

"Throttles are pretty standard equipment." Pearl still spoke to Tulsa. "You need to test-drive a few more to figure out the features that you like. Otherwise one of these days you might end up with the wrong model. Like I did."

"While we're talking," Ruby said, rising, "let's have some dessert."

BJ practically bounded out of the chair. "I'll help serve it."

Pearl suspected that BJ volunteered in order to assure she got the biggest piece of whatever it was Ruby had fixed.

As it melted in her mouth a few minutes later, Ruby's peach cobbler with fresh peaches and whipped cream tasted to Pearl like springtime, all soft and promising. It amazed her that Ruby still professed to enjoy baking. Of course, Ruby hadn't slaved at Sherman's for almost sixty years.

"I can't imagine living like Jocelyn with all that money," she said aloud. "Having your own cook. And getting to travel the world when you're still young enough to enjoy it."

Jen scooted to the edge of her chair. "If I were rich, I'd go to Paris. It seems so romantic. I can just picture walking beneath the Eiffel Tower with Jack."

Tulsa opened her mouth to comment but closed it again. Maybe she was learning verbal restraint, which was a quality she badly needed.

"I'd visit the Holy Land," BJ said. "I want to see where Jesus lived and those lovely churches."

"Well, Clifford and I traveled to most every state we wanted to see," Ruby said. "Never had much of a hankering to go anywhere else. If I were Jocelyn, I reckon I'd stay right here."

Maybe she would now, too, Pearl thought. "I used to want to see the world. Starting with

Nashville. Now my get-up-and-go's got up and gone."

"How about you, Tulsa?" Jen asked.

"I don't know. Alaska maybe. All those rivers."

"All those mosquitoes," Pearl said.

"If I were with Colt Thunder," Jen said, "I'd go anywhere he wanted, mosquitoes and all."

"Me, too," BJ said. "I wouldn't mind having that man scratch my itch."

BJ grinned. Jen giggled. Tulsa smiled. Pearl chuckled. And Ruby laughed out loud.

"I like talking about these books," Pearl said.

"I like reading them, too," Jen said.

"Me, too," BJ agreed.

"How about you, honey?" Ruby asked.

Tulsa looked about as comfortable as a cat getting a bath. "I didn't much like the first book. This one was better. But it was still pretty predictable. Smitten woman wins her man."

Jen looked at Tulsa almost apologetically, Pearl thought, as if to say she was only speaking out of affection. "It's been eight months since you and Warren broke up, Tulsa. Maybe it's time for you to go out on a date."

"I will. When I meet someone who interests me."

"You're pretty and thin," BJ said to Tulsa. "I bet a lot of guys would like to go out with you."

Tulsa waved aside BJ's comment.

Jen spoke in a firm voice. "BJ is right, Tulsa.

You are pretty. And you've gone out with only five or six guys, total. You were choosy even back in high school."

"You're just saying that because I didn't want to date Ellison Owens."

"He was a great guy," Jen said, "and half in love with you."

Tulsa tapped her own head in obvious exasperation. "How could he be in love with me? He hardly knew me."

"I fell in love with Clifford the first time I saw him," Ruby said.

Pearl pointed her finger at Tulsa. "I'll bet you're so particular because you're scared."

Tulsa scoffed. "I'm not afraid of any man alive."

"Not afraid of men, no," Pearl said. "Afraid of being dropped again."

"I'm a big girl. I can stand disappointment."

"Tell you what, then," Pearl said. "Why don't you agree to go out with the next man who asks you?"

"That's crazy."

"No it's not," Ruby said. "You said that fellow Slade asked you to dinner and you flat-out turned him down."

"I was busy, not afraid."

"Uh-huh," Pearl said.

"I'm not. And why are *you* pushing me? You were married to a man you didn't even like."

"True. But your grandmother sure loved Clifford, and you got her genes, not mine."

"And my mom's, don't forget."

"You would never be desperate like your mom," Ruby said.

"Love just makes life so much lovelier," Jen said.

"Try again, honey," Ruby urged Tulsa.

"Time passes a lot more quickly than you think," Pearl said. "You'll be thirty soon, Tulsa. You ought to get back in the game."

"Fine."

Pearl pointed her finger at Tulsa. "So you'll go out with the next guy who asks you?"

"Unless he's crazy, stupid, dull, or mean."

"Hell, with that list, who's left?" Pearl said.

Tulsa looked incredulous. "You want me to go out with just *anybody?*"

"I figure you can protect yourself pretty well. So keep your promise and accept the first invitation you get."

"Unless he's dangerous," Ruby said. "We don't want you putting yourself in harm's way."

Tulsa looked stunned, like she couldn't believe she was giving in. "I don't know who's crazier. You all for demanding this, or me for agreeing to it."

"What are we going to read next?" BJ asked, looking eagerly at Ruby.

Ruby took a stack of silvery blue paperbacks

from the table beside her. "*Montana Sky* by Nora Roberts," she said, passing the books out. "It's about three very different half sisters who inherit a ranch, and the men in their lives."

"*Three* pairs of lovers?" BJ said. "I bet we can learn a lot from this book."

Tulsa frowned. "Learn a lot about what?"

BJ's face turned tulip red. "Oh, you know. Things."

"When are we meeting next?" Jen asked.

"Not around July fourth," Tulsa said. "That's our busiest time."

Ruby looked at a small calendar she'd taken from her purse. "Let's do Thursday the tenth. That's a month. But I should warn you, the book's a little bloody. There's murder in it. Actually more than one."

"Romance and murder? Sounds exciting." Jen stood. "Speaking of murder, I don't like to leave Jack alone with my mom for too long."

"Who do you think will murder whom?" Pearl asked.

"I think three hours alone with my mother might tempt most people."

"You've got a point," Tulsa agreed.

Ruby tutted. "Stop, you two. She's your mother, Jen. Don't joke about those things."

"Sorry," Jen said, but when Ruby leaned over to pick up a plate, Jen and Tulsa grinned at each other.

Pearl was glad Ruby didn't see it. That grin might make her feel old. It reminded Pearl of the secret smiles she and Ruby used to share in the one-room schoolhouse they attended. Thinking about those days decades ago made *her* feel old. *Ah well,* she thought, as they carried their dishes to the kitchen. *Better old than dead.* Though she believed in God, she wasn't all that certain what death would bring. Nor was she sure that Heaven, whatever it proved to be, would be her final destination.

CHAPTER TWENTY
Tulsa

"I've got a bad feeling about this," Tulsa said to Guy as they stood outside on the porch steps the next morning, the day unusually chilly for June. "You sure you don't want me to go with you this afternoon to see Judge Morris?"

"Nope." He leaned against the door and petted Elvis, whose tail thumped the ground. "He'll just make me pay a small fine and go home."

Tulsa sipped coffee, unsweetened, with the fresh cream Ruby kept on hand. "So you're sure Judge Morris isn't hard on poachers?"

"Not a first offense."

"Tell him the truth. That you were going to

smoke the venison for Wanda's grandmother's ninetieth birthday. That should soften him up."

"I'll be fine, but you be careful. They're predicting thunderstorms tonight." Guy ran his fingers through his light brown hair. "Be sure you're off the water."

"Don't worry. We'll be at the take-out at eight." She and Slade were floating downstream this time, from their place to the Possum Springs take-out. Guy would pick them up. The storm wasn't due to hit until midnight, though gray clouds were beginning to form.

"If this weather keeps up," Guy said, eyes seeming to darken, "we're screwed. How far behind are we?"

"We're down over nine thousand from what we expected to bring in."

"Ouch," he said.

"Yeah. The weather's *got* to clear."

"The Farmers' Almanac's calling for clear skies for most of the rest of the summer."

"Good thing." Lucky the clouds were only scattered. Slade couldn't take pictures in the rain.

Guy unwrapped a stick of Juicy Fruit.

"You got any more gum?" she asked.

"Nope, but I'll share." He licked one side of the stick, then handed the gum to her.

She licked the other side and popped the gum in her mouth. "Perfect." The tangy Juicy Fruit was better less sweet.

Elvis barked and ran into the woods.

"Lord, I hope she's not after another skunk," Guy said. "I've cleaned that dog up twice in the past week. How many canoes we got going out today?"

Her body tightened like a bolt being wrenched. "The Smiths want eight. The Livingston family needs ten. Oh, and the high school group wants twenty. That's thirty-eight. Not enough. Not nearly enough. Damn this weather."

Guy frowned. "It's not just the weather."

"Meaning what?"

Guy straightened his lanky body. "Meaning Rich says Clancy's spreading all kinds of lies about us."

"Like what?"

"That we drive drunk. That our bus breaks down all the time. That we make customers wait for hours."

"That son of a bitch!" She punched Guy's arm. Of course Clancy was starting the rumors. "Why didn't you tell me sooner?"

He rubbed his arm. "Rich just called last night."

"You should've called me right away."

"So you could go off half-cocked and do something stupid?"

"Doing nothing would be stupid. I'm not about to stand by and let Clancy ruin us."

"Agreed. But for now let's get the canoes loaded and get through today. After you finish guiding

Slade, we'll figure out what to do about Clancy." He glanced at his watch. "Ruby's not up yet?"

"No. I'm worried about her. She's been sleeping a lot."

"Well, she's almost eighty."

"Meaning what?" Tulsa snapped. She couldn't believe Guy hadn't called her immediately.

Guy held up his hands as if in surrender. "Meaning if either of us has as much energy at eighty as Ruby's got, we should count ourselves lucky."

"Ruby's not eighty. She's seventy-eight. Let's get those canoes loaded." She set her cup on the steps.

As they headed for the boats, Guy began singing "Blue Eyes Crying in the Rain," which was exactly what she felt like doing at the thought of yet another storm.

Guy had a great voice, deep and husky. If he sang to the women he dated, it was no wonder they were devastated when he broke up with them.

Tulsa swung a canoe overhead and thought again about Clancy poisoning their business. Tonight she would pay him a visit. One way or another, with or without Guy, she would find a way to muzzle the man.

Though they'd been floating only a couple of hours, Slade took what Tulsa thought must be his five hundredth photograph of the river's life:

kingfishers in flight, turtles perched on logs, dragonflies resting on canoe gunnels, lesser green herons stalking fish along the shore, tree reflections splintered by her paddle.

A breeze whipped the powder-blue chamois shirt Slade wore over his T-shirt on a day much too chilly for June. Good thing she'd put on a flannel shirt before they left.

He turned and pointed his lens at her. "I bet you were a real Huck Finn growing up," he said. His camera clicked. "Bet you liked to chew straws and skip school."

"What did you do, *Tom?* Con other kids into painting your fence?"

"No. Waxing my car."

A great blue heron landed on the jagged top of a dead tree, which was framed by looming clouds. "On your right," she said. She backwatered to give Slade a better view.

"Terrific shot." He took a dozen pictures of the bird.

The heron's bluish-gray feathers matched the darkening clouds behind it and were a great contrast with the birch's white trunk.

"Can you back us up more?" he asked. "I'd like another angle."

Tulsa brought the stern of the canoe into branches overhanging the bank.

A snake dropped its head in front of her face. Skin splotched like a rattlesnake. Forked tongue flicking. Gold eyes gleaming. Tulsa sucked in her breath. It was a water snake, nonpoisonous, but it made her feel like danger was only an inch away. She started to paddle them forward.

"Wait!" Slade took about a dozen snapshots of her and the snake.

She was relieved when the snake slithered back up the branch.

"Most women I know would've freaked." His glance at her seemed downright admiring. "If you'd been in Eden, the apple would've stayed on the tree."

She was surprised how much his compliment pleased her.

That's when she heard the first growl of thunder. Startled, she kept her eyes on the sky and counted the seconds. She'd reached just thirty when lightning split the clouds. Sound traveled one mile in five seconds, so the storm was just six miles away. Close. Too close. Although rain hadn't been predicted until much later, she should have kept a closer eye on the clouds. She'd let herself get distracted. It was a beginner's mistake.

Thunder rumbled again. It was almost six, and they hadn't even gone halfway. There was no way they could do two and a half miles before the storm hit, but she would get them as far as she could.

"Stow the camera," she said. "It's going to rain."

He took a picture of the clouds. She thrust the

paddle in the water, sending the canoe hurling forward. A few drops of rain spattered them. Slade quickly stashed the camera in its case, then zipped it into a dry storage bag.

Thunder, louder. Lightning followed in twenty-five seconds. When it got to twenty, they would need to get off the water. She leaned forward, dug the paddle as deep as she could. Cold rain struck them.

"I love storms!" Slade sat up so straight she wondered if he was trying to be a lightning rod.

"Paddle," she said.

He hesitated for several seconds, then picked up his paddle and began helping. Between the two of them, the canoe spurted down the river.

They'd covered maybe another mile when the count shrank to twenty. Tulsa beached the boat on a gravel bar. Slade clutched his camera bag.

Thunder shook the air around them. "We need to get away from the water," she said. "We'll shelter below the trees up that draw."

"No way." Slade turned his face to the sky.

It was as if someone unzipped the clouds, for the rain turned torrential, drenching them both. Thunder reverberated. Lightning flashed in jagged streaks. "Come on." Tulsa started for the draw.

He turned from her and strode to the river's edge, where he raised his fist in the air as if in challenge to the gods. "Bring it on!" he bellowed.

The sky bellowed back. Lightning struck a

sycamore across the river. The tree burst into flame. Slade jumped. Limbs splintered and plunged to ground. The air smelled scorched. "Awesome!" he said as if the lightning had electrified him.

That was way too close. Tulsa grabbed his arm and jerked him back. He resisted. The treetop burned. Sparks flew. Embers hit the water, sizzled. The air stank of burned wood. Dry bag under one arm, Slade relented and followed her back into the draw.

The trees that lined the draw were dense, shorter than the sycamores and cottonwoods farther back up the hill. Under the shorter trees was the safest place to wait out the storm. If it lasted a couple of hours, at least in terms of the threat from lightning, and if they both paddled hard, they would be only about an hour late getting to the take-out point. Guy would be worried. Once he saw they were safe, though, he would probably get on her case for not having seen the approaching storm. Well, she couldn't argue with that. She should have. If the lightning had struck their side of the river, one or both of them could be dead.

Slade seemed ecstatic, either unaware of or downright enjoying the danger. "Now, this," he said, lugging his camera bag as they hurried back up the draw, rain running down his face, "is fun!"

It was, in a way, though they were in no shape to enjoy it. Her worry about money and Rupert

Clancy's lies had distracted her so much she hadn't brought rain gear or extra clothes or matches, supplies she routinely took on late floats. Their clothes were soaked. It was sixty-some degrees and would only get colder.

Small nuggets of hail stung them. If the hail grew to golf-ball size, it could cause real injury. Tulsa quickened her pace. She led Slade to a spot where the undergrowth was thickest. They sheltered beneath a small oak that had been stunted by the density of the surrounding foliage. Water dripped on their heads, but the hail was diverted or slowed enough not to hurt. If this were a scene from *Savage Thunder*, the couple would no doubt warm themselves by making love. But it wasn't, and they certainly wouldn't.

"Too bad my camera's not waterproof." Slade wiped his face with his hands. "Lightning striking that tree would've been a sure prizewinner."

"Lightning striking you wouldn't have been so pretty."

He took a deep whiff of air. "Smells great."

He was right. The wet woods smelled fresh, earthy.

"Storms make me feel alive," he said.

"You do realize that could have been you instead of the tree."

Water cascaded from a branch onto his hair. He seemed not to notice. "I'm not living my life hiding from death," he said.

"That doesn't mean you have to issue it an invitation."

He lowered his voice and stepped closer to her, so close they almost touched. "I didn't know you cared."

"You bet. Barbecuing customers is bad for business."

He stepped back. His laughter pealed through the forest. He was hopeless, but she liked the fact he could laugh and that he'd made no complaint about being drenched with the temperature falling. She just hoped the lightning would stop soon. She didn't enjoy canoeing in the dark. The minute it was safe, she would get them back in the boat and on downriver.

CHAPTER TWENTY-ONE
BJ

Matthew Bonner stepped inside her apartment, took a deep breath, and said, "Oh my. I haven't smelled cooking that good in a long time."

Thank you, Jesus. She'd debated whether to wait until he got there to start dinner but had decided it would be smarter to have the aroma of delicious food filling the apartment, a kind of pork chop perfume. "Thanks," she said. "I hope you're hungry."

"Famished." He glanced around the living room. Would he find her apartment as homey as she did? She was proud of the plaid sofa and matching easy chairs, the shag rug, and the ten model churches displayed on TV trays. He walked over to the nearest church. Its white spire and tiny stained-glass windows—colored cellophane, really, though they looked like glass—shimmered from the lighted pole lamp behind it. She preferred to think of it as shining from the Light of the Lord.

"Did you make these churches?" he asked.

"Yes." What remained of his hair, mostly around the sides, was a lovely mix of brown and gray, and while his lips were thin, they looked soft. Kissable. Kissable? She should never have read *Montana Sky* today. The book made her want to be with a man—really be with a man, both emotionally *and* physically.

"From scratch?" he said.

"Yes. And my own designs."

"They're great. Do you sell them? I bet you could get five or six hundred dollars apiece. Maybe more."

"Oh no. I like having them around. They make me feel like my home is God's home." She had no intention of explaining how they also helped her feel forgiven.

"Isn't every home God's home?"

"I guess, sure. But they make me feel like . . . well, like I'm not alone."

"I know what loneliness feels like," he said.

He gave a funny, kind of crooked smile. The left side of his mouth turned up higher than the right. What attracted her was that the lines around his eyes fanned up like they were smiling, too.

He looked back at the scale-model Normandy Church she'd taken almost a year to finish. Sadness seemed to wash across his face. "Catherine sang in our church choir. She had the voice of an angel. Used to walk around the house humming the week's hymns."

It had been just a little over a year since Catherine died. The day BJ found out Buddy had been killed, she'd stopped at the Big Dipper Ice Cream Shop for comfort food. She'd cried so much, the chocolate cone tasted salty, which forever after diminished her enthusiasm for chocolate. How much more Matthew had lost! She admired his love for his wife. She just hoped it didn't take up all his heart.

"Why don't you have a seat at the table," she said, "and I'll serve us." She gestured to the oak dinner table her grandfather had made long before she was born. She'd set out the rooster place mats, white plates with tiny pink roses, and good silver.

He paused at the table. "Can I help?" he asked.

"Oh no. It's no trouble. You go on and sit down."

"Don't mind if I do." He plunked down like a man relieved, like a man who had been on his feet far too long. "I've been cooking my own dinners this past year. Or maybe I should say I've been thawing them."

"Oh dear," she said. "That doesn't sound very tasty."

"Well, Sara Lee's a better cook than I am."

"I'll be right back." She slipped into the kitchen and hummed her favorite hymn, "Where the Soul Never Dies." She might not sing in a choir, but she'd been told she had a nice voice.

She put pork chops on a platter, the garlic mashed potatoes, black-eyed peas, and green beans in bowls, tugged her long shirt down to better cover her extra pounds, and carried the food to the table.

When she was seated, Matthew speared a pork chop for her, then one for himself. "If it tastes half as good as it smells, you'll have made me a happy man."

He took a bite of meat before she could suggest they say grace. She said a silent prayer, *Thank you for this food we eat and for all the blessings you bestow on us,* but she was watching for Matthew's reaction.

He closed his eyes, chewed the pork chop. "Delicious." He scooped up a bite of mashed potatoes. "Oh, yum."

"I used cream instead of milk," BJ confided.

"Everything tastes so good. This dinner borders on the miraculous."

The joy on Matthew's face tickled her right down to her toes. Maybe all her prayers and penitence were paying off. "Tell me about your children," she said.

He leaned back in his chair with the look of a well-pleased man. "I've got two sons. Arnold's a doctor. Jonathan's a lawyer. How about you?"

"Oh, just one son, Guy." When he was little, she used to dream Guy would grow up to be a doctor. One who could heal her ills. But even as a little boy, Guy's favorite toy was his toolbox. In fact, she remembered him toddling out of his room, diaper sagging, clutching his toy hammer. Good thing Guy hadn't had a hammer in his hand when he found his birth certificate. He might have used the hammer on her. Given the ice in his voice when she called him this morning, he still might.

"Isn't he the fellow who can build or fix most anything?" Matthew said.

She tried not to flush with the pride that suddenly coursed through her. "He's pretty handy."

"So I've heard. It's odd: Arnold can repair an artery, but I doubt he could change a flat tire. And Jonathan could prove a guilty man innocent, and I fear he probably has, but when he was a kid he couldn't tell a lie with a straight face. Funny how you never have any idea what your kids are going to grow up to be."

"I know what you mean. I used to wish Guy

would be a doctor or lawyer. Something where he could keep his hands clean. Like his friend, Judge Morris's son, who went into his father's law practice."

"Well, the dishonorable judge has more girl-friends than a trial has jurors. Always buys them shoes. Sends them to my store and has me charge the shoes to him. Not that it's any secret. Even his wife knows." Matthew wiped his hands on his napkin. "Cheaters are beneath contempt."

BJ's cheeks burned. Was it the heat of shame . . . or fever? Could a temperature come on that fast? What if she had the flu? What if she gave it to him? She pretended to push back a wisp of hair in order to feel her forehead. It was cool. The heat must be coming from guilt. Better to shift the conversation to safer ground. "Where do your sons live?" she asked.

They chatted more about their boys over dinner and his grandkids over dessert. She'd made an angel-food cake with butterscotch frosting. It was so moist, it practically melted in her mouth. She stifled a moan of pleasure.

"This cake's sublime," he said.

After dinner she served coffee in the living room, where they talked of how little the town itself had changed and expressed mutual appreciation for the simplicity of small-town living. Matthew looked at his watch. He exclaimed his surprise that it was already nine thirty. He stood.

"I'm an early-morning person," he said, "and I've got to work tomorrow. It was a delicious dinner. Thank you."

He walked toward the door, his back to her. He wasn't going to kiss her, probably wouldn't even want to come back.

"Good night," he said and opened the door to leave.

Tears were forming in the backs of her eyes. No kiss. No promise of another date. Of course not. Who had ever wanted her, really? She'd forced herself on Buddy, and look at the mess that had created. No matter how much she wanted to be wanted, she would not force herself on another man. Ever.

He stopped in the doorway and turned to her. "BJ?" he said.

She stepped toward him. "Yes?"

"I never dated anyone but Catherine." He stopped and looked at his hands. "I don't know how to say this."

She hadn't realized how close she'd come, their faces merely inches apart. "Yes?" she said again.

"Would you . . . Would you like to do this again sometime?"

"Oh yes."

Surprise filled his eyes. "Good. How about Saturday? I'll take you out."

Kisses were more likely in private than in

public. "That's okay. I enjoy cooking. Would you like pork chops again?"

"How about fried chicken? That was the one thing Catherine would never make."

"Fried chicken it is."

And it happened. He leaned toward her. She leaned toward him. They kissed. It wasn't a lip-bruising, Colt Thunder kind of kiss, but a brief, shy one. After he said good night, she ran her tongue over her lips, savoring her first kiss in years.

When her ecstasy had lessened, she walked over to the closest church, knelt, offered up a heartfelt "Thank you, Jesus," then grabbed one of her cookbooks and turned to the section on fried chicken. She'd made fried chicken before, of course—many times—but she wanted it to be so crispy, so perfect, that Matthew Bonner would swoop her up in his arms and kiss her again.

CHAPTER TWENTY-TWO
Tulsa

Rain slapped the leaves they crouched beneath and struck their wet hair, their sodden clothes.

At least the lightning and thunder were beginning to move past. Once they could get back in the boat, paddling should warm them.

"Cold?" Slade said.

"I'm fine." She clenched her jaws tight so that her teeth wouldn't chatter. "How about you?"

"Okay. You do know the best treatment for hypothermia?"

"Stay indoors."

"But outdoors it's bodies cuddling. Naked." He raised his eyebrows as if in invitation.

He was joking, of course, but his invitation sounded halfway appealing. She pictured the two of them stretched out naked in front of a fireplace, warm. No, hot. Very, very hot.

Wow! She must be getting befuddled from the cold. She shook her head to clear it.

What was that sound? There. It didn't seem like thunder. She turned her ear toward the river. It sounded like a boat being scraped across sand and gravel. She listened hard. A motor revved.

"What's wrong?" Slade asked.

She sprinted for the water. Just as she emerged from the trees onto the gravel bar, she saw a canoe disappear around the bend. Not just *a* canoe. *Their* canoe. The noise of an engine told her that someone was towing their boat away. "Stop!" she bellowed. The engine rumbled for a few more seconds, then was swallowed up by distance and the hammer of the rain.

Slade came up beside her. "Somebody must have thought it was a lost boat."

Rain pelted them. Tulsa curled her fists. "Only

one man on this part of the water has a jet boat with an engine like that. Rupert Clancy."

Slade raised his hand to shield his eyes. "Who?"

"Clancy's more of a 'what.'"

"Do you think he was stealing your boat?"

"You bet. The boat has our logo. Notice he didn't check to see if anybody was around."

"Why would he take your canoe?"

"To strand our customers. He's been spreading lies about us. He wants us to fail so we'll have to sell him the land and cabins we just bought."

The minute she reached home, she would see about Clancy.

If she reached home.

It was just eight. They were only now due in. Guy would realize they had to get off the river. He wouldn't start looking for them much before nine or nine thirty. Hypothermia might overcome them before he could find them. Beside her, Slade shivered. Tulsa cursed her carelessness. She took Slade's cold hand in her own and pulled him back up the draw. Though the trees could protect them from the rain, they offered no warmth on this frigid night. Tulsa closed her eyes and willed Guy to sense the danger they were in.

CHAPTER TWENTY-THREE
Jen

Beside Jack on the sofa, Jen munched a handful of buttery popcorn, trying to watch the action movie Jack had brought home for the third time. She preferred romantic comedies. In this movie, there were too many explosions and too few kisses.

Kaboom!

"Yes!" Jack pumped his fist in the air at the same moment Jen's mom hollered, "Yeah!"

"This is a *great* movie," Jack said, looking from Jen's mom to Jen. "Isn't it?"

Jen forced a nod.

"Damned right," her mom said, her hair so lacquered it could probably impale flies. Her T-shirt logo read, *Do I look like your therapist?*

Jen preferred her movie heroes to be gentler. Only halfway over, the movie had a lot of fighting still to come. Jack leaned forward, eyes glued to the screen. She bet he could recite most of the dialogue. Of course, she'd watched *French Kiss*, her favorite movie, four times, but she'd asked Jack to watch it with her only once.

At least the popcorn was good. She chewed a mouthful of crunchy white kernels, drenched in butter and seasoned with plenty of salt. Even popcorn as good as this, however, couldn't make her enjoy another viewing of a movie she hadn't much liked the first time.

"Honey?" She squeezed Jack's firm leg. She loved his body. Loved, too, the spearminty smell of his aftershave. Ever since she started reading romance novels, one whiff of anything spearmint was enough to make her want to ravage Jack on the spot. "Honey?" she said again.

"Yeah?" Jack kept his eyes on the screen.

"I'm going to bed."

"Don't be ridiculous," her mom said.

Jack's brow furrowed. "Don't you want to watch the movie? This next part's great!"

"Well, we've seen it. And I want to read."

He pressed the remote, freezing a building that was being blown into smithereens. "Read?" he said.

"*Montana Sky*. Our book club book. It's really exciting. Just as good as our last one, *Savage Thunder*."

"*Savage Thunder*?" her mom practically brayed.

Jen supposed it was a hokey title, but she still loved the book. And she couldn't wait to get back to *Montana Sky*. She still didn't know who the murderer was.

Jack put his arm around her, pulling her to him, straitjacketing her. "It's more fun to watch movies together," he said.

Lily in *Montana Sky* might not be willing to

defy Adam, but Jocelyn in *Savage Thunder* defied Colt lots of times. That didn't mean she didn't love him. Jen looked back at the screen. *Kaboom!* Jack again thrust his fist in the air, releasing her. Jen bolted to her feet. "I'll see you in a little bit. Okay?"

"Really?" Jack said, looking up, his expression the crestfallen look of a toddler whose hamster just died.

A barrage of bullets onscreen.

"Got him!" her mom hollered.

Jack turned back to the movie.

Jen swallowed her sense of guilt and headed for the bedroom. In the master bath, she brushed her teeth but didn't wash her face. Since she'd started reading romance novels, she never washed her makeup off before going to bed. She enjoyed lovemaking these days even more than she used to. She peered in the mirror, tousled her short hair, reapplied eyeliner and eyeshadow, darkened her lips, dabbed a bit of rose oil behind her ears, and pulled on her negligee.

Jen slipped between the satin sheets and took *Montana Sky* from the drawer in her nightstand. She just hoped none of the heroines or heroes would fall victim to the murderer. Surely not in a romance novel.

She'd always liked cocooning in bed. When she was little, Jen had frequently sought refuge there, as if covers could block out curses. She would snuggle under the blankets, clutch her only doll, listen to her drunken mother scream at the father Jen never knew, and beg God to make her mother nice like the ones in the books her teachers read. God didn't answer. As she got older and started reading magazines about fashion and movie stars, she would daydream of leaving on the arm of a handsome, preferably rich man.

She opened the book and was soon lost in the wilds of Montana.

Calack. Calack. Calack.

Her mother was wheeling the noisy wheelchair toward the bedroom. Jen sat up. The door flew open. "What the hell's wrong with you?"

Jen pulled the sheet up almost to her neck. "Nothing."

Her mother wheeled over to the bed and ripped the book from Jen's hands. "Don't be stupid. Go back to Jack."

"But I've seen the movie. Twice."

"Twice. Three times. A dozen. Men need companionship." Her mother's scowl was intensified by the deep lines under her eyes, the deep creases around her mouth. "If you don't give it to Jack, he'll find someone who will."

Jen's cheeks flared. "No, he won't. He loves me."

Her mother grabbed Jen's left hand. "There's no ring on your finger, Jen. If you don't take care of him, there never will be."

Jen cringed.

"Go back to your man, Jen. Read your damned books when he's not around."

Jen rose, put on her crimson robe, and, shoulders slumped, trudged back down the hallway, her mother *calack*ing along behind her like a dog herding sheep.

The sound of bullets burst from the living room. Jen felt as if they were aimed at her.

CHAPTER TWENTY-FOUR
Tulsa

Tulsa huddled beside Slade, both of them hugging their knees in a vain attempt to retain some body heat. When the rain stopped, they'd left the draw and come back down to the water's edge to be more visible. If Clancy hadn't stolen their canoe, they would be home by now. And warm.

A wafer moon emerged from behind scattering clouds to cast a soft glow, lovely but without warmth. She kept expecting to hear the whine of a motor that signaled Guy was looking for them. It was almost ten. He should have come for them by now.

"You know, hypothermia is no joke," Slade said, "and your teeth are chattering." He put his arm around her.

His arm felt strong, his body firm. He was right. Her teeth were chattering. The cold front must have dropped the temperature into the fifties. She tried to focus on the noises of the night: the river's whisper, the owl's forlorn hoot, the belching of a bullfrog. The crickets' usual din had been silenced by the rain. She imagined a family of crickets crouched around a tiny bonfire.

"Know any camp songs?" Slade said.

"I never went to camp. Only one I know's 'Kumbaya.' How about you?"

"I just remember 'Ninety-Nine Bottles of Beer on the Wall.' "

"Who keeps beer on a wall anyway?"

"Must be the Brits. They drink it warm."

She grimaced. "Sounds awful."

"On a hot day, it is." His eyes took on a dreamy look. "But I wouldn't mind a warm Samuel Smith's Porter right about now."

She hugged her knees harder. "I could go with a mug of hot coffee."

"And a good fire," he said.

"And one of Ruby's quilts." Their breath floated up like tiny ghosts.

"I'd be happy to help warm you when we get back," he said.

"When we get back, I'll have other things on my mind."

"Like what?"

"Like Rupert Clancy."

"Here we have a romantic setting," Slade said, "and a great reason to light some fires, and you're not interested. I must be losing my touch."

"You've lit a lot of fires, have you?"

He grinned. His black hair fell near his eyes, making them seem darker. "Guilty," he said. "Though lately I seem to be less of a pyromaniac. I'm thirty-four now. I've been thinking maybe I'm ready to settle down. With the right woman. Who knows where I might find her? A café in Paris. A shop in Times Square. A gravel bar in the Ozarks."

Though he grinned, he was shivering. It wasn't from excitement. "Where the hell is Guy?" she said. "And why didn't I bring any matches?"

"If it makes you feel any better, I was a Boy Scout, and I didn't bring any either."

"An Eagle Scout?"

"Never got that far," he said. "I wouldn't have gone at all, but my brother got into the whole badges thing."

"What's your brother like?"

Slade seemed to look into the distance with an unfocused gaze. "Identical twin. Only I guess not that identical. I was the goof-off. Brett was the Eagle Scout. The straight-A student. The class president."

"Does he live in Kansas City, too?"

Slade didn't respond at first. It seemed that sadness shadowed his face.

"He died of leukemia. At fifteen."

179

"Oh," she said. She touched her hand to his leg. "I'm sorry."

"Brett was my best friend. I still miss him."

A whip-poor-will started its song, calling its name over and over: *whip-poor-will, whip-poor-will, whip-poor-will*.

Slade turned his head as if to better hear the bird's call, then spoke again. "I kept thinking that since we were identical twins, I'd get sick, too."

"But you didn't?"

"No, though sometimes I still half expect to. It doesn't make sense. We had the same genes. We lived in the same house."

She understood his sadness. His bewilderment. It was similar to how she felt after her mother died. The haunting grief. The desperate need to know why. Not that she'd ever found any answers. "That must have been hard," she said, and waited to see if Slade wanted to say more, but he was silent.

The temperature was still dropping, their shivering becoming constant. Hypothermia could lead to irregular heartbeat, and in extreme cases to brain damage and death. Her teeth chattered harder. "We need to get our blood moving," she said, "or we could get in real trouble. Stand up."

Movement was slow. They lumbered to their feet. Slade slapped his hands against his shoulders. She sprinted up the sandbar, turned, and sprinted back. Of course, Slade couldn't run. His knee wasn't fully healed.

"You've got to get your heart rate up," she said. "Can you do squats or at least walk fast?"

"I'd like to lie down."

"No." She took his arm and pulled him up the gravel bar and back, up and back, up and back, until they were winded. She wanted to keep going but was feeling increasingly drowsy.

They sank to the sand.

"Let's hold each other," he said. "For warmth."

They lay on the soggy ground, her back spooning against him, his arms clasped around her. It had been a while since she'd lain with a man. Her shivering increased.

"Feels good," he said. His voice sounded weak, but he tightened his hold on her. Her heart sped up. That was a symptom of hypothermia. No, wait. A *slower* heartbeat meant your body temperature was dropping.

A new sound brought her head up to listen. She crossed her fingers like Ruby did when making a wish. "Let it be Guy," she whispered. "Please let it be Guy."

CHAPTER TWENTY-FIVE
Ruby

Ruby ran the spotlight along the shore on both sides, but the light revealed only shrubs and trees that at night seemed a dreary gray, like a lifeless face. She bit her lip. Where were Tulsa and Slade? The rain had stopped two hours ago. Could lightning have struck them? Ruby's mouth parched with fear.

"She'll turn up," Warren said. He stood in the stern, steering the boat, tall and string-bean thin, his eyes on the water ahead.

He was right. He had to be. Tulsa would be okay, though she wouldn't be thrilled to see Warren. Still, Warren was the conservation agent responsible for search and rescue on the river. He was also the only man Ruby knew with a jet boat other than Clancy. With Guy in jail, thanks to Judge Morris, Ruby had had no choice but to ask Warren for help.

Brrr. The damp cold pierced Ruby's jacket like fingers from the grave. Good thing that the storm had passed and that it was supposed to warm up tomorrow. If she could just find Tulsa safe, she could deal with anything, even the possibility of losing her home . . . a possibility that seemed increasingly real.

Up ahead on a gravel bar, two people were waving their arms. Ruby shone the spotlight and leaned forward to see better. Tulsa. And Slade. *Thank God!* Warren beached the boat.

"Where's Guy?" Tulsa asked, teeth chattering, as Ruby wrapped her in a wool blanket she had packed while Warren handed Slade another.

Tulsa's eyes fell on Warren, then quickly darted back to Ruby.

"In jail," Ruby said, hugging her granddaughter.

"What do you mean?"

"Judge Morris sentenced him to four days," Ruby said.

Tulsa was trembling, Slade shivering beside her. Their breaths puffed tiny clouds into the air as they both pulled the blankets tighter.

"Four days?" Tulsa looked at Warren. "Why?"

"I don't really know," he said. "It's unusual. I've heard rumors that Clancy is friends with the judge. I don't know that for a fact. But we need to get you two to shelter. Come on."

Tulsa stepped into the front of the boat beside Ruby, Slade the stern. Warren backed them off the gravel bar and started downriver toward the house he shared with his girlfriend. Ruby had left the truck there.

"Where's your canoe?" Warren asked.

Tulsa kept facing forward. "Clancy took it."

"What?!" Ruby said.

"We sheltered up a draw," Tulsa said, speaking

loudly to be heard over the motor. "Our canoe was on the beach. I heard a jet boat. When I went down to check it out, I saw the canoe being towed."

"You *saw* Clancy?" Warren said.

Tulsa faced him. "Who else around here has a jet boat? And who else would take a canoe without checking to see if somebody was around?"

"That's pretty circumstantial," Warren said.

"Maybe so," Tulsa said. "But I'm right."

If Tulsa was right about Clancy, then, given that their logo was painted on the bow of the canoe, it would seem maybe he *had* intended to strand someone. Ruby didn't think Clancy would have known it was Tulsa, but rumors that their customers had been left freezing in the rain would definitely hurt their business.

And worse. If Clancy had deliberately put someone in real danger, the man was even more of a polecat than she'd realized.

Ruby's shoulders sagged. She had never been a night owl, and worry had exhausted her even more than usual. She wanted to put on her flannel pajamas and snuggle beneath her quilt, but she had the uneasy feeling that she was going to have to try to stop Tulsa from going after Clancy.

CHAPTER TWENTY-SIX
Tulsa

Tulsa stopped Big Red in front of their place.

Slade got out and held the door for Ruby.

Ruby didn't budge. "Let it go, Tulsa," she said. "At least till morning."

Tulsa gripped the steering wheel so tight she was surprised it didn't crack, but she kept her voice mild. "Clancy might not expect me tonight. I want to see if he's got our canoe."

Ruby remained in the truck. "If you do something stupid, you could end up in jail with Guy. That would wreck us."

"Clancy needs to know he can't get away with lying and stealing." Ruby looked uncertain. "Give Floyd a call," Tulsa said. The owner of the nearest canoe business stayed up late. "See if he knows anybody who could fill in for Guy this weekend. We're going to need help."

"You promise not to do anything illegal?"

"Sure."

"I mean it."

"I'll go with her," Slade said. "I'll see she doesn't hurt anybody."

"Thank you," Ruby said. "Tulsa, at least change into some dry clothes."

"Every minute I delay gives him more time to hide our boat." The heater blasted warm air, and though it hadn't dried her clothes, at least her teeth had stopped chattering. "I'm fine. We'll just be a few minutes. Call Floyd, then go to bed."

Slade helped Ruby from the truck. Ruby lingered a bit, then headed for the house, which glowed white in the moonlight. Slade hopped up in the truck beside her.

"You don't have to come," she said. "I'm a big girl."

Slade buckled up. "I wouldn't miss this for anything."

When Ruby was inside, Tulsa took the shotgun from the gun rack behind them, slapped in three cartridges, set the safety, and returned the gun to the rack.

"You planning to do anything I wouldn't do?" Slade asked.

"Guess I don't know you well enough to answer that."

She sped the five miles along the main county road to Clancy's turnoff, a steep hill much like the drive to their own place. The instant she drove into Clancy's yard, his two dogs lunged, snapping and howling, at her tires. Lights flooded the area. Clancy had knocked down the old white home that stood on this property for decades and built a sprawling, ultramodern house that she had to admit she admired, its many arches and curves surprisingly graceful.

Clancy emerged to stand in the doorway, his long hair loose about his face, not quite covering his smirk.

"To what do I owe this pleasure?" he asked.

"You stole our canoe."

"Oh? When did I do that?"

"Give me a break."

Clancy leaned against the door frame. "Got any proof?"

"Not yet, but I'm getting out of this truck and walking down to the river to look around."

"That's a bad idea," Clancy said.

She looked down at the huge dogs' sharp teeth. Tulsa took the shotgun from the gun rack, pumped it once—*kachunk*—and handed it to Slade, who looked downright dumbfounded. "If those dogs bother me," she said loudly, "shoot *him*." She pointed at Clancy, whose jaw dropped.

"That's a *really* bad idea," Slade said. He took the gun like it was a live explosive.

"On the count of three," Tulsa said. "One." Saliva dripped from the mouths of the snarling dogs. "Two." She kept her face impassive, but her heart was beating so hard she half expected it to rip through her chest. "Three."

Clancy gave a sharp whistle. The dogs trotted over to him. He snapped his fingers. They sat, growling.

Beside her, Slade held the shotgun out of the window but pointed at the ground. Good man. Tulsa grabbed a flashlight from under the seat. She shoved open the pickup's door, strode to the river, and ran the flashlight around Clancy's yard, then along the bank. No sign of their boat. Or Clancy's. She faced the house. He'd probably hidden their canoe. She walked back to the truck. When she climbed in, relief washed over Slade's face.

"Didn't find what you're looking for?" Clancy said.

"Where's your jet boat, Rupert?"

"I'm having some work done on it. Mind if I go back to sleep now?"

"I wouldn't just yet," she said. "See, there's another problem. Seems like you've been spreading lies about our business."

"It's a free country," he said.

"Slander's illegal."

"That might be, but I doubt you could afford a lawyer to prove it."

The sneer in his voice further rankled her. She had to think of some way to get the man's attention. His immaculate 1966 Mustang was parked by the door. From what she'd heard, he valued that car more than he valued his friends.

"You just wait there," she said. "I'm not going far."

She drove Big Red a little up the hill, stopped,

then put it in reverse. "Brace yourself," she told Slade as she took her foot off the brake. The pickup rolled backward—straight toward the passenger door of Clancy's Mustang. The truck gathered speed. Reflected in the mirror, Clancy's expression changed from arrogant to puzzled to downright alarmed. She hit the brake. Her truck skidded in the gravel, back end swinging left. From what she could tell, it stopped about a cat's whisker away from Clancy's car.

"What the hell?!" Clancy yelled. The dogs howled. "You're crazy!"

"You might want to keep that in mind before you spread more lies or steal any more of our stuff. Just so you understand, if you mess with us in any way, I'll be back. Only next time, I won't hit the brake."

Clancy scowled at her but refrained from speaking, as if he were afraid of pushing her over the edge. She drove the truck slowly up the hill.

After a moment, Slade spoke. "Remind me not to upset you."

"Don't lie, cheat, or steal, and you'll be fine."

"Those dogs could've killed you."

"I didn't think he'd want to go to jail for manslaughter."

"And if you were wrong?"

She shrugged. "I wasn't."

"Good thing. I'm not much of a shot." He shook his head like he was still trying to take in what she'd done. "You also almost wrecked your truck."

"Well, I've been paying insurance on it for thirteen years without a claim. I didn't know how else to make my point short of shooting the man. Insurance won't cover that." At the top of the hill, Tulsa emptied the shotgun of cartridges and put the gun back on the rack.

"I've been on some interesting dates," Slade said, "but nothing quite like this."

"It wasn't a date."

"It's not too late to make it one."

He was certainly right about that: the adrenaline still spurting through her made her feel fully awake. Maybe a date with Slade was worth considering. Seeing Warren had reminded her of what was missing in her life.

The black-silhouetted hills around them rolled like waves to the horizon. It had become a beautiful night.

"It wouldn't surprise me if Clancy put Judge Morris up to jailing Guy," she said.

"Guy *was* poaching, though. Right?"

She straightened. "He shot one deer to prepare smoked venison for a ninety-year-old woman's birthday. There are plenty of deer around."

"Sorry. I shouldn't have spoken without knowing the situation."

"You're right."

Slade's remark had erased any inclination she

might have had to extend this night. She just hoped that Ruby had been able to find someone to fill in for Guy over the weekend.

When she pulled up in front of the house, Ruby came outside. "You should be asleep," Tulsa said.

"So should you." Ruby turned to Slade. "Did she hurt him?"

"No. Scared him a little, though."

"Tulsa, what did you do?" Ruby said.

"Nothing he didn't have coming." Tulsa got out of the truck.

"You're wrong," Ruby said. "I called Floyd. He said he'd found one of our canoes washed up on a gravel bar and towed it to his place."

"What?!" Tulsa said.

"Floyd just got a new jet boat. Said he was so excited to test it out, he forgot to check the weather. He had to beach for a while, too."

"Damn," Tulsa muttered. "But Clancy *has* been spreading lies."

"Tulsa?" Ruby said.

"I know. I know." She hated it when her grandmother used that scolding tone, especially when Ruby was right. Tulsa couldn't believe she had to apologize to Rupert Clancy, of all people. "I'll call him in the morning. Did you find anybody to help us out this weekend?"

"No. Floyd can't spare anyone, and he couldn't think of anybody who's not already tied up.

I'm sure Pearl will help, but she and I can't lift canoes."

"I'll help," Slade said.

Tulsa stared at him. "You?"

"Why not?"

"I thought you had to go back."

"Not necessarily."

"What about your knee?"

"I can lift. I just can't run."

"There's nowhere to stay. The cabins are booked."

"You can stay with us," Ruby offered. "We've got a guest bedroom. Doesn't have its own bathroom, though."

"I don't mind sharing," Slade said, "if you want my help."

Tulsa tried to sort out what she wanted to say. Slade was watching her again.

"We'd be much obliged," Ruby said.

Slade nodded to Ruby but kept his eyes on Tulsa.

The idea of Slade sharing their house made her squirm inside. She just wasn't sure whether she was squirming from distaste . . . or delight. Well, they needed help. "Yeah," she said. "Much obliged."

CHAPTER TWENTY-SEVEN
Ruby

Seated across from Pearl in the kitchen, Ruby took a bite from a bowl of what Tulsa had long ago dubbed Ruby's Ay Caramba Chili. Well, sure it was. Chili wasn't worth eating if it didn't bite you back.

She closed her eyes as she chewed. The spicy flavors of chili powder, garlic, and salsa practically singed her tongue. Delicious, especially washed down with ice-cold lemonade. Good thing the food got her attention, because she was dog tired: if she had flea bites, she'd be too pooped to scratch.

Normally Tulsa and Guy helped out between hauling canoeists. Slade had worked hard all weekend, but his unfamiliarity with put-in and take-out spots meant Tulsa had to drive every trip. Ruby couldn't have managed the phones, the bookings, the sales of soda and ice, the bus scheduling, and the customers' many inquires without Pearl's help.

"You look beat," Pearl said.

"I am a little tuckered. How about you?"

Pearl's eyelids were drooping. "I haven't worked this hard since Sherman died."

"I sure do appreciate your help," Ruby said. Pearl stirred her chili rather than ate it, her eyes moist, like she was on the verge of tears. Was the chili *that* hot? "What's wrong?"

Pearl's spoon *ping*ed against the sides of her bowl. "Daniel's sick," she said.

That boy meant everything to Pearl. "Is it serious?"

"Yeah. He's . . ." Pearl's lip twitched. "He's homosexual."

"Well, sure."

Pearl sat up so straight she looked nailed to her chair. "He told you?"

"No. I just always figured he was. I'm glad he doesn't have some fatal disease."

"Homosexuals go to hell. What could be more fatal than that?"

"Daniel's a sweetheart. He's not going to hell."

"Leviticus says male lying with male is an abomination."

Pearl could probably quote every verse of the Bible, she studied it so much. Ruby was more of an occasional reader, a passage here or there when she was feeling down. "Leviticus is the Old Testament, right?"

"God didn't change His mind in the second half. Corinthians says the unrighteous shall not inherit the kingdom of God, and the unrighteous it lists includes thieves, adulterers, and homosexuals."

Ruby sipped her tart lemonade. She didn't

believe Jonah really had lived in a whale or that a snake had seduced Eve, but Pearl did.

"It's my fault," Pearl said, still stirring her chili.

"What is?"

"That Daniel's . . . that way. I shouldn't have taught him to cook."

Ruby thumped her glass on the table. "Poppycock! That boy was born with a rolling pin in his hand. God made him the way he is. Why would God make somebody something He hated?"

Pearl wiped her hand across her mouth. "I don't know."

Ruby sighed. The Bible should be a comfort, not a burden.

Her friend still hadn't eaten much. Ruby rose. "I've got cherry cobbler in the freezer. I'll heat some up."

"I'm not hungry," Pearl said.

"Starving yourself isn't going to change that boy. Chili or cobbler?"

"Cobbler."

"We'll put a little cream on it. That'll give you some protein." Ruby squeezed Pearl's shoulder. "It'll be okay."

"How?"

"I don't know, but it will. If you try to change him, you're just going to wear yourself out."

"You're one to talk," Pearl said. "You keep trying to push Tulsa into marrying. Being single isn't even a sin."

195

"No, but it sure is a shame."

"You won't give up trying to change Tulsa till that child is married or you're dead. And even then you'll probably haunt her."

Pearl had a point. Tulsa seemed happy enough. Ruby poured thick cream into a pitcher, took cobbler from the freezer, and set it on defrost in the microwave. Fretting about Tulsa didn't help her rest easy, and she'd been so tired of late. "Okay," she said as she took the heated dessert from the microwave. The aroma of cobbler wafted into the room. "Tell you what. I won't mention dating or marriage to Tulsa for a whole week. And if I can do that, maybe I'll try for another."

"I hope you've got yourself a good supply of duct tape," Pearl said.

"You don't think I can quit?"

"I think you had an easier time quitting cigarettes."

Lord. That had taken her years and nicotine patches, lollipops, straws, prayers, and a young Tulsa repeatedly grinding up her Lucky Strikes in the garbage disposal. Pearl might be right. Well, she was committing to only a week of not bothering Tulsa about it. Surely she could manage that.

CHAPTER TWENTY-EIGHT
Tulsa

Moonlight shimmered across the ripples Tulsa made as she swam a slow, lazy breaststroke. Too bad it hadn't been this warm three nights ago, when she and Slade were stranded on the gravel bar. She dipped under, surfaced, dipped and surfaced, the water so soft against her face it was like swimming in liquid velvet.

Jen had introduced her to the marvel of moonlight swims when Tulsa came to live with Ruby. Their night swims made Ruby anxious, worried that *something might happen,* though what that *something* was, Tulsa had never understood. She couldn't remember a time she felt in danger on the river, unless maybe it was when she was trapped with Slade in the middle of the storm. He was a strange man. On the one hand he was cocky and arrogant, but he'd worked hard over the weekend. As Pearl would say, that made up for a multitude of sins. And aside from his tendency to taunt death, he'd been a good man to be stranded with.

She remembered the muscularity of his chest as they'd held each other for warmth and wondered if his chest was smooth or hairy and how it would feel to run her hands over it.

A splash made her look back. Slade was swimming toward her. She switched to the crawl and struck out upriver against the current. Her strong arms and hard kick enabled her to make headway, but slowly. She fueled herself with thoughts of how much she'd hated apologizing to Clancy for being wrong about their canoe. "Better watch that temper of yours," he'd said. "One of these days it might get you into trouble." Clancy's smug tone had made her want to slap him, but he was right that she'd been wrong, at least about the canoe. Still, she didn't regret confronting him. He had better stop spreading lies.

Slade splashed close. She hadn't expected him to catch up. She had to resist the temptation to try to outswim him. He might aggravate his knee injury trying to catch her. She turned over and let the current carry her back. The moon caressed her face.

Eventually she righted herself to tread water. Slade floated toward her and did the same.

"It's a beautiful night," he said.

Smooth. His chest was smooth. "Yeah."

She wanted to run her hands over that sleek, muscled chest. Instead she started to swim away. He put his hand around her ankle, pulling her to him. She let him. His arms encircled her. He kicked to keep treading water. His lips brushed hers. Once. Soft. Twice. Tantalized, she put her hands behind his head and pulled his lips to hers. Their kiss—restrained at first, then harder, deeper—made her dizzy. She was tempted to wrap her legs around Slade and kiss him until the moon set.

Which was a crazy idea.

Or maybe not.

She'd made love with only two men before Warren: Donny and Charles. Donny had broken up with her, she with Charles. She and Warren had shared passionate lovemaking, but look how that had ended. Maybe lovemaking wasn't what they'd shared after all. Maybe it was just sex, and maybe that was enough. Relationships didn't last anyway, not for her. After tonight she would probably never see Slade again. That made it easier. She wouldn't have to wonder whether he loved her.

She swam to shallow water and stood, water dripping down her breasts and legs from the skimpy bikini she'd chosen because it was as close to naked as she could comfortably come when customers might wander down to the river.

"You're leaving?" Slade said as he got out of the water.

The disappointment in his voice gave her a sense of power. She held out her hand.

He took it, pulling her toward him. She kissed him, then pushed him back. "Not here."

"In your room?" he said.

"No. I don't want to disturb Ruby. The people

renting Eagle's Roost cabin have left. I haven't cleaned it yet, but we can put a couple of air mattresses on the deck if you're interested."

"Oh, I'm interested. I'd make love with you in a canoe if you wanted."

"I don't want to make love. I want to have sex."

Slade looked startled. He studied her. "Well," he said. "It's a good place to start."

And end.

She took his hand and strode toward the carport. She tossed air mattresses and sleeping bags in the bed of the pickup, snatched the hide-a-key from the tailgate, and drove them to Eagle's Roost.

When they got out of the truck, Slade grabbed the air mattresses while she took the sleeping bags. They leapt up the stairs.

She opened the cabin. The people who had stayed there had left dirty dishes in the sink, towels on the floor, and crumpled sheets on the bed.

She opened the door to the deck. They quickly prepared air mattresses and spread sleeping bags over them, then faced each other. Tulsa didn't hesitate. She licked Slade's smooth chest. He moaned and put strong arms around her, kissing her until she pushed him away and yanked off his swimsuit. He pulled her bikini top over her breasts and kissed them. She removed her swimsuit bottoms.

She pulled him down onto the air mattresses. He

touched and stroked her, played her. She played him back, ran fingers and lips over his chest, down his stomach, his legs. Then he licked her, from breasts to belly and down. He licked her all over, all over, bringing her, trembling, to the edge. He stopped. He did it again. She positioned him beneath her and did the same to him.

He put on a condom, and then she was on him. She guided him into her. Her hips rose. Fell. Rose. Fell. Gyrated. She practically spun in circles while he thrust hard until they both came, moaning and gasping.

Tulsa collapsed against him. His heart pounded against her breast. Could he feel hers as much as she felt his? It seemed that her own heart had never beat so fast. Not long ago she'd mocked Sandra Brown's phrase "pinnacle of passion." She wondered whether she'd just reached it.

"God," he said.

"Yeah." She clung to him. His heartbeat gradually became faint against her.

"That," he said after a bit, "was practically an Olympic sport."

She pushed herself up enough to see his face. He had quite a grin. "More like a rodeo ride," she said.

"I'd suspected you could be dangerous, but I had no idea just *how* dangerous. A lesser man might have suffered serious injury."

"You shouldn't have opened the gate."

"Are you kidding? I wouldn't have missed that ride for anything."

Neither would she. Every part of her still tingled. She lay on the air mattress listening to the croaking of frogs and the hooting of an owl from deep in the woods. When her body had calmed, she kissed him once, then stood.

"Where are you going?" he said.

"Back."

"Stay here."

"Can't."

"Why not?"

She shrugged. "Ruby would worry."

"She's asleep."

"She gets up a lot to pee."

"I bet she'd be glad you're not in your bed."

Probably true. Tulsa put on her wet swimsuit. "You can stay here tonight if you'd like."

"This is nuts." He stood, pulling on his trunks.

She liked that he was off balance. It made her steadier. The crickets and cicadas chirred from the woods, a lovely symphony that under other circumstances she might stay to enjoy.

"We can leave the bags and air mattresses," she said. "I'll get them in the morning."

Slade put his hands on her arms as if to slow her down. He frowned. "I'm not sure I understand you," he said.

"I enjoyed myself," she said. "Tomorrow's a workday. You'll be heading back to Kansas City, and I won't see you again. There's nothing to understand."

"That's where you're wrong," he said. "I may be leaving tomorrow, but I can guarantee you I'll be back."

Startled, she moved away from him. That wasn't what she'd expected. Of course, talk was cheap. She'd had fun. She doubted she'd ever see Slade again after tomorrow, no matter what he said tonight.

PART THREE

JULY

CHAPTER TWENTY-NINE
Tulsa

The way the yellow bus had been lurching while they shuttled customers and canoes earlier, Tulsa would have thought they'd put booze in the fuel tank. Guy was working on the bus while she covered the office phones so Ruby could nap. With the back of her hand, Tulsa wiped off the sweat that seeped down her face. The temperature had hit 102, you could take a bath in the humidity, and their air conditioner had conked out, but they'd had over two weeks of sunny weather.

July was starting out on a promising note. They were booked for the upcoming Fourth of July weekend. And from what she'd heard around town, Clancy had stopped his lies. All in all, she was beginning to feel hopeful. She hadn't heard from Slade since they'd had sex two weeks before. That was what she'd expected, but her disappointment surprised her.

The screen door opened. Guy walked in, grim-faced, the underarms of his T-shirt damp with sweat, his odor musty, like he'd been rolling in mud. "What?" she asked.

He stuck his hands in his back pockets. "It needs a new engine."

"What!"

"I can't fix it and run canoes. We'll have to take it to Jimmy's."

"For how long and how much?"

"A week or two. Between renting a bus and repairing ours, we're looking at fifteen thousand."

Regret nearly strangled Tulsa. "I should never have let Ruby risk everything."

"That was Ruby's decision."

"I should have talked her out of it. I thought we'd be okay. A little tight at first, sure, but I didn't expect . . . all this."

"Is there enough to pay for the bus?"

She steadied her head in her hands, trying to stop her brain from spinning. "It will use up our emergency fund. When you add that to what we lost during all the rain, we're burning through the money we were relying on to get us through the winter."

Guy sank into the chair across from her. The circles under his eyes were dark. Worry, long hours, and the hot, muggy days were taking a toll. She didn't even want to think about what the heat was doing to Ruby.

"These last two weeks, we've done more business than ever," he said. "Our original figures projected occupancy at eighty percent. If we can keep it up closer to our current ninety or ninety-five, it would help make up for what we've lost."

"True."

Guy leaned forward in his chair. "All the things we've done to advertise are paying off. And we've got this month, August, and part of September before things start slowing down. We'll be okay."

"If nothing else goes wrong."

"We'll just have to see that it doesn't."

"Do you think the engine trouble has anything to do with the water in the tank we got a few weeks ago?"

"Possibly. No way to tell."

Their only hope was to keep their business near full capacity. "I'll call community organizations again," Tulsa said. "And I'll visit every merchant in Fiddle and West Plains. We could offer one free rental for every four boats rented. See if we can't increase our appeal to big groups."

"Go for it."

Tulsa's eyes drifted to the door. The rear of the yellow bus was just visible. "I can't believe it's dying," she said softly. They'd had the bus for as long as she'd run canoes.

"It's not dying," Guy said. "Just ailing."

The sound of tires churning gravel made Tulsa rise to look out the screen door, hoping for new customers. The arriving vehicle turned out to be a bright yellow van with the words *Forever Florists* scripted in green letters on the side. Tulsa stayed where she was.

The driver, a young man so short she wondered how he could see over the steering wheel, wore a yellow shirt that matched the van. He hopped down and took out a vase full of a dozen white roses. "You Tulsa Riley?" he asked through the screen door, his lips spread in an enormous smile.

"Yeah," she said. Did he smile like that for every delivery?

"Got something special for you."

She opened the door and took the vase. "Thanks," she said. They had to be from Slade. Nobody else would send her flowers.

Ruby entered the office. "Aren't those gorgeous," she said.

"They're nice, I guess." Tulsa didn't feel like they were anything that special. She patted her pockets for cash for a tip but had nothing. "Just a minute," she told the driver. There was petty cash in the desk drawer.

"Hold on," the young driver said.

She faced him again.

"Come outside with me," he said.

Tulsa gave him a quizzical look but stepped out, followed by Ruby and Guy.

The driver slid open the van door. It was full of vases of roses. Roses in bud. Roses in bloom.

"They're yours." The driver's smile seemed to stretch right off his face.

"Oh my," Ruby said beside her.

Yellow roses, white roses, lavender, red, orange, pink. Vases and vases of flowers.

Tulsa blinked. "*All* of them?"

"Every last one," the grinning youth said.

Tulsa could see one of the heroes in *Montana Sky* doing something like this, but a real person giving her all these flowers dumbfounded her. She stepped closer to the van and breathed in a riot of color. "Is there a card?"

"Sure is." The young man handed her a small white envelope.

Tulsa opened it, Ruby peering over her shoulder. *Away on business. I miss you. See you soon. Slade.* Beside her, Ruby sighed. Stunned, Tulsa reread the card.

"Isn't this something?" Ruby said.

Guy took a flower from the vase Tulsa was holding. "If he really knew you, he'd buy you a good canoe paddle. Sure seems, though, like the man's getting serious."

"I hope so," Ruby said.

"That's ridiculous," Tulsa said. "I hardly know him." Boy, was that an understatement. She hadn't expected to even see Slade again, let alone have a garden delivered to her door.

"Let's get these flowers inside," Ruby said. She stepped up to the van to take a vase. Guy took two and headed toward the house behind Ruby.

Tulsa picked up a second vase of roses of incredible shading: a blend of red, orange, and pink, like an autumn sunset. The colors of all the flowers Slade had sent mirrored the colors of the sky. The lavender of twilight, the yellow of a setting sun, the white of summer clouds, the pinks and golds of sunrise. She sniffed one flower. Two. Several more. None of the flowers had even a faint fragrance. No thorns either. They must have been bred to look good. Well, appearance wasn't everything.

Maybe she shouldn't encourage such nonsense. Too bad Slade hadn't just given her the money the flowers cost. They could have used it to help pay for the bus repairs. The whole thing was an absurd waste of money. Absurd. Ostentatious. And, yet, on some level, romantic. Incredibly romantic.

Then again, this many roses meant you had a big bank account, not necessarily a big heart. Or a faithful one.

She carried the two vases to the house. Ruby took them and headed to the living room. Guy and the driver had already gone back for more. Tulsa took out a ten-dollar bill to give the driver and followed behind. Once the others had taken more vases, she lifted one full of flowers that were a stunning shade of coral, suggesting the soft hues of early morning. She'd seen plenty of roses, in stores and people's gardens, but she wasn't sure she'd ever really *seen* them.

Of course, morning, though it might splash across the sky, would inevitably fade. Gathering in her arms three vases of roses that were lavender, coral, and pink, Tulsa buried her face in the petals of dawn.

CHAPTER THIRTY
BJ

It was Nora Roberts's fault, BJ thought as she headed for a cart outside the Fiddle Grocery. There had been plenty of lovemaking in the first two novels, but Roberts's *Montana Sky* featured not just one but three heroines, half sisters who meet when they inherit and fight over a Montana ranch. All three fall for dreamy men with whom they have passionate, satisfying sex—a far cry from her own experiences. In the book, even the virgin enjoys herself.

BJ reached for a cart handle. Ow! On this scorching Wednesday after the Fourth, the handle was all but ablaze. She examined her fingers. No blisters, thankfully. She wrapped Kleenex around the handle, pushed the cart through the grocery door and shivered. They had the air-conditioning set too high. That or she was coming down with something. The flu? Pneumonia?

Focus, she told herself. She steered her cart down a narrow aisle, tossed a can of green beans in the basket, and reread the words she'd written beside *green beans* on her grocery list: *flash a female smile.* Whatever that was. It was Nora Roberts's term. Maybe if she tried smiling in front of a mirror, she would get the hang of it.

Matthew had been over for dinner numerous times in the past month and had taken her out every week. They'd graduated from one kiss to several, but it wasn't enough, not by a long shot, not after reading *Montana Sky*.

She pushed her cart to the produce section. Sometimes she shopped at Raley's in West Plains, but she didn't have time today. She had to visit Mildred Clark, who had pneumonia, then Rita Browning, who had fallen and bruised herself. BJ had promised their minister she would look in on the two women and do whatever needed doing. *Peaches,* she noted, smoothing the wrinkled paper, and across from that, *lick his lips*. Good thing she'd thought of pairing steps in flirting from *Montana Sky* with her grocery items. She felt several fuzzy peaches to find ripe ones. Licking a man's lips seemed almost as intimate as actual intercourse. She would have to be sure she didn't serve anything spicy.

The glare of the fluorescent lights made her head hurt. Or maybe it wasn't the lights. Maybe her head hurt from trying to remember everything on her list, a list she wouldn't be able to consult Friday night. She had a lot to learn from *Montana Sky*'s heroines and heroes. True, the murders in the book were bloody—she'd had no idea a romance novel could be so violent—but the lovemaking seemed heavenly.

BJ smoothed the list. She needed all the pointers she could get. Her own mother had been so frazzled raising her, putting in long hours at the hardware store, cleaning house, and cooking dinners, she'd rarely even put on lipstick, let alone taught BJ to. What little BJ knew about attracting boys she learned from Faith. And, now, from the books.

It was possible that sex had been painful for her not just because Buddy and the others knew as little about arousal as she did, but because God was punishing her for her betrayals. So would sex with Matthew hurt as well, even after so many years of regret and efforts at penitence? BJ's hands ached. She realized she was throttling the grocery cart and released her grip. Her list fluttered to the floor.

"Are you okay?"

Matthew stood before her, a stack of Sara Lee frozen dinners in his cart, a look of concern shadowing his face. "Fine," she said, startled. She bent to retrieve the list.

He beat her to it. If he read the list—*chicken* and *slide into his lap*—she wouldn't be able to face him ever again.

He glanced at the paper. His eyes didn't seem to focus on the list. She practically snatched it from his fingers. "Thanks," she said.

"Are you sure you're okay?" He peered at her with light brown eyes beneath straggly, graying eyebrows. "You're awfully flushed."

215

"Just hot."

"It is warm today." He peered in her cart. "Are we still having fried chicken Friday?" He looked hopeful.

Would she really have the courage to slide onto his lap? "I'm planning on it," she said.

"Great! Your fried chicken could win ribbons." He paused like he wanted to say or do something more. BJ shifted her weight, curious about what he might have in mind, but he just gave her a sheepish look. "Well, I'd better finish here and get to work," he said. "See you Friday."

"Oh yes."

As he walked away, she admired the shape of his bottom. It wasn't tight and boyish, but full, manly. He would know what to do in a bedroom. Sex with Matthew would surely bring pleasure, not pain.

She headed toward the baking aisle. She probably wouldn't be having such thoughts if Ruby hadn't started passing out novels that were practically sex manuals. Was there anything sinful in all this? Probably not. Her church wasn't like some, which seemed to condemn anything pleasurable. Her own minister preached that joy was holy, that our happiness made God happy.

Butterscotch pudding—unbutton his shirt.

BJ reached for brown sugar for the pudding. With any luck they would all enjoy themselves Friday night: Matthew, God, and herself.

CHAPTER THIRTY-ONE
Jen

Meghan, who'd just turned seven, and her five-year-old sister, Emily, raced across Jack's lawn and barreled into Jen so hard, she had to grab Jack's arm to keep from falling. "Auntie Jen!" they shouted.

She squatted to hug them, Emily with her missing front tooth and Meghan with bangs she'd mangled. "I love you to pieces, my two favorite nieces," Jen said. Strictly speaking, they were Jack's nieces, not hers, but that didn't matter. The girls smelled like strawberries. Shampoo, maybe. Their silver earrings sparkled in the sunlight.

"Say hi to your uncle," their father, Andrew, reminded the girls.

He and Jack looked a lot alike, Jen thought, both blond and compact, though Andrew was taller.

Emily peeked out at Jack from behind her sister. "Hi," Meghan said to Jack, then turned her attention back to Jen. "Will you paint our nails, Auntie Jen?"

"Sure," Jen said. "Why don't you go in and choose your colors."

Cheering, the girls dashed into the house. Though Jen had begged her mother to be on good behavior, she half expected to hear screams.

"I'd better get going," Andrew said. "Gloria will kill me if I'm late. Thanks, you guys."

Jack walked his brother to the car. Andrew and Gloria were so lucky to have the two girls. Jen thought of the family of half sisters who meet in *Montana Sky* and how much she herself resembled Lily, the sister who liked to fix up her home, the sister who enjoyed being pregnant. Jen inhaled the delicious aroma of the neighbors' newly cut grass, which seemed a world away from the trailer where she'd grown up, with its yard of concrete and gravel.

She and Jack headed inside. "It's going to be a long day," he said.

Jen put her arm through his. "It'll be fun. Besides, it's good practice."

"I'm not having girls," he said. "Not unless they can throw like boys."

"Right." The girls hurtled into the living room. For a split second Jen feared they were fleeing her mother.

"I want this pink one." Meghan held up a bottle of vivid pink polish.

"Very pretty," Jen said.

Calack, calack. Jen's mother rolled her wheelchair into the room, her broken leg propped out, supported by the chair's brace. Her T-shirt read, *Beer's the answer. What's the question?* The girls turned toward her, their eyes widening.

"Girls, this is my mom," Jen said.

"Did you break your leg?" Emily asked, her voice filled with awe.

"No," Jen's mom said, "my arm, but I had a stupid doctor." She cackled. Jack grinned.

"She's just kidding," Jen said.

Meghan stepped forward. "Can I paint a flower on your cast?"

Jen braced herself for a withering response.

"If you want," her mother said.

Jen exhaled. She hadn't realized she'd been holding her breath.

"Me, too!" Emily said.

The two girls painted tiny flowers on the cast with nail polish. Jen's mother drummed her fingers on the wheelchair arm. Jack sank onto the couch and started reading *Sports Illustrated.*

"Those are very pretty," Jen said of the girls' artistry.

"Do you like them?" Emily asked Jen's mother.

Her mother peered at the cast. "They're okay," she said. She shifted in her wheelchair like she was trying to force out different words. "They're . . . nice."

Jen's jaw dropped.

Emily turned to Jen. "Will you do our nails now?"

"Sure."

Emily held up two bottles of polish. "I want one hand orange nails and one black," she said.

Jack looked up from his magazine. "It's not Halloween. And that would look hideous."

"What's 'hideous' mean?" Emily asked. She took Jen's hand.

"It means 'ugly,'" Meghan said. "Like you."

Emily burst into tears. Jen knelt to embrace the tearful girl. "You're not ugly, Em. You're beautiful. Meghan, that was mean."

Jack rose and snatched the polish from Meghan's hand. "You are a very bad little girl. Just for that, you don't get your nails done."

Meghan wailed.

Jen looked up from her embrace of Emily. "Jack, I don't—" she began.

"She called me stupid first," Meghan sobbed.

"Did you call your sister stupid, Emily?" Jack said.

Emily clutched Jen tighter.

"Give me the polish, you bad little girl. Give it to me now!" Jack tried to grab the polish, but Emily held tight.

"Jack, stop." Emily in her arms, Jen stood, aware of her mother watching, silent.

"They'd better learn manners if they're going to visit us." Jack held his hand out to Emily. "You are bad children, and bad children don't get nice things."

Lily in *Montana Sky* would risk anything to protect a child. Jen stepped back so that Emily was out of Jack's reach. "Let me do it," she said.

"Fine."

Jen set Emily down. Both girls ran from the room. "They're just kids." Jen spoke softly to calm him.

"You have to teach kids right from wrong," he said.

He started after them, but Jen stepped in front of him. "I'll get them," she said. "You and Mom go ahead and eat. Lunch is ready."

Jack paused. Jen's mother rolled her wheelchair toward the kitchen. "Come on, Jack. Let Jen deal with the little heathens."

Jack all but stomped into the kitchen.

Would he be that harsh with their own children? Kids needed discipline, sure, but more than that they needed love. Consequences, not condemnation. If he treated their kids like that, he would make a terrible father, one who acted like her own mother.

The sound of crying made Jen hurry forward. She found a sobbing Emily curled up on the rug in the guest bedroom. Beside her, Meghan rubbed her back. "Don't cry," Meghan said. "I bet Auntie Jen will still do our nails."

Jen put her arms around both girls. "Shh," she said. "It's okay. You're not bad. You just made a mistake. We'll do your nails next time. Let's make cookies instead. Cinnamon ones with sprinkles." She heard her own words, but what she found herself thinking was the exact opposite. It wasn't okay. It wasn't okay at all.

221

CHAPTER THIRTY-TWO
Ruby

"I think it might be kind of sexy." BJ spoke in a tiny voice and kept her eyes on the copy of *Montana Sky* in her hands. She'd consumed the strawberry shortcake Ruby had served in what seemed like ten seconds.

Tulsa frowned and took a bite of the short-cake topped with strawberries and cream Ruby had whipped. Jen smiled kindly at a seemingly embarrassed BJ, while Pearl was adjusting her hearing aid.

Ruby loved this room, with its soft colors of peach cobbler. The roses that had survived the week made the room even more welcoming.

"Did you say you think having a man leave bruises on you would be sexy?" Pearl asked BJ.

BJ sank back in the green armchair as if she were trying to shrivel away. "Maybe," she said in an even smaller voice, more a wisp of air than a word.

Tulsa plunked her clean plate on the coffee table. "So then you must have found Lily's ex-husband, the wife beater, *really* sexy."

"No," BJ said, then louder, "No! Ben doesn't beat Willa in the book. He grabs her hips so hard when they're making love that she knows it will leave bruises. And Willa likes it. She's hardly a battered woman."

"It's only a difference of degree," Tulsa said.

"I like the way Adam and Lily make love in the book better," Jen said. "It's passionate but gentle."

"I agree with Jen." Ruby swallowed her last bite of delicious shortcake. "A man can show that a woman is his without grabbing her so hard he bruises her."

"Right," Jen said. "Like he could buy her an engagement ring."

"Well, sure," BJ said. She made eye contact again. "But a *little* roughhousing might be fun."

Ruby turned to Pearl. "You've been quiet. Is your hearing aid working?"

"Just fine. I've been thinking. Sherman certainly thought he 'owned' me. He never proved it in bed, mind you. We were rarely even in the same bed. And I hated the way he was always ordering me around. But I agree with BJ. It could be fun to be with a man who wanted me as much as Ben wants Willa. A little rough passion and a man's 'brand,' as Ben calls it."

"I can't believe either of you," Tulsa said, her gaze shifting between BJ and Pearl. "That kind of possessiveness doesn't stop in the bedroom. In the book Ben's always trying to control Willa." Tulsa sat up taller. "If any man tried to 'brand' me with bruises, he'd be the one who'd end up wearing them."

Jen chuckled. "That's for sure. What do they call those women who have power in S&M relationships? You know, women who whip men and things."

"The word's *dominatrix*," Ruby said. "And a male would be called 'dominator' or 'Dom.' " She loved the astonishment that swept across Tulsa's face. "I read *Fifty Shades of Grey*," she explained.

"I can't believe you read that thing!" Tulsa spoke with vehemence.

"I didn't commit murder, dear; I just read a book."

"Did you like it?" Jen said.

"Well, it's a romance, so parts of it I liked. But I wasn't crazy about all the other stuff."

"What kind of stuff?" BJ asked.

"Spankings, ties, belt whipping. I guess the reason I didn't like it is that, especially as you get older, enough pain forces its way into your life without inviting more."

"Exactly," Tulsa said.

"One of the characters in *Montana Sky*, I forget which, says she thinks a little 'macho arrogance' is sexy," Jen said. "She wasn't talking about bruises, though."

"That's nuts," Tulsa said. "Most men are too macho already."

Jen looked around at the others. "Do you think

things would be different if women had more power?"

"I think mothers would be a lot less likely to send their sons and daughters off to war," Ruby said. "I know I would."

"Me, too," Pearl said. "Besides, women would be too busy gossiping to start wars."

Jen grinned. "That's the truth. I hear so much gossip when I do people's nails, I could tell you all about the private lives of just about everyone in Fiddle."

"Spare us," Tulsa said.

"I used to hear a lot of gossip at the café," Pearl said. "If women ran things, we wouldn't need spies. We could just send out teams of nail technicians and waitresses to all the influential women in the world."

"All two of them?" Tulsa said.

A knock at the door startled Ruby. She jerked, spilling coffee across the rug. "Oh." She started to get up.

Tulsa knelt in front of the dark spots on the rug. "I'll get it." Jen joined her.

Pearl rose. "I'll get the door."

"I'll get some water." BJ headed for the kitchen.

"Strong as you make coffee," Jen said to Tulsa, "it's a wonder it didn't burn a hole in the rug."

"Amen," Ruby said.

Pearl reappeared with Slade. "Ladies, this is Slade. He's come for Tulsa." Pearl grinned.

"Welcome back," Ruby said. She'd expected him earlier and worried he might cancel.

Jen stood. Tulsa remained on the floor, scrubbing at the spill with the water BJ brought. Ruby would swear that Tulsa was deliberately avoiding looking at Slade.

"Pearl said you're having a book discussion," he said. "I don't mean to interrupt. Just stopped by to get the key to Treetop."

"You can stop now, Tulsa," Jen said. "The rug's clean."

Tulsa ignored her. Slade squatted beside Tulsa holding the key Pearl must have given him. "We'll go for a ride when your group's over," he said.

The look that darted across Tulsa's face seemed to Ruby to be part excitement, part fear.

Tulsa stood. "We might go late."

Slade didn't look the least perturbed. "Good. I'm a confirmed night owl." He looked around the room, his gaze seeming to linger on the vases of flowers. "I hope you liked the roses."

Tulsa swallowed before nodding. "Yes," she said. "Thanks."

"Good night, everyone." He turned to Tulsa. "See you later. Just come by when you're done."

They all stared after him until they heard the door close, then every one of them turned to Tulsa.

"Good lord," Pearl said. "I didn't think a real man could be that good-looking."

Tulsa raised her chin and her voice in apparent defiance. "He's not *that* handsome."

Her protest was greeted with a derisive snort from Pearl and hoots from the rest.

"And he gave you all those roses." BJ's voice was dreamy.

"Okay, maybe he's good-looking, and he gave me flowers," Tulsa said. "But that doesn't mean I'm under his spell."

"Really?" Jen said. "Because you sure blushed when you looked at him."

"Your imagination," Tulsa said.

Ruby turned away to hide her smile.

CHAPTER THIRTY-THREE
Tulsa

The engine of the silver Austin Healey 3000 thundered, and the wind whipped Tulsa's hair into her eyes as Slade sped to pass a pickup on the two-lane highway.

"That's what two hundred ninety-six revved horsepower can do," Slade said.

Tulsa pinned her hair with one hand. The headlights of the truck receded quickly behind them and were soon swallowed by darkness. "The cops patrol this road a lot," she warned.

"No way they could catch us. This baby's a rocket."

Slade accelerated. The engine roared. The Healey streaked up and down hills, past farms, fields, and woods. The ride was tight, smooth, the speed exhilarating. When they topped a particularly steep hill, she half expected them to go airborne.

"God, I love how she handles," Slade said. "Let's have some music to fly by."

He pushed a button on his CD player. Electric guitars blared from the speakers. Slade danced in his seat, moving his shoulders to punctuate the beat. "You don't like grunge?" he said.

"I guess not. You do?"

"Sure. I used to play bass guitar in an alternative rock band. We were pretty good. Played a lot of parties. Even had some groupies. We wanted to be rock stars."

"Why weren't you?"

"We weren't *that* good. I miss it sometimes, though."

"What part do you miss most?" she said. "The groupies?"

"Women aren't an issue. I miss the energy I used to have. I'd stay up all night, sleep a few hours, and wake up raring to go. That was fun."

"I don't think I'd have been a grunge groupie," Tulsa said.

"You prefer country songs about trucks, dogs, and cheating women?"

"No, I prefer country songs about trucks, dogs, and cheating *men*."

He switched from the CD to a country radio station. Hank Williams blasted from the speakers. "Love that twang," Slade said.

"Hey, you're a homegrown boy, too."

"I live in Kansas City, remember. It's a *long* way from here."

A bug splatted against the windshield. "You've got a point." Kansas City meant crowds, noise, pollution.

A shrill sound came up behind them: a police car, siren spinning.

"Damn," Slade said.

His eyes flicked to the rearview mirror, to the road, back to the mirror, back to the road. Was he considering making a run for it? Then he slowed and steered the Healey to the shoulder.

The young officer who approached them was clean-cheeked and baby-faced. "Good evening, folks."

"It was," Slade said.

The officer ran his hand over the Healey's silver exterior. "How fast does she do?"

"Up to a hundred and sixty," Slade said. "I wasn't going anywhere close to that. I had everything under control."

"Uh-huh."

"I just opened her up a bit to impress my date. No harm done."

"You know how fast you were going, sir?"

"A hundred?"

"Can I see your driver's license and registration?"

"Is that really necessary?"

The officer just held out his hand. Slade took his license from his wallet and the registration from the glove compartment and handed them over.

"Wait here." The young officer walked back to his patrol car.

"Can't say I didn't warn you," Tulsa said.

"I've got great reaction time, and the car stops on a dime. He should be arresting drunk drivers, not me."

"You worried about the ticket?"

"No. I just hate having to slow down."

"Have you always been rich?" she said.

"Pretty much. My dad made a fortune in commercial real estate. I tripled it."

"You've no idea how the rest of us live, do you?"

"I know most people work hard for not much money."

The patrolman returned to hand Slade a ticket. "I put out a bulletin to be on the lookout for a speeding silver convertible. Have a safe evening, folks." The young man walked back to his patrol car.

Slade just stuffed the ticket in the glove box. The police car headed down the highway. Slade drummed his fingers against the steering wheel.

Tulsa took in the murmur of grass rustling in the breeze and the smell of rich, fertile earth.

Slade stopped drumming. "Tell you what," he said. "I'm going to Paris for an investment conference. Come with me. My treat."

"Yeah, right." She kept her eyes on the road ahead even though the car wasn't moving.

"I mean it. I'd like to get to know you better, and Paris is a great place to get acquainted."

She faced him. "You're crazy. I hardly know you."

"I thought we got to know each other rather intimately last time. Let me remind you." He put his hands on her shoulders and tried to pull her close.

She pushed him away. "Don't." She would be damned if she would play Willa to his Ben.

"Don't what? Kiss you?"

"Don't try to force me. I'm not yours to command."

A smile played his full lips. "I can't imagine that you've ever been anyone's to command. That's one of the things I like most about you. That and the way you make love, which I propose we do again. Now."

"Here?"

"Or at the cabin."

She ran her fingers through her hair. "Make love. Go to Paris. You don't waste time. Tell me, how many women have you taken to Paris, anyway?"

"What does it matter?"

"I'd like to know."

"A few."

"And how many have you loved?"

"I don't keep count. Why? Don't you want to go to Paris?"

"I can't."

"Why not?"

"I have a business to run."

"It'll be here when we get back."

"Actually, it won't. Ruby and Guy can't handle it by themselves. Things are tight. I can't afford to take off for Paris."

"Let me clarify." He leaned toward her. "Are you saying no to Paris, period? Or no for right now?"

"I don't know," she said, surprising herself.

"Good. That's a start. Now how about love-making? Are you saying no to that, too?"

Her head was spinning. She wasn't sure whether what they'd done was make love or just have sex. It was all too much. Too fast.

Too tempting.

"Not tonight," she said.

"Well, then, I've got a meeting in Springfield tomorrow, but how about dinner tomorrow night?"

"Okay."

"And I booked a float with you for Saturday."

"I know."

"Good." He caressed her cheek. "You're sure you don't want to make love tonight?"

She needed space to think. To breathe. "I'm sure."

Slade tilted his seat and leaned back to stare up at the sky. Tulsa left her seat upright, but her eyes took in a million trillion stars.

"On a night like this," Slade said, his eyes still skyward as he took her hand, lacing his fingers through hers, "I can believe in most anything. Love. Peace on Earth. Goodwill toward men."

Tulsa tilted her seat back to get a better view of the sky. With her eyes and soul feasting on stars, maybe anything was possible. Even the possibility that love could last.

CHAPTER THIRTY-FOUR
Pearl

The blare of the phone wrenched Pearl from her reading of *A Knight in Shining Armor*, by Jude Deveraux, the romance Ruby had handed out for the next meeting in a month. It was only eleven, and everyone who knew Pearl knew she didn't go to bed before midnight. In fact, this was the time of night when Daniel often called. She picked up the phone. "Hello?"

A gurgle.

She switched on her lamp. "Who is this?"

"Gran?"

Daniel's voice was a croak. "Daniel? What's the matter?" she said.

"I'm sick."

Dear God, please don't let it be AIDS, she prayed. "How sick?"

"Bronchitis."

"That's all?"

He didn't respond immediately. "'All'?" he said.

"Sorry. I didn't mean it like that. Are you in the hospital?"

"No. I'm home." He wheezed. "Will you . . . make . . . my soup?" he asked in a small voice that made him sound all of about four.

Pearl chewed her knuckle. She'd long ago dubbed her chicken noodle soup Daniel's Delight. She hadn't made it since Sherman died, hadn't made anything she couldn't microwave.

"Gran? Please?" Daniel coughed a wet, phlegmy, miserable-sounding cough. "I'm on antibiotics. The doctor said I'm not contagious."

Pearl's eyes fell on the photograph of Daniel on a shelf above the phone. He was a winsome five-year-old dressed in the things Conrad had insisted Lillian buy: a too-big football helmet, cowboy vest and boots, a toy pistol strapped around his waist . . . and in his arms the floppy-eared stuffed rabbit Pearl had given him. "Of course," she said. "Give me your new address."

When she'd bade him good night, Pearl stretched

back out on the bed. Was the friend he was living with—she wasn't sure if it was a boy or girl—ignoring Daniel's illness? Pearl knew about being sick and alone. When she spent a week in the hospital following a hysterectomy, Sherman labeled it her "vacation." He wasn't joking. It was the only vacation he ever let her take.

Pearl switched off the light and closed her eyes, but her mind raced between anger at Sherman and worry for Daniel. If Daniel's friend wasn't tending him, Pearl would bring Daniel home with her. That way she could keep watch over her grandson, body *and* soul.

CHAPTER THIRTY-FIVE

Tulsa

"Are you sure you want to end this evening?" Slade said as he stopped the Austin Healey at the turn to Guy's cabin.

"No," Tulsa said. "But yes." It was a half-mile hike from here to Guy's. She needed to walk, and she needed to talk to him. She reached for the door handle.

Slade took her in his arms. She yielded. Their kiss made her stomach somersault.

"Do I scare you?" he asked when they separated.

"Of course not."

"So we're on for my cabin tomorrow night at six," he said.

"Too early. Seven thirty."

"Seven thirty it is." He leaned across her to open the car door. "Good night, Tulsa."

She got out of the car.

Slade touched a finger to his forehead, saluting her, then sped off, his stereo blasting grunge rock. She started walking toward Guy's. The swelter of a July afternoon had seeped away, leaving cool air that smelled green and earthy and vaguely sweet. The stars were so thick, they seemed like glitter. Much as she loved morning, nothing moved her like a night sky streaked white with stars.

As she neared, she could hear Guy strumming the chords to "Wabash Cannonball." She climbed the stairs to his deck. Elvis looked up from her spot at Guy's feet and thumped her tail.

"Well," Guy said, still playing his guitar, "look what the cat dragged in."

Tulsa gently tugged Elvis's ears.

"How was your date?" Guy said.

She shrugged. She didn't want to admit that her insides were still somersaulting from Slade's kisses, that part of her regretted not going back to Treetop with him. She took the chair beside Guy's and listened to the music. His long fingers were perfect for picking out guitar tunes. After several minutes she spoke. "Have you ever been in love?"

He didn't answer right away, just kept playing.

"Guess that depends on how you define *love*."

"I'm sure no expert," she said. "Maybe it's when your heart races and you think about the person all the time. You look forward to being with them. And when you wake up in the same bed, you're glad to be there."

"Hell, if that's all love is," he deadpanned, "I've been in love lots of times."

He played the first few bars of "Love Me Tender." She looked again at the stars. She wanted to be loved tender. To be loved sweet. That surprised her. "What do *you* think love is?" she said.

"For one thing, I think it lasts."

"How long?"

"More than a minute," he said.

"Less than a lifetime?"

"Beats me. Some songs say it lasts forever. Others that it's just an illusion."

"That's what I had with Warren," she said. "The illusion of love." Perhaps she'd been so enamored with Warren because he was attuned to nature like she was. Her sadness over losing him had almost totally faded since she met Slade. "Maybe as long as you're happy, it's love," she said, "and when you're not, it's over and you move on to someone else."

"Ruby and Clifford seemed to have loved each other till death did them part," Guy said.

"True. Maybe love's an illusion for everybody

237

except a few lucky people." Romance novels took the easy way out: they ended with proposals or weddings, didn't deal with day-to-day living. Of course, most romance readers would just assume the characters' love lasted.

"What made you so philosophical tonight?" Guy said.

"The stars?"

He played more of "Love Me Tender," looking up at the sky. Her gaze followed his. The Milky Way seemed painted on black velvet.

"Maybe love does last forever," Guy said. "I wouldn't know. But I figure if you truly love someone, it must be like the river: full of hidden surprises and sparkles so bright it just about makes your heart stop."

Guy wasn't drop-dead handsome like Slade, but he had those whisper-soft brown eyes. He could know love if he chose. "Do you want to be in love?" she asked.

"Depends. If love means you act like you're Krazy-Glued to someone, or they act like it, like my mom, then I don't want any part of it. How about you?"

"If I thought love could really last, then maybe, yes."

Guy picked out the melody of "Both Sides Now," a song about love's temptations—and its illusions. His voice was soft, smooth.

When he'd finished the song, he adjusted the

guitar strings, plucking at one, then another. "Do you think you might be falling in love with Slade?" he said.

"That's the crazy thing. I hardly know him. But everything's happening so fast!" She looked toward Guy, wishing he could tell her what she felt. "I've always gone slow, you know? With Slade, part of me says 'Slow down,' but the other part says, 'Fire up the engines and let 'er rip.'"

He stopped plucking the strings. "Don't go rushing into anything. People aren't always what they seem. Some people keep looking the other way and end up loving an illusion. Give it time. You'll figure things out."

She rose. "I'd better get going."

"You want a ride?"

"No, thanks. I could use the walk." It was only a mile. Maybe walking would help calm her down. Her insides seemed stuck in a spin cycle.

Guy strummed his guitar and sang a line about not really knowing what love is.

Elvis rose to her haunches and howled.

CHAPTER THIRTY-SIX
Jen

It would be hot later, but the early morning was clear and nippy as Jen knocked on the familiar door. "Please be there, please be there," she whispered.

Ruby answered still dressed in her pale blue robe over a nightgown spotted with blue flowers, her hair that lovely white.

"Morning," Ruby said, as if Jen showing up on her doorstep at seven thirty happened every day. "You just missed Tulsa. She had to take some folks upriver to put in."

"That's okay. I was hoping I could talk to you." Jen already knew what Tulsa would say.

Ruby tucked her arm in Jen's and they headed for the kitchen. "How about some coffee and a slice of fresh nutmeg raisin bread while we chat?"

"I don't need anything," Jen said.

"Good food isn't about *needing*," Ruby said. "It's about *wanting*."

She patted her stomach, which looked thinner than Jen remembered. "Have you been dieting?" Jen asked.

Ruby chuckled. "You know me better. I think it

must be God's idea of a joke. When you're young and trying to be thin, pounds have a way of piling on. When you're older and don't care, they just fall right off."

The kitchen smelled of nutmeg, coffee, and warm, risen yeast. Its white walls with red trim reminded her of lipstick on a smiling mouth.

"How's your mom?" Ruby asked as she filled two cups with coffee.

"Oh, she's, you know, she's Mom."

Ruby slathered two slices of bread with sweet butter and served them each a piece. All those afternoons Jen had come home with Tulsa after school, Ruby would fix them milk and cobbler or fresh snickerdoodles, Jen's favorite. No matter how bad a day Jen might have had, the treats and milk and kitchen comforted her.

She swallowed a bite of bread without chewing. She couldn't have said whether the seasoning was nutmeg or garlic powder.

"What's wrong?" Ruby said.

Her caring tone unleashed Jen's tears. Ruby reached out her hand to cover Jen's while Jen fought to regain her voice. "Did you and Clifford always agree on things?" Jen managed at last.

"What things?"

"Like how to raise Tulsa's mom?"

"Pretty much. 'Course, Clifford was a pushover. If Faith was in trouble, all she had to do was bat her eyes and he'd give in."

"Was he that way with other people's children, too?"

"Mostly. Why don't you tell me what's eating you, honey."

Ruby's hand was so wrinkled, so worn. So comforting. When Jen explained what had happened two days before, her voice was shaky. "What if it's easier for him to punish kids than to love them?" Jen's mother used to scream at her if she left a towel on the floor and spank her if she cried. "I don't want my kids to be raised like I was."

Ruby poured cream in her coffee. "Most people treat their kids like they treat each other. Do you feel like Jack loves you, honey?"

"I think so." Jen sipped the bitter black coffee. Tulsa must have made it. Jen added sugar.

"How does he show it?"

"He doesn't ask me to pay rent. He let Mom stay with us. He let me paint with bright colors even though he prefers dark. He likes me to do things with him, like watch movies. But sometimes I'd rather read." Jen sipped her drink. Better. If only she could be as strong as Tulsa's coffee. If only she didn't always feel compelled to add sugar. "Did you and Clifford like to do the same things?"

"Mostly. 'Course, he could sit and watch a baseball game for hours. I'd rather watch a dog sleep." Ruby added even more cream to her coffee. "The thing is, you've got to give in at times. Compromise is the key to relationships.

Like watch a movie one night and read the next. But if you always give in, that's not compromise, Jen. It's surrender."

"How do you know which it is?"

"Seems to me it's how it makes you feel. Compromise feels okay. Surrender doesn't. Nobody else can tell you that. Only you know how you feel."

What she felt was small and young and very, very scared. Jen cursed her inability to stand up to Jack. Or her mother. Or her boss, Marianne. Or anyone who mattered in her life. Then again, if she'd gone ahead and polished the girls' nails, Jack might have gotten angry. What if he'd ordered her from his house?

"Lately," she said, "I haven't been as happy with Jack." She clapped her hand to her mouth. Did she really feel that way? And why? Was it the books? "I don't want to lose him, but I want to be married and have kids with a man who's good to them." Adam from *Montana Sky* would make a great father. So would Ty Beaumont from *Sunny Chandler's Return.*

"I had a friend who insisted you shouldn't cook with nutmeg," Ruby said. "My friend claimed nutmeg drowns out every other flavor. But I've always been partial to it. I figure you've got to know what you like. Doesn't matter what anyone else thinks. If you like nutmeg, use it. If you don't, well, there are other spices."

"Not like nutmeg," Jen said.

"Talk to Jack," Ruby said. "Let him know how you feel. Don't hide yourself because you're afraid, Jen. You're stronger than you think."

"I don't feel strong."

"You said you liked Lily in *Montana Sky*. Look at how strong she becomes."

"But I'm scared," Jen said.

"We shape our own romances, honey."

Jen trembled. Even if she could make herself act as strong as Lily, what were the odds that Jack would respond like Adam? Was she willing to take that chance? She ripped off a chunk of bread, put it in her mouth, and realized she didn't really like the taste of nutmeg. Too overpowering. Too brash. If she made breakfast bread, she would stick to cinnamon.

CHAPTER THIRTY-SEVEN
Pearl

The small white clapboard house where Daniel was living featured green trim, a sidewalk lined with marigolds, and roses—lavender, yellow, coral—blooming in front. Pearl got out of her car, lifted up the pot of chicken noodle soup she'd made for him, and walked to the front door, which opened before she could knock.

"Welcome, Mrs. Jacobs," said a short young man with close-cropped hair and a mustache. "I'm Hank. Let me get that." He took the pot from her, smiling a loose, almost goofy smile. "Come on in." He moved back for her to enter. "Daniel will be thrilled to see you."

How nice that Daniel had such a polite friend! Hank led her through the living room; it smelled sweet, like clove potpourri. She registered three butter-yellow walls with white trim, one gold accent wall, hardwood floors, a brick fireplace. Simple. Inviting. They walked by a spotless kitchen. Hank set the pot on the stove and kept going.

They reached a bedroom painted mint green. Hank stepped aside.

"Gran," Daniel croaked.

He looked awful, as pale as the white pillow he lay against, his freckles the only thing giving his face color. His congested lungs rattled.

"Oh, Danny," she said. She should have known sooner that he wasn't well, should have made up with him after the Cindy fiasco. What if she'd lost him?

Hank pulled a chair closer to the bed for her and touched his hand to Daniel's forehead. "I think your fever's gone."

Pearl practically strangled on her own horror. Hank and Daniel were lovers, not friends. Dear God! Daniel wasn't just on the Devil's path. He was living in his lair.

"Did you bring the soup?" Daniel wheezed.

As she sat, she took in the dent in the pillow next to Daniel's. "Of course." Her words came out as little more than a whisper.

"Thanks."

Hank sat down on the bed beside Daniel. "Daniel's a great cook, as I'm sure you know," he told her. "I can grow food, but I've no idea what to do with it." He pulled the blankets higher up Daniel's chest.

On the bedside table, a framed picture showed Daniel and Hank riding a tandem bike, their faces radiant.

Hank stroked Daniel's face. "Would you like some soup now, sweetie?"

Daniel's eyes followed Hank as he left the room. Pearl realized she was breathing so shallowly it was a wonder she didn't pass out.

"He takes good care of me, Gran."

Daniel sounded painfully weak. Pearl took his hand.

"I'm glad you came," Daniel said.

"Me, too." A little white lie wouldn't hurt anything. She squeezed his hand.

"Gran?"

"Yes, sweetie?" She cringed at the thought that Hank had used the same term of endearment.

"I'm happy. Hank makes me happy."

Clearly he wanted her to say she was glad for him, but she wasn't, so she squeezed his hand instead. This wasn't the time to launch into Bible quotations about sin. She looked back at the pillow beside Daniel, pressed down where Hank presumably laid his head. Where they kissed. She suppressed a shudder. "Your mom sends her love."

"And Dad?"

"I don't talk to him," she said. Daniel looked forlorn. "I'm sure your dad loves you, Danny. Deep down. In his own way."

"Like Grandpa loved you?"

"I suppose so."

"Here you go, Danny boy." Steam rose from the bowl of soup Hank carried. The steam filled the room with the aromas of chicken, garlic, and a mishmash of herbs. "Don't you just love microwaves?" he asked Pearl. "They're so fast!"

She did, but she didn't want to agree with Hank about anything. She scooted her chair back as Hank sat on the bed beside Daniel again, couldn't bear to touch him.

Hank blew across a spoonful of soup to cool it. "This smells divine," he said. "What's in it?"

She recited the ingredients. A package of chicken drumsticks. Dried noodles. Carrots. Celery. Onions. Garlic. Parsnips. Turnips. Fresh parsley and cilantro. And the final ingredient: sherry.

"Wow," Hank said. "No germs could stand up to a bowlful of this. You'll be well in no time."

There was something disarming about Hank's openness. He was nothing like Sherman or Conrad, her son-in-law. Well, that was certainly an understatement. But if Daniel's plan was to show her they belonged together, it had failed. Hank might be good *to* Daniel, but that didn't make him good *for* her grandson.

Would she rather Daniel be with a loving man like Hank, or a woman who behaved like Sherman? Well, those weren't the only two choices, thank God. What she wanted for Daniel was a wife who acted like Hank. Her chest felt tight. Surely she couldn't be getting Daniel's germs that fast. She rose. "I need to get going."

"Already?" Hank said.

"Why?" Daniel asked.

"I promised Ruby I'd stop by. She needs some help." Her second lie.

"You'll come back?" Daniel said, his face seemingly paler than when she entered.

"Of course." Her third lie. She was practically turning into Simon Peter, who denied his relationship with Christ three times. Hopefully a little white lie wasn't the same thing as flat-out denial. Then again, it wasn't a total lie. She would come back if Daniel really needed her, but she would make damned sure that Hank wasn't home.

CHAPTER THIRTY-EIGHT
Tulsa

Even though the sun was sinking behind the trees as Tulsa trudged toward Slade's cabin, the temperature still sweltered at eighty-six, cooler than the high that afternoon of 103, but hot. And so humid even the mosquitoes were lethargic. Tulsa slapped one that landed on her cheek. She wiped off its remains along with sweat.

This had been their busiest day so far. So many people had wanted to float, she'd barely had time to pee. After getting only four hours sleep the night before, she was half inclined to go straight to bed.

She'd worn her lightest-weight T-shirt and her only pair of cargo pants. She'd have worn jeans if it weren't so hot. Ruby had urged her to buy a dressier blouse, but Tulsa didn't have the time or inclination to shop.

Treetop loomed ahead. The cabin's red cedar woodwork still struck her as gorgeous, the view from the deck twenty feet above the river as remarkable.

Slade's face brightened when he saw her. "You look great," he said when she reached the deck.

He'd shaved off his stubble. The way he looked

at her, with those gorgeous eyes, that sexy smile, and those soft, smooth cheeks, made her want to skip dinner and go straight to the bedroom, but the aromas of chicken and rosemary stirred her appetite. "It smells delicious, and I'm starving," she said.

"Why don't you pick out some music while I finish the salad?" Slade handed her his iPod.

She scrolled through the albums. Alice in Chains, Corrosion of Conformity, Nine Inch Nails, Smashing Pumpkins. "Butthole Surfers?" she said.

"Good band."

"I think I'd rather listen to the birds and the river right now, though the birds are probably too hot to sing."

"Your wish is my command." He turned off the air-conditioning and opened the windows. The river rushed across rocks below.

"How was your meeting?" she asked.

"Good. Air-conditioned." He touched her cheek. "You're beautiful," he said. His fingers scorched her face, and the heat didn't stop there.

The timer blared.

"This is a pause," he said. "Not an ending."

He served them dinner, then poured them each a glass of Riesling and raised his in toast. "To romance," he said. "And travel. I meant what I said last night about taking you to Paris." He clinked his glass against hers.

She studied his face. There was no hint he was joking. "Why?"

"Because you intrigue me. You're beautiful. Funny. Independent. Ballsy. Passionate about the people and things you love. You're not hung up on money. Or artifice. You're different from the women I usually date. I like that."

"I get it." She sipped her wine. "I'm a novelty."

"Nothing wrong with being different. Nor with being sexy." He held up his fingers like he was sizing her up for a photograph. "Dressed up, you'd really be dangerous."

"I already am."

"You can say that again."

The salad was wonderfully dressed, the rice moist, the game hen delectable. If anything, Slade was a better cook than Ruby, his use of herbs more tantalizing.

"Tell me about your family," she said, taking a bite.

"What do you want to know?"

"What are your parents like?"

Slade swirled the wine in his glass before answering. "My father was a generous man who enjoyed making money. My mother enjoyed spending it. They were well matched. After my brother died, they were pretty miserable. What about yours?"

"My dad died before I was born, my mom when I was ten."

"That must have been rough."

"I always knew Mom loved me. When she died, Ruby adopted me and I had the river. That's more than a lot of people get."

By the time they finished, darkness had settled in, bringing a cooling breeze. The glow of lightning bugs dotted the night. In the distance an owl hooted.

"I brought you something," Slade said.

"Oh?"

He handed her a silver gift bag that held a book of some sort. She pulled out a bound, hardcover blue book. The cover had a cutout space in the center that featured a photo of a great blue heron perched on the jagged top of a dead birch. She opened the book to the cover page, the heron photo captioned *The Sweet Oak River. Photographs by Slade Morrison. River guide, Tulsa Riley.* Flipping through the book's pages, she saw stunning shot after stunning shot. There were photos of kingfishers and dragonflies, ripples and flowers, turtles and snakes, locusts and otters, river grass and woods, shots of sky, shots of her. Each picture seemed like a small poem, an ode to the river and the life that flourished around it.

"These are remarkable," she said, her eyes lingering on the last photo, a shot of dark storm clouds gathering overhead.

"I thought you might like them," Slade said.

"I really do. Did you win the photography contest?"

"I got too busy to even enter."

She looked up at him, this man who cooked such artful meals and took such artful pictures. He removed the book from her hands and set it on the table, then opened a gold box of chocolates, took out a piece, and rubbed it across Tulsa's lips. She licked them. She wanted him.

He put the chocolate in her mouth, stood, and took her hand. As she rose, she looked out at moonlight rippling across the water.

They sank onto the sofa. He touched his fingers to her face. Tulsa started to open her arms to him, but he stood up. Disappointment swept her.

"Don't go anywhere," he said. "I'm just going to put on some music."

He didn't walk so much as prowl, moving on the balls of his feet as if ready to spring. She expected rock music, but the songs were slow jazz and deep sax, full of longing. When Slade came back to the couch, he took her hand. "Not here," he said.

They hurried to the bedroom and fell onto the bed. Their kisses tasted of wine and chocolate. Their lovemaking became increasingly passionate. Once again every part of her tingled. Though she'd enjoyed sex with Warren, it hadn't come close to this.

Slade nuzzled her neck. "Stay the night," he said.

"I should go back. We've got folks floating at eight."

"*Should* is a dirty word."

"Sometimes." Well, why not stay? He was a sexy man and surprisingly thoughtful. She lowered herself back against him. She was always up by five. That would be plenty early. And she wanted to make love again.

He yawned, seemingly sleepy. Though she was ready for more lovemaking, he was clearly not. His yawns eventually slowed her own pulse, making her realize how tired she really was. She moved off him and listened to the rush of the river, the croak of a frog, and the lovely *chirr*ing of crickets and cicadas outside the cabin.

Slade put his arm around her, pulling her to him. "Damn, those bugs are loud," he said.

CHAPTER THIRTY-NINE
BJ

It was the pudding that gave her courage. The soft flavor of butterscotch, hinting of caramel, so tasty, so familiar. So right.

"This pudding's delicious," Matthew said, seated at her table in the dining room.

How could her fantasies for this night go wrong? Surely she deserved to know what it was like to be sexually fulfilled at least once in her life. She wanted Matthew to enjoy himself as well. He probably hadn't made love with anyone since Catherine died. "I've got something even better." She hoped she sounded flirtatious rather than pathetic.

He leaned back in his chair and patted his pudgy stomach. "I'd better not eat another thing. The way you feed me, I'll be two sizes up in no time."

"It isn't food," she said.

"Oh? What could be better than your cooking?"

What did Tess do first when she seduced the lawyer in *Montana Sky*? Ah yes. Stand in the doorway and *flash a female smile*. BJ still wasn't sure what that was, but she rose on the pretext of carrying a plate to the kitchen, set it on the counter, then did indeed stand in the doorway and give a smile she hoped was feminine.

The problem was, Matthew wasn't looking her way. He stood and started stacking dishes to carry them from the table. That pretty well negated step two, which involved pulling her dress up her leg just enough to seem sexy, though since she didn't have a romance heroine's figure, she'd wondered whether to attempt that move anyway. Unfortunately steps three and four required that he be sitting, but he was walking toward her carrying dishes. What had she been thinking when she'd studied the novel? That he'd have studied it, too?

He set the plates on the counter and started to roll up his sleeves to wash.

Think, BJ, she urged herself. "Let's let those

wait," she said in a voice she hoped was husky. "I'll do them later."

"You sound a little hoarse," he said. "Are you feeling all right?"

She nodded.

"And you're sure about the dishes?"

She nodded again.

He rolled his sleeves down. "Okay, thanks."

She opened a bottle of brandy she'd bought at the supermarket because Tess served brandy when she seduced Nate.

"I'd better not have any," he said. "I've got to be at work early for inventory."

Was he really thinking of leaving? Now? Her heart galloped. There must be some way to convince him to stay. What would Tess do? BJ set the bottle on the counter, turned, took hold of his lapels, pulled him to her, and ran her tongue over his lips. Although her action was bold, her body quivered, less from desire—though there was some of that—than from nerves.

Matthew pressed his lips against hers. His eyes closed. He kissed her lip to lip for so long BJ almost wondered if he knew how to French kiss, but when she ran her shaky fingers through his hair, his tongue at long last roamed her mouth. She reciprocated. She tasted coffee and butterscotch.

She wanted to move beyond kisses, but how? *Butterscotch pudding,* she thought. *Unbutton his shirt.* That might work. It took her a minute to summon the courage. She undid his top button. *Jell-O. Run your hand over his chest.* She brushed chest hair that was a lot more plentiful than the hair on his head. He put his hand over her breast and moaned. So he was enjoying this, too. Good. She arched her neck so that he would kiss it. She wanted to feel him kissing her neck, her breasts, her private parts, just like Colt would. Or Adam. Or Ben. Or any other romance novel hero.

Matthew fumbled with the buttons of her blouse. She should have worn a T-shirt. His fingers were clumsy. She tried to undo her own buttons, but her fingers were clumsy, too. Maybe it would be easier in the dark. She took Matthew's hand in hers, ran her lips over his fingers, and led him to her bedroom.

He reached for the light switch. She took his hand. "No," she said. If he saw her, really saw her, all her excess pounds, her wrinkles, her folds, he might laugh. "Let's leave it dark."

"But I want to see you."

"Please?"

"Well, okay."

They stood facing each other in the darkened room. Who should do what next? Nothing seemed right, even when she silently recited her entire grocery list. Matthew removed his shirt and let it drop to the floor. She did the same with hers. Her bra followed. His chest wasn't muscular, but it wasn't soft either. Her bare breasts felt heavy, exposed. Cold. He turned away. Her chest clenched. Was he rejecting her? But he unzipped his pants and let them, too, drop to the floor. She had the feeling a romance heroine would have unzipped the hero's pants or at least taken off his underwear, but it was all she could do to take off her own.

When their bodies were cloaked only by darkness, Matthew sank onto the bed, pulling her with him. "Are you sure about this?" he said.

"Oh yes."

He kissed her. The fingers of his hand moved between her legs but only briefly, only enough to make her want more. He shifted his hand to cup her breast. "Ready?" he asked.

She was too stunned to say no.

He was on her and then he was entering her. She was mostly dry. It didn't hurt like it had when she was seventeen, but it didn't feel good. He moved inside her. Tears sprang to her eyes.

He came and collapsed against her. She lay under him while he panted.

"Oh, wow," he said when his breathing slowed. "That was great!"

It was? Wasn't she supposed to feel something more? The main thing she felt was a pounding in her head that seemed to worsen with every breath she took. A massive headache was the first sign of a brain aneurysm. Should she ask Matthew to take her to the hospital?

He began snoring.

She slipped out from under him and stumbled to the bathroom, where she yanked open the medicine cabinet, grabbed her bottle of aspirin, and took four. If it was an aneurysm, she would soon black out. If it was just a bad headache, the pain should start to lessen. Leaning against the sink, she waited, trembling, as she prayed silently. *Please, Jesus, please don't let my brain explode.*

CHAPTER FORTY

Tulsa

The banging on the door woke her.

"Tulsa!"

Guy. Why was he hollering? Beside her in bed, Slade stirred.

"Come on, Tulsa," Guy yelled. "Get up!"

"Just a minute," she called.

The banging stopped.

"Good morning." Slade brushed his lips against her hair.

"Morning." His well-defined chest gleamed in the morning light. The way he grinned reminded her of the intimacy they'd shared. She was tempted to share it again.

"Hurry up!" Guy yelled.

She grabbed a shirt hanging over a chair, Slade's

blue linen shirt, and buttoned it as she staggered to the front door. "Stop hollering," she said. On the other side of the screen door, Guy wore jeans and an old T-shirt that was slovenly compared to Slade's shirt. "What's wrong?"

He scowled. "One, you're here shacking up when we got a busload of floaters scheduled in fifteen minutes."

She'd overslept. *Damn.* "Sorry," she said.

"Two, the toilet's backing up in the house."

That woke her. "What?!"

He didn't elaborate.

"Shit," she said.

"Yeah. A lot of it."

She didn't bother to ask if he'd called Roto-Rooter. He or Ruby would have done that immediately. "Is it leaking in the backyard?"

"Not yet."

That was a partial blessing. At least if the sewage stayed inside the house, customers wouldn't smell it.

Slade came up behind her. She didn't turn around. If he was butt naked, she didn't want to know.

"You pumped the septic tank lately?" Slade asked. He moved beside her, dressed in a shirt and shorts, thankfully.

Guy's eyes shifted to him. "Yeah. Probably a combination of tree roots, too much rain, and aging."

"I need to change," Tulsa said, opening the screen door for Guy to come in. "I'll be quick."

He backed up. "I'll wait in the truck."

She gathered her clothes from the living room floor and hurried to the bedroom.

Slade put his arms around her. "You sure you want to go?" he said.

She pushed him away. "Not *want* to. *Have* to." She dressed quickly and started out.

He held the bedroom door closed. "My office called yesterday. I've got a deal that's foundering. I need to head back to Kansas City."

Was this a *Wham, bam, thank you, ma'am?* She was stunned by the intensity of her own disappointment. "Suit yourself," she said.

He put his hands on her shoulders and nuzzled her ear. His black hair tickled her neck. "If I was going to suit myself, I'd stay right here, and so would you, and we would make love all day long."

She yielded at first but then once again pushed him away. "I can't."

"I know. I'll be back soon. Like I said last night, this is a pause, not an ending."

She looked into his blue, blue eyes. "Good," she said. On her way out she grabbed the photo book. "Thank you again for this."

Slade just smiled. "My pleasure."

The instant she jumped up in the truck beside Guy, he floored it. They bounced along the rutted

261

road. Each jarring made her feel like a nearly empty ketchup bottle someone was pounding.

"When did it back up?" she asked, clutching the book Slade had given her.

"Couple hours ago. It's got to be the leach field. It's a wonder it lasted this long. They're good for only about thirty years, and Ruby said they got plumbing in the fifties. It has to have over fifty years on it."

"You should've come sooner."

"Uh-huh."

His expression was grim. "I'm sorry," she said. "I should've been there to help you and Ruby." His face relaxed a bit, but his expression still seemed strange, almost possessive. Apparently he was taking his brotherly role seriously.

"I got the trailer loaded. Just have to haul them upriver." His jaw tightened again. "If we have to replace the leach field, we're looking at around ten thousand."

"Ten thousand?" Tulsa paled. "On top of every-thing else? We'll run out of money by March."

"You could see if the bank would give us an extension on the payments."

A particularly rough patch of road made Tulsa's teeth clatter. "No. George and Clancy are buddies. If Clancy finds out how close we are to going under, he might try something to make that happen."

"Let's focus for now on keeping up business this

summer," Guy said. "A lot could happen between now and March."

"Yeah. Something else could go wrong."

Guy rammed the gearshift into a lower gear. He didn't respond. Tulsa gritted her jaw and stared out the window at a smashed deer on which buzzards were feasting.

PART FOUR

AUGUST

CHAPTER FORTY-ONE
Pearl

Darkness shrouded her house. Love songs sung by June Carter Cash played softly on her stereo. The rocking chair where she sat reading *A Knight in Shining Armor* creaked. There'd been a break-in a couple of blocks away just a few nights ago at the home of a ninety-year-old widow, so of course Pearl kept the windows and doors locked. Though it was only ten and the first of August, the night seemed so much darker than it should. She half wished that she had someone like the title character of *Knight* to live with.

She turned back to the latest romance. The story of time travel involving a sixteenth-century knight and a modern young heroine who grew from doormat to assertive woman through the power of love, the book was a little strange—time travel?—but still fun.

A knock on the door made her heart lurch.

Another knock, followed by another, in rhythm with the pounding of her heart. *Thump. Thump.* Why wasn't the person using the doorbell? She stood. Wished she owned a gun. She hurried to the kitchen and removed the butcher knife from its block, then walked to the door. Knife clasped in her fist, she steeled her voice. "Who is it?"

"Daniel. Let me in, Gran!"

Daniel? She lowered the knife, flipped the dead bolt, unlatched the chain lock, and opened the door. Daniel stood before her, a look of outrage on his face. "What's wrong?" she said.

That's when she noticed his battered brown suitcase.

"I left Hank."

She wanted to fling up her arms and shout, "Hallelujah!"

"Can I stay with you?"

"Of course. I'm glad to have you." Her heart raced like she'd just done a thousand jumping jacks. If he stayed with her, maybe she could protect him from his errant desires.

He set his suitcase by the door. He smelled of something citrusy. Orange, maybe. Or grapefruit.

"Why are you holding that knife?" he asked.

The large blade glinted in the overhead light. "Can't be too careful these days." She set the knife on the coffee table. "What happened?"

Daniel ran his hand through his curly red hair. "Hank plans every Saturday without asking me what I want. He insists the silverware be separated in the dishwasher. That the newspaper be refolded perfectly. That the towels be squared on the rack. He's a control freak, Gran. He bosses everything, just like Dad bosses Mom, and Grandpa used to boss you."

She certainly knew about being bossed. To their customers, Sherman was an easygoing man; they'd had no idea he was so controlling, any more than she would have guessed that about Hank. She'd buried Sherman with a spatula in his hand. A bullwhip would have been more appropriate, though of course he'd never laid a hand on her. She'd let him control her simply with the whip of his personality, something the heroines of the romances they'd read would never have done, not by the end of the books.

"I'm glad you left him," she said. At least now her grandson had a chance of returning to normal. "Let's have a cup of hot chocolate." She linked her arm through his and headed toward the kitchen. Hot chocolate with whipped cream. What could be more normal than that?

CHAPTER FORTY-TWO

Jen

On her back in bed, Jen reread the last few pages of *A Knight in Shining Armor*, closed the book, and wiped away tears, clasping the novel to her heart. The other romances had been wonderful, filled with passion, both emotional and sexual, but love spilled off the pages of *Knight*. The bond between the heroine, Dougless, and her knight, Nicholas, was a bond so strong it transcended centuries. Lasting love—maybe not through centuries, but at least through a lifetime—was what she'd always dreamed of. What most women she knew dreamed of.

Was that what she had?

She scooted farther under the covers, sliding down the soft satin sheets. She opened the book and reread the passage where Nicholas told Dougless she was selling herself short by clinging to Robert, the boyfriend who wouldn't marry her. Nicholas's words seemed intended for her own ears. She, too, was cheapening herself for a man, giving Jack all he wanted without commitment. While marriage brought no guarantees, if a man and woman truly loved each other, it should be a natural step, not something to avoid like a skunk's stench.

Of course, for Dougless the choice was easy. She dropped a halfhearted boyfriend only after her knight had wooed her. If Jen gave Jack an ultimatum and he spurned her, then what? She would never find another Jack, let alone her knight. But Ruby was right about surrender: it didn't feel good. She'd surrendered to Jack for far too long.

She threw off the covers. If she was going to do this, she should look her best. She applied eyeliner and eye shadow, brushed her hair a hundred strokes, sprayed her favorite, rose-scented perfume on her neck, and applied the cherry-flavored lipstick she used so that their kisses would taste good.

Summoning every bit of courage she could muster, she forced herself, slow step by slow step, to the living room. Jack's attention seemed divided between a baseball game—the score on the screen was five to two—and the newspaper in his hands. She cleared her throat, where it felt like her heart had stuck.

He looked up.

"I have to talk to you," she said.

He set the newspaper down.

Calack. Jen's mother rolled her wheelchair into the living room, a plate piled with Oreos and potato chips on her lap. She was wearing her white *I'm sorry I hurt your feelings when I called you stupid—I thought you already knew* T-shirt.

She couldn't do this with her mother there. Jen straightened. "Mom, I need to talk to Jack privately."

Her mother's eyes darted from Jen to Jack and back. She set the plate on the coffee table. "Come with me," she said, and wheeled her chair down the hallway toward the spare bedroom.

"I'll be there in a few minutes," Jen said.

"Now!"

Jen stood frozen. Jack picked up the paper and started reading again.

"I'm waiting," Jen's mother called.

Jen plodded down the hallway. The instant she entered the bedroom, her mother closed the door and turned her chair to block Jen's exit. "What are you thinking?" she said.

"What do you mean?"

"I know you, Jen. I see that look in your eyes that says you're about to do something stupid."

Could her mother read her mind? "I'm not going to do something stupid."

"Uh-huh."

"I've lived with him for two years, Mom. It's time we got married."

"Yep, just like I thought. Stupid."

Jen put her hands on her hips. "That's my decision."

"I'm not going to stand by and let you ruin your relationship."

Jen almost laughed. "Since when do you care what I do?"

A look of surprise briefly creased her mother's face. "Stupid, Jen. It would be stupid."

With her mother blocking the door, Jen was tempted to open a window and climb out.

"Listen to me," her mother said. "Don't confront Jack."

"It's time he made a real commitment. And I want to start a family."

Her mother snorted. "You think kids are the answer?"

"I know you didn't want me," Jen said. "But I'm not like you."

"You're right. I didn't want to be a single mother. You made my life hard, Jen. Maybe you didn't mean to, but you did."

"I *want* kids."

"Jack's not ready."

"You've talked to him?"

"No, but I know men, and if you confront Jack, you might lose him."

Jen sank onto the bed. "How long am I supposed to wait?"

"Until he pops the question. If you force him into marrying you, he'll always resent it. You've got it good. You've got a nice house. Comfortable furniture. Carpeting." She gestured toward the window. "A real yard. Why risk all that?"

"Because I want more."

"If you force Jack to choose right now, you might end up like me: living in some dumpy trailer with only the TV for company."

"You don't think he loves me?"

"I don't know. But give him time."

"I'm almost thirty. I can't just twiddle my thumbs and wait while my childbearing years go by, hoping he will one day decide he wants kids."

Her mother rolled her chair away from in front of the door. "It's your life, Jen."

Jen rose, her legs so shaky she almost sank back onto the bed. She looked at her mother.

"Don't blow it," her mom said.

Jen opened the door and walked down the hallway. Jack was still splitting his attention between newspaper and television. If he remembered that she'd wanted to talk, he didn't show it.

Calack.

Go back to living in a trailer? Jen shuddered. Her mother was right. She would just have to be patient. She looked at the television screen. The umpire motioned over his shoulder: strike three. Batter out.

CHAPTER FORTY-THREE
BJ

BJ slumped in her car outside Dr. Newman's office, half wishing the tests had shown something wrong, something fixable. But no. There was nothing physically wrong. So why, each time she'd made love with Matthew over the past three weeks, had the only part of her that throbbed been her head? She shifted positions, her legs making a sucking sound as they pulled away from the hot vinyl seat. She couldn't bear another night of hopes dashed. Of headaches so severe she thought her head would burst. She covered her face with her hands and cried.

When her tears subsided, she thrust her car into

gear and drove slowly home. Inside her house, she collapsed on the scratchy plaid sofa. Her gaze drifted to the book on the coffee table. *A Knight in Shining Armor*. How many climaxes did the heroine of that novel supposedly have in one night? Three? Six? Fifty-four? BJ hadn't had even one.

If there was nothing physically wrong with her, then why couldn't she feel like she was supposed to feel, like the women in the novels? After all the volunteer work she'd done, after all the model churches she'd built, after so many years of being careful not to smile at another woman's husband or boyfriend, surely God wouldn't still punish her for sleeping with Travis and Buddy.

Or maybe the pain wasn't from God. Maybe it was just her own messed-up wiring. Which would never change. She'd tried everything. She took extra-strength aspirin those nights Matthew came over. She drank diet colas, hoping the caffeine would help. She applied ice packs to her head after lovemaking. Nothing worked. Nothing.

There seemed to be only one choice: end their relationship. And yet . . . Matthew was a good listener. A kind man. And she'd eaten so many dinners alone before he came into her life. So many lonely dinners. Being with him, she felt buoyed, connected. Did she really want to go back to eating alone six or seven nights a week?

Tears again spilled down her cheeks. If she

confessed her pain to Matthew, he might wonder whether he'd ever satisfied his wife.

If only she could talk to Catherine. BJ would ask her whether she'd enjoyed lovemaking with Matthew, and if she had, what she'd done to make it pleasurable. While Matthew hadn't had the lovemaking skills of Colt or Ty or Nate or Ben or any other romance novel hero, he'd done some things that should have pleasured her. Licked her breasts. Touched her there, if only briefly.

After the first night, BJ had pretended to enjoy herself, terrified of losing Matthew if he knew she was frigid.

Frigid. That's what she was.

The phone's ring startled her. She picked it up. "Hello?"

"Hi. It's Matthew."

She pictured his face, his eyes framed by lines that turned up when his lips did. His warm, lovely face.

"Where would you like to go for dinner Friday night?" he said.

Tears scorched her eyes. Her head began to pound.

"BJ? Are you there?"

"I'm sorry," she said, "but I'm busy this weekend."

Silence.

"Does that mean you're busy this weekend, or you're busy, period?" he said.

He would be happier with a different woman. One who wasn't frigid. One who would welcome lovemaking. "I think we should stop," she said.

"Did I do something wrong?"

His directness surprised her, as did the sadness in his voice. "No. It isn't you. It's me."

"I don't understand."

She twisted the phone cord around her fingers so tight, the tips turned red. Like her face. She could not bring herself to confess her frigidity or her past sins. Surely Matthew would judge her. And if he told others in town, she would hear snickers wherever she went. "It's something I can't explain."

"I think I get it."

"You do?"

"I know I'm not anyone's idea of handsome."

"That isn't it, Matthew."

His voice was soft when he spoke again. "Then what is, BJ?"

"I'm sorry," she said.

"I'm sorry, too."

The phone clicked when he hung up. She hadn't wanted to hurt him.

Her head continued to throb. Her neck and back began to do the same. The refrigerator beckoned. She took out a quart of vanilla ice cream, spooned butterscotch syrup over it, and took a large bite. Tasteless. She might as well be eating cotton balls. Had she lost even this little bit of satisfaction? She pictured Matthew's sweet round face and sobbed.

CHAPTER FORTY-FOUR
Tulsa

Tulsa let up on the throttle of the riding mower she was steering around the campground and wiped away the sweat that had beaded her forehead and was seeping down her cheek. She would be sure to shower before Slade came tonight. Just thinking of him made her grin. Ten days ago he'd had taken her parasailing, which had exhilarated her. She figured it was the closest she would ever come to seeing through a heron's eyes.

And then, three days ago, she'd received his letter. Her first thought had been that he was writing to break up with her. She'd been surprised how much that possibility had hurt. Far from ending their relationship, however, he'd said that he missed her and was falling in love with her. *My heart's moving faster than my Austin Healey,* he'd written, *and no siren is going to stop it.*

Those words had startled her so much, she'd looked down at her hand and seen that she'd crumpled his letter. Immediately she set it on the desk and rubbed her palm over the letter repeatedly, trying to smooth out the wrinkles. Slade was coming back tonight. She wasn't sure whether her racing pulse as she thought of him now meant she was eager or terrified.

It was late afternoon when Guy drove his pickup into the campground, parked, and got out. Tulsa stopped the mower near his truck. Elvis bounded over to her. Tulsa bent to ruffle the dog's head. Elvis's stomach and nipples looked swollen. "She's pregnant?" Tulsa said. She dismounted the mower.

"Yep," Guy said. "I think the culprit's Jim Lacy's mutt. Damned hound ran off a few weeks ago from Jim's and came calling."

"Think the pups will be born blind?" Tulsa asked, stretching.

Guy ruffled one of Elvis's ears, Tulsa the other. "I hope not," he said. "Can you imagine eight blind pups? Be hard to give them away. Might have to drown them."

"You'd sooner drown yourself."

"Don't tell anybody. It might damage my image."

"You're a bigger softie than Ruby. But don't worry." She put a hand over her heart. "Your secret's safe with me."

"Thanks." Guy's T-shirt was damp with sweat, his smell musty. "You know, we've been running at ninety-six-percent capacity the last three weeks. If we can sustain that and bring in another thirty thousand or so this winter, we just might make it."

"We'll need to target people who will still be

free to vacation once school starts. That's mostly older people, so I thought I'd come up with a flyer to post in retirement communities and senior centers."

"Good idea." Elvis barked and plunged into the woods. "Lord, I hope she's not chasing skunks again," Guy said. He shook his head as if in lament. "Slade still coming today?"

"Uh-huh." Her heart had started to race again at the mention of Slade's name.

"What are you going to be doing this time?"

"I've no idea."

"That man sure changes hobbies a lot," Guy said.

"That he does."

Guy clasped his hands over his head and stretched.

When he spoke, Tulsa was sure he was trying to sound nonchalant. But failing.

"I wonder if he cycles through women as fast as he does hobbies," Guy said.

She shrugged, though she'd wondered the same thing. If Slade did cycle through women, she didn't want to let her feelings for him intensify. "I've got to finish the mowing. What about you?"

"The newer chain saw's not running right. I'm going to take it apart and see if I can fix it. If I can't, we'll need to replace it."

The chain saw wasn't that old. She half wondered whether Clancy had messed with it, but she hadn't seen him in weeks and fortunately hadn't heard about any more incidents of his rumormongering. Still, even though the chain saw would run only about $200, it was money she would rather not spend.

"If anyone can fix it, it would be you." She started to remount the lawn mower.

Guy put his hand on her shoulder. "You be careful," he said. "I don't want to see you get hurt."

She turned back to him. "Hey, I've been on riding mowers since I could sit up."

"That's not what I mean, and you know it."

"Don't worry. When it comes to romance, 'careful' is my middle name."

CHAPTER FORTY-FIVE

Ruby

Tulsa came down the stairs, freshly showered and smelling of an herbal fragrance but wearing a green T-shirt and jeans with a grease-smudged stain in the approximate shape of Mississippi.

Ruby steadied herself against the banister. She'd told Tulsa that Slade had called to say he was arriving soon. "Oh, honey," she said, "surely you're not going to wear that."

"Why not?"

"If I have to spell that out, you're not as smart as I think."

"Slade knows who I am. And I'm not a girly girl."

A car door slammed outside. Ruby glanced at the grandfather clock on the mantel. Their friends would be arriving soon for the book group. That gave Tulsa and Slade only a few minutes.

"Why don't you skip our discussion tonight so you can spend more time with Slade?"

"No." Tulsa's eyes darted between Ruby and the back door. "I'm not going to ditch my friends for a man."

"Everyone would understand. We do talk about *romance* novels."

They heard a knock at the back door. Tulsa's eyes brightened as she started toward the office to answer it.

Though Ruby was tempted to spy, she imagined Clifford at the top of the stairs, beckoning her up. *Don't,* he'd say. Of course, that was easy for him. Men were less curious than women, at least about people. The question of how an engine ran could intrigue Clifford for hours, but he wouldn't lose any sleep over what makes people tick. Still, he was right. She would go upstairs and knit for a bit. She paused at the bottom of the stairs; too bad her bedroom wasn't on the first floor. She felt so tired, what she called cooked-spaghetti tired. Limp. It was such a long way up. Using

282

her right hand, she pulled herself up the staircase.

When she reached her bedroom, Ruby sank onto her bed, made soft by a foam topper that cushioned her bony body. She picked up the photograph of Clifford from her nightstand. He hadn't been a romantic in the same way as Slade, but he'd certainly won her heart. He had it still. If she closed her eyes, she could hear his voice, with his Georgia drawl. City folks thought Ozarkians talked funny, but an Ozarkian's twang didn't come close to a Georgian's. *Let me light your far,* Clifford used to tease. *Want a far in the farplace?*

She missed his teasing, his dopey grin when he thought he'd said something funny. At least she had memories. It was strange how love both filled you up and hollowed you out. Well, that was just how life was. Downright ornery.

She hadn't been interested in any man since Clifford died. Except for Ed. That night the winter before when he'd stopped by to talk about building a new cabin, she'd walked him to his truck, snow falling soft and fluttery against her cheeks. New. He'd kissed her. She'd kissed him back. It had felt so good and seemed so natural. Until she remembered Clare, Ed's wife.

Ruby had pulled away from him. Much as she would have liked to keep kissing him and see where it led, she couldn't do that to Clare. She told Ed not to kiss her again. He hadn't, but that didn't mean she didn't sometimes wish he could.

She'd never told anyone, not even Pearl. It felt like she'd been unfaithful to Clifford, though it wasn't like she loved her husband any less. Well, it didn't really matter. She wouldn't be kissing Ed again, unless he ended up single someday. She expected to die a widow. Not anytime soon, hopefully. Tired though she might be, she was still enjoying herself. The time to die was when you weren't.

CHAPTER FORTY-SIX
Tulsa

Tulsa didn't know whether to throw herself into Slade's arms or run the other way. He stood at the door, grinning. Two things kept tumbling around in her mind: Guy's warning that Slade might change women as fast as hobbies, and Slade's letter saying that his heart was moving faster than his car.

"Hey, beautiful," he said, stepping from outside into the office.

"Hey." She remained where she was: behind the desk.

"You playing hard to get?"

"No," she said, though she didn't leave her sanctuary.

He strode over to her, put his arms around her, pulled her to him, and kissed her.

She was finding it hard to think straight.

His mouth roamed her neck, her ears, her eyes, her lips, his hot breath stirring her. He pressed her back against the desk. The map of Dallas County open on the desktop crinkled beneath her.

She took his head in her hands, held it steady, and kissed him hard. He tasted of peppermint and coffee. She kissed him harder.

She was vaguely aware of the sound of car doors opening and closing.

While they kissed, he jerked her T-shirt down so her shoulder was exposed, then ran his tongue along her clavicle as he moved one hand between her legs.

"Oh," she said and touched him back.

A knock.

Tulsa nudged Slade back and straightened just as BJ came through the door, giving them a wide-eyed stare. So did Jen. And Pearl.

After the others had passed through the room, Slade put his arms around her again. Tulsa's throbbing body almost hurt she wanted so badly to climax, but she pushed him away. "Stop," she said.

He moved back. "Come with me to Treetop." He took the cabin key from the antler rack. "I came down on my new motorcycle—a Yamaha Star Bolt. Fast bike. Let's go fly around curves."

"I can't."

"Sure you can."

"No."

"Why not?"

"I'm not going to walk out on my friends." Tulsa straightened her shirt. "They matter to me."

Slade moved close. "Do I matter to you?"

"Maybe."

He leaned back against the wall, his eyes traveling her whole length. "Guess that's why you dressed up," he said. "Been kneeling in an oil slick?"

"Hey, this is my good pair."

"You sure know how to impress a man."

"This is who I am."

"I know. You're the woman who braved snarling dogs and nearly crashed her truck into a vintage Mustang." He moved close. "Why is it I can't stop thinking about you?"

"Beats me. Have you tried therapy? Or aspirin?"

"You think aspirin's a cure for love?"

Tulsa's back went rigid. He'd used that word again.

"I'll see you later," he said. "After the group. If you want to, that is."

"I'll come," she said.

"You certainly will. Several times."

He pushed open the door, swaggered toward his black-and-silver motorcycle, tossed the cabin key high, and snatched it in midair. How could she fall for such a presumptuous man? She tugged her jeans away from her tingling crotch, dropped her shoulders, and headed toward the living room to discuss knights in shining armor. Much as she mocked the book's suggestion that love could endure through centuries, she wanted to believe it could at least last a lifetime.

CHAPTER FORTY-SEVEN
Jen

In the living room, Tulsa sat with her hair disheveled and an expression in her eyes that Jen thought could only be called wild.

Pearl held up her copy of *A Knight in Shining Armor.* "You practicing for the movie version?" she asked Tulsa.

Jen couldn't recall Tulsa ever turning red like that before. "Sure," Tulsa said. "The audition's tomorrow."

"Looked like it was tonight," Pearl rejoined.

BJ pointed at Tulsa. "We saw the way you kissed him."

Why did BJ, who was wearing baggy sweats and no makeup, sound so accusatory? "Who wouldn't want to kiss him?" Jen said, then turned to Tulsa. "Is Slade your knight?"

Pearl fooled with her hearing aid.

"No, he's my lover," Tulsa said. "There are no knights in shining armor."

"What I think's ridiculous," BJ said, "is the way the men in these books supposedly make love. Nobody does that. Besides, I think the serving lady has it right when she tells Dougless that a woman should give her heart to God. That's the only way to be really satisfied."

Pearl's chuckle shook the flap of skin beneath her chin. "Satisfied by who? The Holy Ghost?"

"Satisfied with Jesus." BJ put her hand to her neck.

It had been a while since BJ had talked of Jesus, let alone sounded so bitter, Jen thought. Something must have gone wrong with Matthew. Jen took in the aroma of ginger coming from the fresh-baked gingerbread in the kitchen.

"I don't think many men automatically know how to satisfy a woman," Ruby said to BJ.

Ruby looked pretty tonight, her hair white and soft, her face made warm by the lines around her eyes. She seemed a little wan, though.

"I had to teach Clifford," Ruby admitted.

BJ's face wrinkled in apparent disgust. "I'm not a car. I shouldn't need to give a man a driver's manual. Not a mature man. Dougless's knight didn't need directions."

"Jack sure revs my engine," Jen said. "That's one of the things I like about him."

"If I'd had a manual, I'd have gladly given it to Sherman," Pearl said. "He wasn't much of a driver. But then, I was no Corvette."

"Is Slade a good driver?" Pearl asked Tulsa.

Tulsa shrugged. Then nodded.

From the woods an owl called. Its deep-throated hoot sounded like it was whispering the word "love" over and over.

"Sex is a small part of love," Ruby said. "I would have gladly given it up if Clifford could have lived a few more years."

"Then why do you give us books that are so full of sex?" BJ said.

"Because they're also full of love."

"Nobody's forcing you to read them," Pearl said.

"Maybe I just won't." BJ edged back in the green sofa chair, her face set in a sulk.

"What I found unbelievable in the book," Tulsa said, "is that Dougless would put up with her loser of a boyfriend, Robert, or think for one minute that he was going to marry her."

Ruby gave Tulsa a fond look. "Most of us love first with our hearts. It takes the brain a while to catch up."

"Besides," Jen said, "Robert does propose to Dougless eventually."

"In real life, he wouldn't," Tulsa said. "The Roberts of the world don't."

"The gingerbread smells so good." BJ sniffed the air. "Do you think we could have some now?"

"Sure," Ruby said. "And we'll have milk with it. Gingerbread just demands milk."

"I'll get it," Tulsa said.

Jen rose, too. "I'll help."

In the kitchen, Jen poured glasses of milk while Tulsa cut slices of warm gingerbread, releasing the fragrances of ginger, clove, and cinnamon and the dark aroma of molasses. "Do you think Jack's a Robert?" Jen asked.

Tulsa looked at her. "I don't know, Jen. Do you?"

Jen filled a glass. "Sometimes," she said, sipping her milk so it wouldn't spill.

Tulsa stared at her. "You should have a husband who's worthy of you," she said.

"Are you saying Jack's not?"

"You're so giving, Jen. I worry that Jack is . . . different from you."

"He's given me a lot."

"I know. And I know how much you want a nice place to live. But a house isn't the same as a home."

In her longing for a husband and stability, was it possible that she was doing exactly what Tulsa feared?

A few minutes later they were all eating and drinking. The pungent gingerbread—rich, moist, and bittersweet—melted in Jen's mouth.

Ruby raised her glass of milk in a toast. "To knights in shining armor and love that lasts."

All but Tulsa pantomimed clinking glasses. "Come on, Tulsa," Jen said. "You, too."

Tulsa looked reluctant but lifted her glass.

Ruby winced.

"What's wrong?" Pearl said.

Ruby gave a short gasp. She dropped her glass, clutched her shoulder, then slumped in her chair.

Tulsa bolted up, dropping her own plate and glass, strewing milk and gingerbread across the rug. "Ruby!" Tulsa screamed, shaking her.

Ruby didn't respond.

CHAPTER FORTY-EIGHT
Pearl

The ICU doctor had said Ruby wouldn't survive, but doctors were human despite their white coats and air of omnipotence. They could be wrong. They had to be wrong.

"Wake up, Ruby," Pearl urged. She looked for some sign the unconscious Ruby had heard her. Ruby didn't stir. Her face seemed sunken, her breathing so shallow it was almost invisible, her skin such an ash white, she looked already dead. So many tubes ran into the unconscious Ruby— dripping things into her, draining things out— that it was hard to know where to touch her. Pearl had only five minutes in the ICU. She picked up Ruby's inert hand, the one with just a single tube strapped to it, and gently squeezed.

How did you say good-bye to someone with

whom you'd shared so much, someone who had always believed in you? When Pearl's dreams of performing at the Grand Ole Opry seemed washed away by scrubbing and scouring, only Ruby had understood how bereft Pearl felt. Ruby had thrown her arms around Pearl, hugging her close. "Turn on the radio and sing along," Ruby had said. "Practice. You don't have to have a diploma for Nashville." That's all that sustained Pearl over the next four years of endless chores. Her knuckles grew raw, but her voice grew strong. "You belt out a song like a star," Ruby said.

Ruby's love had been real, even if Pearl's talent wasn't.

Unlike her own hands, Ruby's had been so lovely—smooth and plump. Now, like her own, Ruby's hands felt bony. "There's something I never told you," Pearl said. "Something I never told anyone. But I'm not confessing till you wake up, Ruby." The doctor had said it would take a miracle for Ruby to survive. *Please, God,* she prayed. *You led Daniel from the lion's den. You parted the waters of the Red Sea. Please help us now.*

Pearl's eyes grew teary. For the first time, she missed Sherman. He might not have been the most sensitive man around, but he would understand how much Ruby meant to her. For all his faults—and her own—he would have understood that.

Whatever energy had sustained her seemed to

drain away. She sagged. She needed to go so the others could come in. She would have to leave Ruby's fate in God's hands. There were so many bad things God allowed to happen, things that surpassed her own understanding. Surely He could work this one little miracle. It wouldn't begin to compensate for all the evil in the world, but it would certainly bring joy to herself and all those who loved Ruby. It didn't seem like too much to ask.

CHAPTER FORTY-NINE
Jen

Jen touched Ruby's hand, struck by how tiny and still it seemed—a doll's hand. Ruby's hands had always been busy—baking treats, wiping away Tulsa's and Jen's tears. If only Jack were here to hold her. When she called, he'd said it was late, that she should come home, that he would wait up for her. He'd said he had an aversion to hospitals.

Who didn't? Jen breathed in the stench of antiseptic and desperation, probably her own.

If Jack did wait up, would he hold her the way she needed to be held?

She looked back at Ruby, the closest thing to a loving mother she'd ever known. Jen didn't believe in God like Pearl and BJ did, but she thought maybe she should pray, just in case. *Please, God, if you're there, help Ruby recover.*

Jen opened her eyes. If Ruby would just wake up, Jen could explain that she suspected Jack was less like Nicholas, the loving knight who cherishes the heroine of *A Knight in Shining Armor*, than Robert, the boyfriend who doesn't love the heroine nearly as much as he loves himself. Ruby would ask the questions that would help Jen decide whether she truly loved Jack—and he her.

She couldn't imagine life without Ruby there providing counsel; she didn't want to imagine life without her. She looked at the clock. She needed to leave so Tulsa could come back in.

This was probably the last time she would see Ruby alive. Jen's heart seemed to lurch. For an instant she thought she was having her own heart attack, but no, she was grieving, not dying. She leaned over and kissed Ruby's wrinkled forehead. A tear slid down Jen's cheek and landed on Ruby's. "Thank you for all you've done for me, Ruby," Jen said. "I love you."

CHAPTER FIFTY
BJ

BJ clutched the railing of the unconscious Ruby's bed, looking down at her tiny form, wiping away tears. It wasn't fair.

Oh, it wasn't so bad for Ruby. BJ had no doubt that if Ruby died, she would soon be with the angels, and one of those angels would be Clifford. But what about all the people she was leaving behind, bereft, like herself and Tulsa and Guy, Pearl and Jen? It wasn't right that some bad people, people who beat their children or started wars, lived into their nineties, while Ruby hadn't even reached eighty. God should keep the good people on Earth and take the rotten ones.

Just before BJ moved away from Fiddle some thirty years before, Ruby had stopped by to bring her a baby quilt. It was a beautiful quilt, which Ruby had sewn in lovely blues and greens that reminded BJ of her beloved Ozarks and the home she didn't want to leave.

"We all make mistakes," Ruby had told her. "You just have two things you need to do now. Love your baby. And forgive yourself." The first had been easy. BJ wasn't sure she would ever manage the second.

She had always thought she would confess all her sins to Ruby—the truth about Buddy and about Travis. Now there would be no chance to tell Ruby anything. She rubbed her aching head. What she needed wasn't aspirin or Tylenol. What she needed was someone to comfort her. She longed to see Matthew.

Bowing her head, she clasped her hands and prayed. "Please don't take Ruby, Jesus. We need her here."

BJ straightened. She clenched her hands. Did she dare call Matthew after breaking up with him a week ago? Would he be willing to see her . . . or hang up in her ear? She'd never been particularly brave. But maybe, just maybe, she'd learned enough from the bold fictitious heroines of the novels they'd read to become a bolder, real woman.

She leaned over the bedrail and kissed Ruby's forehead. "Good-bye, Ruby," she said. "Godspeed."

CHAPTER FIFTY-ONE
Tulsa

Tulsa gripped Ruby's hand so hard in an effort to tether her here, she was afraid she was hurting her. The slack expression on Ruby's face didn't change.

Guy sat on the arm of Tulsa's chair. She was

glad for his company. Curtains separated the beds of the five other patients. None of them had visitors, which wasn't surprising given that it was almost one thirty in the morning. Two nurses conferred at a desk at the nurse's station in the center of the ICU. There wasn't anyone else. Still, Tulsa would swear that someone was with them by Ruby's bed, someone unseen.

A monitor beeped. A blood pressure cuff *whoosh*ed as it inflated and deflated. An oxygen mask forced air into Ruby's lungs, while tubes dripped liquids into her veins.

One of the nurses signaled that they needed to leave. Tulsa held tight. She would not let Ruby die alone. "I'm staying."

"Me, too," Guy said.

The nurse gave them what seemed like a sympathetic nod. "The doctor needs to check her. You can come back when he's finished. It'll just take a few minutes."

Guy put his arm around Tulsa's shoulder and steadied her as she reluctantly stood. She leaned against him. His T-shirt smelled of sweat, which she found comforting amid the gleaming sterility of the ICU.

In the hallway, the others gathered around, Slade closest to her. She was glad to see him, but Guy loved Ruby, too, and he tightened his grip. It was comforting to nestle against him.

"Is she gone?" Pearl asked.

"No," Tulsa said, her voice breaking.

"They're checking her," Guy said.

A few minutes later a skinny doctor with a distracted air emerged from the ICU. Tulsa stepped out from Guy's arm and asked the question that terrified her. "Is there any improvement?"

"I'm afraid not."

"So there's no hope?" Jen said.

"Her heart attack was severe," the doctor said, "and she's got pulmonary hypertension, which is a narrowing of the arteries in the lungs. That makes it worse. I recommend you say your good-byes if you haven't yet."

They stood gathered in the hallway after he left. "Thank you all so much for everything," Tulsa said. "It's late. Go on home."

"What about the folks coming to float today?" Pearl said.

Tulsa had completely forgotten this was Thursday. Or rather, that it was now Friday morning. They had a lot of canoes booked. They desperately needed the business, but there was no way she would leave.

"I can cover the office," Pearl said.

Pearl looked so sad. It occurred to Tulsa that Pearl and Ruby had been best friends for years, before she had even been born.

"I'll help," BJ offered.

Slade took Tulsa's hand, his grip gentle but firm. "I'll handle the canoes."

"Thanks," Tulsa said, then turned to Guy. "You should go, too. Slade can't manage the canoes alone."

"I don't need to leave yet," Guy said. "I'll stay awhile."

"I'll go home for a shower and a nap," Jen said, "then I'll pick you up some clean clothes and come back."

"Don't you have to work?"

"I'll deal with that."

Tulsa wasn't sure what made her look up. Maybe it was the sound. What she saw was someone coming toward them on crutches that thunked against the bare floor: Jen's mom.

Eyes narrowed, forehead creased, Jen straightened as if expecting to be slapped.

Though Tulsa wondered how and why Jen's mother had come, she was more concerned with Ruby. Jen went to greet her mother, Guy to find coffee. BJ and Pearl left.

Slade touched his fingers to Tulsa's cheek. "Hang in there."

She leaned into his hand, then thanked him and returned to Ruby's side. Tulsa squeezed her grandmother's hand so Ruby would know she wasn't alone. Ruby's face was so gray. Had she looked that gaunt before? Had Tulsa just not paid attention, allowing Ruby to wither away?

She closed her eyes, yearning to hear Ruby's voice, but the only sound she heard was the whoosh of the blood pressure machine. She felt so tired. Maybe when Guy came back with the coffee, however bitter, she should pour a little in Ruby's IV.

Tulsa stroked Ruby's cheek as gently as Ruby used to stroke hers when she was sad or sick. "Ruby," she said, "if you can hear me, I'm not ready to say good-bye. Please Ruby, please, please, please don't die."

CHAPTER FIFTY-TWO

Jen

Jen peered over her mother's shoulder down the beige hospital hallway, half expecting to see Jack, even though he'd refused to come. "How did you get here?" Jen asked.

"Drove Jack's car," her mother said, leaning on her crutches.

"Jack let you?"

"He was zonked out on the couch."

"Oh." At least he hadn't gone to bed. "You aren't supposed to be driving yet, Mom."

Her mother harrumphed. "Since when did I pay attention to what I'm supposed to do?"

The white letters on her mother's purple T-shirt proclaimed, *Queen of the Trailer Park.*

"How's Ruby?" Jen's mother said.

Jen blinked back tears. "Not good."

"I'm sorry, Jen." Her mother held her gaze for a long moment, then looked away.

Jen was so tired she half wondered if she was hallucinating her mother. "I'm surprised to see you," she said.

Her mom faced her. The bags beneath her eyes weren't as deep as they'd been when she came to stay with them, her face less puffy. Tonight her hair, not lacquered for once, looked soft. "I never was mother material, Jen. That's just who I am. But Ruby, well, she should've had a dozen kids. And so should you. I figured tonight you needed someone to show up."

Jen sucked in air to keep from sobbing. "Thank you," she said, her voice unsteady.

"Are you staying here tonight?"

"No," Jen said. "I need to go home and take a nap, then I've got to go pick up some clean clothes for Tulsa and come back."

"So you're ready to head home?"

Jen nodded.

Her mother turned toward the exit. "You got your car?"

"Yes."

"I'll drive Jack's back to my trailer. He can pick it up in the morning."

The thought of her mother alone in her dump of a trailer renewed Jen's tears. "Why would you go back to that awful place?"

301

"You knew I was moving out tomorrow. I've got the car now, and I was already packed. Besides, you and Jack need some privacy." Her mother started toward the door, her crutches thumping the linoleum.

Jen grabbed her mother's shoulder. "Mom?" she said.

Her mother stopped. "What?"

"You haven't had a drink in over two months."

"Yeah. Two *long* months."

"Don't start drinking again. Please."

"It's too late for me, Jen."

"No, it's not."

"Yeah, it is." She resumed thumping toward the door.

Jen kept pace beside her. When they reached Jack's car, her mother leaned her crutches against the back door and clambered into the driver's seat. Jen handed her the crutches.

"You take care of yourself," her mother said, staring out the windshield. "Lord knows, you've always had to."

Jen watched her start the ignition, put the car in gear, and screech from the lot. She raised her hand in farewell even though she knew her mother couldn't see her.

A few minutes later she sat in her car in Jack's garage listening to Celine sing the love song from *Titanic*, one of her favorite movies.

If Jack was awake, he would have heard the car.

He would know she was home and grieving, that she needed him. She sat, waiting to see if he would open the door.

He didn't.

The song ended. Jen entered the house, the television blaring some program or other. Jack was sitting up on the couch looking sleepy. She turned off the TV.

"How's Ruby?" he said.

Ruby's name brought tears. "Not good."

Jack stretched, yawned, and stood. Though he was a relatively short man, he towered over her. "I'm sorry," he said. "I know you hate to lose her, but she's had a long life. I'm really beat. Let's go to bed."

Jen stepped back. "I'm not coming."

"Why? It's late."

He was right. It was late. She should have done this months ago. "I'm leaving," she said.

He blinked. "What?"

"I want more."

He ran his hand through his blond hair. "More what?"

She remembered what Tulsa had said. "I don't just want a house. I want a real home. For me and someday for my children."

Jack's face was a picture of confusion. "I said we'd have kids someday."

The memory of Jack trying to wrench nail polish from five-year-old Emily reminded her of the kind of father Jack would be. If, indeed, he ever actually decided to have children. "That's not enough. I'm sorry, Jack, but I want a husband who will love me and our kids the way we deserve to be loved."

"You've been reading too many romance novels," he said.

"I've only just started." It was time for her to ride to her own rescue, to become the heroine of her own life. She headed for the bedroom to pack.

"I don't even charge you rent," he said, his voice sounding indignant. "What do you think you can afford on your own?"

She would stay with Tulsa until she could find a place—probably nothing more than a tiny studio apartment, but at least it would be hers. She took her suitcase from the closet shelf.

"Be reasonable," Jack said. "Where do you think you're going?"

She smiled to herself. "Home," she said.

CHAPTER FIFTY-THREE
Pearl

The scrambled egg was so runny, it slipped through the tines of Pearl's fork. This was her first time back at Sherman's—now Lavelle's—since Sherman died. For some reason, she'd wanted to come here, to orange Naugahyde and buttery biscuits, but the biscuits were burned, the eggs undercooked, the bacon limp. The café stank of grease and a cloying floor wax. Sherman would be turning over in his grave. Pearl set down her fork and cupped her hands around her third mug of hot chocolate. It was hard to ruin cocoa.

Across from her, Daniel talked with his mouth half-full. Flecks of toast dotted his tongue. "Are you okay, Gran?"

Pearl's head hurt. She'd slept for just four hours. It was hard being sad and alone, with Ruby hovering between life and death, so she was grateful for Daniel's company, but oh, how young he was. It was difficult to remember ever being that age. "Just tired. And sad." She wished she had someone to hold her. How much she'd missed of life by marrying a man who could no more reach out to her than she could to him. We create our own stories. She wished she could write another draft.

"I'm sorry about Ruby," Daniel said. "I know how much you love her."

It was odd to think that Ruby had been more of a sister to her than her own sisters, who were so much younger. If only Ruby would rally.

Behind her, the café door creaked open. Sherman had oiled those hinges every day. Apparently Lavelle didn't bother.

"Why won't you return my calls?"

Hank. She hadn't seen him enter.

Daniel didn't even look at him. "There's nothing to say."

"How can you just leave?" Hank said. His grimace of anguish made Pearl flinch.

Spots of color dotted Daniel's cheeks.

"Look at me," Hank pleaded.

Daniel looked at the table. Hank's eyes filled with tears. Shoulders slumped, he left the café. The door creaked again on his way out.

Pearl remembered the tenderness on Hank's face when he took care of her sick grandson. "You never talked to him about why you were leaving?" she said.

"There's no point. People don't change. Look at Dad. And Grandpa."

"It was as much my fault as your grandfather's, Daniel." If only she'd realized a long time ago how true that was. "And it's your mom's fault as much as your dad's."

"You didn't boss Grandpa around. And Mom doesn't give orders to Dad."

"No, but we let them boss us. I should have refused. So should your mom." How different her own life might have been if she hadn't been raised to believe that the husband was head of the house. She would give anything not to have passed that belief on to her daughter. Thank God her grandson didn't share their submissiveness, but maybe he'd gone too far the other way. She looked up. He was studying her, his hazel eyes locked on hers.

If she told him that she thought he should stand up to Hank, that he should talk to him, argue with him, she would be driving Daniel back toward damnation.

"What?" Daniel asked.

"Nothing," she said.

CHAPTER FIFTY-FOUR
BJ

Head propped on one hand, BJ swirled syrup over the banana pancakes in front of her, too tired to lift her fork and too sad to swallow.

"You need to eat something," Matthew said.

His eyes were the color of perfectly browned toast. That's what her mother used to fix for her when she was sick: golden-brown toast spread with tasty homemade apple butter. BJ had called Matthew when she woke up after just a few hours' sleep. He'd met her here. There was something so comforting about him. The gentleness in his voice. The warmth in his eyes. He was like a hot-water bottle, the kind Ruby and Pearl talked about having used as kids to warm their beds. BJ realized with a start how much she'd missed him.

"If you don't eat," he said, "you'll just feel worse."

She cut a bite of pancake, tasted syrup, chewed, and swallowed. The food stuck in her throat. It was like she'd swallowed a wad of Kleenex. She gulped water to wash it down.

"I know what that's like," Matthew said. "The last few weeks with Catherine, I lost twenty pounds."

Her eyes fell on the book beside her plate. She'd brought *A Knight in Shining Armor* to reread in case she arrived first. She hadn't wanted to just sit and wait, certain she would keep picturing Ruby, who was still on the brink of death. "I could stand to lose a few pounds," she said.

"You're fine just the way you are." Matthew handed her a glass of orange juice. "At least drink some juice."

She sipped it. For all she could taste, it could have been tomato juice. Or motor oil.

"Just before Catherine died," Matthew said, "she saw her mother, who'd been dead ten years. Catherine looked so happy. It made me think that death is a peaceful passing."

"But it's not fair." Even to her own ears, BJ thought she sounded all of about five.

"I don't suppose we're ever ready to lose the people we love."

Her lips trembled. She certainly wasn't ready to lose Ruby, and neither were Tulsa or Guy. Or

Pearl or Jen. Thinking of Guy made her check her watch. It was almost eight. She needed to be heading out to help with the canoe business. "Thanks for meeting me," she said.

"I'm glad you called."

She unzipped her purse to get out her wallet. He covered her hand with his own. His hand felt callused. Strong.

"I got it," he said.

"You're sure?"

He nodded.

"Thanks." She didn't want to take her hand from his, but she needed to. "I'd better go." She scooted to the edge of the booth.

"BJ, I . . ." He seemed to hesitate, but only briefly. "Can I call you?" he said.

"You really want to?"

"I'd like to see you again. I like you."

"Me? Not my pork chops?"

"I like you both. Your brisket's not bad either."

He smiled, and it seemed to her that his smile was as comforting as his perfectly toasted eyes. "Okay," she said.

"Great! When you're feeling up to it, we'll go out. You need a break from cooking."

"Okay. Thanks." He looked so happy. It had been a long time since she'd made anyone look that pleased. Despite her own gloom, she felt a flutter of pleasure at the thought of seeing him again. Of course those flutters had always ended in disappointment and pain. But maybe Ruby was right and you had to teach a man how to please you. Not that she was an expert on that subject. Nor did she know how to go about teaching him. Verbal instructions would be weird. Maybe she could just moan loud when something he did felt good.

"I'll call you tonight to see how you're doing," he said. "And if you need me, please call. Anytime."

"Thank you, Matthew."

She walked out to her car in a daze, opened the door, and got behind the wheel. She'd left her book on the table. Well, the waitress would find it. She could get it later. She'd read it anyway, and she was too tired to go back. She reached into her purse for her bottle of aspirin and shook two pills into her hand. Wait. Did her head even hurt? She dropped the pills back in the bottle.

Matthew didn't have a hero's looks or skills in bed, but he was a good man. When you really thought about it, maybe it was more important for a man to be a friend than a knight in shining armor. Important for a woman to be the same. Sexual pleasure mattered less than loving and being loved. BJ wished she'd been less selfish with Faith and her cousin Marjorie, two people she had loved, but maybe it was time to forgive herself and hope God would do the same. She put her car in reverse and backed out of her spot.

CHAPTER FIFTY-FIVE
Ruby

One minute soft grass tickled her bare feet while mud squished between her toes. The next she was balloon-light and aloft, floating farther and farther from the Earth. Below her a canopy of green lined the gleaming river.

Above her, someone beckoned, vague and indistinct.

She caught a whiff of a familiar aroma, one she'd always loved: cherry pipe tobacco. She looked up. The fragrant tobacco told her who was beckoning her. She reached for him.

"Ruby, please don't die."

She stopped. Torn between wanting to be held in his arms and wanting to hold the granddaughter she loved, Ruby hovered, looking up, looking down.

"Live, Ruby. Live."

CHAPTER FIFTY-SIX
Tulsa

Six cups of bitter vending-machine coffee hadn't staved off Tulsa's exhaustion. She lay her aching head beside Ruby's shoulder and dozed, dreaming that she and Ruby were floating down the river in a canoe. "The leaves are turning," Ruby said in the dream. At Ruby's words, Tulsa looked up at the branches overhanging the water. The leaves were, indeed, turning, their edges hinting at the yellow that foreshadowed the brilliant hues of October, the shriveled browns of November, the barren branches of winter. Despite the sunlight, cold, damp air bit into her, making her shiver.

"Tulsa?"

Ruby wasn't speaking in the dream now. She was just smiling up at the leaves. Tulsa struggled to make sense of her dream, to determine who was calling her name.

"Tulsa?"

She made herself wake. Ruby's eyes looked into her own. "Ruby?" Adrenaline surged through Tulsa. "Ruby," she whispered, afraid that if she spoke too loud she might startle her grandmother into another heart attack. Ruby was alive. Alive!

"Autumn's coming," Ruby said, her voice shaky, weak.

Tulsa took Ruby's hand and looked around the ICU: there were no windows. Ruby must have been dreaming, too. "It's still August. Don't rush winter, Ruby. I'm not ready."

A gray-haired nurse materialized. "Well, I'll be." The nurse checked the monitors above Ruby's head. "Anybody who doesn't believe in miracles ought to work in the ICU. Bless you, dear." She studied Tulsa. "And you, too. You look like we ought to hook *you* up to some oxygen."

"I'm fine." Ruby alive was the only medicine Tulsa needed.

"I'll let the doctor know." The nurse bustled away.

Tulsa leaned her head against Ruby's hand. Tears spilled down Tulsa's cheeks. It seemed odd to cry now, but she couldn't help herself.

"What?" Ruby said.

Tulsa wiped away her tears. "I thought I'd lost you."

Ruby closed her eyes, opened them. "Saw . . . Clifford," she said. A look of immense peacefulness smoothed Ruby's face.

"You did?"

Ruby's eyes closed again. "Sleepy."

"I love you so much," Tulsa said.

Ruby fell asleep, her face still pale but with a hint of color in her cheeks. Tulsa was eager to call

Guy and their friends but would wait for the doctor to confirm that Ruby would survive. She turned the brass wedding band, loose on Ruby's withered finger.

Ruby had seen Clifford. After more than thirty years, her grandmother still loved him. Tulsa thought of Slade and of roses. Thought, then, of *A Knight in Shining Armor*. Dougless and Nicholas loved each other so much, their love endured centuries. Of course, they were fictional characters, but Ruby's love for Clifford was real, and it had survived decades after his death.

Tulsa doubted she could ever love a man that much, but it was time to try.

PART FIVE
SEPTEMBER

CHAPTER FIFTY-SEVEN
Tulsa

George Calhoun leaned back in his desk chair in the small office of the Bank of Fiddle, his girth protruding between the chair slats, and tutted. "I'm afraid I can't do that," he said.

Tulsa's pulse hammered her neck. They had brought in enough business to cover the loan payments through December. But Ruby didn't have prescription drug coverage. The doctor had told Tulsa he would be prescribing Ruby several medications. That meant their finances would be hit even harder. With Labor Day weekend having just passed, their business would drop sharply. Barring a miracle, they would run out of money by the first of the year.

Tulsa didn't want Ruby to worry about the possibility of defaulting on the loan. Stress was hard on the heart. She leaned forward in her chair. "I'm just asking for an extension of a few months. We're keeping the cabins open year-round. We'll be in good shape by spring, I'm sure of it."

A fountain on George's desk—water trickling down a copper slate—gurgled. The sound soothed her. Surely George would agree to an extension. He had to.

George rested his hand on fingers clasped as if in prayer. "You were sure buying Ed's was a wise thing to do, too."

"It was. It is. We just need a little more time."

George nodded like he was listening, truly listening. "Do you think maybe you made some bad business decisions?"

"Not really. I mean, what were the odds that it would rain so much, the sewer would need replacing, the bus would go out, and Ruby would have a heart attack?" Tulsa had dressed up for this meeting in her best cargo pants and a button-down white shirt she'd bought at Goodwill.

"A good business plan anticipates contingencies," George said.

"We did. Just not all of them at once."

He unwrapped a piece of heavily scented cinnamon candy. The wrapper crackled. He didn't offer Tulsa any. That's when she knew they were doomed. Still, she had to try. "Look at our numbers." She pointed to the page on which she'd calculated their likely income over the next year.

George ran his fingers down the page. Whether he was motivated by economics or his friendship with Clancy, Tulsa didn't know, but she suspected he was only pretending to check the numbers.

"Impressive," he said, sucking audibly on the candy.

For an instant she let herself hope.

George shook his head. "Unfortunately, they're

just numbers. You need dollars. I'm afraid I can't grant you an extension."

"You mean you won't."

"No." George's double chin jiggled as he shook his head. "I mean I can't. It wouldn't be in the bank's interest."

"The bank's? Or Rupert Clancy's?"

"Rupert and I are good friends, but this is strictly a business decision."

"Ruby's been doing business with this bank for years. Decades. Our credit's always been good. There's no sound financial reason for you to deny us an extension. We're good for it."

George picked up a trout paperweight on his desk. He said nothing. He was going to refuse.

"Please," Tulsa said.

"Sorry."

"We'll keep current in our payments through December, then we'll pay January, February, and March in April and May. That's no time. Just the snap of a finger." She snapped two fingers together to illustrate. "Ruby could die from the stress." Her voice broke.

No response.

"You don't care if Ruby dies, do you?"

"I hope Ruby lives a long life. But I run a bank, not a charity."

"What happens if we fall a month or two behind?"

"The terms of your mortgage give us power of

sale if you miss even one payment. I suggest you make all of your payments on time, or you won't even own your place by April."

Tulsa stood. "There are other banks around."

George unwrapped another piece of candy. "Good luck. No bank will loan you a dime. You're too leveraged and close to falling behind on your payments. But feel free to waste your time." He tossed the candy into his mouth.

Tulsa couldn't even breathe. "I'll find a way to make the payments," she said when she could. "And in the future, we will give our business to another bank."

"What business?" George's smile was so smug, it was all Tulsa could do to restrain her urge to slap the man.

She stepped outside into sweltering heat and closed her fingers into fists as she walked along the cracked sidewalk. She licked lips dried by weeks of summer. In a few minutes she was due to meet Slade at the rehab center to bring Ruby back to the home they would soon lose, and it was all Tulsa's fault. Her grandmother may have decided to take the loan out, but Ruby had done it for *her*.

Tears filled her eyes. How had she been so blind to the truth? The river hadn't been her lifeline all these years. Ruby had. Ruby's love had saved her. Ruby's steadfast love. Tulsa had repaid that love by allowing—wanting, really—Ruby to risk everything. She climbed into her pickup. Dread made her limp, and she rested her head against the steering wheel. She'd told George she would find a way to make the payments. Big talk. Oh, she would try the banks in West Plains, but she suspected George was right, that they would turn her down. The Sweet Oak River Oasis was going to sink, and there didn't seem to be a damned thing she could do to save it.

CHAPTER FIFTY-EIGHT
Ruby

Ruby sat on the edge of the bed and watched Slade look at Tulsa, his eyes lit up like a man in love. Tulsa's eyes, however, seemed to be looking everywhere but at Ruby's. "What's wrong with you, Tulsa?" Ruby said.

"Nothing."

"Then why won't you look at me?"

Tulsa's eyes darted to Ruby's and darted away.

Dr. Phillips appeared in the doorway, beckoning Tulsa with his finger. *Nuts,* Ruby thought. The doctor's big bald head reminded Ruby of a pancake. She had a suspicion of what he would say, but she just looked out the window, hoping she was wrong.

The smell of Dr. Phillips's cologne lingered after he disappeared, the overpowering clove aroma of Old Spice. Well, it was better than the room's normal smell—vaguely moldy, like there was a leak somewhere. Or maybe it was just the smell of old people. Her roommate, who was off doing physical therapy, was even older than she was.

Ruby raised her feet back up on the bed.

"You have everything?" Slade asked.

Ruby looked around the white-walled room that had been hers for almost two weeks after ten days in the hospital, bare of the many cards and flowers she'd received from friends and customers. "Yes indeed." At Ruby's request, Tulsa had already given the flowers to other patients. "If we don't get going soon," she said, "I'm going to meet myself coming back."

"How are you feeling?" Slade asked.

"Fair to middling," she said.

"That's good. You beat death, you know."

"Nah. I just postponed it a bit."

"A long bit, I hope."

Ruby closed her eyes. The darkness was restful. "We all die. It's just part of life."

"It's the opposite of life."

"It's the natural ending. Nothing to be afraid of." She opened her eyes. Slade was studying her, a pensive look on his face.

"I don't know that I'm afraid," he said. "Just unwilling. When it's my time to go, it'll be under protest."

Ruby remembered Tulsa saying that Slade's twin brother had died young. What could she say now to make him realize how peaceful death could be? "I saw Clifford, you know. My late husband."

"When?"

"When I was dying. I—"

Tulsa returned to the room, her face scrunched in what looked like bewilderment. "What do you mean, you're not going to take your medicine?" Tulsa said.

"What?" Slade said.

"Ruby told the doctor she didn't want prescriptions." Tulsa spoke to Slade, but her eyes accused Ruby.

Ruby locked her eyes on Tulsa's. "That's my decision, honey."

Tulsa's whole face seemed to tremble. "But why?"

"Did he tell you what all those pills cost?"

"I don't care what they cost."

Ruby lowered her voice. If she spoke softly, perhaps Tulsa would hear her better. "The pulmonary hypertension drugs run ten thousand a month. No way we can pay that. We'd lose our place for sure. You'd have no home, Tulsa."

"But you can sign up for Medicare D," Tulsa said. "Doctor Phillips said it's the open enrollment period. And there's supplemental coverage available for what D doesn't cover."

"Yes, I can sign up now. But it wouldn't take effect until January. That's forty thousand dollars we'd have to pay before it kicks in. We don't have forty thousand dollars, honey."

"I'll get it somehow," Tulsa said. "Do you think I'm going to just let you die?"

Ruby had known this would be hard, but she wasn't going to live forever. "I'm going to die sooner or later. If it's sooner, you won't lose everything. And the bank won't foreclose and sell our whole place to Clancy."

"I can lose everything else. I can't bear to lose you." Tulsa held up slips of white paper. "Dr. Phillips gave me the prescriptions."

Ruby folded her arms over her chest. "I won't take them. And I can be just as stubborn as you."

Tears welled in Tulsa's eyes. "Please," she said.

"There's a simple answer to this," Slade said.

He'd been standing quietly. Ruby turned to him. "What's that?"

"I'll pay for them."

"Thank you," Ruby said, "but I can't take your money."

He smiled and raised his shoulders almost in apology. "I've got plenty."

"I know. But it wouldn't be right."

"Would it be right if I were your grandson-in-law?"

"If . . ." Ruby looked at him, then at Tulsa, who was staring at Slade, an expression of what Ruby thought was incredulity etched on Tulsa's face. "Well," she said, "I reckon that's a horse of a different color."

Tulsa still stared at Slade. It was one of the few times Ruby had seen her speechless.

"I'd envisioned a slightly more romantic proposal," Slade said to Tulsa, "but this seems like a good time." He looked around the room like he was searching for something to give her—roses, maybe, a ring, but the only things left were a hospital bed, a tray, and a can of Coke. He ripped off the tab. The Coke fizzed and foamed, dripping down the sides. Slade knelt in front of Tulsa, taking her hand in his. "Marry me," he said as he slid the tab onto her pinky.

Tulsa's face blotched red, like she had a bad case of poison ivy. Her mouth was half-open, but no words came out.

"Do you love me?" Slade asked, still kneeling.

Tulsa looked like she'd been shot with a stun gun. "I don't know. Maybe. But I haven't even seen where you live."

"We can fix that," he said. "As soon as Ruby's comfortable, you can come to Kansas City to meet my friends and see my home."

"You'd be willing to live here?" Tulsa said.

Slade stood. "We'll talk about where to live after you've seen my place."

Slade lifted Tulsa's chin to his and flashed her his wide smile. Tulsa's expression now seemed closer to relief than joy. The last thing Ruby wanted was for her granddaughter to marry the right man for the wrong reasons. Or the wrong man for the right reasons. Ruby wanted Tulsa to be all dazzled like a romance heroine. Not begrudging. "Say yes only if you love him," Ruby said, hoping she did, more for Tulsa's sake than her own.

"She does," Slade said. "She just doesn't know it yet. But I'm a patient man. She'll realize she loves me. And in the meantime"—he lifted the prescriptions from Tulsa's fingers—"I'll get

these filled." He turned to Ruby. "Two months' worth, to give Tulsa time to sort things out." He winked. "Deal?"

"Deal," Ruby said.

CHAPTER FIFTY-NINE
Jen

The fact that Ruby felt good enough to have everyone over to dinner two weeks after coming home—BJ had cooked, baking the chicken instead of frying it and preparing the mashed potatoes with skim milk—was a hopeful sign, Jen thought. The rehab facility must have really restored Ruby's health. That or she was just tired of Tulsa's cooking.

Good thing Jen had had vacation time coming. She'd taken off the first week Ruby was home, staying there to cook, help tend Ruby, and handle phones for the canoe business. It had been good for everyone, Jen included. Helping Ruby took Jen's mind off her grief over Jack. Though she never doubted she'd done the right thing in leaving him, she missed him. Tulsa had said Jen was grieving what she and Jack hadn't had as much as what they had. Tulsa was probably right.

When she went back to work, the widowed Delilah Foster offered Jen the in-law apartment in her house at reduced rent in exchange for yard work. Jen was thrilled to accept. Mrs. Foster had let her paint the one-bedroom apartment however she wanted. Jen had chosen apricot for her living room, turquoise for her bath, and bright yellow for her bedroom. Coming home to such welcoming colors made her smile.

Ruby was chewing her chicken with her eyes closed as if to savor the taste: tangy with garlic powder and lemon. She'd regained much color in her cheeks and seemed to be getting stronger every day. She'd even resumed answering the phone and handling reservations for cabins, campground, and canoes.

"This chicken's delicious," Ruby said.

Everyone else—Jen, Tulsa, Pearl, Guy—nodded in agreement. BJ looked pleased.

"It smells great, too," Jen said. The garlic

chicken, the lima beans, the mashed potatoes and gravy, the fresh corn on the cob. "Funny how much certain meals just smell like home."

"Yep," Pearl said, then turned to Tulsa. "You should get this recipe. The way to a man's heart is through his stomach."

"I'd say Tulsa's already got Slade's heart," Ruby said.

Guy sliced off a chunk of chicken, frowning. Something was bothering him.

"Where does Slade want to take you for your honeymoon?" BJ asked Tulsa.

"There may not be a honeymoon. I haven't said yes." Tulsa shrugged. "I know he loves Paris."

Jen pictured museums, the Eiffel Tower, and walks along the River Seine. "I'd love to see Paris."

"Heck, I'd have liked to see Knott's Berry Farm," Pearl said.

"But doesn't Paris sound especially romantic?" Jen said.

Guy set his knife and fork beside his plate and wiped his lips with his napkin. "You're talking about marriage to a man you hardly know."

Tulsa tilted her chair back. "Not true. He's practically lived here the last few weeks. I've gotten to know him well, and I like what I've seen."

"Liking someone isn't the same as loving him," Guy said.

"You should talk." Tulsa's nostrils flared. "You spend every night at Wanda's. Is that liking or loving?"

"Neither. We broke up."

Tulsa went wide-eyed with astonishment. "You did? When? Why?"

"A couple of weeks ago. It wasn't working. And at least Wanda belongs here. Slade's a good guy, but I checked him out on the Internet. He lives in the penthouse of a high-rise and hangs out with society types. That's not your world."

"And your point is?"

"My point is that if you could be happy living that life, then you're not the woman I thought I knew."

It *was* hard to picture Tulsa in high heels in a high-rise with high-society people. Still. Slade was such a catch! Tulsa had confided in Jen how close she and Ruby were to defaulting. Slade could certainly take care of that. If Tulsa decided she loved him, Slade could take care of a lot of Tulsa's needs.

"Who I am isn't etched in stone," Tulsa told Guy. "I'll see Slade's place and then decide what I want. Besides, we'll live here."

"Yeah, right. Slade's going to want to live here. You need to slow down and think things over."

"Hey, I'm not rushing into anything," Tulsa said. "I haven't made a decision."

"Life isn't a romance novel," Guy said.

"Really?" Tulsa's sarcasm was obvious. "I didn't know that."

If only Slade had fallen for *her,* Jen thought. She wouldn't need to debate his proposal.

"Speaking of romances"—Ruby reached over to the hutch beside the table and picked up a stack of four books—"here's the next one."

She handed each of the women a white paperback with a castle on the cover. *The Secret* by Julie Garwood.

Jen didn't much care what book they read. She was just happy that Ruby felt up to it. "It's been too long since our last book," she said.

"True," Ruby said. "How soon shall we meet?"

"Soon," Pearl said. "A month's too far apart. Especially at our age."

BJ scooted forward. "A week?"

Ruby looked bemused. "Jen?"

"Yes to a week."

"Works for me," Pearl said.

Tulsa riffled the book pages. "I'll be in Kansas City this weekend. I don't know how much time I'll have to read."

"Monday the twenty-second it is, by popular demand," Ruby said. "If you don't get it all read, honey, that's okay, but I bet you can." She turned to Guy. "You can borrow my copy if you want to read it."

Guy wrinkled his nose. "No, thanks." He stood.

"Where are you going?" Tulsa asked.

"I got a date with Elvis. I understand *her*." Guy started for the door. Jen half expected him to slam it on his way out, but he didn't. The others sat in silence, looking at the place where Guy had been.

BJ bolted to her feet. "I'll be right back," she said.

Jen expected BJ to head for the bathroom, but instead she rushed out in the direction Guy had gone. Much as Jen would love to know what was up with the two of them, it wasn't her business.

Pearl picked up the book Ruby had chosen. "What's this one about?"

Ruby glanced down at the cover as if to remind herself what book they were reading. "Love. And friendship. It takes place in Scotland. In medieval times."

"I hope it's as good as the others," Jen said, then turned to Tulsa. "Did Slade say what he has planned when you go to Kansas City?"

"He's throwing me a party to meet his friends."

"You're not intending to wear jeans and a T-shirt, I hope."

"Why not?"

"I'm sure Slade dresses down when he comes here." *Slade in a tux: wow!* "You need to dress up when you go there. I'm thinking a basic black dress for the party. Simple but classic."

Tulsa ran her fingers through her hair. "You know I don't do dresses."

"You want to make him feel proud for his friends," Jen said.

"He should be proud of who I am, not what I wear."

Ruby leaned toward Tulsa. "Honey, that may be a little naive."

Pearl grunted. "A *little?*"

Jen pointed her fork at Tulsa. "You are going shopping. Tomorrow. With me. For a dress."

"My gosh," Pearl said. "Something sure gave you spunk, Jen. I don't recall ever hearing you give Tulsa orders."

"Me neither," Tulsa said.

Jen didn't flinch. "Don't dodge the issue. What time tomorrow?"

"Noon, I guess," Tulsa said. "After we put in all the canoes and before we have to pick anyone up. But I'm not getting a black dress. That's what you wear to funerals."

Jen just smiled. "Fine," she said.

"Do you feel swept up like the women in the books?" Pearl asked Tulsa.

"Not exactly," Tulsa said. "I guess I'm excited, sure." She stabbed lima beans with her fork, then raised her eyes to take them all in and spoke in a plaintive voice. "But what if I marry him and the sparks die out?"

No one answered her immediately. "With Clifford, the sparks changed to a warm glow," Ruby said. "I think that's what happens with love."

"Besides, if the marriage goes bad," Pearl said, "you've got choices we didn't have. Like divorce."

Tulsa sat straighter. "No way. When I give my word to marry till death do we part, I intend to keep it."

"Then give *me* your word," Ruby said.

"What?" Tulsa's eyes darted toward the door, as if she were looking for a way out.

"Give me your word you won't marry Slade just for my sake," Ruby said. "That you'll say yes only if you really love him."

Tulsa stood. "I'll get the coffee."

"Tulsa?" Ruby said.

Tulsa paused, uncertainty clear on her face. "Okay." She spoke so softly, it was almost inaudible, then started toward the kitchen.

"Say the words," Ruby insisted.

Tulsa didn't turn around. When she did speak, it was a mumble. "I promise."

"Look me in the eyes and say it again."

Tulsa turned slowly—reluctantly, Jen thought.

"I promise," Tulsa said.

Ruby settled back in her chair. "Good. Let's have some dessert."

"I'll help Tulsa." Jen stacked plates, then carried them to the kitchen, where Tulsa was fumbling with a serving spoon. "What's wrong?" Jen asked.

Tulsa scooped up pudding and plopped it into

the first dessert bowl. "If I don't marry him, we'll go under. I think we would be okay if we could get through to spring, but without Slade's help, there's no way. And Ruby . . ." Tulsa buried the spoon in the bowl of pudding and shook her head.

Tulsa had told Jen about Ruby's insistence that she wouldn't take the medicine she needed if it meant losing their home. "I wish I had the money to help," Jen said.

"I know."

"Slade's a good man."

"I know that, too."

"*Do* you think you love him?" Jen asked.

"Maybe. But it's happening so fast. Do I feel like I might love him because I really do, or because I'm so afraid of what will happen if I don't? Ruby's shown me once again how much you can love someone. The sacrifices you're willing to make. I don't know if I could ever love Slade like that."

"Don't try to figure things out right now. Go to Kansas City. Listen to your heart, not your head. It will tell you what to do."

"And if it tells me that I don't love him?"

Tulsa both looked and sounded frightened. Jen covered Tulsa's hand with hers. "I don't know, but you're not in this alone. All of us love Ruby. We'd figure out something."

Tulsa looked doubtful.

Jen handed her two bowls of pudding and picked up the other three. With any luck, Tulsa would discover that she truly did love Slade. If the opposite proved true, there would be plenty of time to panic.

CHAPTER SIXTY
BJ

Elvis was just jumping into the bed of Guy's pickup when BJ came outside. Guy had to have seen her, even in the murky light, but he slid behind the wheel and started the engine. BJ jerked open the truck door. It creaked. "Stop!" she said.

He didn't look at her. "Go back inside, Mom."

"Not until you tell me what's eating you."

"Nothing." He pulled the door shut.

The truth struck her hard. "You love Tulsa," she said through the partially open window.

Guy's arms flexed. He must have tightened his grip on the steering wheel. He kept his eyes on whatever he was seeing through the windshield. "I gotta go."

"I'm not blind, son. I'm going to go right back in there and tell them the truth. Tulsa needs to know *before* she decides about Slade."

Guy turned his head to face her. Meeting BJ's

eyes, he said, "We agreed not to hurt Marjorie, remember?"

"I care more about what's best for *you*. It's long past time I told the truth."

"No!" The word came out like a gunshot.

"Why not?"

"Tulsa needs to decide whether she loves Slade without any distractions."

"Distractions?" she said.

Guy's face contorted in the same anguish she heard in his voice. "If Tulsa does love him," he said, "Slade could provide for her and Ruby in a way I never could."

"But what if she doesn't really love him?"

"She's got to figure that out for herself."

It made sense in a way, what he was saying. But Tulsa would never even consider her options if she didn't know the truth. Just as Guy hadn't started to see it until her secret had come out. "Are you sure?" she said.

"I'm sure. I appreciate your offer, Mom, but you need to respect my decision. No telling Tulsa or any of them. Agreed?"

Although part of her was relieved—the part that didn't want to confess to her cousin and her friends the shameful truth—what he was asking of her felt wrong. She hesitated, hoping he would change his mind. Her breath fogged up the car window.

"Mom?" he said.

"Okay," she said after a long pause. "But I think you're making a mistake."

He nodded at her, then put the engine in gear. It made a grinding noise, almost as if the truck were protesting.

She waited in the yard as Guy drove off, staring after the truck, just in case he turned around.

When she rejoined the others, they all looked at her with questioning eyes.

"What's eating Guy?" Tulsa asked.

BJ couldn't look her in the face, so she stared just above Tulsa's head, hoping it seemed like she was not as flummoxed as she felt. "Nothing really," BJ said. Not one of them looked convinced. She had to come up with something to throw them off the scent. "He'd had an argument with some guy who stiffed him on some work he did. And I needed to ask him something about my car."

"Your pudding's delicious," Ruby said. "Thank you."

The others nodded in agreement.

"Glad you like it." BJ turned to Pearl. "Too bad we don't have any of your blackberry–sour cream pie. Dot Grafe asked me just last week if I had your recipe. I told her the only people who know it are you and God, and neither one's talking."

"If you want to tell someone a secret," Pearl said, "tell God. He's the only one I know who won't blab."

BJ shot to her feet. "I need to use the ladies' room." She practically sprinted for the bathroom. If she was going to keep her promise to Guy, she needed to take a few minutes to herself.

In the bathroom she doused her face with cold water and stared at herself in the mirror. The lines around her eyes seemed to have multiplied in the last few minutes. A few more and she would look as old as Ruby and Pearl. Strange that silence had been so easy for her all those many years. Strange, too, that lying still came easy, though hopefully for a better reason than shame.

CHAPTER SIXTY-ONE
Tulsa

On Thursday, when she drove into the garage of the towering converted office building where Slade lived in the heart of downtown Kansas City, Tulsa was half tempted to drive right out. Every other vehicle—convertibles, sports cars, sedans, and SUVs—looked freshly laundered. Even the sprinkling of pickups appeared polished. She parked between a gleaming green Jaguar and a glistening black BMW. Well, Big Red was an Ozarks truck. Dust was its natural color.

Tulsa took her battered duffel bag from the seat and walked to the spacious lobby. An ornate crystal chandelier glinted off a floor inlaid with huge tiles. A doorman cleared her to take the elevator to the penthouse. She punched the button for the top floor, wondering what she would find.

The elevator door opened; Slade's unstubbled face gleamed like the well-kept cars. "Welcome to my world," he said, and took her in his arms.

His chest felt firm, solid, his arms strong around her. They kissed. He tasted of wintergreen. Something about him smelled melony. His hair, maybe? He looked, tasted, smelled, and felt so good, she was tempted to rip off his shirt and make love right there by the elevator.

"I don't know whether to ravage you first or show you your future home," he said.

She stepped back. "My *home?*"

"I guess it would actually be more of a base of operations."

"I never said I'd live here. We said we'd talk about it after I visited. I thought we'd live at the river. Most of the time, anyway."

"I have to live here. My business is here."

"What about *my* business?"

"Running canoes? I'd think you'd welcome the chance to give that up."

"I happen to like running canoes. And I have no interest in closing my business."

He held up his hand. "We'll talk about it after you've been here a couple of days. I'm offering you a better life. A *much* better life." He took her hand. "Come see."

He ushered her through the doorway of his condo. The floor-to-ceiling windows, impeccably clean, commanded a sweeping view of the sky and looked out toward the Missouri River. Elongated clouds spread across the horizon, brilliant reddish-orange clouds that reminded her of a million roses on fire. "Wow," she said. You didn't get this kind of view at the river, where trees blocked so much of the sky.

Slade put his arms around her from behind. "There's a world out there waiting for us."

She thought of mountains and jungles and deserts, and of oceans teeming with fish as colorful as the blouses Jen wore.

"We can go anywhere," he crooned in her ear. "Anywhere at all."

She turned toward him, her eyes searching his. "I can't just go off and leave Ruby alone."

"Not yet. How is she? Still improving?"

"Yes, thankfully."

"So we'll go a little later. If we need to, we can hire someone to live in with Ruby. She wouldn't want you to limit your life."

Tulsa turned back to the living room: cherry-wood floor, white stone fireplace against a white wall, white couch, white chairs, white hallway. She half expected that Slade burned white logs, which would produce white flames. Even dirt in this room would probably turn white. It was a long way from the Ozarks. She started to walk toward the windows, but Slade restrained her.

"Wait." He squatted and unstrapped her Tevas, then guided her feet into a pair of silky red slippers. "They keep the floor cleaner." He tilted her chin up and kissed her. She kissed him back but not as fervently. When they kissed at home, the only witness was the river. Here it seemed like they were on display to the whole world.

"What's wrong?" he said.

"I feel exposed."

"Not exposed enough. Let's finish the tour, then see about a little more exposure."

He showed her an ultramodern kitchen with spotless stainless-steel appliances, a huge office with a modular glass desk, and a guest bedroom bigger than much of their downstairs at home. The master suite featured a tantalizing Jacuzzi almost as deep as the river, a gorgeous black-marble fireplace, a walk-in closet with enough clothes to stock a Macy's men's department, and a gigantic abstract painting with squiggly lines.

"That's a Thomas Karpa piece," Slade said. "Like it?"

"Reminds me of an electrocuted porcupine."

He glanced back at the painting. "It does?"

Tulsa looked out at the broad, rolling Missouri River, the sky beginning to gray.

Slade gestured around the room, with its shiny

surfaces and zapped porcupine. "What do you think of all this?"

"It's quite . . ." She wasn't sure what word to use. *Overwhelming* sounded too negative, *lovely* not even close to what she felt. She didn't know what she'd expected. Maybe it was the altitude that made her dizzy. "It's impressive," she said. "But it takes some getting used to."

"We've got the rest of our lives." He put his arm around her and guided her back to the living-room couch. They sank onto it, but the iceberg cushions didn't give.

Slade pulled her to his chest and reached under her blouse. His fingers fluttered over her back. She pressed her lips to his. He thrust his hands inside her pants to cup her rear.

She sat up.

"What's wrong?" he said.

The windows were just so huge. "People can see us."

"With binoculars, maybe. I say we give them a good show."

"Let's move to the bedroom."

"The windows are just as big in there."

"You don't have curtains?"

"And block the view? It's like being on top of the world."

"On top of it, not in it," she said.

A look of pride crossed his face. She pulled away.

He glanced at his watch. "It will be dark soon," he said. He sat up and took her foot in his hands. He massaged the arch, the ball, the heel, the arch again. "Feel good?"

"Oh yes."

When darkness finally hid them from others' eyes, they stripped off their clothes. He signaled her to wait, reached under the couch, and brought out a towel.

"Really?" she said as he spread it beneath them.

"Part of my Boy Scout training. Be prepared."

How often had he made love on this couch? She was tempted to ask, but as his tongue roamed her, she soon forgot her question. When he entered her, she gyrated her hips like she had before. He thrust like he had before. Her climax felt good, but she didn't reach the same pinnacle she had when they'd made love at the river. Well, that wasn't surprising. Every time couldn't be a medal winner.

Slade's soft, steady breaths told her he'd fallen asleep. She studied the view outside the windows, locating the old Power & Light Building. Did its spire still change colors at night? When she was a little girl, her mother often walked with her to a nearby hill to view the lights. She'd not understood that spotlights bathed the spire in red, then white, then green, then amber. Awed by what seemed like magic, she'd believed she could grow wings and fly, ride a dragon, or swim across the

Milky Way. Then her mother died. For a long while she hadn't believed in much of anything.

Now the view made her feel like she could grow wings and fly again.

Slade startled awake. "We've got dinner reservations at the Savoy." He sat up. "Have you eaten there?"

"Nope." The Savoy was one of Kansas City's most expensive restaurants. On those few occasions when she had to visit the city, she opted for fast food.

"You're in for a treat. Hungry?"

"Starving."

"Good. Let's get ready."

Slade changed into a pair of expertly creased tan slacks and a gray linen shirt with a leather aviator's jacket. Tulsa switched into her favorite bronze T-shirt and a brand-new pair of cargo pants, then picked up the backpack she used as a purse.

He didn't move. His eyes surveyed her.

"What?" she said.

"Did you bring something dressier?"

"A dress for tomorrow night's party."

"Let's see."

Her shoulders tightened. "That feels a little weird."

"The Savoy's classy. And I'm eager to see you dressed up." He set her backpack on the kitchen table. Unease made her shoulders even tighter, but she opened her duffel bag and took out the green rayon dress Jen had helped her choose. Long sleeves. Plain buttons. Straight skirt that fell to her knees. The only thing dressy about it was the silver belt buckle, which was shaped like a crescent moon.

Slade's face was slack. "What?" she said.

"Nothing. It's an okay dress."

"Okay?"

"It'll do for tonight. Tomorrow we'll pick you up something a little more elegant for the party. My treat, of course." He held up his hands and framed her as if for a photograph. "Black dress and pearls. With the right jewelry, you can go anywhere."

"You do realize that I don't wear dresses? This is the first one I've owned in years."

"It's a good start."

"And I don't wear black."

"Why not? You'd look great in black."

"Black reminds me of funerals, which I can't stand. And rain, which isn't high on my list either."

He put his arms around her. "Am I high on your list?"

"You were."

"I'll just have to see what I can do to get back on top."

"Oh? What if I fancy the top?"

"Top. Bottom. I'd settle for anything."

"Good." She held up the dress. "Settle for this."

He kissed her neck. "It's fine for tonight. Hurry and switch. I'm starving."

345

The dress was fine for tonight *and* tomorrow night, assuming she didn't spill anything on it. He would just have to accept that. Yes, it was simple and no-frills. But then, so was she.

CHAPTER SIXTY-TWO

BJ

BJ flipped the pork chops that simmered in the skillet and filled the kitchen with the delicious aroma of sizzling meat. Though Matthew had taken her out to eat several times since Ruby's heart attack, this was the first dinner she'd cooked for him since they'd resumed sharing meals. She had no hidden agenda other than to thank him for being so supportive about Ruby.

BJ's eyes fell on her copy of the white-covered romance, *The Secret*. She sighed. There was much she could relate to in the novel. Like the heroine's uncle, she'd told her son tales of his father's heroism—not slaying dragons for the king like in the book, but fighting evil for his country. Boys needed fathers they could be proud of. And, of course, she'd also lied about who Guy's real father was, just as the heroine's mother in *The Secret* lied about who the heroine's father was.

The doorbell rang. BJ opened the door for

Matthew. He looked almost dashing in a dark blue shirt that contrasted well with his graying hair.

He sniffed the air. "Pork chops?"

"Yes."

His eyes lit up. "Wonderful! Here. You left your book at Myrtle's."

He handed her *A Knight in Shining Armor*. She'd forgotten all about it. "Thanks."

In the kitchen she set the book down and took the grocery bag he was carrying. It felt cold. Peering inside, she saw a gallon of butterscotch ice cream. She'd told him she was serving pumpkin pie for dessert. He must want pie à la mode, but pumpkin and butterscotch? Stranger still, when she served the pie, Matthew refused even a single scoop of ice cream.

After dinner he said, "You look lovely tonight."

Surprised, she looked up from her plate. His golden brown eyes seemed to shine. "Thanks," she said.

She used to enjoy kissing him, but he hadn't so much as kissed her since the last time they'd made love. There was no point. Why play a drumroll if you weren't going to reach a crescendo? If in fact your head was going to hurt, really hurt? She rose to clear the table.

Matthew rose with her. He came around to her. "I'll do the dishes later," he said, and brushed his lips across her ear.

It tickled. Did she really want to get all excited for nothing but a splitting headache?

She was stunned when Matthew unbuttoned the top buttons of her blouse, more stunned still when he kissed her neck. It felt good, but not as good as his fingers felt when he moved them between her thighs. She clung to him until his touching brought her to the brink. The brink of what, she wasn't sure. She'd never felt like this. The one thing she was certain of was that she wanted him to finish what he'd started, right then, right there.

To her dismay, he backed away. "Don't stop," she said.

He took her hand and led her to the bedroom. She started to reach for him, but he caught her hand. "Not yet," he said. "Let me. You just enjoy yourself. And let's leave the light on low."

He slowly disrobed her, unbuttoning her blouse, unfastening her bra, unzipping her pants. All the while, he caressed her most erotic places. Had he been taking lessons? BJ didn't know whether to beg or scream. It was part pleasure, part pain. "Don't move," he said when they were both naked. "I'll be right back."

"Hurry!" Her head wasn't hurting so far, not one little bit.

He soon reappeared holding something behind his back. "Close your eyes."

Curious, she did as he said. The bed creaked

when he sat on it. Something cold dropped on her breasts. Cold. Wet. She smelled butterscotch.

"Whoops," he said. "How messy of me. Let me clean that up." He began licking. "How does that feel?"

She moaned and opened her eyes. He was watching her with a confident expression as he spooned ice cream onto her womanly parts. Her heat melted it; the ice cream dripped down. And then—much to her amazement, much to her delight—he licked that off, too. It struck her that Nicholas and Dougless made love using ice cream in *A Knight in Shining Armor.* Had Matthew read the copy she'd left at Myrtle's?

What he did next removed any doubt.

It made her quiver. It made her moan anew. It catapulted her into the unbridled ecstasy described in romance novels. In her mind BJ thought, *Thank you, Jesus,* but the only word she uttered was "More!"

CHAPTER SIXTY-THREE

Tulsa

Whether the women in Slade's photograph albums wore formal gowns, ski outfits, safari jackets, or parachutes, everything about them—earrings, hair, makeup, nails, skin—attested to a glamour

Tulsa didn't possess or care about. Obviously Slade did. Why on earth had he proposed to her?

Before Slade left on an errand, he'd told her to feel free to look around. She'd been glancing over the many books on the built-in shelves in his study—travel guides and travel tales, mostly—when she came across the photo albums. They were separated by continent. Curious to see some of the places he'd mentioned, she took down South America and Europe. Each contained stunning photos of jagged snowy peaks, vibrant turquoise seas, sunny green countrysides, and storybook villas and towns. They also contained shots of women. Beautiful, glamorous women.

Tulsa sipped the rest of the latte he'd made her. The espresso tasted like chewing a mouthful of coffee beans. Delicious.

She looked back at the album, wondering whether Slade was attracted to her differences, or if he expected her to become like the women in these pictures. Guy had long ago warned her about Slade's changing enthusiasms. Was she anything more than the flavor of the month?

Tulsa let her eyes take in the living room, with its enormous windows and its enormous whiteness. She wasn't convinced she wanted to live here, away from the Sweet Oak, or that she wanted to spend weeks or months traveling. Most people probably would, but how she was going to decide whether this was the life she wanted, she didn't know.

Last night's extraordinary dinner had been a window onto Slade's world. The crab cakes, the tarragon vinaigrette on fresh greens, and the asparagus hollandaise were pungent and delicious, unlike anything she'd eaten. The lobster, which looked like a giant crawdad, was surprisingly tasty. The chocolate hazelnut torte with raspberry sauce would do Ruby proud. It was a long way from Swanson's chicken potpies or Big Macs.

Between their meals and the bottle of wine they shared, most of which Slade drank, the bill must have come to over $300. He'd left an eighty-dollar tip. The waiter had been attentive, though she wasn't sure he'd worked any harder than a waitress in an Ozarks family restaurant, where a twenty-percent tip for a family of four probably wouldn't reach much more than ten dollars. Still, she liked Slade's generosity.

It had surprised her that her gurgling stomach didn't disturb him last night. She'd lain awake, wired, while he slept, his arm around her. She'd kept asking herself the same question: Did she love him? And she kept reaching the same conclusion: I don't know. He was essentially a kind man, fun to be with, passionate about certain things. She wasn't even sure what love was. In the novels they'd recently read, the heroines all chose men who preferred a simple lifestyle. If she married Slade, she'd be doing the exact opposite.

"Hey, babe."

She hadn't heard him come in. Her heart fluttered. God, she loved those eyes! "Hey."

He was carrying several bags. "I'll be right back." He disappeared down the hallway.

"See anyplace you'd like to go on a honeymoon?" he asked when he returned, sitting beside her.

"I don't know if we're getting married, let alone where to go if we do. But there's a lot of beautiful scenery in these albums. And beautiful companions."

He shrugged. "Passing fancies."

"Did you propose to any of them?"

He sat beside her. "Two, I think."

"They turned you down?" That was hard to imagine.

"No, I changed my mind. When I was younger I was a little impulsive."

"So would you like to take back your proposal to me?"

He lifted her hand and kissed her bare ring finger. "No way."

"Why, Slade? Why me?"

He trailed his fingers lightly over the soul of her foot, tickling it. "Like I told you at the river, you're different. You're fierce. Passionate. Loving. Independent. Not after my money. And you're beautiful. Plus, I suppose I'm a little different now, too. I'm ready to settle down. To one woman, that is. Not one place." He stood and held out his hand.

Rising, she entwined her fingers in his. He led her down the hallway to the master bedroom. Set out on the bed were a strapless black dress, two necklaces of black pearls, and a small pearled black handbag.

"May I?" he said. He twined one of the necklaces around her arm. "Makes a great bracelet, no?"

She took it off. "I've been choosing my own clothes for a long time now."

"I know. But you'll look great in this."

She searched his eyes for some speck of doubt, some indication that he'd heard her the night before. "I told you I don't like black."

"Just try it on. If you don't like how you look, you don't have to wear it."

"I don't have to wear it, period."

"I'm not trying to boss you. I just want my friends to see the woman I see."

"Do you see me, Slade? Or do you just see the woman you want me to be?"

He locked his eyes on hers. "I see who you are. Which I like very much. And who you could be if you wanted. Some of the time. Please. Just try it on."

"And if I say no?"

He waved his hand as if to make the dress vanish. "Then you can wear jeans and a T-shirt." He stepped closer. "Or nothing at all." He kissed her neck.

Jen seemed to whisper in one ear that she needed to dress up for Slade, while Ruby hollered in the other: *compromise*. She took the dress.

"Hey," he said as she walked toward the bathroom, "no need for modesty."

She ignored him. In the bathroom she took off her jeans. When had she last worn a dress before last night? Wasn't it at her mother's funeral? She tugged on the dress, running her hands over the poppy-soft silk that caressed her. She faced the mirror. Slade was right. The way the dress clung flattered her.

The expression on his face when she stepped out of the bathroom stopped her. It was a mixture of open astonishment—and admiration. "God, you're gorgeous." He put his arms around her and turned her to face the huge mirror over the dresser.

In the reflection, a handsome man embraced a chic woman who looked like the women in his photographs: she barely recognized herself.

He lifted her hair off her neck. "How about braiding this?"

"Don't push your luck."

"Okay, but there is one more surprise." He opened a shoe box containing a pair of high heels that looked like they could pierce armor.

"You're kidding," she said.

"Can't wear sandals with this outfit."

"I've never worn heels."

"They're only an inch. And we won't be dancing. You'll like them. You'll see."

"They're nice, Slade," she said. "It all is. But I don't like pretending to be someone I'm not."

"I know this isn't your usual style, but wear it for me tonight. It'll be fun."

She told herself she was being silly. It was just for one night. For his friends. If she truly loved Slade, then she should be willing to do this for him. After all, he was willing to take care of Ruby.

He fastened the pearls around her neck, his fingers brushing her skin like a whisper. The pearls glistened. They were stunning. So why did she feel like she was choking?

In the high heels, Tulsa's feet felt as if they'd been run over by a forklift. Slade, across the room, stood surrounded by a group of his buddies, while she was with a gaggle of women wearing jewelry that twinkled almost as much as the lights outside the window of the banquet room, which was ten floors down from Slade's penthouse. She wasn't sure how the migration of sexes had occurred, but she would probably feel more at home with the men. She would certainly rather be in their shoes.

"We just bought a villa in Sicily," said Kimberly, a woman whose face was unlined but whose neck was wrinkled, as if maybe she'd run out of money halfway through plastic surgery.

Tulsa thought Kimberly might be older than most of the others.

"I thought you liked Paris," said a woman named Lauren, who wore so much heavy perfume, Tulsa felt her nose clog.

"We're keeping our apartment there, but our tastes are changing," Kimberly said. "Less butter and cream. More tomatoes and basil."

"Which do you prefer?" Lauren asked Tulsa. "Sicily or Paris?"

"I haven't been to either."

"Slade will take care of that, I'm sure," said a woman with a ring so huge, it could deck a moose. "You must be thrilled about marrying him."

"I haven't said I would."

"My God." Lauren looked astonished. "How could you not? I can't tell you how many women would love to be in your place."

Tulsa couldn't begin to explain to them how she really felt—the dismay as well as the excitement. She couldn't even explain it to herself.

The group of women parted slightly. A woman with a long neck, thick glistening black hair, and a dancer's sensuous carriage glided toward them.

"I'm Melissa," the woman who had joined the group said. She reached out a hand with long, manicured nails.

"Tulsa." She extended her own callused hand to meet Melissa's smooth one. Jen, who had wanted to do Tulsa's nails, would love Melissa's manicure.

"So you're Tulsa." Melissa ran her eyes up and down Tulsa's body. "A lot of women in this room hoped to marry Slade. Tell us, how did you land him?"

Given Melissa's easy elegance, Tulsa suspected the woman had hooked plenty of men. Why not Slade? "That's a good question," she said.

"Oh, come on, it's just us girls. What's your secret?"

Tulsa turned her palms up to show she really had no answers.

Melissa leaned toward her. "Help us out here. Some of us are still single, while you landed one of Kansas City's most eligible bachelors. Tell us how *you* trapped him. I just can't imagine Slade spending more than five minutes in the *Ozarks*."

If there was no sneer on Melissa's face, there was certainly one in her voice. Tulsa had no intention of allowing this woman to humiliate her. "I used a coon trap," she said, laying on a hillbilly accent.

"A what?"

"Ain't you ever had raccoon steak?" Tulsa said. "It's almost as good as snake possum stew."

"What a quaint sense of humor." Melissa's lip curled. "Slade said you run a . . . canoe business. Is there any money in it?"

"By Ozark standards."

"Enough to buy you a trailer home?"

"Don't forget the whiskey still and banjo."

"I like your spunk," Melissa said with a chuckle. "I'm beginning to see why Slade fell for you."

One of the other women, who wore a white sequined dress, stepped partially in front of Melissa and faced Tulsa. "I'm Genevieve. If you haven't planned your honeymoon, I highly recommend the Bliss Resort in Fiji."

"There may not be a honeymoon," Tulsa said, not wanting these women to keep assuming she would say yes.

"No woman in her right mind would turn Slade down," Genevieve said. "That man is a catch. And like I was saying, at the Bliss Resort, one whole wall of your villa opens up, and you're right on the ocean. It's a little pricey at twelve thousand but well worth it. After all, you only get married once."

"Says who?" Melissa winked at Tulsa.

"Twelve thousand a week?" Tulsa said. "A lot of people in the Ozarks live on less than that a year."

Melissa's eyes glinted with amusement.

"Not a week," Genevieve said. "A night."

"I think Bliss might be a little too much for our guest." Melissa ran her hand over a jeweled bracelet. "She doesn't want to spend her honeymoon in sticker shock."

Tulsa decided she should introduce Melissa to Rupert Clancy. "You're right," she said. "I don't want to spend my honeymoon in much of anything. But like I said, it's premature to talk about honeymoons when I haven't even agreed to marriage."

Melissa looked her up and down. "Your little black sheath is so elegant. Is it a Dior?"

"I've no idea."

"If Slade picked it out, it must be. He's bought so many Dior dresses, he must own stock in the company."

"Lay off, Melissa," Lauren said. "You're just jealous."

Melissa's full, glossy lips tilted up. "Of course I am, darlings. Aren't you?" She turned and headed toward the men.

"Ignore her," Lauren said. "Slade dropped her."

"Who's she going after this time?" Kimberly asked.

"Probably someone with a wedding ring." Lauren turned to Tulsa. "Melissa loves a challenge."

Melissa touched Slade's shoulder and ran her hand along his arm. Slade stepped away from Melissa, who said something that made the men burst into raucous laughter.

"We've got a little place outside Cannes you could use for your honeymoon," said a woman with eyes so dark they looked like shadows. "*If* you decide to marry Slade. And if you don't, I recommend you see a therapist."

The others grinned. Tulsa listened as they—who knew nothing about her—argued about whether she and Slade would most enjoy Cannes, Sicily, Geneva, St. Martin, London, or Rio. It was all so far from anything she'd ever dreamed about. These were Slade's friends. Their world was his world. Did she really mean to leave the river for this?

"Excuse me," she said, and started toward Slade, whose back was to her.

"It's a pretty river," she heard Slade say to Melissa, "but I wouldn't want to be stuck there."

The heel of Tulsa's left shoe caught. She tripped and pitched forward into Melissa, who grabbed Slade's arm. Melissa steadied herself with one hand and Tulsa with the other.

"Whoa, partner," Melissa said, a mock twang in her voice.

Slade put his hand on Tulsa's shoulder. "You okay?"

"Yeah." She nodded to Melissa. "Thanks." The left heel had snapped. The instant Tulsa removed the shoes, her feet stopped hurting. "That's much better," she said.

"You look like you're my size," Melissa said. "Would you like to borrow some heels? I just live a few floors down."

Tulsa massaged the arch of her left foot. "No, thanks. This feels just fine."

"Are you sure?" Slade asked.

"Yep."

"Barefoot," Melissa said. "You really are quaint."

Slade's smile seemed forced. Perhaps her going barefoot embarrassed him. Well, the heels had almost crippled her. If he wanted glamour, there was plenty of it elsewhere in this room. Maybe he needed to take another look around. Maybe she did.

CHAPTER SIXTY-FOUR
Pearl

Seated in Ruby's cheerful kitchen, with its red-trimmed white walls and the furnace cranked up high, Pearl peeled back the plastic covering their TV dinners: roast beef, mashed potatoes and gravy, green beans, and apple dumplings. The steam that rose from their plates carried aromas of beef and baked apples.

"It's not as good as your cooking," Pearl said, "but it's a whole lot easier to fix."

"It's just fine," Ruby said. "Thanks for bringing dinner and for keeping me company."

"You heard anything from Tulsa?"

"No, and I haven't called." Ruby cut up her roast beef and mixed it with the potatoes and gravy. "I'm trying to do like we said a while back and not push her. I do like Slade, though. I hope he could make her happy."

"Seems to me Tulsa's already happy."

"I suppose, though I don't know why she doesn't want a family. It's unnatural."

"I can't see Tulsa being happy barefoot and pregnant in the kitchen," Pearl said.

"I can't see Tulsa doing anything she didn't want to do."

Pearl put butter on her potatoes, let it melt into the gravy, then took a bite. *There.* The creamy flavor of sweet butter made most anything taste good. "Lucky thing Tulsa wasn't born in the Middle Ages," she said, thinking of the world depicted in *The Secret.* "They'd have called her a witch and burned her at the stake."

"You're right," Ruby said. "Imagine, pregnant women back then weren't allowed into church because they were considered unclean. Now, that's just nonsense."

"And priests condemned women who didn't scream in childbirth because they thought that women were *supposed* to suffer to pay for what Eve did. I sure hollered enough birthing Lillian to pave my way into Heaven." The green beans were as mushy as the mashed potatoes and didn't taste much different. "You think it's true, what *The Secret* says the church preached back then?"

"I expect so. Heck, women in this country didn't even get the right to vote until a few years before you and I were born. In some countries, they still can't."

"Imagine if your mama died in childbirth," Pearl

said, "and the church said it was because God was punishing her."

"I'm not sure I'd have believed in God if I lived back then," Ruby said.

Pearl drank milk to help swallow the stringy meat. When she spoke, her voice sounded shaky. "Do you ever wonder . . . I mean, if the priests back then were wrong, maybe they're wrong about things now, too."

"Like homosexuality, maybe?" Ruby said.

It seemed that Ruby's face was full of affection and understanding. "Well," Pearl said, "but the Bible does condemn men laying with men."

"The Bible condemns a lot of things," Ruby said. "Doesn't it say you'll go to hell if you eat shellfish?"

"Well, that's right. It does."

"And it says that wives are supposed to submit to their husbands. Look at how Sherman ordered you around and how Conrad bosses Lillian. Do you think *God* really wants men to rule over women?"

"No." Pearl leaned toward Ruby. "I think the Bible would've been a whole lot different if women had written it."

"Why are you whispering?" Ruby asked.

Pearl hadn't realized she was. "It seems blasphemous to question God."

"You aren't questioning God. You're questioning the men who wrote the Bible. They were just humans. Like Rupert Clancy. And Conrad. And Sherman. You want to follow rules written by them? Heck, Sherman even kept you from singing. Now, *that's* a sin."

Pearl froze.

"What?" Ruby said.

When Ruby was in the ICU, Pearl had promised that if Ruby lived, she would confess the truth to the secret she'd kept for over fifty years. Well, Ruby was alive. "Sherman never heard me sing," she said, letting her shoulders droop.

"He was that set against music?"

"What I mean to say is, it wasn't his fault I stopped singing."

Ruby set down her fork. "I don't understand. Whose fault was it?"

Pearl stirred the food on her tray, mixing together the remaining roast beef and potatoes, the green beans and apples. "My own."

"But you were so happy when you sang."

"When I moved to St. Louis," Pearl said, "some folks from the Grand Ole Opry came to hold auditions. I was sure they'd want me. I sang my favorite song, 'I Fall to Pieces.'"

"You used to sing that song sweeter than a bowlful of honey."

"The Nashville folks didn't think so. They said I didn't have enough range or tonal quality. Said there was no way I'd ever be good enough to sing on the radio."

"Oh, Pearl. I had no idea."

Pearl wadded the napkin in her lap into a tiny ball. "I didn't want folks to know. I wanted them to go on thinking I sang like a radio star. That's why I kept it a secret. I wanted to feel special."

"Is that why you never joined the church choir?"

"I guess so."

"Oh my."

They didn't speak right away, not until Ruby broke the silence. "Your singing used to make me feel so good," she said. "It made a lot of folks feel good, including you. You never should've stopped."

"Maybe not."

"You don't even sing at home?"

"Not since that audition."

"That just breaks my heart. You ought to sing again, Pearl. The world needs music."

"I'm not sure I could even carry a tune anymore."

"I'm betting you could," Ruby said. "You ought to at least try."

Pearl looked at her hands. "All those years, it was easier to blame Sherman. And I guess it was easier to let him boss me."

"Well, it's one thing to *let* someone boss you," Ruby said. "But to say God *wants* men to rule? The Bible's just plain wrong about that."

"Maybe so."

"No 'maybe' about it," Ruby said. "It's wrong. Of course, I know plenty of women who do the wrong thing, too. I like to think that God forgives all of us our sins."

"What sins have you ever committed?" Pearl said. Ruby lowered her face. Was Ruby blushing? "What?"

"I kissed Ed once," Ruby said.

"When?"

"A couple of years ago. For a minute I plumb forgot he was married."

"I always knew Ed had a spark for you," Pearl said. Ed's eyes shone whenever he looked at Ruby. "But I didn't know you felt the same about him."

"If he weren't married, I'd kiss him again. Not that he could replace Clifford. Nobody could do that. It's just that sometimes, the nights get mighty lonely."

"I'm sure God's already forgiven you for that kiss," Pearl said. "You've done so much for other people. You're a good-hearted woman, Ruby Riley."

"Well, so are you," Ruby said. "And your Daniel's a good-hearted young man. Even if homo-sexuality is wrong, and I'm not so sure it is, don't you think God would forgive him?"

Pearl wanted to think that God would love her grandson no less than she did. She looked into Ruby's gentle, loving eyes. Wouldn't God's eyes be just as gentle? Maybe He really wouldn't condemn homosexuals to hell. When you got right down to it, it was awful hard to see how loving someone could ever be a sin.

CHAPTER SIXTY-FIVE
Tulsa

Slade was breathing through his mouth, exhaling little puffs of air with each breath. Tulsa slipped out from beneath his arm, grabbed *The Secret* and underpants from her duffel bag, and tiptoed from the room. The view outside the living-room windows—millions of city lights—made it seem as if the Milky Way had come to Earth. She couldn't see a single real star. At first she thought it was because the city masked them, but then she spotted the clouds racing across the crescent moon to fill the sky.

She slipped into her underpants, then sank onto the hard couch. If only she could sleep. It was after midnight, and she was tired. She rubbed her feet, which ached from the heels she'd clomped around in for far too long. Closing her eyes, she leaned back on the couch and tried counting trout. They swam off. She tried counting bullfrogs. They hopped away.

She sat up. Milk sometimes helped, so she went to the kitchen, opened the refrigerator door, and wrinkled her nose. It smelled like something had died in there. There was wine and beer, meat, vegetables, pâté, and fruit. And a strong, stinky cheese. What she longed for was some of Ruby's cobbler or BJ's butterscotch pudding. Or Pearl's blackberry–sour cream pie. Not cheese that belonged in a casket.

Back in the living room, she pulled the afghan over her and scanned again the ending of *The Secret*. The married heroine, Judith, thinks how she's part of a family, home at last.

That was not how Tulsa felt.

Judith chose a simple life with her new husband far away from the land where she grew up. To Judith, home was where her husband was. Tess in *Montana Sky* opted to abandon a fast life of luxury in Los Angeles for the slower life of her lover on a Montana ranch. And Dougless in *A Knight in Shining Armor* was willing to forgo the conveniences of the twentieth century to live with the man she loved in the Middle Ages. All three women were willing to give up the worlds they'd known for their men.

Rain began to spatter the windows. Tulsa rested her head against the glass. She wanted to feel the rain on her skin. Needed to feel it. Needed to think. She thought best outdoors.

If she went back in the bedroom for her clothes, she might wake Slade. She wasn't ready for that. She took a flannel shirt and dark jacket of Slade's from the hall closet. Both fell below her knees. She didn't want to ruin a pair of the silk slippers he kept on hand, so she grabbed the spare key and slipped out the door barefoot.

The elevator seemed to descend in less than a heartbeat. She told the guard at the desk that she was going for a walk.

He raised bushy black eyebrows. "It's not safe alone. Or barefoot," he said.

"I'll be fine."

Tulsa pushed open the lobby door and stepped outside. Rain pelted her head. It was a mid-September night, hints of autumn in the chilly air. She remembered when she first began to fall for Slade that night on the river, stranded and joking, then hugging as the temperature dropped.

She started down Walnut. The sidewalk felt so different from walking barefoot at the river, where blades of grass tickled her feet and, after a heavy rain, mud squished between her toes. Of course, walking on river rocks sometimes hurt. While the city sidewalk felt rough, wet, and cold, it didn't pain her.

A homeless man huddled under a blanket in the doorway of an office building. The rain seemed to spread the stench of urine. Tulsa felt in the pockets of Slade's jacket, hoping to find cash, but there was nothing. She couldn't very well give the man the jacket, but at least she could make eye contact. "Good evening," she said to him.

The man shrank back and pulled the blanket over his head.

She walked on. Shielding her eyes, she looked

up at the clouds. There was so little sky visible. It was like being on the river, only there, trees blocked her view. Here buildings, slabs of steel and concrete towering above her, hemmed her in. Home at the river smelled of honeysuckle and rich earth, the city of urine and muck.

An occasional car passed, tires swishing against the wet pavement. It seemed she'd been away for only a few minutes, but a bank's clock indicated it was nearly one. More than half an hour had passed; she'd been walking in the rain lost in a fog of her own.

"Hey, baby." A man leaned out the window of a Corvette. "Looking for some action?"

She glanced around to see if there were lights anywhere in case she had to run for it. None. She ignored him and kept walking.

"Night, beautiful."

The Corvette sped down the street. She stopped. Slade's jacket wasn't rainproof. The flannel shirt was damp now. She was chilled, and it probably wasn't all that wise to be walking alone.

She headed back toward Slade's building. The homeless man still huddled, blanket over his head.

"Find what you were looking for?" the lobby guard said to her.

His question startled her, but maybe she had. It wasn't just the look, feel, and smell of the city. It was everything: the penthouse, towering above and sealed off from the world. The black dress and high heels. The debate about whether they should honeymoon in Rio or Rome. The fancy restaurant. The silk slippers. None of it was who she was—or who she wanted to be. "I believe I did," she said to the guard. "Good night." She took the elevator back to the penthouse.

When she unlocked Slade's door and stepped inside, he was pacing, the plush white guest robe over one arm. Shirtless and dressed in his creased tan pants, he looked incredibly sexy.

"Where have you been?" he said, helping her off with his wet jacket and shirt, then wrapping her in the robe.

"Walking. Thanks." She clung to the front of the robe, so soft it was like being cloaked in a cloud.

"You shouldn't be out there alone at night," he said. "This isn't the Ozarks, you know."

"I do know that, yes." At home they didn't lock their doors. She never feared darkness.

Slade studied her with a wary expression. "What?" he said.

She didn't respond immediately.

He held out his hand. "Let's go back to bed so I can warm you properly. We can talk there."

She didn't take his hand. "I can't live here, Slade."

"What?" Mouth open, he looked bewildered.

"I know you love the city."

"Music. Art. Stores. Theaters. Restaurants. What's not to love?"

"Crowds. Clutter. Concrete. Noise. Traffic jams. Crime."

"It beats living in the Ozarks." He sounded angry. "Going to bed with the clamor of bugs and waking up to the same thing day after day."

"But it isn't the same," she said, wanting him to feel the river as she felt it. "Things change with the seasons. The river changes. The trees. The birds. Everything's always changing."

"Oh, please."

His tone of disdain surprised her.

"I'm talking real change," he said. "The Amazon flows through jungles. The Nile through deserts. The Po through the Alps. How can you even begin to compare all that to one little river? You need to travel the world. To taste more of life."

His tone grated her already raw emotions. "Don't tell me what I need," she snapped.

"To compare one river with all the rest of the world is pretty damned provincial." Slade paced a few steps in one direction, then back, then another. He stopped near her. "Are you afraid of travel? Is that it? Because with a few precautions, it's safe."

"No, I'm not afraid."

"I guess not. Your fearlessness is one of the things I love about you. So if it isn't fear, then what is it?"

She wasn't sure he'd ever understand. "I'm not a rolling stone. I want to gather moss. It's soft and it's green, and I like the way it feels."

He put his hand on her forearm. "I get it. It's change that scares you. Of course. You moved so much growing up, it's no wonder. But that was different. You had no voice then. You do now."

She gave his hand a gentle squeeze. "Yes, and I like my life. I like waking up to herons fishing, and birds singing and mist rising off the water. I like waking up to Ruby's French toast and Guy's jokes. To fresh air and kingfishers swooping along the river."

"You'd still have all that, just not as much. I hate to be trite, but I can show you the world and help you become a fuller person."

Tulsa took off the robe and stood before him in her wet underpants. "I'm not a doll for you to dress up or a broken window for you to fix."

"I know that." His eyes roamed her.

"Do you? I told you I don't like black dresses, and you deliberately went out and bought me one."

"You looked gorgeous."

"I'm not glamorous, Slade, or sophisticated. I'm a country girl. A river rat. And I'm fine with that. I'm sorry you aren't."

"What exactly are you saying?"

She swallowed hard. "I can't marry you."

He scoffed, his features creasing in an angry frown. "I'm sure glad I wasted all that time in the Ozarks."

His words stung. "Wasted?"

"I thought you loved me."

She took a deep breath to steady herself. "I did, too. But Ruby always says that compromise is the essence of any relationship. The fact neither of us is willing to compromise proves that while we may care for each other a whole lot, it's not enough to make a marriage work."

"Most of the women at that party would marry me in a heartbeat," he said.

"And they'd be lucky to. But I'm not most women."

"Which is what I love about you."

"I'm sorry. I don't like hurting you."

Slade crossed his arms and shook his head.

Tulsa felt her chest tighten. "You've helped me understand what I want and what I don't want, which things I can compromise and which I can't. And I've learned how much I want to love someone, really love him, with all the joy and all the heartache that love demands. So thank you."

"I'm glad you were able to use me."

"That's not fair, Slade. I'm grateful for all your help with the business, but since neither of us is willing to give up our homes, we didn't use each other. We really cared for each other, just not enough."

He turned his back to her. Rain struck the large plate-glass windows and slid down.

"What will you do about Ruby?" he said.

Tulsa closed her eyes and tried to take a deep

breath, but the most she could manage was a shallow catch. "I don't know, but I'll find a way to pay you back."

He spun around. "Do you think that's what I want?"

"No, I guess not. I'm sorry."

"I'd write you a check right now to buy the pills till Medicare kicks in, if Ruby would take it."

"Thank you. But she wouldn't, and she keeps the books. She'd know. You have a generous heart."

His eyes brimmed with tears. Or maybe she was just seeing him through her own.

"You're leaving tonight, aren't you?" he said.

"I think I should."

"So I'll never see you again." His voice caught.

Tears spilled down her cheeks. "Please don't say that. I'd hate to lose your friendship."

"There's nothing I can say or do to change your mind?"

"No. I'm sorry, but no."

"Well then, I'm going to my study," he said. "I can't bear to watch you leave."

"Will you hug me first?"

He put his arms around her and gave her a stiff, brief hug, then released her and walked briskly from the room.

She wiped away tears, put on her jeans and T-shirt, stuffed her things in her duffel bag, and stood in the bedroom asking herself if she was making a mistake. The clang of heavy-metal music burst from the other room, almost a scream.

She slung her duffel over her shoulder and walked out.

The cold parking lot, with its low ceiling lit by fluorescent lights, stank of exhaust and motor oil. She hurried to her dusty old Ford pickup parked amid the gleaming cars, started the engine, and steered Big Red toward home.

CHAPTER SIXTY-SIX
Ruby

The creaking of the stairs that woke her before six in the morning sent Ruby leaping from the bed to grab her shotgun. There was no way she would lie there like a patsy while someone robbed her blind. Or worse.

The stairs creaked again. Ruby clutched the wood fore-end of her Remington, pumped a round—*kachunk*—and flung open her bedroom door.

The intruder froze, hands raised in surrender. "Don't shoot!"

The familiar voice slapped Ruby fully awake. "Tulsa? Why are you creeping up the stairs? And why are you home at this hour?" Ruby remembered the gun. She set the safety and leaned it against the wall. Tulsa's eyes were welling with tears that could mean only one thing. "Oh, honey," Ruby said, opening her arms.

Tulsa fell into her embrace. Ruby patted her granddaughter's back. "What happened?" she asked softly when Tulsa's crying subsided.

"I don't want to live Slade's life," Tulsa said. "I know you wanted me to marry him. And I wanted to, I really did. For both our sakes. But I don't love him. Not enough."

"It's okay." Ruby took a wadded-up but unused tissue from her nightgown pocket and handed it to Tulsa. "I'm proud of you, honey."

Tulsa wiped her eyes, then the dribble beneath her nose. "For what?"

"For having the courage to follow your heart."

Tulsa squeezed Ruby's hand. "I'll figure out some way to bring in money," she said. "But you've got to promise me you'll keep taking your pills."

Ruby squeezed back. Tulsa gave a tremulous smile and her shoulders slumped. She must be interpreting Ruby's squeeze as agreement. If so, she was wrong, but they needn't deal with that now. There would be plenty of time to set Tulsa straight.

CHAPTER SIXTY-SEVEN
Tulsa

A day later, Tulsa hung up the phone after telling Rupert Clancy she wanted to see him and wiped her lips. Good God. Was selling Clancy the land and cabins they'd bought from Ed really the only way to save Ruby?

Tulsa had reminded Ruby earlier that she'd agreed to keep taking the pills. Ruby had just smiled. Tulsa knew what that smile meant: Ruby would take the pills she had, but she wouldn't buy more. Deciding whether to sacrifice Ruby, their home, or the Sweet Oak River Oasis canoe business had been easy.

But Clancy? Ruby might never forgive her. The six realtors Tulsa had called yesterday had all said the market for Ozark land was slow, and that the cabins raised the price beyond most buyers. In all likelihood, it could take a few months to sell off the property they'd bought from Ed.

They didn't have months.

If only she'd loved Slade enough to marry him, she wouldn't have had to call the one man she loathed. The thought of Slade's infectious smile made her so sad she nearly cried.

"Good morning." Guy was at the door.

"Is it?" She leaned back in the chair as Guy entered the office. She took in the antler rack with cabin keys, the smell of cherry pipe tobacco, the window framed by maples and oaks. She would have to leave all this, but at least Ruby could stay.

Guy sat on the desk near her. "Hard, huh?" he said.

There was such warmth in his voice and his soft brown eyes. She wanted him to hold her, but she didn't dare ask. This wasn't the time to cry. She made her voice sound gruff. "I'll be fine." And she would. Of course she was sad, but she would get over Slade, just as she'd gotten over Warren, who wasn't really the man for her either. Maybe no one ever would be.

"Did you love Slade?" Guy asked.

"Not enough, apparently."

"I'm sorry it's hard."

She brushed away tears.

"We've just got a few canoes going out today," he said. "I'll handle them."

"Okay, thanks." She stood. "I need to run into town."

"What for?" Guy said.

"Jen lost her copy of the book for tonight's discussion. I told her I'd drop mine off." Her face felt hot. Had she ever lied to Guy?

"What?" he said softly, his eyes locked on hers.

"Nothing." She grabbed her keys off the rack

and shoved open the screen door. "I'll be back in a bit."

"Tulsa?"

She stopped but didn't turn around. She wasn't sure she could face him and keep lying.

"It's Slade's loss," Guy said.

While she drove toward Clancy's, Tulsa's mind raced and circled and tripped on itself. At the top of the hill that led down to his place, she pulled over. The woods that flanked the road were thick, the once vibrant green leaves dotted with the early yellows of autumn. A woodpecker drummed its unseen presence. If only it were tapping out Morse code from the universe telling her how to save the Oasis.

She hadn't told Ruby her plans. Hopefully, with the sale of Ed's and the closing of the canoe business a done deal, there would be no point in Ruby's refusing to take her pills. Of course Guy would be furious, though not as furious as Ruby.

Although marriage to Slade would have made this trip unnecessary, and although she would miss him, she didn't doubt that she'd made the right choice.

In an early chapter of *The Secret*, the heroine declared that she'd never let herself fall in love because it meant too much heartbreak. It was true that love could break your heart, but her relationship with Slade had brought hints of how much love could also fill it. A man didn't have to be rich and handsome or a knight in shining armor. He just had to be the right man for her.

A crow flew by, cawing like it was scolding her for stalling. If she delayed much longer, Clancy might leave. She was already twenty minutes late, and she needed him. She put the truck in gear.

The dogs soon materialized, barking, lunging at her tires. Clancy's version of a welcoming committee. It figured.

He was sitting on the porch stairs of his sprawling, cedar-planked modern house, so unlike the compact one- and two-story white houses that dominated the Ozarks. His long hair half hid his face. She stopped her truck. Clancy made no move to calm the dogs. So that was how he intended to play it. Fine. She turned off the ignition, leaned back against the seat, closed her eyes, and waited while the dogs howled. The minutes stretched like hot taffy.

A whistle silenced the dogs. She opened her eyes. The dogs trotted to the porch and lay beside Clancy. She had no intention of starting this conversation. It was bad enough that she would have to close the business. Thankfully Guy had the skills to find work locally: carpentry or mechanics. She'd scanned the want ads. There was nothing around unless she could get hired on at Roto-Rooter, and she wasn't sure they even hired women. She would have to move away.

Clancy didn't rise, but he signaled her to roll

down the truck window, which she did. "What did you want to see me about?" he asked.

A thrill spurted through her. She'd won the first round, though there was a long way to go till the final bell. "I'm considering selling the land and cabins we got from Ed."

"Why?"

She made herself shrug. "Too much work."

He barked a laugh. "Scared of losing your place, more likely. I heard Ruby's sick."

"She was. She's fine now."

Clancy spat on the ground. His saliva dampened a small spot of dirt. Damn the man. She started the engine, shifted the truck into reverse, and began to back out, half wishing he'd let her go.

"Hold on," he said.

She put the truck back in park and turned off the motor. "I'll take what you offered Ed," she said.

"Seven? You won't get it from me."

"Why's that?"

He took a minute to answer; his pale green eyes studied her face. "Ed wasn't desperate. You're sweating desperation. Why else would you sell to me?"

She'd lost that round. "Land's worth the same now as it was then," she said.

"Not to me. See, I don't really want Ed's now."

"What!"

"Nope. I want all of it."

"All of what?"

"Ed's place. *And* yours. Your business. Your house. I want every goddamned acre of land and plank of lumber. Oh, and I want all your canoes and gear."

He couldn't be serious. "That's crazy."

"The way I hear it, you're going to lose it all soon."

"No, we won't." If only she believed that. Clancy was right; she was sweating desperation. "You were willing to buy just Ed's place before."

"Then, yeah. I knew there was no chance you'd sell everything. Now you don't have much choice."

Tulsa clung to the steering wheel. "Losing our home could kill Ruby."

Clancy unwrapped a wad of bubble gum and stuck it in his mouth. "Ruby convinced Faith to leave me. I lost her. And you. I would've married Faith and adopted you, you know."

"Yeah, right. From what I heard, you never wanted me around. You always left me with Ruby."

"Sure, when you were a baby. But I'd have loved to have a little girl to spoil. And besides, you already know I hate the canoe business. All that racket on the river. Once I own your place, I can sit back and enjoy the peace and quiet."

Tulsa couldn't have swallowed even a sip of water, her throat was so tight. "Please. If you saw me as your daughter then, help me now."

He blew a large bubble, then popped it. "Too late for that." He rose slowly, the dogs rising with him. "I'm just going to wait it out and help myself to your place when the bank forecloses."

"So why did you agree to see me?"

He shrugged. "I was bored."

Tulsa wanted to appear tough, but at that moment she felt so vulnerable, she suspected her voice sounded like a six-year-old's. "You know, Rupert, you're a leech, sucking the life out of good people like my mom. You made her leave you. Not Ruby. You're just not man enough to face it."

Clancy shrugged. "If I were you, I'd stop wasting time and hightail it home. Enjoy your place while you can. You won't have it for long."

The slam of the screen door when Clancy went inside triggered the dogs into frenzied barking. One of them leapt up against the truck, its snarling mouth with its pointed teeth only inches from her throat. She rolled up the window.

CHAPTER SIXTY-EIGHT
BJ

BJ squirmed. Why did Ruby have all the living-room lights on? It was too bright. She couldn't stand the way everyone but Tulsa was looking at her: Ruby, Pearl, Jen. Could she help it if she had a different opinion of *The Secret*? Oh, they all liked the book; their discussion had made that clear. However, everyone but Tulsa—who for some reason looked like she was sitting on thumbtacks—disagreed with her about the possible merit of keeping at least some things secret.

"I'm just saying that secrets aren't necessarily lies," BJ said, patting the book's cover.

"How are they different?" Jen said.

"Well, like if you kept your birth date secret. That's not a lie."

"We're not talking about birth dates," Pearl said. "We're talking about big lies. Like in the book. They lied about who Judith's father was. They kept the truth secret from her."

BJ's face felt hot. Hot. Hot.

"Are you okay?" Ruby said. "You look awful flushed."

"Oh, I'm fine. Just a hot flash." She undid her top two buttons to be more convincing about the hot flash. "You know, there are *some* secrets that are good. Would you want to know who your mother was if she was, say, a serial killer?" There. She'd proven her point.

"Yes," Jen said, and everyone but Tulsa nodded.

"Well, I wouldn't," BJ said. "Some lies are more comforting than the truth."

"You know something you aren't telling?" Pearl asked.

BJ shook her head so hard, her brain seemed to rattle. What she didn't understand was why Tulsa was so red-faced.

"I sometimes tell customers their haircuts look good even when they don't," Jen said. "I guess some lies are just kindnesses."

BJ jabbed a finger at Jen. "Exactly."

"Don't do me any kindnesses like that," Pearl said. "I don't want to go around looking like a poodle."

BJ undid another button, realized it made her bra show, and refastened it.

Ruby frowned.

"What's wrong, Ruby?" Tulsa said, anxiety in her voice.

"Nothing," Ruby said. "And if you don't stop hovering, honey, I'm going to go drown myself just to get a little privacy."

"That's not funny," Tulsa said.

"It wasn't meant to be."

Jen scooted to the edge of the sofa, shifting her gaze back and forth between them. "It's like Lily in *Montana Sky* when she goes stir-crazy. Remember? She's recuperating and nobody will let her do anything till she blows up at them."

"Yeah, but that's a novel," Tulsa said. "It's your own fault, Ruby. When I asked if you felt okay before your heart attack, you always said you did. You kept how you really felt secret."

"Tulsa's got a point," Pearl said.

Ruby just smiled. "Let's get back to the book," she said.

"There's a difference between a white lie or a little fib and a big lie," Pearl said. "Not telling someone who her father is, like in *The Secret*, that's a game stopper."

If only she could dunk her own hot face in a bucket of ice, BJ thought. She didn't know whether to keep up the lie about Guy's father, as Guy had insisted, or risk alienating her friends—and her son—by telling the truth.

The outside office door flew open. Guy burst into the living room, his hair tousled, his eyes wild. He looked like he'd just been blown in on a tornado. Guy glared at Tulsa. "Clancy's bragging that you tried to sell him Ed's, and he laughed in your face."

"What!" Ruby said.

Tulsa raised her chin. "I thought I could save our home. And Ruby."

"What are you talking about?" Ruby said.

"You'd close the Oasis?" Guy said.

"Sell to Clancy?" Ruby said. "What in tarnation were you thinking?"

Tulsa's eyes avoided Ruby at first, then locked on her face. "I know you, Ruby. I know you won't take your pills if it means losing the Oasis. There's no way I'll let you die."

"Die?" Pearl said.

"We all die," Ruby said. "I've had a good life."

Guy towered over the seated Tulsa. When he spoke, his voice was softer. "I'll take a job with a contractor. The pay's decent. Between that and odd jobs, I might be able to bring in enough so you could keep the Oasis going."

BJ fell back in her chair, her hand on her heart. Her son, who hated taking orders, would willingly get a job working for someone else away from the river?

"No," Tulsa said. "I'd take a job bartending or something if it would bring in enough, and *you* could keep the Oasis going."

Watching Tulsa and Guy square off over who was going to take a job neither wanted, it struck BJ just how much Tulsa and her son loved Ruby. And each other. Should she confess to Tulsa and the others despite her promise to Guy to stay silent? Would Tulsa ever talk to her again, or would she be like her mother, Faith, who was so angry about Buddy she wouldn't even take BJ's phone calls? Confessing was the right thing to do, but having just been able to forgive herself and to feel forgiven by God, she dreaded the possibility of renewed blame. Look at the book. Judith would never forgive her mother. Never. And what would BJ's cousin Marjorie say?

"I've done the calculations a thousand times," Tulsa said. "Neither of us could make enough. We'd have to triple our expected off-season business. And if we did, we'd need both of us to handle things. The house and business are all bundled together in that loan. If we can't keep up with the payments, we lose everything. That's why I went to Clancy. I thought maybe he'd be willing to buy what was Ed's and let us keep the rest."

No one spoke for a while. The silence seemed to suck the air from the room.

Tulsa looked at Ruby. "It's all my fault. I should never have let you take out that loan."

"That was my decision," Ruby said. "And it's exactly why I'm not buying any more pills."

"Now, that's just nonsense," Pearl said. "Nobody's going to let you kill yourself."

"I'll do whatever it takes to save you, Ruby," Tulsa said.

"I know it's not the same as living at the river, Ruby," Pearl said, "but you could always come live with me."

Ruby looked like she was trying to skewer Tulsa with her eyes. She answered Pearl without glancing around. "Thanks, but that won't be necessary." She kept her gaze on Tulsa. "I can't believe you'd go behind my back like that. And to Clancy!"

Tulsa glared right back. "And I can't believe you'd think I'd just let you die."

"You should at least have told me, Tulsa," Guy said. "Not gone off on your own. That was just plain stupid."

BJ's eyes fell on the soft white cover of *The*

Secret. When Judith learned the truth, it made her stronger. Besides, lies were wrong. Big lies, anyway. Very, very wrong.

"Tulsa, Guy's not your brother," she blurted out. Or thought she did. Nobody reacted. Maybe she'd just said it in her mind.

"I forbid you from selling to anyone, especially Clancy," Ruby said.

Tulsa held Ruby's angry gaze. "I will *not* let you die. And mine's the only name on the deed now, remember?"

"Tulsa, Guy isn't your brother." BJ was pretty sure she'd said it aloud this time.

Tulsa, Ruby, and Guy looked on the verge of arguing further . . . until what she'd said sank in. They turned to stare at her. Everyone did. BJ picked up her copy of *The Secret* as if the book could explain it all. No one spoke. They all seemed frozen in place. "What I mean, Tulsa, is that Buddy wasn't Guy's father."

Tulsa's mouth practically hung open. "Who was?"

"Travis," BJ said.

"Who?" Ruby said.

BJ looked at the book in her hands. Confession hadn't been this hard in the book. "My cousin Marjorie's husband, Travis."

No one said anything for a moment.

"You slept with your cousin's husband?" Pearl said.

"*And* Buddy?" Ruby said.

BJ felt herself shrivel. She riveted her gaze on her clasped hands as she confessed the truth about Buddy and Travis.

When she had finished, Tulsa turned to Guy. "Did you know about this?"

"For the last three months," he said.

"Why didn't you tell me?"

"Travis is scum," he said. "But I like Marjorie. And I didn't think it made any difference."

Summoning all of her strength, BJ said, "I was so ashamed. And I never *said* Buddy was Guy's father. But, Tulsa, your mom told everyone what I did with Buddy. I didn't want people to know I'd betrayed Marjorie, too, and I didn't want Marjorie to know. Everybody just assumed Guy's father was Buddy. I didn't think it would hurt anything."

"I don't believe this," Tulsa said.

The chair felt so hard. BJ shifted position. "I'm really sorry. I almost told everybody years ago, but Travis and Marjorie lived outside West Plains, and then they moved to Arkansas. And we moved. Buddy was gone. And Faith. There didn't seem to be any point in telling. And I was still so ashamed."

"So why are you telling us now?" Tulsa said.

BJ didn't want to put ideas in Tulsa's head. Maybe she was just imagining things, but it seemed that all of their lives would take different turns if the truth came out. She looked back at *The Secret*, still in her hands. She'd been wrong to keep Guy's real father secret, let alone sleep with

Travis and Buddy, but the truth about what that would mean for everyone else was theirs to hash out. She held up the book. "It just seemed like time to confess."

Tulsa and Guy looked at each other, then looked away. It was the first time BJ had ever seen them embarrassed with each other. If only she'd been honest from the start. Still. It had taken her almost thirty years to forgive herself. She thought Guy and God had forgiven her. Maybe the others would, too. Even Marjorie. If not, she would still have done the right thing in confessing. She would have to tell Matthew as well. Hopefully he would understand, but if he didn't, then he didn't. She sat up straight. For once nothing about her hurt. Not her back, not her throat, not her shoulders, not her feet, not her head. In fact, she felt a whole dress size smaller knowing she'd finally come clean. She should have told the truth a long time ago.

CHAPTER SIXTY-NINE
Tulsa

Tulsa put her hand on the back of an easy chair to steady herself. Guy scowled at her. She scowled right back. She may not have told him she was going to Clancy's, but at least she hadn't neglected to tell him they weren't related.

"Well, now, that *is* a real humdinger," Pearl said to BJ, "but let's back up a minute. Ruby, how many days' worth of pills have you got left?"

"Thirty-one. And I can promise you all that I won't take anything if Tulsa sells the Oasis, especially to Clancy."

Tulsa reached for Ruby's hand, but her grandmother kept both buried in her armpits. "You're my oasis, Ruby. I can lose the business. Not you."

"How much do the pills cost?" Jen's face looked full of the same fear Tulsa felt.

"Ten thousand a month until Medicare D kicks in," Ruby said, "which wouldn't be until January. Slade paid for two months, but that's still twenty thousand we don't have. Plus we've used up most of our savings that we needed to get us through the off-season."

Pearl whistled.

"I wish I were rich," BJ said.

"Ruby, please." Tulsa heard the desperation in her own voice. "Let me buy your pills."

"No," Ruby said. "Twenty thousand dollars for pills means that much less for the business, and it's in real danger."

They all fell quiet. The only sound in the room was the rumble of someone's stomach.

Pearl broke the stillness. "Remember the old pie suppers folks used to have?"

Tulsa frowned. Pearl shouldn't be talking about pie at a time like this.

"That was a long time ago," Ruby said.

· "A supper of pies?" BJ looked downright eager.

"Folks used to raise money for people in need by auctioning off pies at a special dinner," Pearl said, scanning all of them before turning back to Ruby. "We could hold an old-time pie supper to raise money for your pills."

"But how would that bring in more than a few hundred dollars?" Tulsa asked.

"We'd make it a real shindig," Pearl said. "Offer a barbecue. Some prizes. Sell raffle tickets."

"For the pies?" Jen said.

"Those and anything we can get folks to donate," Pearl said.

Ruby blinked. "Whose pies?"

Pearl raised her hands, palms up. "I could make a few."

Silence again settled over the room.

Ruby looked almost as stunned as she had at BJ's confession. "You swore never to make another pie," Ruby said.

"I suppose I'm allowed to change my mind."

"Lots of folks would buy raffle tickets for a chance at one of your pies." BJ leaned forward as she spoke. "I will. I'll buy several."

"We could sell tickets in Fiddle and West Plains," Jen said. "Through the stores."

"And the churches," BJ added.

Jen nodded. "We could raffle off a year's worth of my manicures and pedicures, too."

"Heck," Pearl said, "we might as well auction off the recipe for my blackberry–sour cream pie."

Someone gasped. Tulsa wasn't sure who, but the gasp certainly expressed her own astonishment.

BJ bounced in her chair. "That's a prize I'd like to win! And we could sell my churches. We could get six or seven hundred dollars apiece. I've got ten. That would buy some pills."

Tulsa's pulse jackhammered. Guy's eyes looked about to explode out of his head. Their questions came out simultaneously. Hers—"Really?"—and Guy's—"You'd give up your churches?"

BJ sat straighter. "I don't need them anymore. I've got God in my heart."

From what Tulsa had heard, she wasn't sure if it was God or Matthew filling BJ's heart, but she didn't care. If the churches sold, it would help buy the pills Ruby needed and maybe buy them enough time to save their business.

"Are you sure you want to sell your churches?" Ruby said.

"I am. It's a little bit of penitence for my lies."

Tulsa wasn't sure she was ready to buy BJ's penitence, but she would think about that later. "We could raffle off some free float trips," she said.

Guy nodded. "And a guided float trip. Plus a weekend in one of the cabins."

"Good."

"I'll bet a lot of merchants in West Plains and

Fiddle will donate prizes," Jen said. "Ruby, you've got a lot of friends."

Pearl seconded Jen. "More than you know. I'm sure we can get all kinds of things donated to raffle off."

Guy began pacing. "Wanda's brother works at the paper. I bet he'd write up an article. And I bet we could get donations from a lot of outdoor-gear stores, sporting-goods stores, and fly shops. Maybe some would even sell raffle tickets."

Ruby took a tissue from her pocket and dabbed at her eyes. "Thank you. Thank all of you." Her voice quavered.

Ruby was always urging her to open herself to love, Tulsa thought. Though Ruby meant with a man, what Tulsa felt at that moment was an opening to the love that was in this room, the love of their loyal, generous friends. "When would we hold it?"

"October eighteenth," Pearl said. "That gives us about a month to get things organized and have the raffle before you run out of pills."

Ruby sat straighter. "We should call the day something."

"You mean like Super Saturday?" BJ said.

"More river-oriented. Like River Delight. Only not that."

"River Escapade?" Jen said, then frowned. "No. No pizzazz."

"People would know it's at the river," Tulsa

said. "Maybe we should mention autumn to remind folks they can still float after summer."

Pearl clicked her tongue. "How about Autumn Delight? Nah."

"Autumn Ecstasy?" BJ suggested.

"Close," Ruby said.

Nobody spoke for a minute. Tulsa thought of Autumn Pinnacle but dismissed it as not quite right. "Autumn Rapture," she said. Good God. She was thinking like a romance novelist.

"Would it make folks think of the end-of-the-world Rapture?" BJ asked.

"If it does," Pearl said, "it oughta get their attention. Great title, Tulsa."

"I'll raffle off working on cars and doing home repairs," Guy said.

He wasn't her brother. Tulsa's thoughts tumbled around her mind. How had BJ managed to keep his real father secret for almost thirty years? And could a raffle possibly bring in enough money?

"We'll need to raise a lot," Ruby said. "We've got to bring in enough to keep the business going, too. Twenty thousand won't do it."

"I'll talk to merchants in Fiddle and West Plains about raffle prizes," Jen said.

"I'll help," BJ said.

"Good," Pearl said. "I'll check with the local churches about supplying food."

Guy looked at Tulsa. "Bet we could get more

fly shops to sponsor us if we offer free publicity."

"You're right. And we'll mail out letters to anybody who ever floated with us."

"It just might work," Ruby said, her face lit up so bright, it was like the sun was shining through her eyes.

Tulsa gave a short cough before speaking. "There's so much to do. I say we hold off on the next book until after Autumn Rapture."

"Agreed," Pearl said. Jen and BJ nodded.

Ruby, however, was looking at her with narrowed eyes. "You're not trying to end the group, Tulsa. Are you?"

"No." The next words tumbled out before she had time to think about them. "I wouldn't, even if I could."

Ruby smiled. "Thatta girl."

Guy crossed the room to stand in front of Tulsa. "You don't sell. Not to anybody."

"I won't if we make enough. Providing you promise not to take another job."

"For now. But if we don't bring in enough, you still don't sell."

"Especially not to Clancy," Ruby said.

Pearl held up her hand to still them. "Let that dog lie for now," she said. "We'll give this our best shot and then see where things stand."

Pearl was right. "Okay," Tulsa said, "but, Ruby, you keep taking those pills. Promise?"

"For now."

Tulsa opened her mouth to protest but then closed it.

Guy began ticking off the steps on his fingers. "We contact merchants, churches, customers, and friends to get prizes to raffle off, make flyers, print tickets."

"Wait." Tulsa rummaged through an end table drawer until she found a notepad and pen. "I'll write down exactly what we need to do to pull this off." She began to jot down ideas. "We're not leaving anything to chance."

CHAPTER SEVENTY

Pearl

Pearl's eyes drifted to the white cover of *The Secret* beside her on the kitchen table. The story haunted her. She squirted whipped cream into the ritual bedtime cups of hot chocolate she'd fixed herself and Daniel. Daniel had glowed when he was with Hank.

"I'll help you bake the pies," Daniel said. He dipped his spoon into the drink and licked it clean, catlike.

Daniel was a lovely young man, sweet and caring. It was better for him to be true to himself. She hadn't been. She'd wanted to live a big life, to sing and travel, to see the world, or at least parts of it. Instead she'd allowed Sherman to take that away from her. She'd given him the authority in order to spare herself her sense of failure. She'd surrendered so much. And yet, she'd also helped raise Daniel, helped shape him into the gentle young man he was. Maybe her life hadn't been small so much as ordinary.

"How many pies should we make?" Daniel said. "Ten? Twenty?"

"We'll start with a dozen." Steam rose from the cups, carrying the sweet fragrance of the drink. She wasn't sure which she liked more about chocolate, its taste or its aroma.

"Mom called me," Daniel said, his voice wistful. "Dad doesn't know she did."

"Good for her! What did she have to say?"

"She wants me to come for Thanksgiving, but Dad says no."

It struck her then, the thought that if she were pregnant in medieval Scotland, Daniel's father would have been the priest who called her unclean and forbade her from entering his church, just as surely as he'd forbidden Daniel from entering his home. And he would have quoted the Bible to back him up.

"You said you left Hank because he was bossy?" she asked.

"Just like Grandpa. And Dad."

She pressed the nozzle on the whipped cream can to add more topping. It made a familiar whooshing sound. "You told Hank how you felt? You argued with him?"

Daniel frowned like she was making as much sense as a talking poodle. "If you really love each other," he said, "you don't have to fight. You understand each other."

"Honey, who told you that? The tooth fairy?"

"But you never fought with Grandpa, and Mom doesn't fight with Dad."

He was right on both counts. Unfortunately. "That's not true love. It's surrender. Jocelyn and Colt fight all the time. So do Ben and Willa, and Nicholas and Dougless. Sunny and Ty. Judith and Iain."

"Who?"

She'd forgotten they weren't real. "The lovers in romance novels. They argue a lot. But they love each other."

"Romance novels?" Daniel's skepticism was as apparent in his voice as on his face.

"If I'd argued with your grandfather, maybe we'd both have been happier."

Daniel scratched his head, mussing his red hair. "Gran, what are you telling me?"

Did she really want to say this? Well, it seemed right. How did anyone ever know for sure? "Give it another try with Hank, Daniel."

"What?" He gaped like she'd just told him to shoot her.

"Fight with Hank. Not physically. Argue. Maybe

it won't work out. Maybe it will. But if you don't try, if you don't talk about the things that rile you, then your relationship doesn't have a chance. And neither will any other relationship."

She stood and walked to the shelf that held her romance novels. Any of them would do. She pulled one out. *Savage Thunder*. "Read this," she said, handing the book to him. "It might give you some ideas." And while she was at it, she would go ahead and send her daughter her copy of *The Secret*. Maybe the book's story of how one woman risks her marriage to stand up for herself and other women would help give Lillian some gumption.

Daniel ran his fingers over the cover of *Savage Thunder*, with its image of a half-naked man and woman embracing. "Colt Thunder? He looks hot."

"Read it. And go back to Hank, Daniel. I'm going to bed." She set her cup in the sink and started out.

"Gran?"

She looked back at him.

"I love you," he said.

"I love you, too." He was so young, her grandson. Sometimes she forgot that. "Good night, Danny."

"Sweet dreams, Gran. See you in the morning."

"Don't take this wrong, sweetie, but I really hope not."

PART SIX

OCTOBER

CHAPTER SEVENTY-ONE
Tulsa

An unusual early October storm whipped the trees in gusts up to forty-five and dropped nearly two inches of rain in just a few hours. Three days after that, the river was clear but still high and running fast. Tulsa hadn't seen much of Guy since BJ's stunning confession some two weeks before. He'd spent most of that time driving around the western and southern portions of the state, talking with outdoor gear and fly shop owners. Most had been willing to sell raffle tickets, and quite a few had donated prizes.

Tulsa missed Guy, but she had welcomed time alone to try to adjust to the fact they weren't related. Hopefully he would be back before the weekend, however, when they had a troop of Girl Scouts scheduled. Given that it was especially vital to keep the river safe in the colder autumn weather, when overturning a canoe could be dangerous, she had decided to float the most popular six miles of the Sweet Oak to be sure the storm hadn't brought down trees or limbs that would create hazards for floaters.

Tulsa turned in at the Peterson place and drove to the river's edge. She unloaded the canoe off the top of Big Red and took out the paddles, chain saw, and hatchet she'd brought in case she needed to clear fallen trees or branches. Breathing deep, she inhaled the fragrances of wet autumn leaves and a vague hint of apple.

The wind gusted, and she buttoned her bulky jacket, a lumberjack plaid wool. Though it was a brilliant autumn day, the sky a radiant blue, the wind made it feel more like winter. In heavy rubber boots that came almost to her knees, she waded into the clear water. Tulsa's shoulders dropped, her body relaxing for the first time in a long while.

She positioned the canoe into the current and lifted herself in over the stern. The water flowed fast in this stretch. She easily maneuvered the canoe around a rock. She'd floated the river so often she could practically do it with her eyes closed.

Sunlight seemed to set the surrounding trees ablaze, deepening the rich hues of crimson, orange, and gold, weaving a tapestry of leaves as comforting as one of Ruby's quilts. There was little sound except the quiet gurgle of the river and the swish of the canoe passing through water. *God, it's beautiful,* she thought. She wondered what Slade was doing, whether he was wining and dining some woman in Kansas City. Or Paris. In the eighteen days since she'd broken up with him, she'd found herself missing him less, though sometimes the thought of his fabulous smile and beautiful eyes made her wistful for love.

Log ahead on the right. She backpaddled to angle the canoe around it.

She floated the first three miles without thinking about much, which was fine with her. In the fourth mile she came to the heron rookery, which she and Guy both loved. It felt like he'd been gone for-ever. She missed his reassuring calm, his shared love of Ruby and this place.

Rapids hurtled her around a bend. A freshly fallen sycamore sprawled across the channel. The current carried her into the tree's grasping branches. Tulsa backwatered hard. Trapped in the branches, the canoe tilted and went over, spilling her into the frigid water. *Cold. So cold.* The swift, swollen current swept her downstream.

Her boots and jacket weighed her down and made it impossible to maneuver. She struggled to take off her coat. Stuck in her jacket, her arms wouldn't move. She went under. Kicked her way up. Choked. Struggled. Went under again. The roar of rushing water filled her ears as water forced her forward, pushed her down. Her lungs ached. If she couldn't free her arms, she would never see Ruby or Guy again.

She strained hard, kicking just enough to clear the water's surface. She sucked in air, but the current again forced her down. And again. And again. *I'm going to drown.*

No! Tumbling in the fast water, she thrust her arms behind her and yanked on one sleeve. Her jacket held. Light-headed, lungs airless, she was close to blacking out. *Pull,* she told herself. *Pull.* Her sleeve began to come off, inch by inch, as the water hurled her against a rock. She bounced off. Her shoulder throbbed, but she tugged harder. One arm came free. She kicked and pulled herself to the surface, gasping. She jerked her other arm loose.

Summoning every shred of energy she had, Tulsa managed to pull and kick her way to shore. She crawled from the water and collapsed, gulping in air on the riverbank. She was alive, thank God! Her pulse raced, her heart pounded. She relived the boat capsizing, when she thought for sure she would drown. Closing her eyes, she tried to take a breath deep enough to still her trembling, adrenaline-crazed body.

Eventually her gasps subsided. She shivered, cold. No, freezing. She clambered to her feet. Her canoe had been swept away. It was at least a mile's trek to her home. Dizzied, she leaned against a nearby tree, its orange leaves brilliant against the blue sky. The rough bark pressed into her wet clothes. She shivered harder. It would be difficult going in these boots, but she was alive. So were Guy and Ruby. He might not be her brother, nor Ruby her own mother, but she loved them both.

Tulsa started hiking through the woods in her sodden clothes, her feet kicking up leaves, creating whirlwinds of color on a dazzling October morning.

CHAPTER SEVENTY-TWO
Jen

Jen half expected the slight man seated behind a desk in the small office of the West Plains Cinema to sound like a munchkin, but he boomed out, "Can I help you?" in a voice deep enough to narrate army commercials. He looked to be near her own five foot one, his nose so skinny it barely supported his glasses.

She entered the office practically drooling from the smell of popcorn coming from the machine in the lobby. Popcorn was one of those aromas—like baked bread, freshly ground coffee, and warm snickerdoodles—that was nearly impossible to resist. She took in the movie posters covering the office walls: *Titanic*, *French Kiss* (her favorite movie of all time), *Runaway Bride*, *The Bodyguard*, *Sleepless in Seattle*. A romance novelist could have chosen those posters. So, for that matter, could she. "Are you Pete Wexler?" she asked.

"Sure am," he said. "What can I do for you?"

Jen explained her mission, that she was soliciting raffle prizes to save a life.

"Whose life?" he said.

"Ruby Riley's."

"Any relation to Clifford?"

"He was her husband."

"Clifford used to fish with my father when they were boys. Take a chair."

For an instant she thought he was offering her one of the folding chairs as a raffle prize, but then he gestured for her to sit down. She did.

Pete took out a pack of gumdrops. The scent of sugar perfumed the air. "I quit smoking last year and got addicted to these." He held the bag out to her.

"No, thank you," she said.

He popped several into his mouth. "My lungs are healthier," he said, "but I'm probably rotting my teeth."

"It's good you quit smoking." His shirt matched the color of the purple gumdrops.

"My daughter threatened to take up the electric guitar if I didn't quit." He shuddered. " 'Electric' and 'guitar' go together like . . . what?"

"Liver and licorice?"

He chuckled. "I was going to say my ex and me, but liver and licorice is much more original."

Funny. She and Jack had gotten along for the most part. In the more than two months since she'd left him, however, Jen had come to understand that the reason why they'd gotten along so well was that she pretty much just went along with whatever Jack wanted. Except for paint color. She'd stood up for that. In her next relationship, she would need to assert herself far more.

Maybe if she'd stood up for herself with Jack, he would have acquiesced. Maybe not. Jen missed him: the way he smiled at her in the mornings, the way his face lit up when she fixed his favorite foods. Missed, too, her belief that they would eventually start a family and live happily ever after. It had surprised her, though, how quickly she'd come to regard her in-law apartment in Mrs. Foster's house as home.

Pete's gaze rose to the wall behind her head, then fell back on her. He seemed startled. "I knew you reminded me of someone." He pointed to the poster behind her.

She looked around. *French Kiss*. She was pleased that someone besides her saw her resemblance to Meg Ryan. "Without the millions or the leading man," she joked. Instantly she regretted it. What was she thinking blurting that out?

"Romance seems to work better on-screen," Pete said with a rueful look.

"Or in novels." She rose to leave before she further embarrassed herself. "Any donation would be great."

Pete opened a desk drawer. "When's the raffle?"

She told him about the upcoming Autumn Rapture on the eighteenth, only eleven days away. He seemed to listen closely. He held out four theater passes good for an entire year. "These are great!" she said. She put the passes in an envelope. "I hope I win one."

"Would one be enough?" he asked.

She told herself she was imagining things. He couldn't really be flirting with her. Could he? "At the moment." She could swear he appeared pleased. He was nowhere near handsome, but he seemed genuinely nice, and he had a thrilling voice—and a daughter with whom he spent at least some time. "Thanks," she said. "There'll be a list of all prizes and donating merchants in the *Gazette* Friday. Tickets are five dollars." Checks had been coming in for raffle tickets from people around the state who had floated with the Oasis but couldn't attend Autumn Rapture.

"What other prizes do you have?" He walked beside her as she left the office, his head reaching just above her own.

She listed the donations they'd come up with so far: gift certificates from every single merchant in Fiddle and a bunch from West Plains, Pearl's pies, free fly-fishing gear and floats from fly shops and sporting-goods stores around the state, their own guided float trips, a free weekend at a Sweet Oak River Oasis cabin, and innumerable things made by Ruby's friends: quilts and sweaters and paintings, a hand-carved child's rocking horse, a gorgeous wooden rocking chair, and BJ's churches. Plus the secret recipe to Pearl's blackberry–sour cream pie.

"Wow," he said. "That recipe alone will sell a lot of tickets."

"It already has." Her own mother, who barely scraped by on disability, had bought five tickets, saying she figured if she won, she could sell off Pearl's recipe for a lot more than twenty-five dollars.

"Give me twenty tickets," Pete said. He pushed buttons on his cash register in the lobby and took out five twenties.

The smell of buttered popcorn again made Jen's mouth water.

He scooped her up a bag of popcorn. "On the house."

She hoped she could keep from cramming the whole thing in her mouth. She'd skipped lunch to solicit raffle prizes, and she had to drive back to Fiddle to work. "Thanks."

"Anytime."

She headed for the door.

"Wait," he called. She turned back to him. "What's your name?"

She couldn't believe she'd forgotten to tell him. "Jen Haskell."

He leaned against the counter. "Will you be at the raffle, Jen Haskell?"

"I'm giving free pedicures."

"I guess kids are welcome?"

"Definitely. We'll have face painting, too, and all kinds of activities."

"Autumn Rapture, huh?" He took a package of gumdrops from the concession stand, ripped it open, and tossed one in his mouth. "I'll look forward to it."

So will I, she thought, munching the crisp, buttery kernels. She stepped out into a mostly cloudy October afternoon; it had been sunny earlier that morning. On her way to her car, she passed by a new, ultramodern salon, with its bright colors and sleek look. An appeal to Marianne's compassion wouldn't work. Jen could hear Marianne's haughty voice. *I'm a businesswoman, not a social worker.*

The thing to do was to price out the improvements she wanted to make: paint the walls brighter, offer coffee, feature a bookshelf like the post office had and a CD player with a selection of love songs. Most of the things she had in mind could be purchased used. She would be glad to help paint. Naturally Marianne would resist. That's why Jen needed to list the costs—and calculate the potential for increased profits. If Marianne hoped to compete with the new West Plains salon, she needed to make changes. Jen pitied the woman. She didn't seem to understand the most basic truth: if you spread sunbeams in others' lives, you spread them in your own. It might be a cloudy day, but in her own world, the sun was shining.

CHAPTER SEVENTY-THREE
Tulsa

Two days after capsizing, Tulsa sipped thick black coffee and sat on the rock watching the mist rise, the river breathe. BJ's news from over two weeks before was feeling a little less weird. If people could adjust to things like getting fired or losing their house in a tornado or some far worse calamity, she supposed she could adjust to the fact she didn't have a brother. After all, she hadn't even known she supposedly had one until a year ago.

The sycamores across the water shimmered yellow, while the sugar maple hanging over her head blazed orange and red. It was a mid-October morning, chilly but not the bone cold of winter. The air smelled of river and the musty earth of autumn.

It was too bad Guy despised his actual father. She regretted never getting to meet her own. Still, she was lucky. Her mother had loved her. So had Ruby. She still had Ruby. And Jen. And Guy.

A kingfisher swooped along the shore, its flight fast and darting; its angry cry split the silence. The sound of gravel *ping*ing against metal told her that a vehicle was approaching. She hoped it was Guy. She hadn't seen him since he'd returned the day before from his trip soliciting raffle prizes and ticket sales.

Sure enough, Guy's truck soon stopped near her. He lifted Elvis from the passenger seat. The dog was so huge with her pregnancy, Guy apparently didn't want her jumping. He set Elvis on the ground. Tulsa buried her face in Elvis's soft fur as an unfamiliar shyness overtook her. The dog licked Tulsa's cheek.

"Morning," Guy said.

There was still a strange note to his voice. A politeness, an awkwardness that mirrored her own. "Morning," she said. "How are you?"

"Okay."

Elvis backed away and swayed toward the patch of trees bordering the river. Guy squatted beside the rock, unwrapped a stick of Juicy Fruit, and offered it to her. She shook her head.

"What's the latest ticket count?" he asked. He popped the fragrant gum into his mouth.

"Sold over sixteen hundred. Pearl and your mom and Jen are really working hard getting raffle prizes and selling tickets. Most of the fly shops you went to are reporting sales, too. Somebody told Slade about it. He donated an all-expenses-paid weekend at the InterContinental Hotel on the Plaza in Kansas City."

Guy whistled. "Fancy place. I bet that sells some tickets."

"Yeah."

"Did you talk to him?"

"Ruby did. I called but got his voice mail. I left a message thanking him." Hearing Slade's voice on his message had made her tear up.

He stared at his hands. "Wish I didn't look so much like my damned father."

"What's the resemblance?"

"I've got his forehead, his eyes, his chin."

"But not his heart," she said.

He smiled. "I hope not."

"Has your mom told her cousin the truth?"

"Yeah. Marjorie wasn't all that shocked about Travis, but she was pretty disappointed in BJ. Seems she found out about Travis messing around a few years ago. She was going to divorce him when their son, Barry, graduated from high school, but Barry got a girl pregnant and married her. I guess Travis is a terrific grandfather. He really dotes on their granddaughter. Marjorie didn't like being betrayed like that, but to Mom she sounded more resigned than angry."

"Your mom must be relieved."

"She is."

"So you have a sibling after all." Their eyes met and flicked away. "Did you know him before?"

"We've met a couple of times. Don't know him well, but I like him okay. I stopped by there a few days ago to say hi. He's going to come for a float trip after Autumn Rapture." Guy spat. "I still don't understand how a married man can mess around like Travis. Don't get married in the first place. That way you can do what you please without hurting anyone."

"Kind of lonely, though," she said, hearing the wistfulness in her own voice.

Guy whistled low. "You've sure changed your tune," he said. "You used to swear you'd never marry."

"I used to swear I'd never have a period, kiss a man, or open myself to love."

"You've done all that, have you?"

"I believe I have."

"Well, that's good."

Sunlight pierced the mist and streaked light across the water. He stood; his jeans rustled. She scooted over, though the rock seemed startlingly small. She half hoped he would take his usual perch beside her so things could be normal again and half hoped he wouldn't because they weren't normal.

Enough river gazing. She stood. "We better get to work."

Guy gestured her forward. "After you."

She wanted to tell him to stop being polite, but the words stuck in her throat.

A mournful wail pierced the air. "What's that?" Tulsa said.

Guy listened. Another wail. "Elvis."

They dashed into the house. Guy filled a bucket

with water. Tulsa grabbed towels and hand sanitizer, then dumped books from a cardboard box. They sprinted into the woods following Elvis's cries.

The dog writhed on the ground. Tulsa had witnessed plenty of animals give birth. The only times she'd seen one thrash like Elvis was when there was a problem. Elvis's contractions had happened too fast, were coming too hard, and were shaking her whole body.

"Something's wrong," Guy said.

They knelt together beside the brown-and-white dog. "Easy, girl," Guy said. He ran his hand along Elvis's stomach.

"Breech birth? Pups too big?" She didn't bother to suggest a vet. They didn't have time.

Guy cleaned his hands, then pushed one into Elvis.

"Can you feel it?" Tulsa said.

"Barely." He shoved his hand farther inside.

Elvis yelped. "Easy, girl," Tulsa said. "He's going to help you."

Elvis raised her head, her milky eyes unseeing.

"I got it," Guy said. "It's big and it's breeched."

He didn't have to tell her to take Elvis's head. Tulsa cupped it between her hands and kissed the dog's muzzle. "Hold on," she urged.

Guy somehow leaned even farther into Elvis, his face straining like he was the one giving birth. He closed his eyes and pulled.

He emerged with a blood-smeared arm and a

brown puppy that looked two sizes too big to be born. Elvis immediately began licking the pup when, grinning, Guy set it beside her.

"Thatta girl," Tulsa said, cutting the umbilical cord. "Good job," she told Guy.

He stuck his arm in the water bucket, then squirted sanitizer over his hands. "Remind me to get this dog spayed," he said.

Without a word they spread a towel on the ground, slipped their hands under Elvis, and lifted her onto the towel, setting the puppy beside her. Elvis chewed off the membrane that coated the pup.

"Let's call this one Sunny," Tulsa said, surprising herself. The name made sense, though. This pup had resisted birth just like Sunny Chandler had resisted love. Like she herself had.

"I sure hope there's no other breeched ones." Guy pet Elvis's head.

The puppy wiggled beside Elvis. Both Tulsa and Guy ran fingers along Sunny's soft, sticky fur, a large pup still so small, a birth that seemed miraculous. Tulsa's eyes met Guy's over mother and pup.

Elvis whimpered. "Here we go again," Guy said, kneeling by Elvis.

Tulsa knelt by Guy. Their shoulders brushed. Guy's smile—framed by lines that reminded her of sliver moons—answered her own.

CHAPTER SEVENTY-FOUR
Tulsa

At four in the morning the day of Autumn Rapture, Tulsa gave up trying to sleep. She was too wired. She slipped into her jeans and flannel shirt and tiptoed down the stairs so as not to wake Ruby or Guy, who had stayed in the guest bedroom to get an early start with the final preparations.

But not this early.

She fixed a cup of instant coffee and went to sit on her favorite rock overlooking the river. The crescent moon cast a pale light. Two owls traded hoots. The river *shusssh*ed along. A lone bullfrog croaked. Gone was the din of crickets and cicadas, muted by the changing seasons. Tulsa breathed in the smells of clean water and the musk of autumn, her heart racing.

From far off she heard a noise she couldn't identify. She turned her head and strained to hear better. It sounded like a motor or engine, but nobody would be mowing or plowing at this hour.

She turned back to the river. Lightning bugs glowed, then dimmed, then glowed again. She tossed a small stone into the water. It fractured the reflections of stars, creating swirls of silver.

They'd sold over four thousand tickets so far,

but that wasn't close to enough to buy Ruby's pills and make their initial off-season loan payments. Fortunately many people had pitched in to help: donating prizes, selling tickets, posting flyers, writing letters to the editor urging others to come. Guy's computer friend, Rich, reported that people were spreading word of the raffle on Facebook and Twitter, neither of which Tulsa had ever used.

Women's societies from several churches had contributed chicken and hamburger patties to barbecue later, cold cuts, cheese, bread, salads of all kinds, deviled eggs, beans, rolls, chips, and a slew of desserts. The food had been picked up and delivered in ice chests Friday afternoon by high school students. The church ladies would set out the food and sell tickets for it on the tables she and Guy had already set up. Jen would arrive by nine twenty with fresh doughnuts contributed by the bakery in Fiddle.

Tulsa loved Ruby, but she'd had no idea how many other people loved her, too.

Footsteps. She scooted over. Guy sat beside her and sipped from a glass of iced tea.

"Couldn't sleep, huh?" he said.

"No. I hope I didn't wake you."

"Nah. I haven't slept much either."

Guy looked out at the river, his hair falling over his eyes, his body beside her compact and warm. They sat in silence for a while, listening to the sounds of the night.

"What if we don't sell enough tickets?" she said.

"We will."

Tulsa heard Guy's words, but she also heard an unfamiliar waver to his voice. Well, of course they were scared. To bring in another $15,000, they'd need to sell another three thousand tickets. If only a hundred people showed up, there was no way they'd make that much. Not even close. Tulsa clasped her arms around herself, not sure if she was shivering from the chilly autumn air or nerves.

Guy took off his denim jacket and put it around her shoulders.

"Thanks," she said, moved by his kindness, wanting to clasp it to her as a shield against failure, "but aren't you cold?"

"Nope," Guy said. "I keep going over everything to be sure we haven't forgotten anything."

"Me, too. Over and over."

It seemed like hours before dawn crept in. Birds woke—fewer than in the summer, but cardinals stayed year-round. Their lilting songs, a series of melodic whistles, soon heralded the sunrise. Mist floated up from the water.

Tulsa stood. "Time to get to work."

Guy rose, stretched, then touched his glass to hers in toast. "To Autumn Rapture," he said.

She'd consumed all her coffee long before, but she went through the motions of toasting, licking a last drop from the cup and hoping that toasting with an empty glass wasn't a jinx.

By nine thirty, ten minutes after Jen was due, a half hour before Autumn Rapture officially began, all was ready. They'd displayed the actual prizes they had, such as quilts and furniture, on long tables borrowed from Fiddle's churches. Other prizes, like Slade's gift of a Kansas City weekend, were advertised on posters they'd created. They'd also set out coffee and food, and put up signs designating three tables for pedicures, face painting, and the sale of raffle tickets. Ruby was bustling around the kitchen making snicker-doodles by the dozens.

By 9:40 nobody had arrived, not even Jen.

Or by 9:50.

Tulsa would have expected a few early arrivals, not to mention Jen. She tried calling Jen's cell, but it went straight to voice mail. She went back outside and paced.

Ruby came out and shaded her eyes against the bright sun. She looked up the hill. Tulsa did the same.

No one.

The kitchen timer sounded. Ruby squeezed Tulsa's hand and went back inside.

"Maybe people are waiting for lunch," Tulsa said.

"Yeah," Guy said. "It's too early to panic."

Hopeful words, but Guy looked as close to panicked as Tulsa had ever seen him.

Ten o'clock.

What was that?

Tulsa squinted. It looked like someone was walking down the hill toward them. Was it a mirage? Surely if she was going to hallucinate, she would imagine cars coming down the hill, not a single straggler.

"Guy?" she said, pointing up the hill.

He squinted, too.

"It's Jen," Tulsa realized. Jen stumbled. Tulsa broke into a run.

Guy reached Jen first, but not by much.

"What happened?" Tulsa said.

Jen doubled over, gasping for air.

"Are you hurt?" Tulsa asked.

Jen shook her head, wheezing out her words. "Trees. Cut down. Blocking . . . road."

"How many?" Guy said.

"Four or five." Jen straightened.

"How far back?" Tulsa said.

"Where it gets too narrow to turn around."

"That's over two miles." Tulsa looked at Jen's feet, clad in strappy pump sandals. "You walked two miles in those?"

Jen looked down at her feet.

"Damn," Tulsa said. "If we had cell coverage, you could have just called." Tulsa patted Jen's shoulder. "Go inside and let Ruby take care of you."

Jen started limping toward the kitchen.

"And, Jen," Tulsa called, "we owe you."

"Big-time," Guy said.

"If people hear about the blockage," Tulsa said, "they might not even bother to try to come."

She and Guy grabbed chain saws from the carport and put them in the bed of the truck. Thank God they had a winch on Big Red.

"It has to be Clancy," Guy said.

Tulsa remembered the motor she'd thought she'd heard. Maybe Clancy had figured out a way to defeat them once and for all.

The sound of tires churning gravel made Tulsa look up.

"Well, I'll be damned," Guy said.

Tulsa followed his gaze. Jen's car was coming down the hill, followed closely by a line of cars and pickups. Judging by the dust cloud that rose like smoke as far up the hill as Tulsa could see, there were a whole lot more cars coming down. As they arrived, some people honked, some shouted, some waved.

Calvin Stuart, Ed Logan's straw-skinny eighty-five-year-old cousin, who had made a killing when he'd sold his five hundred acres, much of it riverfront land on the other side of the river, was driving Jen's car, followed by Ed.

Ruby and Jen came out to join Guy and Tulsa. Ruby put her hand to her heart. "Oh my," she said.

Ed and Calvin reached them first.

"How did you get through?" Guy asked.

"Just walked down the line of cars till I found a couple of people with chain saws," Ed said, pulling his Stetson down, his eyes constantly darting back to Ruby. "Then a whole lot of folks joined us to cut and carry. Good thing those trees weren't old growth, or we'd still be sawing."

"Were there a lot of cars?" Tulsa asked.

"Line went as far back as I could see," Calvin said. " 'Course, I got cataracts."

"No worries," Ed said. "Somebody on a CB said cars stretch back out to the highway."

Four miles. "Thank God," Tulsa said, sagging with relief. "And thank you both so much."

"Yes, indeed," Ruby added.

"Those trees were deliberately cut," Calvin said. "Ain't no doubt about that." He spat on the ground. "Had to be Clancy. Man's gotten rabid. It's about time we straightened his ass out."

Tulsa wished she knew how to do that.

"Don't go breaking any laws," Ruby said. "I've had enough stress."

People were gathering in clusters, laughing and talking, looking around at the tables with prizes and coupons.

"I'll get the doughnuts." Jen hurried toward her car.

Ed tugged on his Stetson again. "The only reason Clancy's dangerous now is because of George Calhoun. Calvin, if you could round up a bunch of business folks to pay George a visit at the bank and tell him that if Clancy messes with Ruby and Tulsa any more, you're all going to take your money out of his bank, he'll change his tune real fast. Without George, Clancy will be toothless."

"Consider it done," Calvin said.

"Thank you," Tulsa said. "Both of you."

"For you, anything," Ed said, though his eyes were only on Ruby.

"You bet," Calvin agreed.

Both Ruby and Guy were grinning. Tulsa smiled a smile that felt every bit as wide as the river. "Sweet," she said.

CHAPTER SEVENTY-FIVE
Ruby

Seated on a stool by the bonfire, Guy sang love songs, ballads, and blues in a voice like creamy butter. Ruby looked around the fire at the fifty or so people who remained from Autumn Rapture. Most sat on blankets listening to Guy, some roasting marshmallows on sticks, the smells of burning wood and sizzling sugar filling the night air.

Ruby still couldn't believe how successful the day had been, how gorgeous the weather, how much money they'd made. Many of their steady customers and quite a few new ones had driven in from Springfield and Kansas City. Local folks had flocked in as well, drawn by the free floats and the raffle prizes, the activities, and the food donated by Pearl's and BJ's churches, not to mention Pearl's pies. Her blackberry–sour cream pie recipe had accounted for at least five hundred tickets.

Between all the raffle tickets they'd sold today and previously, plus the sale of all ten of BJ's model churches, they'd taken in over $34,000, which would buy the needed two months of pills and pay the next three loan installments. Better, they'd booked all four cabins for every weekend and even some midweek days through Thanksgiving—and beyond. With any luck they could build enough business to sustain the Oasis through the entire off-season.

Guy's eyes roved his audience while he sang. Beside Ruby, Tulsa was staring into the fire. Ruby wished Clifford sat on her other side. He would have loved this day. Still, she could wait awhile longer to be reunited with him.

Jen seemed to be enjoying herself, her face glowing orange in the light from the flames as she roasted marshmallows with Pete Wexler, whom Ruby recognized from the movie theater, and his daughter. Of course Ruby had no way of knowing whether Jen and Pete would actually date—let alone fall in love—but Jen certainly looked happy. Ruby would keep her fingers crossed.

Then there was BJ, sitting hand in hand with

Matthew Bonner, who seemed the epitome of a gentleman. BJ looked relaxed and content, like a woman well satisfied.

Pearl was perched on a padded folding chair next to Daniel and Hank. Her lips were moving, though she wasn't making a sound. Maybe Pearl was mouthing the words to the song Guy was singing. Ruby vowed that the next chance she had to make a wish, it would be for Pearl to sing again.

Sadly, the one person in the group who was alone was Tulsa. Ruby had to admit, though, that she felt selfishly glad Tulsa hadn't gone off with Slade to roam the world.

Guy finished a song to enthusiastic applause, which he raised his hand to stop. "I used to do it a lot smoother."

"There's a whole lot of things we used to do a lot smoother," Ed said.

"Not me," said Rich, Guy's friend. "I'm like a good wine. I keep getting better with age."

"Yeah." The woman with Rich laid her hand on his knee. "This guy don't have no trouble popping his cork."

Loud laughter rose from the circle. Ruby looked at her watch. Heading toward midnight.

Guy launched into "Desperado." His voice was full and soft. He sang the first verse with his eyes closed. Tulsa looked back up at the stars.

Guy opened his eyes at almost the same moment that Tulsa lowered her gaze. Their eyes met. Both of them looked startled. More than startled. They kept on staring at each other. Then Guy smiled his warm, creased smile. Tulsa smiled back.

Tulsa and Guy? Well, why not? When they first got the news almost a month ago, it would have seemed a little strange. Not now. It wasn't like they'd been raised together. And they shared so much, in particular their passion for the river. Guy and Tulsa made sense in a way that Slade and Tulsa hadn't. Since they didn't share a father, maybe there was nothing that ought to keep them apart.

Guy looked around at his audience and launched into what he said was his last song. It was a song about trusting the singer when he said "I love you." The fire danced and flamed and crackled, as if in time to the music. Guy sang without once looking at anyone other than Tulsa. She looked right back.

What was that novel about flying? Danielle Steel was the author, Ruby was sure. It was the story of a young woman in the 1930s and '40s with a fierce love for flying and the much-older man who loves piloting just as much as she does. The book had a one-word title. *Flight*, was it? No. *Pilot*? No. Oh, why couldn't she remember? *Wings*! That was it.

If the possibility of romance between Tulsa and Guy was only in her own, at times admittedly fevered, imagination, no harm could come of handing the book out for the next group. It wasn't the same as telling Tulsa to date Guy. She'd sworn off that kind of interference.

After *Wings*, maybe they'd read something by Jayne Ann Krentz. Or Barbara Cartland. Or Fern Michaels. Or Judith McNaught. There were so many great writers out there, so many wonderful stories to read. *Long live romance,* Ruby thought. *Long live love.*

ACKNOWLEDGMENTS

Whatever delights this book offers were created with a dazzling array of help.

My editor, Tara Parsons, who pinpointed what needed to be revised to make this novel work. (And thanks to the whole enthusiastic team at Lake Union.)

My agent, Meg Ruley, and the rest of the cast at the Jane Rotrosen Agency, for their remarkably cheerful and insightful guidance.

My freelance editor, Heather Lazare, who made such a thorough map of what needed changing in earlier drafts, that I couldn't possibly get lost.

Myron McKee, who arranged the interviews that led to the idea of a romance novel book group, and who, with his wife, Ann, runs the delightful River of Life Farms cabins and canoe business that inspired the Sweet Oak River Oasis.

My longtime writers group, talented writers and good friends all: Mike Karpa, Wendy Schultz, Tarn Wilson, and, of course, Madelon Phillips, through daily sharing of our characters' stories . . . and our own. The group's astute feedback helped my characters cease to be acquaintances and become my friends. I'm grateful that no one set upon me with rabid dogs for subjecting the group to 63,047 versions of chapter 1.

My MPC writers group (also a talented bunch), whose frank responses lovingly guided my (many) revisions: Anna Dabney, Margaretha Derasary, Jeanne Dunn, Jean Gregory, Margaret Irvin, Bonnie McManis, Sharon Noteboom, Carol Peacock, Bertha Reilly, Martha Tilmann, and Ellen Woods.

The other two members of our Writers Trio, Bea Pompa and Kathy Hrastar, for terrific edits and moral support.

My seventh-grade English teacher, Mrs. Lee, who first told me I could write. High school teachers Ken Williams and Ron Clemons, who showed me the possibilities—and, yes, joys—of revising, and who helped me believe in my own abilities.

Talented editors, who weighed in on various aspects of the novel: Tanya Egan Gibson, David Groff, Jordan Rosenfeld, Liz Rosner, and Wendy Tokunaga.

My brothers: Ron, for a thorough and insightful edit plus unflagging support; and Steven, for story suggestions that were so right on. Those Zeke and Rafe tales could be books in themselves.

My sister-in-law, Sandra Stites, for cheering me to finish rewriting and submit the thing.

My longtime friend, Ernie Grafe, who can listen to descriptions of problems in the book and pinpoint what doesn't work and why.

Joan Diamond, patron of the arts, whose enthusiasm (and artful aging) have inspired me.

Early readers who helped me believe in the potential of this story and gave invaluable suggestions for how to realize it: Lynn Beittel, Francie Chan, Dianne Elise, Debbie Hernandez, Karen Johnson, Lita Kurth, Ann Reis, Jean Roggenkamp, Sierra Stites, Ailea Stites, Marcy Stites, Ruthann Taylor, and Jean Walker.

Jai Jai Noire, for the author interview videos and for making me think. And laugh.

So many friends, who have taken my writing seriously and helped me to do the same.

Above all, my husband, Bert, for a plethora of fruitful brainstorming sessions that truly helped this book sparkle, and for such generous love that makes my own world do the same.

If I have omitted anyone who should be on this list, I apologize. Please know it's a failing of my head and not my heart.

Reading the Sweet Oak
DISCUSSION QUESTIONS

1. Who is your favorite of the women characters? Why?

2. Do you think BJ was right to keep her secret for so long? Could you have done that? If not, when would you have told?

3. If you were Guy, could/would you have kept BJ's secret?

4. Were you surprised by Jen's mother's actions in her last scene? Were they believable?

5. Who, if anyone, did you view most harshly? Did your opinion change by book's end?

6. The characters in the book are changed by reading romance novels. Have you read any books that have changed your life? Which book(s)? In what ways were you changed?

7. Several characters in the book keep important things about their lives secret. Have you ever kept secrets that you later wished you

hadn't? Whose secret in this book do you feel may have done the most damage?

8. Pearl and Ruby have been friends since childhood. Have you maintained friendship with a childhood friend? In what ways, if any, do you think longer-term friendships differ from newer friendships?

9. Tulsa at the beginning has pretty much sworn off romantic love. Have you ever felt the same?

10. Whose actions most surprised you?

11. Pearl's experiences with her grandson challenge her beliefs. Did you grow up with biases you have since thrown off?

AUTHOR INTERVIEW:
Jan Stites

Where did you get the idea for your novel?
I grew up in Missouri. My family always spent our vacations camping in the Ozarks, and I came to love canoeing and swimming on those beautiful, tree-cloaked Ozark rivers. I still do. For a long time I've wanted to set a book there, but the Ozarks remained a rich setting in search of a story until a canoe-rental business owner requested that I record the stories of older Ozarkians before they passed away. I interviewed mostly female Ozark residents and really enjoyed those interviews—getting to hear people's stories about life in times of Prohibition and moonshine, one-room schools, outhouses decorated with newspaper, and so much more. I also learned how much many of the women enjoyed romance novels. That gave me the idea to center the book around a romance novel book group.

So are some of the characters based on real people?
None of them is based on a particular person, no. That said, the interviews certainly provided me with material to help flesh out my characters.

How did you go about developing the characters and the story?
Almost as soon as I decided to center the book around a romance novel book club, Tulsa's name popped into my mind, as did the knowledge she would be an independent, romance-skittish main character. I also knew she lived with an older relative, who became Ruby. I wanted a friend of Ruby's age and one of Tulsa's in the group, as well as Guy's mother. I didn't know any of the characters well, however, until I began reading romance novels. Almost immediately I found myself responding as the characters: Tulsa would say *this* about that passage, Pearl would say *that*. I also discovered that different books would give various characters insights into their own lives. So reading romances was the gateway to key elements for both character and plot.

Do you have a favorite among the women?
Not really. I like things about all of them. I like Tulsa's spunk and independence, Jen's giving heart, Ruby's gentle wisdom, and Pearl's more caustic wit. I also can identify with BJ's struggle to forgive herself for her past shames.

Was it hard keeping track of five women with their individual stories and their different points of view/voices?

I didn't have any trouble differentiating their stories. The voice of each character developed more clearly with each draft and with a whole lot of input from my writing groups.

Do you read a lot of romances?
I'd read only one when I started working on this book. Then I read maybe two dozen looking for books that would make good selections for my characters. The books I read were quite fun. I wondered and still wonder why it is that romance novels have such a bad rap. Critics complain that they're predictable. Of course, mysteries are every bit as predictable in that you know that in most of them the good guy will triumph, just as you know that in romance novels love will triumph. Are there poorly written romances? Sure. Most of them aren't. Are there poorly written mysteries? Sure. Most of them aren't. But it seems to me to be a very real double standard.

How long did it take you to write this book? Did it change much along the way?
I spent a little over four years on it, but I was also working on other projects. The book underwent some major changes, yes. For instance, at one point I had a physical fight between two of the male characters but took that out fairly early on. I tend to write fast and then revise a lot. I wrote twenty-one completely revised drafts and probably

redid the first chapter over five hundred times if you count the fine tuning.

Pearl's story involves her rejection of her grandson's homosexuality. Why did you include that in a novel about romances?

First, Pearl's grandson's story does involve romance. Also, my book isn't a romance novel but is more general women's fiction about a romance novel book group. I felt free to include whatever struggles women might have that would be affected by reading romance novels. I agree with those who believe in the importance of equal rights for LGBTQ people, but I didn't always feel that way. In grade school I remember joining those who scoffed at the "effeminate nature" of a boy in our fifth-grade class. I also shared the horror of other Girl Scouts who were scandalized by what today would be called a "butch" counselor. Then I moved to California and lived for a while in a shared housing situation with people I didn't previously know. I just assumed all were straight, having never to my knowledge really known someone who wasn't. When one of my house-mates came out as gay, I was flabbergasted. He was a gentle, playful guy whom I adored. Since then I've loved many people who are LGBTQ. Had I not included them in my life, I would have deprived myself of some of the loveliest relationships I've known. When we cut ourselves off from a group of people—whether based on sexuality, gender, race, nationality, or religion—we render our own lives more barren.

What's your writing process like?
I prefer starting early in the morning. We get up around five or five thirty. I eat a quick breakfast, then write for four to eight hours. I know some writers say you should write every single day, but that doesn't work for me. I generally write five days a week, sometimes six, but I have to have at least one day of downtime to recharge my batteries.

What's the hardest part of writing for you?
Conflict. Years ago, when I began writing screenplays, an agent told me that I was a terrific writer with all kinds of potential but asked, "Do you by any chance avoid conflict in your personal life? Because you sure avoided it in this screenplay." He was absolutely correct. I loathe conflict, whether personal or fictitious. I still have to watch my tendency to want to end a scene just when things start to get conflicted. Now when I do scene notes, where I have headings for various elements such as sensory detail in that scene, what changes, etc., the first element on the list, in big bold capital letters, is CONFLICT. I squirm when I'm writing intense conflict, but at least now I'm less likely to skip it completely.

You mentioned scene notes. Do you outline before writing?

I do, yes. I generally begin by writing first-person autobiographies of my characters in their voices, or at least as much in their voices as I've acquired early in the process. Doing the autobiographies helps me come up with ideas for plots. Then I make note cards with one scene per card in the manner many authors do. That way I can shuffle the scenes around as seems appropriate. Once I have a broad outline of the story, I will then do the scene notes I mentioned above. When I actually start writing the first draft, however, I don't just follow the outline. Story is fluid. Scenes and sequence change considerably in the actual writing of a draft.

What do you say to writers who believe outlining spoils the creative process?

I think different techniques work for different people. I have the worst sense of direction, geo-graphically speaking, of anyone I know. The sun could be setting and I'd probably have a hard time pointing out which way was west. Okay, maybe not quite that bad. I have a similar sensibility (or lack of one) in writing. If I had no idea of my destination or route, I'd probably write in circles for months before I realized my narrative was hopelessly lost.

What's the easiest part of writing for you?
I don't know why, but dialogue is easy for me. Maybe that came from starting out writing screenplays. Also, I taught screenwriting for several years at San Francisco State University. One way to learn a skill is to teach it. In preparing classes on dialogue, I picked up plenty of pointers.

What aspect of writing a novel do you most enjoy?
The brainstorming process when I'm just getting to know my story and my characters but am not trying to actually write a draft. The freedom and creativity feed my soul.

Are you in a writing group?
Yes. Three. Some of us in one group met in a novel-writing class over twenty years ago. In that group we generally send one another ten to thirty pages in advance of our monthly meeting and critique closely on the page, then get together to compare notes and talk writing. In another group, which meets twice a month, we read four to five pages aloud. I love the two different approaches. In the first we submit more pages and receive copious notes. When you read aloud, as we do in the second, you get to hear your fellow writers' responses. Are they laughing at what you thought was funny? Are their eyes glazing over? Of course, I can't do a whole novel that way, because

it would take forever. The third group just meets sporadically to talk about writing and exchange a few pages.

What qualities do you tend to prefer in novels?
Compelling characters plus strong story, setting, and voice. I especially love emotionally evocative novels, where I both laugh and cry.

What are some of your favorite novels?
These aren't in any particular order: *The Art of Racing in the Rain* (Garth Stein), *The Guernsey Literary and Potato Peel Pie Society* (Mary Ann Shaffer and Annie Barrows), *The Jane Austen Book Club* (Karen Joy Fowler), *The Unlikely Pilgrimage of Harold Fry* (Rachel Joyce), *We Are Water* and *She's Come Undone* (Wally Lamb), *Water for Elephants* (Sara Gruen), *Firefly Lane* (Kristin Hannah), *The Rosie Project* (Graeme Simsion), *The Accidental Tourist* (Anne Tyler), *Love and Other Impossible Pursuits* (Ayelet Waldman), *The Wednesday Sisters* (Meg Waite Clayton), *Big Little Lies* (Liane Moriarty), and *Good in Bed* (Jennifer Weiner). I hesitate to make such a list because I know I will have accidentally skipped some titles that I love. Also, I read a fair amount and am always discovering new favorites. But then, that's one of the great things about Facebook. I can update my author page with new recommendations as I find them.

ABOUT THE AUTHOR

Jan Stites is the author of the novel *Edgewise*. She received a BA from the University of Missouri and an MA from Purdue University, both in history and English. Jan has worked at a multitude of jobs, including screenwriter, screenwriting instructor at San Francisco State University and UC–Berkeley, waitress, secretary, middle-school teacher, scuba-diving travel writer, journalist, transcriber for doctors and for documentary filmmakers, and teacher in Kenya and the Yucatán. Jan also served as a translator for American doctors in Mexico. Her greatest nightmare is that she may have inadvertently translated "brain tumor" as "toothache." Jan is from Missouri, where she has vacationed extensively in the Ozarks. She lives with her husband in Northern California.

Center Point Large Print
600 Brooks Road / PO Box 1
Thorndike, ME 04986-0001 USA

(207) 568-3717

US & Canada:
1 800 929-9108
www.centerpointlargeprint.com